Bones of the Fair

by Andrea K Höst

Bones of the Fair
© 2013 Andrea K Höst. All rights reserved.
ISBN: 978-0-9872651-6-6
www.andreakhost.com

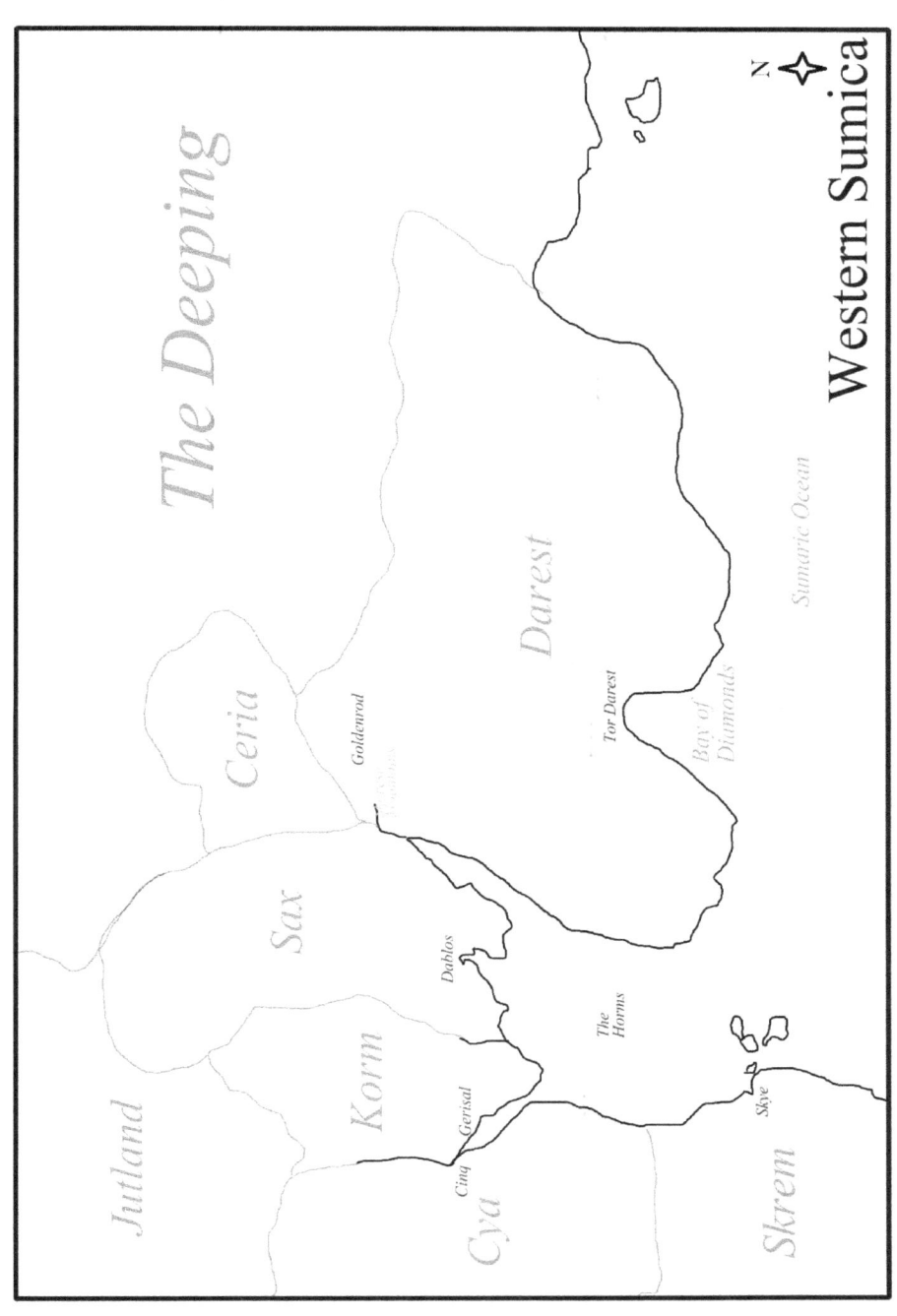

The Deeping

Jutland

Ceria

Sax

Korm

Cya

Cinq
Geirsal

Dablos

Goldenrod

Darest

The
Horns

Tor Darest

Bay of
Diamonds

Skve

Skrem

Sumaric Ocean

N

Western Sumica

Chapter One

Looking north, Gentian Calder could make out the shadow of land. Sapphire Point. Soon they'd enter the Bay of Diamonds, and dock in Tor Darest. After fourteen years, Gentian was coming home.

She would pay for it. No true-mage could go back on their sworn word without some kind of consequence, and since it was her self she was breaking faith with, it would be a very personal cost. All for a mere possibility.

News of the Rathen King's return had reached her the previous autumn. A man transported out of the past, who'd seen an end to the tainted Couerveur Regency, won a vital diplomatic concession from The Deeping, quite turned the failing kingdom's fortunes around. Gentian had been glad, but it had made no real difference to her. Then, during another of her mother's attempts to lure her home, she'd been given a piece of news that hadn't made its way south to Atlarus. This Aluster Rathen had also destroyed one of the old enchantments protecting Darest: a spell woven into the very fabric of the land that had warped and corrupted over the centuries.

How long had she hesitated? A moment? Two? She hadn't even needed the bait her mother had dangled before her, had taken first ship north, every league equal parts anticipation and dread.

The line on the horizon crept closer, and then shifted to the left as they drew toward the gulf known as the Bay of Diamonds. The *Waraga* was a small ship, the wind unfavourable, so it was late afternoon before Gentian felt the shift of territory as they crossed an invisible border, and she tasted Darest for the first time since she was fourteen.

A tiny sigh escaped her, and she stood gripping the rail against her disappointment. There *was* an absence, something different, but It was still there. Darest still hated her. She'd been mad to think that victory would simply be handed to her, that It could ever be vanquished.

Into her regret burst a flare of power, unexpected against the unwieldy tide of the ocean's magic. It drew Gentian's startled gaze down to the bow-wave of the *Waraga*, to look into the eyes of a corpse.

The body was being dragged along as if it had been tied somehow to the hull, drowned face shadowed by the spray. Leaning over the rail, she saw a slight figure with short brown hair. Blindly staring eyes looked out of white flesh so bloated the features were almost lost. But still, after a moment's disorientation she recognised them. The face was her own.

"Sea-fetch."

Naming the fetch broke its casting. The apparition sank into the spray, leaving her only a glimpse of fin and flicking tail, and an uncharacteristic taste of foreboding. A sea-fetch was one of the few true seers, and this visitation was a warning of impending danger. Those who saw their deaths in a fetch's eyes were on the brink of mortal peril. Ill-luck, ill-will – something – would try to strike her down.

If this was the consequence of breaking her vow, it certainly hadn't wasted any time. But it provided a counterpoint, distraction from defeat, and Gentian smiled for the first time since her return journey had begun. Did threats matter? She had gambled, she had lost, and Darest was still far greater than anything she could defeat. So she would go to the meeting which was her excuse for returning, visit her parents because she had promised, and finally see her longed-for home steading. Goldenrod. She would never bond with a place more, never feel more centred and herself than she had there. But then she would leave.

Darest was a hopeless fight.

ooOoo

Resolution was struck an immediate blow when they drew into the harbour of Tor Darest, the capital of Darest, and Gentian set eyes on the excuse. On Vostal Hill, close by the palace, it caught her up and left her staring open-mouthed.

"Quite a sight, isn't it?"

"Wonderful."

The *Waraga's* first mate laughed at the reverential note in her voice. "We were in port when it happened. Didn't take more than a few moments for the thing to grow. Ten day wonder."

The 'thing' was a pavilion fashioned from four massive trees: coin-leaf lorams set on the very crown of Vostal Hill's grassy bulk. Black trunks reached straight and slender for the sun, but then bent unnaturally in toward each other, branches twining together into a peak. In autumn the light green leaves would brighten to a vivid yellow-gold. In Winter bare black branches would be filigree grace.

She wanted it.

"Filled with blue light, it was," the first mate commented, watching her face quizzically. "The Fae Court, come to Darest."

"There's something inside," Gentian said slowly. "Seats."

"Now how'd you tell that? Yes, a throne for the Fae Queen, and a throne for King Aluster. Ah, I'd have given a lot to be a fly on the wall for that meeting, to see our King make the Fair eat crow. It'll be the last trees they give us, that's for sure."

The woman chuckled appreciatively while Gentian sharpened her sight further, to gaze at two far-distant thrones, also fashioned from living trees. Maple, perhaps, or sellac. Lovely.

The King wanted to turn the entire hill into a garden. Gentian, thanks to the exertions of her mother, was here to consult on the project. The Fae pavilion had been mentioned, but no-one had *explained*.

She allowed her sight return to normal, and made herself look away. But her head was already filling with images, with possibilities and the need to give them substance. Walking away from Vostal Hill's crown would be an act of sheer will.

"Neatly caught," she murmured, with the softest of laughs. "Well done, mother."

"Pardon, Miss?"

"I see they've been clearing out the docks."

"They have. The restoration's been running smooth as silk since the snow melt. Timber arrives from the Tongue, they build new houses just south of Belsen Cove, and pull down a few more of the shanties in the docklands as soon as the residents move out. See there? Not fancy places, but there's few who'll baulk at taking them, specially since there's a yard-grant of land to go with it. And they've already started work on Belsen Cove. Going to build ships."

There was open satisfaction on the first mate's seamed face as she looked west to a community growing around the beginnings of a dry-dock. Gentian hadn't been to Darest's capital since she was twelve, but vivid images of grace and neglect had remained with her. Back when Darest had been more than wealthy the Rathen rulers had set a fashion – or dictated it, given the tales of Rathen autocracy – for style to never be sacrificed for utility. The result was beautiful. Tor Darest flowed over the hills at the mouth of the Eldavar River, full of marvellous lines. The foreshore featured a wide promenade of the warm honey sandstone used for most of the buildings, with a deliberate contrast of dark grey stone that Gentian found particularly pleasing. It had been an airy, expansive city, well sewered, with plenty of parkland and marvellous views across the glittering bay.

Since the last Rathen King – bar this reappearing Aluster – had died two hundred years ago, Darest had steadily declined. Bad luck blighted every venture, an enchanted forest known as the Tongue had overtaken the north-east, and farm and orchard workers had been driven from their land: out of the kingdom altogether, or to Tor Darest. The docks particularly had struggled to accommodate the influx, become more shanty town than functioning port. Cracks had been left untended, were followed by weeds, dirt, and a general shabbiness had crept across the city.

A single winter could hardly wash all that away, but clearing out the docks made a marvellous difference. The wood for the new housing came from the Tongue: the Fae kingdom to the east had finally been forced to admit their responsibility for the forest's encroachment and were now obliged to chop it down, restore the orchards, even prepare the lumber for building. Judging from the number of ships in port, and the busy crowd on the foreshore, Gentian was not the only one to return hoping to enjoy altered fortune.

The sails cracked in a freshening breeze and the first mate tipped her cap before hurrying off to bark orders. Gentian watched the *Waraga's* crew swarm over the rigging, then turned her thoughts to the immediate future. A place to eat, a place to sleep.

Too late to escape that.

Chapter Two

It struck. Gentian woke with a sharp intake of breath, shuddering at her heart's own assault, hearing nothing over the pounding of blood, every jangled nerve shouting aloud: Fight! Flee! Foe!

Another breath, as memory flooded past shock; the same progression she'd followed so many times. First a hammer of loathing, the pre-dawn blow of a vast, inimical giant. Next a sense of being wrung like a rag, trapped beneath a black weight, desperate for escape. Fear made exquisite by urgency.

A third breath, as racing dread collapsed to shaky aftermath. Taut muscle dissolving, pain vanishing to memory, skin damp with a lightning-flash of sweat gone cool. Sick disorientation. A wash of revulsion for all the world. So utterly familiar.

Her fourth morning back, her fourth waking. She would endure this every day she remained within the borders. Even that wood-wrought pavilion could not hope to balance it.

Darest.

There was a tang of blood at the back of her throat, a variation on her morning trial. She had grown more sensitive to It. A sip of water thinned the taste of iron, but left her impatient to get on, so as soon as she was able she dressed, packed her belongings, and slung the bags about her shoulders. Today she was to meet the King, and would start out for Goldenrod immediately after.

Though the morning had barely crept past dawn, half the inn's staff were bustling when Gentian came down to settle her account. The kingdom was in the grip of industry, all eager preparation for a grand spring festival to celebrate the rediscovered King. The flatlands between the city's northwest and Belsen Cove were being prepared for a sprawling market fair, and the festival boasted sword matches and races and duelling illusionists, all with truly excessive prizes.

The big event might be weeks away, but Tor Darest was already crowded. The prize purses would be easily made back in harbour fees and fairground taxes, and it was pleasant to see the city so alive and eager. Walking out into streets glistening with early rain, Gentian watched the stir approvingly.

After settling at a harbour-front bakery, balcony tables already filling with an assorted crowd of breakfasters, her gaze strayed inevitably across the bay to the palace and its glorious neighbour. Waiting for the King to schedule their meeting, she'd spent the past few days circling that sight: wandering the wealthy suburbs directly north of the palace, then the sheep-dotted hills to the south and east. She'd finally walked the quiet beach which ran around the base of the hills, and onto Vostal Hill itself, tasting it. Darest, this particular part of Darest, absorbed her fully.

The hook was firmly embedded, right in that spot behind her breastbone. Always, when her particular weakness had her in its grip, she felt it there most. Need for what could be, waiting to be born. She'd sometimes not won a commission for a garden, but she'd never turned her back on one before.

Nor had she yet. Though she loathed her mornings in Darest, Gentian longed to stay, despite vows and resolutions and a straightforward sense of self-preservation. Vostal Hill, that glorious crown, was tipping her into self-doubt. She had endured fourteen years of Darest, had grown strong in her fourteen years away. The hill would take months, but she wanted what she could make of it, what should be made of it for Darest's own sake.

Gentian spent a lazy morning, eating a sumptuous half dozen of the Darien pastries she had missed most. And reconstructing a semblance of resolve. She loved it and longed for it, but Darest was not good for her. Her garden, the vision that living crown had inspired – well perhaps for the first time she would merely provide a design, but not oversee construction.

It was time to see the King.

ooOoo

"You understand, of course, that His Majesty is very busy with preparations. It shouldn't be much longer."

"Of course," Gentian said absently. She cared less about delays than the neatly drawn plans her mother's friend Chult – the palace's Master Gardener – had presented her on arrival. A design for Vostal Hill, well thought-out, showing a certain flair and sense of balance.

Rolling them up, she glanced down the busy hall to the closed doors of the throne room, where two guards in black and brown uniforms were alertly watching the passing throng.

Lips pressed together, Gentian turned away, walking to the far end of the hall and into the stone-bounded garden itching at the very boundaries of her senses. The massive enchantments of the palace were almost entirely gone, but an echo lingered here of the deep-throated murmur she remembered from her childhood visit. She closed her eyes to feel it better: a well-worn groove, like the bed of a dry river. It would be years, perhaps centuries, before the shape of it was gone, with or without the living plant. This place had become the Rathen Rose.

With considerable interest she studied the thorny tendrils twining about the arches of the paved garden. A vessel to bear the force of the enchantment that had protected the palace, the Rathen inheritance, and the very borders of Darest until it had warped and been destroyed by the new King. Gentian puzzled over its leafy husk until an approaching swirl and murmur of bound power warned her the time for reverie was at an end.

"Perhaps a Kedristan red, Master Chult?" she asked as she turned to look out into the hall.

"Do you think so?" Chult sounded startled. "I've never considered what species it might be."

"Father would probably be able to tell," Gentian mused, tapping the Master Gardener's arm to warn him of the arrival announced by bound power. "I'll have to ask him."

"Does it matter?" asked the lead of the trio entering the garden: a tall, lean man with hair and eyes near-matching shades of blue-black.

Gentian automatically swept into the neat little bow she'd perfected for use on monarchs. It was, she reflected, the first time she'd used it on one of her own.

"Certainly," she said. "The Kedristans prefer intense pruning."

"Pruning?"

Dismay from the second of the trio, standing to the King's right. A woman almost as tall as he, her grey eyes and braided black hair complemented by a surcoat of black chased with gold and silver. The uniform suited her build and colouring, giving her a dignity Gentian associated with idealised marble statues. It also served to nearly hide well-advanced pregnancy. This, then, was the traditional champion of the Rathen rulers, once part of the kingdom's enchantments. There was a space in the taste of the garden which matched her shape.

She was also one of the sources of bound power. Close now, Gentian could hear its intent:

"See them, see it, see there, see now, see this, see here, see that, see, see, SEE."

A strong, circular binding that would last several days, prompting Gentian to study the woman's grey eyes, discovering a fixed lack of focus and dilated pupils. Blind. The spell replaced her sight.

"It's, what?" Gentian said. "Six, seven hundred years old? Centuries past its usual span, and the maintenance structure suddenly gone. Unless you're planning to just uproot it, you'll need to replace that. Otherwise it will–" She looked away from the clear discomfort on the Champion's face and surveyed the tangle of vines, the canopy of thorn and serrated leaf. Behind them, the worn grooves of function, a sense of absent purpose, and a yearning ache reaching out to fill the space where the Champion should stand. "It's vulnerable."

Eloquent little silence. Gentian didn't know the details of how the Rose's enchantment had warped, but plainly it had left its scars.

The awkward moment was broken by the third member of the trio, standing a little behind the other two, to the King's left. He was a smaller man, and should surely recede into the background beside the force and height of King and Champion. Instead, clad all in white to highlight porcelain pale skin and white-blond hair, he provided contrast and counterpoint, while his sheer presence, a singular self-possession, threw his companions into shade. He was slender, with finely drawn features, compact chin, a truly beautiful mouth, and the most strikingly vivid eyes: dark rims circled irises of deep sapphire, with a crystalline corona, blue-white, radiating from the pupils. Eyes that, if you looked into them too long, might send you blind.

"You have inherited Laeth Varpatten's sensitivity, Magister Calder?" he asked. An innocuous, tension-breaking question in a perfectly polite tone of voice. And yet there was a glitter in those eyes, a sweetness to the curve of that mouth, which turned the words into an opening thrust.

"And Frid Calder's strength," Gentian replied promptly, entertained by the censure she detected. "But none of their passion for Shaping. Only for the gardening itself."

A fractional drop of eyelash dusted amused contempt. "Do they approve?"

"My parents find any true-mage who doesn't Shape unaccountable, Lord Magister."

The man's lips made another infinitesimal shift, marking a point scored in the unspoken language of a supreme courtier. Gentian had recognised him from his resemblance to his mother, the former Regent. This was Aristide Couerveur, heir to one of Darest's sixteen baronies, current Councillor of Mages, and owner of a reputation for high magery and ruthless ambition.

Since Lord Aristide would have ruled Darest if Aluster Rathen had not reappeared, Gentian would have wondered at the King appointing him to any position of power in the Court, let alone to his left hand. But the roaring whisper of another enchantment provided confirmation of the explanation. She could feel the gale-force power of it centred around an intriguing knot of lines curling beneath the skin of his right palm: a *saecstra*, tightly knotted auditor of intent, and permanent shackle to earn the trust of a King. It would snuff his life if he broke whatever vow he'd made.

Then Aluster Rathen was back to the fore, brusquely impatient as he announced they would go out on Vostal Hill. Gentian made no objection, trailing the picturesque trio into a cloud-scudded afternoon, listening to the King point out the location of particular features he wanted.

Aluster Rathen was no gardener. Informed, yes. Perceptive and decided in his opinion of what a garden should be, but he was more a man who wanted a garden about him, finding pleasure in experiencing it rather than in getting dirt beneath his nails. She doubted he'd ever personally put seed to earth.

"You've viewed the plans?" he asked, when they finally reached the shade of the hill's crown.

"Yes, indeed."

King Aluster gave her a sharp look for the bland tone she'd used. "What do you think?"

"They work in their setting. I would enjoy visiting them. I fail to see why you're consulting me." She glanced up at his still face, and added by way of explanation: "Master Chult is perfectly capable of producing that garden. If you have a design already, why call in a designer?"

"Because there's something missing." The King spoke with frank frustration, and no sign of offence for her plain speech. "Something I can't capture. I don't know what it is."

Gentian decided to approve of her new King. Whatever Rathen flair had led to the creation of Tor Darest persisted. He reached.

Which, for her, was not a good thing. When Chult had shown her the design, irritation had been followed by the realisation that it was the key to walking away from Vostal Hill. Not now. Still–

"Do one of two things," she recommended, deliberately terse. "Leave it as it is, because standing alone it is a perfectly stark loveliness, and anything you do to the hill will detract from that. Else–" Gentian called will and power into conjunction and set an illusion between them, a globe looking into the vision that had grown behind her breastbone.

She'd left the crest of the hill untouched, because no frame or embellishment could match those four loram trees. A thick cross of grass interlaced with flat beds and paving, producing a frame of green and sandstone. Clean lines for the beds, filled with dark flat foliage and massed flowering plants hardy enough for a seaside environment. Golden paths and terraces to match the lines of the city, growing ever more complex the further down the hill the eye roved, until finally a sea-foam filigree of arches, trailing vine and covered walks to froth at the hill's base, just above clean white sand and shimmering water.

Illusion casting required a great deal of concentration to produce unblurred detail, but once she'd settled the image Gentian was able to fix it, and then enjoy the expression on Aluster Rathen's face. Absorbed, intent. No false raptures, just a kind of acceptance that Gentian appreciated more than words. Whatever he'd been reaching for in his design, he'd found it here.

"You appear to have lost the New Palace," said a silk-smooth voice, and Gentian glanced away from the King to his Councillor, who was looking pleased in the way of a person expecting the worst and meeting it, lips curved into a highly satirical smile.

"It is, after all, very ugly," Gentian replied. "Nothing done to the harbour area can be anything but lessened by it." Philosophically she adjusted her illusion, replacing the dark, blocky building rising above the palace walls. "There are a few things that might be done to it externally, to mitigate its effect, but really, you should consider just knocking it down."

"That *is* a solution, certainly." Edged amusement again, but the look Aristide Couerveur was giving his king held careful assessment. Aluster Rathen was evidently not so mindful of the purse strings as his Councillor.

Gentian glanced at the Champion's face, to gauge the third of the trio's reaction, and found her wry, tolerantly listening to the by-play between the pair. Her focus was not on the garden.

Suddenly weary of this always-tiresome stage, when patron weighed up purchase and usually tried to modify a design already complete, Gentian unrolled the plans they had given her, and began speaking in the language of power.

Each syllable, produced with craftsman's care, eased its way out of her mouth like glowing, expansive gas that doubled, tripled in size even before escaping the gate of her lips. An elegant little casting she'd learned in the East, it sent the illusion sinking onto the reverse of the plans, light staining paper in gradual steps until she had a perfectly rendered image she could roll up and present to the King.

"I will be travelling to my parents' steading, and returning around the time of this spring festival. You could, perhaps, give me your decision then?"

"I'll do that," Aluster Rathen said, with just the faintest shift of his eyes toward Aristide Couerveur. It was not the decision, but the detail he would need to settle.

About to bow and make the usual polite noises, Gentian was distracted by a pinpoint of power blooming at the King's right elbow. Both King and Councillor reacted to it, drawing power automatically into shields, then relaxing them once again when it became clear it was sigil-communication, not an attack.

Gentian politely withdrew to stand with Chult on the far side of the pavilion, studying the thrones fashioned from living trees. Certainly some kind of maple. Occasionally she glanced back at the King, engrossed in conversation with the air, but for the while she allowed herself to construct the possibilities of her garden, her frame for this pavilion.

When the solid hum of the communication magic died as abruptly as it had sprung to life, King, Councillor and Champion fell into terse discussion, faces set. Evidently not good news. In dumb show she watched a plan of action formulated, decided upon. Then, to her surprise, the King turned in her direction.

"Magister Calder – you said you were about to leave for Goldenrod Steading?"

"Well, yes." Gentian was aware of a sudden stiffness in her voice. Had something happened to her parents?

"We've just had news of a Saxan barge gone missing in the Galassas. They've asked for our help searching for the passengers. As you are travelling in that direction, I would appreciate you assisting Magister Couerveur in the search."

It was a command couched as a request. "Of course," Gentian said, blankly. The Galassas was the river which ran out of the Skorese Mountains, then along the border between Sax and Darest. It would mean a dog-leg in her journey, but no great detour.

He nodded curtly, and then turned to take his Champion's arm, escorting her back down the windswept hill. Gentian wondered vaguely why a wedding wasn't included in the festival's arrangements, and then shifted her attention to Aristide Couerveur.

"Fleeting Hall in an hour, if you would," he said. "We should make Estharos before dark, at the least."

"Who was on the barge?" It had to be someone important, to provoke this response.

"The Atlaran ambassador. Chenar and Rydan of Sax. Aloren of Ceria. Kestia and Jurasel of Cya. Half the heirs of the western kingdoms, vanished without a trace."

"What were they all doing on Darest's border?"

He was barely listening, thoughts obviously on the task ahead. But then the corners of that superb mouth lifted, curved up into a smile of singular sweetness. It was not at all a nice expression.

"That is a question to answer."

Chapter Three

At the precise moment the palace bells struck the allotted hour, Aspen Choraide snapped shut an exceedingly tedious treatise on the formulation of permanent enchantments and turned to the immeasurably more fascinating task of choosing just the right thing to wear. The divine Aluster's love of unembellished black had seen the demise of the lush and sumptuous fashions of Arista Couerveur's regency, and with the Court slavishly following the new Rathen's lead, or cleaving to the Diamond's pristine whites, the new styles were all too predictable. Of course, due homage was half the point, and Aspen was tall and fair and could bring all that black and white off to his advantage. But how, how to stand out?

A pleasant interlude followed, leaving Aspen's ordinarily tidy room strewn with a good deal of expensive linen. Still, nothing quite satisfied. He would have to find something new for the Festival Ball.

Restlessly he looked outside. He had of late moved his mirror over by the window so that when he dressed he could see the exercises in the barracks yard, and watch the faces of the guards when they noticed him. Guards were great fun: so stern and serious and determined to be correct. There was one in particular, a tall woman who would survey him coolly and then make a point of ignoring his window...but she wasn't there today.

Dissatisfaction was cut short by a sharp rap on the door. Aspen spun across the room and pulled it open on a man dressed in grey, a nondescript creature with regular features and a permanently unobtrusive manner. Born to live in the background, and yet one of the most powerful servants of the Court. Aristide Couerveur's factotum.

"Well, Vaselte!" Aspen watched with quiet glee as Vaselte's eyes flicked from the whirl of clothing about the room to their absence from the room's sole occupant. There was a little matter of a stolen kiss between him and Vaselte, and it was about time he took up that chase again. "To what do I owe this pleasure?"

Vaselte was no easy target, his face resuming that bland lack of personality all the Diamond's servants affected. And then all thought of baiting the man went out of Aspen's mind:

"Lord Aristide is journeying to the Saxan border," Vaselte said. "And would be obliged if you would join him. He leaves in an hour. Wait in Fleeting Hall."

"What?!" Aspen caught at Vaselte's sleeve before he could turn away. "The Diamond, going to the border? Why?"

"Perhaps you should ask Lord Aristide." Vaselte tugged his arm free, nodded with an echo of his master's pointed courtesy, and walked off.

Aspen stood in the doorway staring after him, and then caught the appreciative eye of a passing matron, dropped into a flourishing bow, and retreated. His mind was awhirl, all disbelief and anticipation. Travel to the border with the Diamond? The invitation was almost as surprising as the journey itself. Aristide Couerveur had scarcely budged from Tor Darest since he'd returned from his 'prentice tour. Something particularly momentous must have happened, for him to go off on an hour's notice, a scarce month before a festival he'd been planning since the previous autumn. And Aspen for some reason had express permission to tag along, to observe the Diamond Couerveur outside his natural environment. To perhaps finally realise a long-held ambition.

What to wear suddenly took on a whole new light. Aspen stared around at the chaos of his room, and slowly shook his head.

ooOoo

"Hello, Nixie."

"Aspen." That slow smile, touched with warm amusement. Soren would know why he'd gone straight to her. No doubt she'd waited in her book-lined receiving room in anticipation of his visit, for he and the Champion were friends, allies: they went to each other for comfort and support and, most importantly, information. Between them they had a straight line to all the palace gossip.

She still turned her head toward the person she was talking to, even though the spell that let her see had nothing to do with direction. But it was becoming more and more a perfunctory gesture, leaving her oriented on something just a little to one side of the person she was talking to. Aspen hated that, loathed the reminder of what she'd sacrificed. He fully understood why King Aluster's darkest moods followed those occasions when his Champion's sight spell lapsed while he wasn't around to immediately renew it.

The person least bothered by her loss of sight seemed to be Soren herself. She'd expected to die destroying the Rathen Rose, had told Aspen how astonished she still was to be breathing. When she said things like that it always left Aspen with an impulse to wrap her tight in his arms and regret missed chances. But the King was sadly territorial, leaving Aspen to languish in the role of devoted friend, taking comfort from the delights of the Court. Which, as Soren had once pointed out, was exactly how he liked it.

"Well?" Aspen demanded, when Soren didn't immediately Tell All. "How, what, when, why? No particular order, I'm not fussy."

He loved that he could make her laugh, but her amusement was short-lived and she frowned as she gestured for him to sit down.

"A message came from the Saxan King while we were out on Vostal Hill. His sons were hosting some sort of boating party on the Galassas River, with ambassadors and neighbouring royalty along for the ride. They were sleeping on a barge, with enough guards camped along the bank to take a small city. It's foggy along the river near dawn, but the barge was within hailing distance and there was a lantern set into the bow which could be seen through the mist. The mages in the guard party had no warning of someone casting. They felt a surge of power and saw the lantern was gone, the barge was gone. No trace."

Aspen had not expected his love of drama to be so bounteously fulfilled, and struggled not to gape. "This was this morning?"

"Yes. They scoured the riverbank, cast whatever one would cast in the circumstances. Nothing. Part of the search party headed upstream, but they've run up against the point where the Galassas leaves the Saxan border and heads up into the Skorese mountains. So they wanted permission to cross into Darest." Soren shook her head. "We gave it, of course, and sent word to the nearest guard post to assist wherever possible. King Meneth was all very polite, made no accusations, but, well, it's Darest. The Fair might have given it over to humans centuries ago, but even Dariens are convinced there's Faerie sorcelment at every turn. And those mountains have a reputation."

"Sun." The possibilities unreeled in Aspen's mind. "No wonder the Diamond's bolting to the scene. The entire West will think Darest has stolen their best and bravest. We can talk about haunted mountains, and they might even accept that our re-found Rathen has nothing to do with it–"

"But they'll blame us all the same." Soren's hand absently touched the swell of her stomach. "Aristide will mainly be fielding the diplomatic crisis. He'll investigate, of course, but the West has a dozen mages for each of ours, and if the guard party's mages have been searching all morning with no result, what chance do we have of finding the lost?"

"You'd be surprised." It never paid to underestimate the Diamond Couerveur. Aspen's thoughts hit a snag there and he lifted his head sharply. "Why has he invited *me* along?" For while Aspen had an excess of magical strength and a modicum of talent, he was still no more than a Maistrice, an apprentice, and far less advanced than he should be. All those tomes of word-magic it was necessary to plough through to be passed up to Maja or Magister rank had never held much attraction, and it was only a cunning plot to get closer to the Diamond that had seen him tediously studious these past few months.

"The King ordered it. You and this gardening mage both. Protection, don't you see?"

"Gardening mage?" Momentarily diverted, Aspen lifted his brows. "Do you mean this consultant Chult called in about the King's garden? She's a mage?"

"Apparently. Her parents are some people called Laeth Varpatten and Frid Calder. Aristide was being rather pointed about them, from which I gathered that they and this gardener must be fairly powerful."

"I didn't even know the Goldenrod Shapers had children," Aspen admitted, a shade annoyed. "They're a married couple with a steading in the northwest, Shaping exclusively with plants. Incredibly boring stuff like frost-resistant apples and flax that comes out in a different colour than off-white. The daughter must have the strength, at least, if she's to fly to the border with us." Then he thought it through a little more and laughed. "*She* won't be popular with the Diamond. The only reason he's held out this carrot of possibly-maybe-sometime taking me on as 'prentice is because he's trying to stop Darest haemorrhaging mages. A powerful Darien true-mage who gads about making gardens! That won't go down well at all." He grinned. "No competition for me."

"You are nothing if not persistent," Soren said. "I'd wish you luck, but, really, I dread to think what would happen if you actually sparked some interest from Aristide."

"Happen?" Aspen gave her a pitying look. "My dear child, what have you and the King been up to for the last six months? Hours of lustful abandon, that's what would happen. The shrieking of my name in ecstasy. A good deal of parading about naked, and many tender confidences where he tells me all his secrets."

"Are we talking about the same Aristide Couerveur?" She was giving him that tolerant and doubtful look, the same one she'd worn before the King showed up, when Aspen had been trying to get her to take him just seriously enough. But then, Soren could be stubbornly earnest, and Aspen had never been able to make her see bed-games for the sport they were.

Before she could start telling him not to get in over his head he abandoned his chair and bent over her hands, relishing her embarrassment as he kissed them. "Now that I've a better idea of what to expect, I can start packing. Take care of yourself, O Champion. I'm holding you to that promise of a dance at the Festival Ball."

It was meant to make her laugh again, but she gripped his hands in return, looking far too solemn and stern. "Take care of *your*self, Aspen. And watch Aristide's back. I'm not entirely certain we could manage Darest without him."

ooOoo

It had been an uncomfortably honest thing to say, and it niggled at Aspen while he ran about begging, borrowing and pleading for the essentials necessary to face the world beyond the Darien Court. King Aluster's popularity waxed ever greater, but the success of his reign was without doubt to the credit of Aristide Couerveur. The Diamond owned the Court, served Darest with unparalleled virtuosity, and could never be its King. Not while Soren's lover and child lived.

Aspen had long coveted the Diamond, and thought he understood the man well enough to recognise the logic, not to mention the devotion to Darest, which had led him to bind himself with the *saecstra* rather than risk his kingdom in a battle for the throne. For it was *his* kingdom: he'd been raised in the expectation of ruling it, had fought and won its battles for years, had lived and breathed Darest his entire life. The Diamond Couerveur and the new King were working well together, and there even lingered rumours about them eventually marrying, but the most upright creature in the world would surely chafe at the turn of fortune, and search for a way to alter such a sour fate as eternal second.

The thing that should not be forgotten was that Aristide Couerveur was a pragmatic man. The whole Court knew anyone fool enough to manoeuvre against him was swiftly and thoroughly made to regret it: an object lesson to other conspirators. Pointedly polite, wonderful to look at, and carrying a tangible air of menace. Just the thought of bringing him to his knees tied Aspen's stomach in tingling knots. He was the ultimate challenge.

The familiar thrill came as the Diamond emerged from the Councillor of Mages' apartments. Without the usual tightly tailored demi-robe, his clothes were unexpectedly like the King's. He'd even abandoned white for a charcoal grey that made his pale skin glow. This alone was enough to set every second person in Fleeting Hall to taking second looks, sparking a wildfire of speculation that would probably reach the border before they did. Aristide, utterly self-contained, strolled toward the room's centre, Vaselte following with travelling bags slung on either side.

Aspen hurried his step to beat the Diamond there, joining what must be the third of their merry band. At first sight not too daunting: a small woman with delicate features, her soft brown hair feathered close to a fine-boned skull, and her figure hidden by travelling clothes and packs.

As Aspen came up alongside her she switched her gaze to him and suddenly he was uncertain. She might remind him of a solemn child, all big hazel eyes and unsmiling little mouth, but there was something of the Diamond's total self-possession about her, a centred authority that suggested she hadn't ignored her studies with anything like Aspen's devotion.

"Hello," she said, with an air of careful good manners. "Are you coming too?"

"I am." He dropped into a flourishing bow, casting a glance up through his lashes as he did so, but catching no change of expression. "Aspen Choraide, at your service."

"Gentian Calder."

"I have to admit, Gentian Calder, I didn't know you existed till a few minutes ago. You did your 'prentice work out of Darest?"

She left a pause before replying: "Most of it. My parents taught me a great deal, but I don't think I could have escaped Shaping if I'd 'prenticed with them. I studied in the East, then went to Atlarus for a few years."

Not freshly passed up then, which meant she was probably older than his own twenty-five years. But true-mages rarely looked their ages, and this one could be mistaken for a schoolroom inmate. "No desire to follow in their footsteps, keep us in coloured flax?" he asked ingenuously, very aware of the Diamond just reaching earshot.

And he'd been too obvious. A flicker of amusement touched green and brown-flecked eyes, but she just said "Shaping can be monstrous dull," and turned to make her courtesy to the Diamond.

Aristide Couerveur's opinion of mages who deserted Darest was evidently not preoccupying him at that moment, though the glance he threw Aspen suggested that he, too, had found the ploy transparent. But a mere mis-step could not dampen Aspen's spirits this afternoon.

"All present and correct, M'Lord," he said, almost unable to keep from smirking openly.

"So it appears," Aristide replied, considering Aspen's motley collection of borrowed bags and satchels. He had this trick of lifting one corner of his mouth, just a tiny fraction. It was no doubt designed to make encroaching courtiers feel like idiots, but had always struck Aspen as a strangely compassionate expression.

The Diamond was in too great a hurry to waste any more time sending darts Aspen's way. With a polite nod for Magister Calder, he said, "Estharos with certainty, somewhere in Runath if the winds are favourable, heading out again at dawn tomorrow. We'll leave from the west stable yard."

Flying. Every gift of honey had its gnat to mar golden sweetness. Aspen had the strength for flying, and most fortunately had freshly reviewed the various methods as part of his hopeful preparation for winning 'prenticeship with the Diamond. But if there ever was an exhausting, unpleasant way to rush to the border, it was hurling yourself through the air.

Short hops were quite different. You rose gracefully from the ground, grandly ignoring the people gaping in awe, and wafted gently to your destination. Pleasantly invigorating, really. But distance travel in a hurry, where you had to sling all your belongings about your shoulders and go for hours on end, buffeted by inevitably frozen gales while you discovered that the boundless and bare skies were seething with more grit and insect life than seemed possible, all of it intent on colliding with your face, forcing its way into your mouth or piercing your eyeballs – no.

Out in the stable yard, they made preparations for the ordeal. Vaselte furnished Aristide with a heavy cloak, then a backpack and three long-strapped satchels to sling over his shoulders. This was followed by thick gloves, a scarf wound about the neck and finally a supple leather faceguard which left only a slit for those marvellous eyes. Aspen owned one, and had searched fruitlessly for too long before recalling turning it to more exotic purposes a year or two before. He had to make do with several layers of scarf, wound round and round his head. Hardly ideal, but sustained flying required all your energy, so there wasn't even hope of casting a basic shield to keep the worst of it away.

The little gardening mage watched him mummifying himself with a kind of absorbed interest, and then unhooked from one of her arms what Aspen had taken to be a strange kind of basket. Instead it revealed itself to be a leather helmet, which she plonked unceremoniously on her head, tightening a strap beneath her chin. As well as the usual nose-guard there was, Aspen saw with a sudden pitch of envy, a pinkish-purple glass covering most of her face.

Perfectly aware of his reaction, she treated him to an unexpected grin, wicked and engaging after all that staring solemnity. "All the rage in Atlarus this year," she explained. "Hard to believe no-one thought of it before."

"A mere oversight." Aspen let his voice drop to an intense whisper. "Guard yourself well tonight. That *will* be mine."

"For the warning, I thank you." She'd gone all unsmiling again, but there was laughter in the tone. Then she looked aside, and a moment later Aspen felt the trickle of drawn power. The Diamond was casting, and Aspen wasn't sure he'd even noticed their by-play, his mind already at the border.

That was sobering. No time for games. Lost heirs and political crises and who knew what kind of traps and mare's nests waiting for them to stumble into? Aspen remembered Soren's face, worried and pensive as she told him to watch the Diamond's back. The Lord Aristide had his enemies among the Western kingdoms, opponents who'd be only too pleased to see him exposed, without sufficient guard. Watching the Diamond's back had never been a trial, but for once it could be important, critical. And an unparalleled opportunity.

Rising rapidly into the air, Aspen focused on the black-swathed figure, and anticipated protecting him closely indeed.

Chapter Four

Gentian had long ago learned not to move until her heart stopped racing. The shock of waking always left her wanting to fling herself out of the room, to run away, to get out under the sky and breathe free, but actually doing so would prolong the after-effects of the morning's attack. So she would lie still and take careful breaths until she could move without shaking. Going back to sleep after was something she'd rarely even attempted.

Her fifth morning back in Darest, and she at least had reason to be up and about so early. Good winds had seen them well past the town of Estharos by sunset. When the moon had risen clear and large, Lord Aristide had decided to press on through the night, and they'd ended just shy of midnight in a village in the Barony of Runath. They were to depart an hour after dawn, and expected to reach the border by late morning.

While she washed and packed, muffled noises began to drift up to her narrow room. The single hostelry of the village had been ill-equipped to cope with a trio of mages literally descending on them just when they were turning out the late drunks, and had reacted to the prospect of hosting the kingdom's infamous Councillor of Mages with poorly concealed horror. Gentian had been too limply drained from hours of flying to properly appreciate their haste to relocate an unlucky family to provide sufficient beds, or even to listen to the tumble of apologies that had accompanied the spicy pot-scraping, tough bread and cold apple pie.

Heading down as the light shifted out of grey, Gentian glanced toward the bustle in the kitchen, then left her bags on one of the tables and went out. The air was sharp and crisp, making her nose hurt with the memory of winter, and clouds had come and gone between midnight and dawn to leave everything wet and glistening. She inhaled deeply, letting the slight, honest pain banish that day's serving of hate, then set out at a fast walk along the road.

Runath was a place of fields and farms, dark earth squelching with spring melt, and every view bright with vivid green shoots. And it was Darest, far more Darest to Gentian's mind than the capital, for here familiar laceblossoms embroidered every ditch, and mountains cut the horizon. Those were the Skorese, which had loomed over the southwest of her childhood and were close to due north from this part of Runath. The familiar peaks, even from a different angle, struck her with sudden loss. Home, in the Barony of Dwyallin, was just beyond them, and though this place did not speak to her in quite the same tones – for nothing spoke to her like Goldenrod – it was like a cousin, and had the power to make her chest ache for those fourteen years of exile.

A hurried patter of steps brought Gentian's attention back to her immediate surroundings. A loaded basket was coming down the road toward her, the boy struggling to hold it upright little more than legs bowed beneath its weight. One of the hosteller's children, sent to fetch the village's finest in hopes of pleasing a guest second in consequence in the entire kingdom, not to mention being a great-mage and heir of the former Regent, Baroness Couerveur. The Diamond they called him, and loved and feared him, and until yesterday he'd probably been little more than a myth to these people. She wondered how many, in the days and months to follow, would visit the village to hear just how he had looked and acted. If he had any sense the hosteller would seize fortune's gift and charge an extortionate price for folk to sleep in, to even see the room, the very bed where Aristide Couerveur himself had slept. The idea made her laugh.

With a gasp, the approaching child gave a violent jerk and more or less hurled his burden forward. He let out an anguished wail even as the basket left his hands, eyes round with dismay at what he'd done. They went wider still as the spray of eggs and onions, leeks, cheeses and jars slowed, came to a gradual stop, hesitated, then arranged themselves tidily back into the basket.

As his reassembled burden drifted back into his arms, the boy gaped numbly, but he had the wherewithal to clutch the basket tightly when it bumped against his chest.

"I'm sorry for startling you," Gentian said, and watched him shiver and gulp and almost set a few eggs tumbling again as he bobbed a hasty courtesy. Awe and terror competed for dominance on his face as he hastily circled past her and made his escape.

With a twist of her lips, Gentian walked on, idly picking flowers and wondering what it would be like to not be a mage, to fear even benign ones. To not be able to reach out and catch a falling egg with will and power alone. Only true-mages could do that, could feel the magic that was everywhere in the world, and draw on it without device or the use of word-magic. She'd felt the nature of places since birth, and had been little more than six when she'd grown strong enough to start really pulling at it, flexing those muscles that made her true-mage. It was as much a part of her as her sense of smell, or her fingers.

Atlarus had been a good place to live, for the use of word-magic was far more widely spread, less jealously guarded. Most everyone had the inner strength to carry off spoken magic of some sort, and in Atlarus straightforward, useful spells were taught to all who had the patience to learn the exacting rules of pronunciation. *Tekla*, they called it: hearth magic. Atlarus was full of magic, and very far away, and she had often found herself happy there.

Pushing aside the bad decision of her return, Gentian spoke a few words of power, and then traced a glowing symbol in the air to focus a sigil-call. Soon her mother was looking through a square of light before her, dragging curling blond hair off a sun-burned and drowsy face. "Gentian," she said, pleased but frowning. "Where are you?"

"Runath. But I've been diverted into some problem on the border and don't know when I'll get to Goldenrod."

"Yes, we heard about that. Wait – Laeth wants to talk to you."

A few moments later Gentian's father's face, so like her own, swam into focus, the image wavering as it tried to stay with her mother.

"Daughter," Laeth Varpatten said, in his subdued way.

"Father," Gentian replied with perfect solemnity, enjoying the pleasure this small ritual of naming gave him. "Is the redvine flowering well?"

"It buries us. The birds drop from the sky with its scent. The kingrod will be in bloom within a week, and the trees are in their prime. We are putting on our best plumage for you."

Goldenrod was blue, crimson and gold in spring, all heady scents. "I'll try to be there as soon as I can," she said. "Tomorrow, if I can manage it." Today, even, if her luck was good.

"I will look for you." There was an ache in her father's eyes, one that had been there since she'd first crossed Darest's border and refused to return. "Gentian, I felt something yesterday morning. A burst of power in the mountains unlike anything I've ever encountered."

"*In* the mountains? This barge went from the river flats."

"It felt closer than that, though not a great deal. I could not feel any intent from it at all."

"I see." Her father was far from the strongest mage in Darest, but his sensitivity to the arcane was renowned in all Sumica. He was close enough to the Skorese to have felt a major casting there, though she didn't understand why he couldn't sort out the intent.

"Take especial care of yourself, daughter. You have been away too long, and Goldenrod is uneasy."

"I will." She broke the casting, glanced toward the snow still sitting on the peaks of the Skorese, then turned and walked back to the hostelry.

Standing in splendid isolation just outside the front door was a figure in charcoal grey. Gentian had met his mother a long time ago, and took a moment to compare the two and commit to memory this vision of Aristide Couerveur: white-blond hair sleeked back from porcelain brow, elegant outline framed by a rough wooden building, dripping trees, and a few cows looking curiously over a fence. Alien, yet not at all out of place, for he was one who existed by sheer force of self. Mud could not overset him. It was far more difficult to picture the Lady Arista in the same place.

"Research, Magister Calder?"

Gentian blinked, then looked down at the forgotten bouquet. "I will certainly need to put a great deal of thought into the exact choice of plants," she replied, bland in the face of the highly misleading expression of polite attention he was directing at her. "If the King has a penchant for wildflowers, I imagine a salt-resistant strain of laceblossom could be produced."

"I trust this little matter will not greatly discommode you."

"Not at all," she replied as gravely as she could. "The banks of the Galassas teem with life. I will not be wasting my time."

"You must consider Maistrice Choraide at your disposal."

"Oh, I'd not deprive you of him, M'Lord. And, well, not a gardener, don't you think?"

Was that a quiver of genuine amusement? Whatever his opinion of her profession, Aristide Couerveur enjoyed fencing over it. "Perhaps an as-yet undiscovered talent?" he suggested.

She laughed, appreciating this sudden show of humanity, but set the game aside. "I have just spoken to my father," she said. "He told me he sensed a burst of power in the mountains yesterday morning. He felt that it was closer than the flatlands where the Galassas runs along the border."

Aristide Couerveur's gaze became momentarily abstract, then he nodded. "That fits with what we've been told. The searchers have been heading upriver, despite cascades that would logically founder any barge. We will join them, rather than visit the site of the original disappearance."

Gentian nodded, and preceded him back inside. Somehow, she doubted she would reach home tomorrow.

ooOoo

There were more than sixty people scattered along the river, working their way up a series of small waterfalls among the foothills of the Skorese, many miles inside Darest's border. Sax, Cya and Ceria, all missing their heirs. It occurred to Gentian that some of the people here would have been sent in hopes of making sure they didn't come back.

She'd felt the search party before she'd seen them. There were a lot of mages down there, a great many active enchantments. The sight of three flyers set off a swirl of new activity, though the power spent in flight and the near presence of Aristide's *saecstra* made it harder than usual for Gentian to sort intent. Shields mainly, and one or two – over there to the left – who had darts of force ready to loose. And others with arrows set to bow, or hands near sword should magic fail. This was a search in company with suspicion and threat.

They moved into near range, but Lord Aristide made no attempt to draw shield, to establish any kind of magical protection. Calculated good sense, since he had a fair chance of countering anything thrown at him, and risked provoking attack by displaying his defences. Descending a little short of the vanguard of the search took them down beside a group of eight men and women wearing the grey and black of Darien swear-swords.

"My Lord Aristide." The rangy blond woman wearing a lieutenant's badge sounded purely relieved as Aristide tugged loose his flight mask and surveyed their surroundings. They were standing atop a flat rock where the river tumbled over a six foot fall. Most of the search party was spread over the two tiers below, but just across the fast, narrow river was a cluster of ten people in the process of hauling a corpse from the water.

"Couerveur."

The speaker was a woman: compact and vigorous, her clothing spoke wealth while a touch of grey speared through gold-brown curls framing pale eyes. Her face was set, mouth a flat line and, even over the rush and gurgle of the river, tight anger was clear in that single, clipped word. Something about her reminded Gentian of her father. Loss. But where Gentian's father mourned his daughter's absence with quiet sorrow, black pain was pent in this woman's blue eyes.

"Queen Myentra."

This, then, was the Queen of Ceria, come to search the Galassas for the body of her child. Aristide's own voice had held none of her hostility, but little sympathy either. He crossed to the nearest point of the riverbank, his attention on the limp wet form between the feet of two Cyan guardsmen. It was the body of a long, lean man clothed in a saffron shift, his dark skin battered purple. Atlaran.

"Is this the first?"

"The first?" Queen Myentra echoed. "By the Moon, Couerveur–"

"Yes, this is the first."

The speaker, blunt and businesslike, was a man in the green and tan uniform of the Saxan guard, though his accent was Eastern. There were shadows of strain beneath dark eyes and his narrow face was stubbled. He touched a hand to his brow in neutral salute.

"This is Kenetet Vye," said another of the group. An Atlaran woman, elongated and magnificent, wearing the robes and strapping of the imperial honour guard. She stooped and brushed her fingers against the corpse's shaved skull, tracing the crescent of the Moon. "Body servant to the ambassador."

A tiny cough from a grey-haired man with a Cyan way of dress. "There has been, also, some wreckage." His tone was apologetic, as if he pointed out some social solecism. "Fragments, carried on the current. It is what led us upstream, against all logic. We have cast again and again for their location, but these mountains...well." His hands sketched a kind of pitying forbearance. "I understand it is quite the tradition to become lost in these parts."

Queen Myentra took a restive step forward, casting a glare of obvious dislike at the Cyan before facing down Aristide once again. The set of her jaw was pugnacious. "I would have an explanation for this, Couerveur. What excuse can you give for this attack?"

Gentian was not alone in paying close attention to Aristide's response. Darest's relationship with the Western Kingdoms was characterised by the Western monarchs being a little too pleased to see a once-great power struggling, probing weakened defences with increasing avidity. Darest had long enjoyed the tenuous protection of its connection with the empire of the Fair, but this fantastic disappearance might actually unify the fractious West into an invasion. To prevent that, Darest would have to walk a tightrope between soothing suspicion and not exposing its throat.

Aristide Couerveur looked away from the tableau on the opposite bank and studied the tumble of the Galassas River. His gaze roved to vertical walls cut into the dark mountain rock, where ferns clung damply in a mist of water spray. Then the foothills that grew beyond, ever more jagged, reaching lofty slopes patterned white. Superbly indifferent to an impatient audience, to the dripping corpse, to any notion of appeasement. Those fine-cut lips, whose subtle shifts Gentian was increasingly enjoying, curled minutely at both corners.

It was a slap in the face, deliberate and precisely underscored. A proclamation that Aristide was a Darien on Darien soil, one called on for assistance and greeted with discourtesy. Never mind what the West had lost, what they suspected, what forces they could bring to bear: they had best remember their manners.

And it worked. The Queen looked taken aback, swallowed an initial response, then adopted a tone of reluctant conciliation. "*If* you please, Couerveur. We would appreciate any aid or guidance you can offer in this. If there is any light you can shed on this situation, we would be glad to hear it."

Again, that tiny shift of lips. A fuller curve this time, to signify approval, a kind of 'well done' of the sort a teacher would offer a laggard pupil who finally grasps a lesson. It was masterful, shifting control of the scene firmly into Aristide's hands, relegating searchers to the role of petitioners and never-you-minding the question of numbers and justifiable outrage. Gentian supposed it would be taken amiss if she applauded.

"I am told that a burst of power was detected yesterday morning, some short way into the mountains." Aristide employed a blandly informative tone. "I suggest that seeking out the source would be more productive than collecting your barge piecemeal. We will follow the course of the river from the air."

This plan of action was eagerly adopted, and the four disparate groups on the opposite bank turned to relaying orders to the rest of the searchers. Aristide, his tall apprentice dogging his elbow, turned to the Darien soldiery waiting his orders and asked for details of those missing.

"Too many, M'Lord," the woman in charge replied, standing up very straight. "It was one of the grand barges and there were more than thirty on board. The Atlaran ambassador. The Saxan Crown Prince, his brother and entourage. The current Cyan Crown Prince, Jurasel, as well as the eldest Cyan princess, her wife and their children. The Cerian Crown Princess, a couple of cousins and hangers-on. Each group had a limited number of attendants and at least one guard. Also a small crew."

Gentian turned away, dangling her helmet by its straps as she watched the Atlarans carrying away the remains of the ambassador's body servant. She wondered if it was at all likely that the ambassador was not in a similar condition. The Arachol would not appreciate losing one of his emissaries, and she did not like to examine the idea of the Atlaran imperial temperament turned on Darest. Atlarus was less likely than most to flinch from the idea of offending The Deeping.

Closing her eyes, Gentian shifted her internal attention to the *place*, to the mountains themselves. They had a distinct presence, but mountains usually did. She'd rarely encountered a mountain that didn't watch, didn't lean ponderous attention on any who ventured its slopes. These did not welcome, but it was an attitude without any overt hostility. Rather, she felt as if she stood before a group of giants, shoulder to shoulder, a living wall. A blocking stance, weighty rejection without malice. *No, they said. Go away.*

Something was wound through this, an insubstantial thing Gentian's mind interpreted as a trace of scent. Or a faltering thread of light, a glinting secret sewn through fractured rock, marking a path, whispering. *This way. Over here.*

Puzzled, she opened her eyes and looked at the channel the river had cut into the slopes ahead.

"Are you familiar with the Skorese, Magister Calder?"

Aristide Couerveur stood at her elbow, watching her face as she had watched his. She wondered what his ear for power was like, and if he was sensitive enough to touch the places he travelled.

"I've travelled the far foothills," she replied, and gave him a sideways glance. "Family expeditions hunting out interesting plants. But Goldenrod tends to keep clear of the mountains proper. My twice great grandmother supposedly got herself lost when she was a girl. The usual story – abandoned all sense of direction and ran in circles. Mist and clouds and divinations making nonsense of themselves. They call them the Veiled Mountains in Dwyallin."

He shifted his gaze back to the ranked peaks. "There's a strong keep-away, well-documented, focusing on the northern mountains. The mines just east of here aren't troubled, nor are larger expeditions. Thorough exploration has been made of the entire range. There's nothing to be found."

"I've not heard of barge-loads of people vanishing before."

"No. What do you see on the river?"

Sharp creature, to read her that well. Gentian could usually keep her thoughts to herself. Or perhaps he merely remembered her parentage, and was wise enough to ask.

"A lure? Some kind of marker? Recently worked power, though not laid down today."

"Footprints?"

He meant betraying signs inadvertently left by a casting mage. "It could be. But it seems more deliberate."

"Then be wary of traps."

Gentian nodded absently, thinking of the fetch. She might not have a horde of enemies on her own account, but she was being pulled into someone else's schemes. She'd best not let herself be dragged under.

ooOoo

The Galassas flowed in stages from a lake high in the heart of the mountains, carving its way through the southern foothills before spreading and slowing as it ran toward the sea. A pool the maps noted as the Cauldron lay at the point where the river tumbled from the shoulder of Mount Hestas to the lower hills. Twin falls thundered to either side of a block shaped like the prow of a massive ship, churning the water of the pool to a swirling frenzy before it finally escaped in another cascade.

The search party settled on the wide rim of the Cauldron to either side of the outfall. No-one spoke. What could be said before so much death?

The barge itself was partly intact, jammed up against the outfall so that the water had to surge to the rim to squeeze around it. This plug kept the debris, the pieces of clothing and personal belongings – and the bodies – trapped in the pool's violent whirl.

They were naked. Gentian didn't understand that, and paused in confusion while people began to speak to each other in shocked little murmurs. They'd hardly *all* be sleeping bare, certainly not the crew. No. Stripped by the force of water alone.

"Blood magic?"

It was the Easterner in the uniform of Sax, grim and blunt. A handful of voices immediately responded in the negative, and Gentian shook her head in her own denial. Whatever else this was, the power of these deaths had not been wrought into some casting. There was no stink of that kind of atrocity.

Nor would it make any sense: to have lifted that great hefty river-barge and brought it long miles upriver and dropped it here – smashed it, by all appearances, against that prow-like rock – would require an immense amount of power, beyond a single caster. Even the deaths of mages, princes, would scarcely compensate for the cost.

Not that Gentian could produce a better explanation.

"What then?" The Queen of Ceria, now stark with loss confirmed. "Why has this been done?"

"Simple murder?" The Cyan mage, in a most colourless tone.

"Nothing simple about this." The anger had gone of out the Cerian Queen, and the look she turned on Aristide was one of appeal. "I can't grasp this, Couerveur. Does someone move against the West?"

"I have no answer for you, Majesty. Not yet." Aristide was considering the tangled wreckage below as if it were a game-board, and a move had been made that did not fit to rule. "Closer investigation might make matters clearer." His blue-white gaze lifted, and he said with a civility which left aside past skirmishes: "Then we will recover the bodies."

The cluster of searchers who had been mage enough to fly the course of the river gathered together and began to discuss divinations. Gentian ignored them, curling down to wrap her arms about her knees and stare at the froth of water and flesh while she carefully sorted all that her senses were telling her.

That thread of power still teased the edge of perception, whispering *This Way* straight into a wall of rock. Dark marks scored the lichen there, sole sign of the impact of solid wood. The mountains lowered, close and disapproving. A few dozen castings made background chatter, ranging in strength from Aristide's *saecstra* to little vanity castings to keep clothes clean and make mages prettier. She tracked three or four sturdy enchantments in the water below, attached to objects tumbling in the lower currents.

The deaths were star-bursts, just beginning to fade. Some clustered on the far side of the pool before the prow, but most below. They'd survived the impact, fallen with the barge into the water, and drowned.

"Feeling sick?"

Lord Aristide's apprentice, Aspen, mixing curiosity with concern as he bent down beside her. She had yet to quite work the man out. He seemed powerful enough, but was old to have not been passed up at least to the journeyman level, Maja.

"Were none of them mages?" she asked. Rhetorical question. Gentian knew full well that the Cyan princess at least was true-mage, and odds were the others as well. Royalty and mage-craft were an almost sure admixture as power sought power.

"Well, of course some of them were!" Aspen replied, giving her a sharp look. "Crown Prince Jurasel and Princess Kestia. Most of the other royals I should think."

Gentian nodded. "Can you feel the deaths?" she asked.

Uncertainty now on those clean-cut features. Perhaps wondering if her mind was touched. But he nodded. "Yes." His voice dropped. "How can I not? Like scars on the skin of the place."

It was a good description, much better than the usual ripples-in-a-pond metaphor. "Death leaves claw-marks," she said, glancing past the apprentice to where his master had stopped speaking and turned. "Punctures in this world, little implosions of living magic as Lady Moon takes back her own."

"That is what we see here." It was the Atlaran guardswoman, looking down from her great height. But the shadow of comprehension had touched her face and she frowned out at the seething pool.

Gentian nodded, and encountered the apprentice's confusion again. "You see a lot of death in Atlarus," she explained. "All that public duelling, the honour battles. You can taste it for days, and this is very much what I would expect to feel if a random group of people had died here yesterday morning."

"But not mages." Aristide, gone very still indeed.

"No." She closed her eyes, searching again and finding nothing which fit. "Mages, true-mages who die, pull on arcane magic in reflex, and warp great gouts of it. They imprint their deaths on the world. You can feel it for weeks after. Years, in certain circumstances."

She stood at last, feeling the protest of her knees, and met the assembled hope and disbelief of four kingdom's searchers.

"If there were true-mages on that barge, and they died, they didn't do it here."

Chapter Five

"Kidnapping then."

Her Bluntness, the Cerian Queen, had broken the stretched-taut silence. All gruff and business still, but her eyes shone, and the whole way she stood had changed, shouting relief, precious hope. Aspen liked her the more for it, though from all accounts her relationship with her daughter was no display of matched minds.

"Who could have the power for it? Or the reason?" This from the Easterner playing Saxan guardsman, looking uneasy among his betters.

"Skrem?"

The chief of the Cyan mages dropped the word into play with a kind of distasteful dusting of his fingers. It produced a most interesting effect, a kind of stifled exchange of glances that went beyond the usual attitude that all Skremman were marginally less pleasant company than a well-shaken sackful of snakes. Aspen hadn't heard anything tasty about Skrem for months, not since they'd buried their last monarch and started the long-winded search for the next. Say what you would about the Rathen Rose: at least it had managed succession without periodically sending an entire country on a frantic treasure hunt.

The Diamond, with a superb failure to acknowledge any undercurrents, turned back to contemplation of the Cauldron. "If this is a kidnapping, the trail has already cooled. Perhaps speculation can be postponed until the preliminary investigation has been made?"

That got them moving again, and left Aspen caught between hovering uselessly in the background and attempting his own divinations. He had the basic ones by heart, but would achieve nothing sullying already muddy waters with low-level casting. Better to concentrate on the physical, to search about for subtle clues. He had already added to his list of ambitions the opportunity to produce some devastating statement which would make everyone gape at him, amazed.

But the thrill of adventure had been cut sharply by the discovery of the barge. Aspen couldn't quite recapture the same sense of excitement, for all he searched diligently about the immediate area, peering into whatever nook or cranny came to hand, and studying with particular care anything that might hold a footprint. But whenever he turned his head he would catch a glimpse of an arm, an elbow, a sleek, wet flank. A wreckage of people.

Quite against his best intentions, he found himself close to the upper fall, staring back down into the pool. The bowl of the Cauldron was not entirely smooth, and every so often one of the tumbling figures would strike a rock or a fragment of barge. He wondered if, left long enough, there would remain only pieces. A kind of soup.

"They'll take them out soon."

The little gardening mage, standing at his elbow like some spirit conjured by discomfort. Aspen decided that spooky, wide-eyed gaze had to at least in part be deliberately cultivated.

"And put them where?" he asked. "Keep them how?" He looked about at vertical black rock, broken irregularly by clumps of grass and something heathery. Damp, deserted and unwelcoming: no frame for mourning. A feeling of acute distress threatened to embarrass Aspen, and he combated it by gazing across the Cauldron at the Diamond's glorious profile: a sight to settle any amount of nerves.

"They don't feel it," said the gardening mage. "Just shells, like those you find on a beach. Does it really matter to those who've returned to Lady Moon, what happens to the husk?"

"I'd object to every degree if *my* 'husk' were not at least in one piece when carried before my grieving parents." He paused, considering the gravity of the occasion. "And decked out in something well-cut in black. With a few of the more presentable of my lovers wailing in the background, and maybe a single great bell tolling in the distance."

Her face went blank at this and she blinked those big eyes, then said: "And perhaps a five-year child of extraordinary beauty following along behind, clutching some particular keepsake of yours against his chest."

Aspen was taken by this idea. "A sword would be perfect; one almost too large for him to hold." The Diamond had a sword with him, and Aspen was longing to see him in action. "I'll have to take it up."

There was a slight noise behind and below them, and they turned in time to see the Saxan guardsman moving away, back stiff. Aspen pulled a face.

"I gather he's in command of the Saxan security escort," the gardening mage said. "His life forfeit if his charges aren't delivered home safely."

"*We* have a kingdom at stake."

"Do you really think the West will invade?"

"Not really," Aspen admitted. "Not invade. Everyone's convinced The Deeping would take Darest back if it were overrun by another land. And of course Sax couldn't stand Cya gaining territory and vice versa; repeat in endless variation substituting Korm, Ceria and Jutland. But with the Treasury scraped clean and the bare minimum complement for the garrisons, we're ripe pickings for punitive raids.

"There's a time factor as well. With the return of The Deeping's oh-so-reluctant support, it's only going to be a matter of years before we're far less vulnerable. Half the world seems to be on its way to the Spring Festival, and there's opportunity oozing from every doorstep, giving folk reason to stay. I'd bet my best robe that this unlikely little boating party involved more than a bit of half-spoken probing to see what everyone thought about forgetting regional tensions in favour of an all-out sacking of Darest. You notice it's only the heirs? To make it a little less official and obvious. Though, Sun knows, it's an odd gathering, whatever the cause."

"Odd how? I know Sax and Cya will never exactly be friendly – they'll never agree over their borders – but it's been, what?, almost twenty years since they were officially at odds."

"Yes, but Kestia *and* Jurasel? For that matter, Jurasel and Chenar? *With* Aloren?"

"What do you mean?"

From the look on her face, Aspen suspected that most of these names meant nothing to the woman. Totally out of touch. Well he always enjoyed playing tutor.

"For a start both Sax and Cya are courting Ceria: pushing for alliances political and personal, particularly in the person of Crown Princess Aloren. She's apparently very good to look at, but completely indolent, and more interested in the latest offering of the playhouses than the running of her country. Naturally this makes her irresistible to Sax and Cya both. They're as anxious to stop each other as to win points themselves, and with Sax hosting this little get-together, Cya's Jurasel is the *last* person I'd expect on the invitation list."

"Perhaps he gate-crashed?"

"Now *that's* an idea." Aspen barely resisted patting her approvingly on the head. "That would explain Kestia. You know Cya's laws of succession mean Queen Rithana can declare any of her immediate kin her heir? Well she does. Often. Kestia's the eldest of three daughters and two sons and from all accounts the Queen doesn't really like her, and uses her as a fall-back position to bring the others to heel. They jump through hoops to please her – except for Kestia, who just gets on with whatever she thinks wants doing, never mind buttering up Mama. She handles a lot of business, whether she's in favour or not, and probably *would* be the one sent to make nice with ambassadors and eye off Darest. Jurasel's the current heir and nothing would solidify his position like winning Aloren. I wonder who was less pleased to see him there – Kestia or Chenar? The entire balance of the West might shift if Aloren could be won."

Gentian looked down at the swirl of flesh and flotsam. "It mightn't be an issue any more."

On that doubtful note, she began picking her way back around the rim of the Cauldron, catching up with the Saxan. Aspen trailed them, trying to gauge the progress of the divinations still underway, eyeing the small clusters of mages. It was no company of friends. Had the heirs been plotting an invasion, all together on Darest's border?

The Diamond was talking to the Cyan and the Atlaran, but turned to Gentian as she came up. "You've not attempted divination, Magister?" he asked, with only a whisper of silk. Aristide Couerveur might consider mages who made their living outside Darest something akin to traitors, but he wasn't unwilling to use them while they were on hand.

"No point," was the reply. "It's all been...rubbed over somehow. There's precious little trace of casting here. Nothing not left deliberately."

"There is a trail leading across the pool," said the Atlaran, her Sumican of markedly Cyan dialect, but still understandable. She pointed toward the central rock with the iron-bound staff she was holding. "The faintest of things, but there. You do not consider it a footprint?"

"Oh no." The gardening mage was blithely confident. "It's a lure. It wants us to go over to that big rock and touch it."

"As the barge did." The Atlaran took this revelation without surprise. "And share its fate? Or those of our missing charges?"

"It may well be the only way to learn it," murmured the Cyan.

The Saxan guardsman looked with a gathering frown at Aristide. "It may be precisely what the kidnapper wants us to do."

Aspen particularly enjoyed the Diamond's habit of listening without comment until a group actually turned to him and waited for him to say something. It was a marvellous device, investing whatever he eventually did say with added authority.

When the pause became tangible, the Diamond Couerveur inclined his head the tiniest of fractions, every inch the King he'd never be.

"We will experiment."

ooOoo

After a discussion equal parts caution and a surging desire to crash ahead, it was decided that the search party would split into two: one group to probe this lure directly, the other observing from a short distance. A pause followed, while reports were made and orders given. The Diamond moved out of earshot and sigil-called King Aluster.

Aspen plotted. He was fully aware that he'd given the Diamond Couerveur cause to think him more interested in gossip than service to the kingdom. Perfectly true, of course, but no reason why he shouldn't start being all hard-working and serious now. At least long enough to slip beneath the man's guard. The little gardening mage had already made the assumption that Aspen *was* the Diamond's apprentice. Maybe, by being helpful at the right moments, he could turn this almost-'prenticeship into a formal arrangement.

He just had to find something useful to do.

The Diamond's relentless self-sufficiency was one of the reasons the man was so deliciously compelling. The

ultimate in untouchables. But it did leave a body
scratching for a suitable service. Aspen was doubtfully
eyeing the neat pile they'd made of their belongings when
what should the man do but walk up and layer himself in
his bags?

When the gardening mage followed suit, Aspen hastily
grabbed up his own collection. If the Diamond thought
this lure might whisk them off somewhere, Aspen would
be prepared for the event. But could they really expect to
be conveniently taken after the missing heirs? Wasn't it
more likely that touching that rock would trigger a trap
and provide the Cauldron with a few true-mage deaths?

With this consideration in mind, Aspen began casting
one of the most reliable of the word-magic shields. His
reward was a brief blue-white glance, and the faintest nod
of approval. Aspen gloated. One small step taken – and
surely not too early to plan the first seduction scene?

Visions of a naked Diamond were a little *too*
distracting, and Aspen had to start his spell again, then
hastily re-established his flight spell, aware that most
everyone else had finished and a final round of discussion
was underway. He'd barely let the last word escape his
mouth when they all began launching out over the
Cauldron.

Nothing would be worse than to have the Diamond
vanish, leaving Aspen behind with this unhappy crowd.
He made haste to get himself right up the front of the
investigators, floating to within a foot of the scratches left
by the impact of the barge, trying to feel what Gentian
claimed was there, while ignoring the scars of death. But
the so-mysterious rock was dumb, revealing no lure, no
trap, no whisper of intent.

Because he would *not* let his gaze stray to the horrid
soup below, Aspen glanced around at the little crowd that
had followed the Diamond's lead. The gardening mage
was looking, of a sudden, decidedly unenthusiastic.
Beside her the Atlaran guardswoman frowned at the heavy

staff she carried, concentrating on some divination. A pretty redhead was the Cerian contribution, with Her Bluntness watching from a safe distance. The self-effacing Cyan mage had tidied himself well to the back of the group, closer to the outfall than the rock. And the stolid Easterner made up the last of the experiment, hand gripping the hilt of his sword as if that could make some fraction of difference.

The observers were gathered on the far rim, scattered in pairs and trios. Aspen was quite unable to resist lifting a hand to wave, but never finished the gesture as the charming vista of searchers framed against a cloud-specked sky was blotted out by a sudden obtrusion of wall.

He started, hearing one of the others gasp as they all stared about at the pearly-white corridor that had replaced the mountain and tainted falls. Aristide, Gentian, the Saxan and the Atlaran were with him, but not the Cyan or Cerian. Aspen had felt no arcane surge to warn of or explain the transition, but discovered instead a lingering feeling of absence. Not at all what his training and senses had taught him to expect at such a profligate display of power.

"Well that was a little lacking in drama," he said.

Then his flight spell cut out and the weird sense of absence began to translate into realisation of a thing which was distinctly and monstrously wrong.

"Sun's teeth!" the Easterner gasped, as he also dropped to the floor, stumbling. The others, after the briefest of hesitations, landed just before the castings keeping them aloft imploded into nothing. Their shields went a moment later. Because there was nothing for them to feed on.

Because, wherever they'd been brought, there was no magic.

The Easterner clutched his sword uselessly, white to the lips, and the Atlaran woman said something in the language of her Empire. Unfazed, the Diamond turned his head, surveying the gently curving passage. It narrowed sharply at the ceiling, forming a smooth and unnatural triangle that glowed with milky light.

Then the little gardening mage took a step forward, looked at the Diamond's hand held loosely at his side, and asked: "How long?"

It was possible for blood to congeal in living veins. Aspen stood with his chest fusing solid, staring at Darest's precious Diamond Couerveur as he lifted his right hand and looked down at the swirling twists and spirals of a death sentence.

Enchantments ran out. It was one of the first lessons taught a mage. Free magic was everywhere in the world, there for you to shape directly with your will, or with words, or runes. To last, that casting had to be fed.

You could set it so it endured as long as you directly stoked it with power: that was how flight spells usually worked, limited only by exhaustion. But with most enchantments, those on objects or on other people, it was far more practical to stockpile power at the time of casting, so the enchantment would last until the stockpile ran out. Those castings were ones of long preparation and effort, ones you had to return to and refurbish, or simply let lapse.

For the grand, important spells, the vital ones which had to last indefinitely whether you had time to tend them or not, you created a stockpile with a feeding mechanism. The Rathen Rose, late, unlamented protection for Darest's border, had drawn on every man, woman and child of the Rathen bloodline. It had stockpiled their power drop by drop, tapping living Rathens until at its height it had been a defence beyond compare.

The *saecstra* with which Aristide Couerveur had proven his loyalty to the new Rathen King worked the same way. It periodically added to a stockpile of magic devoted to sustaining it, using Aristide's true-mage ability to draw power. A very necessary thing, for a *saecstra* was above all things permanent. The enchantment would kill him if he tried to unmake it.

In this place where free magic inexplicably was not, it would soon find itself starving.

"A day or two?" Those incomparable eyes glittered, and he curled his fingers, then opened them again. "You will know as soon as I."

The reaction was pure Aristide, and Aspen tried to draw confidence from it. If anyone could find an escape from this trap, it would be the Diamond. He had to: Darest would not be the same without Aristide Couerveur, and besides, it was surely against The Rules for anyone that delicious to die before Aspen tumbled him. Worse, Aspen simply couldn't face the thought of telling Soren and her King how inadequate his protection had been.

They all stood there looking at the finely-made fingers which shaded a knot of intertwined lines. Aspen was relieved when, after a measuring survey of Aristide, the Atlaran woman reached out to touch the nearest slab of white.

"These walls must have access to power. Perhaps they draw it all into themselves. I have heard it was possible to create a void such as this, though I never imagined one on such a scale. If we break the walls, we should no longer be blocked."

"We just need a battering ram and a few dozen strong shoulders." Aspen could see nothing but wall in either direction. The far distance was hidden by the gradual curve, but he was fairly certain that the corridor was going to go on for absolutely ever and that there would be no battering rams. Just a long long walk, with every step taking them closer to the unthinkable. Wholly pointless guilt clutched at his stomach, and he had to turn so he could no longer see that figure in black.

"Perhaps we should follow this?"

The Easterner, stolidly indifferent to impending disaster, pointed to a few strips of cloth practically under Aspen's feet. They were roughly formed into an arrow.

"Ah!" Shifting instantly from repose to action, the Atlaran woman stooped and lifted one fragment of light yellow. "Those who were lost must have left this marker. It is well." She nodded in evident satisfaction, and replaced the strip of cloth, tidying the arrow into cleaner lines as she did so. "We will go after them."

"Shortly." The Diamond was gazing down the corridor, but turned and made a formal gesture of greeting to the Atlaran. "Introductions are in order first."

"Of course." The Atlaran woman's full lips curved with just a suggestion of quizzical amusement as she looked down at the Diamond's slender figure. "I am Rua Ketu, Second Se of the Hapt of Dest. Hapt-lo Dest and First Se Manetat were with the Ambassador at the time of the taking, and I assumed command of the Hapt in their absence."

The Easterner let go his sword and executed one of the clipped little bows popular in the lands beyond the sprawl of The Deeping. He looked six days short of sleep, scruffy, uninviting and exhausted. More guard dog than mage, he must barely have had the strength to make the flight to the Cauldron.

"Leton Djol, Captain in the Saxan Royal Bodyguard. I would appreciate knowing your opinion of our situation. Is this a place suspected to be in the Skorese Mountains? Are we even in Darest?"

"Yes."

Both the Diamond and the gardening mage had answered, and they glanced at each other. With his particular, pointed courtesy the Diamond inclined his head to her before looking back at the Easterner.

"This is Magister Gentian Calder. And Maistrice Aspen Choraide. We have not left Darest, though this place is not known to me even by rumour. As to our situation: we will find that answer the sooner we look for it." This last contained an edge of reproof, for the Diamond was not overfond of flinging about guesses.

"Then shall we start?" the Atlaran woman suggested easily. "Leave the arrow for any who come after us." She nodded at Gentian, adding: "I have seen the valley you created for the Ambassador, Magister Calder. It is a fell place."

Aspen, glancing at the gardening mage, discovered her eyes wide and disconcerted.

"Do you mean to say that the Arachol has made Aurak Bes one of his ambassadors?" she asked. "I would never have believed it."

"The Aurak expressed a desire to see the North."

"He could have had better timing." The little gardening mage threw a glance at Aristide, frowning. "You comprehend *that* situation, I presume? What the Arachol will do?"

The Diamond responded with the smallest of nods, looking surprisingly austere. Aspen stared from one to the other in confusion. "What will the Arachol do?" he asked.

"Retrieve him." It was Rua Ketu who answered, relaxed but grave. "The Aurak is *ajudica,* and revered among our people. To the Arachol he is both guide and mentor. There is no cost to weigh against his recovery."

For once Aspen could find nothing to say. The others started off, and he followed, mind busy with an image of an army of Atlarans pulling the Skorese down stone by stone.

ooOoo

After what seemed an eternity of walking and was probably at least an hour, Aspen decided everyone had had enough time to dwell on less than palatable thoughts. True, they were trapped in some unknown part of Darest, denied the resources of magic and racing time to prevent the Diamond Couerveur's death and an invasion by either the West or the entire Atlaran Empire. That was no reason to march along as if they'd taken a vow of silence.

"So why didn't the other two come with us?" he asked, glancing around.

"Perhaps they were not close enough?" Rua Ketu answered. Aspen was liking her. She was a comfortable, genial creature, stretched tall as most Atlarans were, but attractively muscular. Her hair was twisted into tufty little knots and her skin was on the darker end of the range of black. It was a pity she'd learned her Sumican from a Cyan, but Aspen would forgive her the accent if they happened across somewhere a little more private.

"Magister Enricar was closer than I," Leton Djol pointed out.

"Was she true-mage?" the gardening mage asked, adjusting the straps of her bags. She carried them with an indifferent ease Aspen couldn't help but envy. He was already thoroughly inclined to dump his entire load.

No-one knew whether the red-headed Cerian mage had been true-mage or only a word-mage, but apparently the Cyan had been true. "But he *was* further back," Aspen mused, then let the point drop. "You made an entire valley into a garden?" he asked instead.

"No. Or yes, though I don't suppose most would consider it that way." She glanced sideways at Rua Ketu. "A 'fell place' is as good a description as any."

"And what's that mean?" Aspen swore she was being mysterious purely for the sake of it.

The gardening mage shrugged instead of answering, but then Rua Ketu volunteered that she had been sent there before the Aurak journeyed north. Aspen suspected the Atlaran shared his disinclination to walk on in silence: there was something about the endless pearl-white absence that clawed at the senses.

"The valley lies a half-day's walk into the hills south of the Aurak's Seat," Rua Ketu continued, touching the sand-coloured cloth wrapped around her wrists. "I left at midday and reached it as the sun set.   A small valley, almond-shaped, veiled with a rising mist." The curve had flattened out of her full lips, but she continued her story in a tone of steady honesty that commanded attention. "My pack was heavy and my feet regretted the instruction not to make the journey by air. The place looked damp, and stones of all sizes lay tumbled about, grey and spattered with lichen.   There was no brightness in the place, only low, dark plants almost covering a faint track winding round to the base. I was not impressed.

"I had been ordered to spend the night beside the pool at the valley's heart, and started down in an ill humour. It was quiet, and the mist curled without breath of wind. And I, who can kill with hand or stave, or a thousand ways with magic, found myself with my neck stiff from anticipation of a blow, looking among those stones for an enemy.

"Neither sight nor spell would reveal who watched, and imagination conjured a thousand monsters from shadow on rock.   I thought I could smell blood.   I cast every protection known to me, and followed the path in the certain belief that the Aurak had sent me to my death."

"Had you given him reason?"

At the gardening mage's question, Rua Ketu's expression set into stone lines. "I had broken a precept," she said, with immense gravity.   "I knew myself in the right, weighed the cost of delays, and took a man's choice from him. I believed that need outweighed the law. What harm to use magic to make a fool see reason?" She sighed. "I was the fool. I had admitted my act, knew the disappointment of my teachers, but I did not own the fault in my heart. The matter had been urgent, my reasons good. It was necessary. I told myself this again, as I walked down into that valley. I told myself that I was true-mage and great, and that I would undergo trial by combat, be proved in the right, and return with honour.

"I was at fever-pitch when I reached the pool at the valley's base, and turned with my staff in my hands ready to face anything. And there was only mist and shadows, and a thousand stones in every direction, leaning down on me. I watched them until dawn. The longest night of my life."

The gardening mage had tilted her head a little to one side, looking up at Rua Ketu with an abstract air. "Did you return with honour?"

"I returned to the Aurak and asked his forgiveness. I have not yet regained my honour. But I strive toward it."

Aspen gave up. "Am I the only one completely lost?" he asked. "What did the ambassador have you do to this valley, Magister Calder? It doesn't sound the least like a garden to me."

"It does depend on what you consider a garden," she agreed, all solemn, but he could see laughter in her eyes. Aspen grimaced at her, but was privately pleased. This was prime distraction from the prospect of invasion, death and an interminable hike along this endless corridor.

And the Guard Dog at least was equally confused. "A garden of stones?" he asked.

"Why not? Stone and lichen, and creeping sage, which is why Se Ketu thought she could smell blood. It grows over that path, and as you walk down you crush it. Scent is a wonderful thing. I once made a maze entirely from rosemary. A tight, twisted maze, tall and close. You can't help but brush against the plants, and the smell is overwhelming." She smiled with simple pleasure. "Though I count the maze as one of my failures, because people invariably come out of the thing longing for a meal of roast lamb, which wasn't quite the intention. Creeping sage isn't unpleasant, but it's unsettling."

"The point of the valley is to make people nervous?" Djol sounded incredulous.

"In a way." Though she didn't smile, she was obviously enjoying their reaction.

"A place of punishment. Can that even be called a garden?" Djol asked, as if it mattered.

"Unless you count vegetable gardens, all gardens are, at their core, an arrangement to evoke a response. An art of environment. But yes, it was an unusual commission. Not a place of punishment, though. The Aurak uses it himself, rarely sends other people there. He is a very powerful man, and all Atlarus has hoisted him on a pedestal and done their best to worship him. He asked me to make him a place that made him feel small."

At this Rua Ketu let out a shout of laughter. "That is what it does, very much so. Small and defenceless, a mouse before a cat. And that he asked for this, that is what proves the Aurak's greatness. He is *ajudica*."

Aspen had heard the term before, though he wasn't clear on the details. "I'm not up on Atlaran philosophy, sorry."

"You do not know the precepts? They are the path through the burden of power."

"At least a way to try to stop history repeating itself," Gentian added matter-of-factly. "True-mages rule Atlarus in context of a series of rules to govern all born with the burden of power. To follow them well is to be *justra*, one who achieves. To embody the precepts, to not strive but actually *be* them, that is to be *ajudica*."

She gave the word a remarkably cynical flavour, but Rua Ketu's response was only a quizzical: "You disagree? The course Atlarus has taken has kept us from past excesses, and the *senserel*, those without power, are well cared for, kept safe. They are no longer play-things to our excesses."

"In power, responsibility. In absence of power, what? I don't like the precepts because the *senserel* aren't expected to live by them. It's just another way of saying true-mages are a more exalted race, held to a higher standard."

The Guard Dog, with what was obviously a habitual frown, asked: "What exactly did you do to make the Aurak Bes feel small?"

"More than plant creeping sage? Telensar Valley – my garden of stones – is a place of judgment. It looks at every creature that enters it and asks them what right they have to exist. Valleys aren't usually like that, don't often turn their attention to those who pass through them. I'm told it's been that way for centuries: true-mages who went there felt uncomfortable, and rarely lingered. But they could not understand the source of the discomfort, since outside the Fair there's few who really feel places.

"My father's family is a sensitive one, and we feel place very strongly. We've been working with the character of our steading, Goldenrod, for centuries, until even people who aren't true-mage can feel it. You can't change the nature of a place, not really, but you can strengthen or modulate it. Sunlight to hearten or a mist to chill. Scent, to conjure countless associations. Objects arranged just so, pleasing or dissonant. Emphasising part of a place's nature until it becomes dominant, or countering some negative aspect until it recedes. People react, and then it feeds in a circle as the place responds to their reaction. The key to Telensar Valley was those stones, and the lichen. I spent an inordinate amount of time arranging them. Bulky, grey, hunched, all patches of shadow and ambiguous outline. Things that crouched and waited. Things that watched. Shapes which could be claws, teeth, the line of a brow. Nothing but lichen and hollows in stone, which fear made into something more. I gave Telensar Valley *eyes*."

Aspen, though he'd no inclination to visit dank and unlovely Atlaran valleys, was delighted by the idea of terrifying the grand and mighty true-mages of Atlarus with a bunch of rocks. "And you said you weren't a Shaper."

"Did I?" She gave him that grave, sideways glance. "Well I'm not, according to my mother. And there *is* a great deal of difference between creating new breeds of plants and animals, and working with the spirit of a place."

Aspen had thought the Diamond to be only half listening, but looking past the little gardening mage he saw that his mouth had taken on a curve instantly recognisable to any veteran of the Darien Court. It gave the man a look of ineffable sweetness, and was reputed to have once caused the Baron of Segai to drop a full glass of wine, then flee the kingdom. It was the expression Aristide Couerveur wore when considering an opponent's destruction.

"And did your design for Vostal Hill involve any tampering with its character?"

The tone was purely polite, with not even a hint of blade. Aspen could only see the side of the little gardening mage's face as she turned her head to meet the Diamond Couerveur's brilliant gaze, but he thought it possible she didn't quail. At the very least her voice was light and unperturbed when she said: "Of course. Why else would I do it?"

"You fascinate me Magister. And what modulation do you propose to make?"

Her pace slowed as she continued to survey his expression. Perhaps it was only then that she realised her danger, recognised how truly little tolerance the Diamond Couerveur would have for someone meddling with the nature of any place in his kingdom, let alone one set flush up against the palace. Her reply was steady, but far less light.

"The first thing I saw when I reached Tor Darest was a Fae temple on Vostal Hill. Stark and exposed, glorious and inescapable. The Queen of the Fair may have made Darest over in gift to Domina Rathen, and centuries of human rule might have blurred the things that made it part of The Deeping, but Vostal Hill's crown strips that away, exposing the true nature of this kingdom. Right there in the heart of the capital, kitty-corner to the palace, a thing which said: this land is Fae. My design takes its shape, and echoes of the city, and gives the hill a cloak of human-kind. Makes it into a declaration, even a celebration of that Fae past, but a past merged with present. The shift I hope to make is one of acceptance." She paused, lifted a hand, then dropped it. "For, believe me, this land has never forgotten what it once was."

Before the Diamond could react with more than a narrowing of those eyes, she added: "We're getting near something – there's active enchantments ahead."

It was well-timed distraction. Aristide looked away from her, and the sense of approaching crisis waned.

"I feel nothing," Rua Ketu said.

Aspen suspected the Diamond didn't either, but he did study the far curve of the corridor before saying, "We must talk of this later," quite as if he hadn't been contemplating Magister Calder's immediate destruction a moment before. And then: "Tell me, Se Ketu, Captain Djol, to what purpose did your charges gather on Darest's border?"

The two guards had drifted a little behind, and Aspen missed their immediate reaction. A glance over his shoulder showed the Guard Dog looking like his bowels had blocked up, while Rua Ketu had returned to that quizzical expression.

"The Ambassador, guesting with the King of Sax, joined a boating party," she said. "I am sure many discussions of trade and mutual interest were held."

Leton Djol didn't answer, and the Diamond actually stopped walking and waited for his answer.

"I have neither the knowledge nor the authority to give you an answer, Lord Magister," the Guard Dog said.

"Do you not? Very well. Tell me instead exactly where this barge was anchored."

"Where? The nearest town–"

Aspen realised where the Diamond was heading. "Which bank were you closer to?"

"We followed standard practice." This wasn't a stupid man. He didn't let his eyes waver from the Diamond's as he added: "Dead centre."

There was no need to say anything more. The barge had been in the centre of the river, and the vagaries of the current might take it entirely into Darest. Aristide turned away, and they trailed after him, looking anxiously down the corridor in the hope that the missing occupants of that barge were indeed ahead.

Aspen saw them before he felt the enchantments they carried: four figures walking along the pearly-white passage toward them. A woman striding before three much taller men, one of them Atlaran. The Atlaran was dressed much like Rua Ketu, in sandy linen with heavier cloth bound about wrists and shins. The other three were dressed in lighter robes, sleeping garb.

Snatching another glance at the Diamond, Aspen caught a very rare change of expression indeed. The faint smile faded completely, and his face went still. Then his mouth curled up into full and vivid appreciation, and his eyes blazed.

Confused, Aspen studied the four. The Atlaran was obviously another guard, and hardly likely to surprise the Diamond. The woman was a smallish brunette, only a little taller than Gentian, with an attractive figure and a brisk carriage. The other two men were almost as tall as the Atlaran, with the fair skin and brown-red hair common to Cya. Both handsome, broad-shouldered, though otherwise dissimilar. One wore a neat, close-trimmed beard, and walked with a snapping energy that threatened to take him ahead of the other's relaxed stroll. There was something faintly familiar about the last man, and Aspen uneasily noted the moment when he in turn must have recognised Aristide. He checked his stride, and his precisely cut features took on an eager, almost hawkish cast.

When the four stopped a short distance away, it was this man who stepped to the fore to incline to a brief and very mocking courtesy, surveying each of their faces in turn.

And with a broadening smile he said: "Hello, brother."

Chapter Six

Aristide Couerveur had gone to what Gentian was beginning to think of as 'full glitter'. "Seylon," he said, sounding very pleased. "I trust you've been enjoying your visit to Darest?"

"Immeasurably," the tall man replied, with an expansive gesture at his rumpled bed-robe, strained companions, and the stark corridor. His accent revealed him to be Cyan, and though his face was built on stronger lines, the shape and colour of his eyes were a darker version of Aristide's: the eclipse reflected in a deep pool. Familiar too was the sugared acid as he added: "Though I could wish for more notice in future."

Gentian vaguely recollected that Lord Aristide's father had belonged to the Heresar family of Cya, and supposed a brother wasn't a surprising thing. From the highly portentous expression Aristide's apprentice was wearing, she guessed this Seylon was not even close to a potential ally.

"A lapse on my part," Aristide said, sketching apology. "Let me know, next time you wish to view Darest, and I will make better arrangements. But we mustn't lose ourselves in pleasantries," he added. "I own, the role of rescuer is new to me, and you may have to prompt me. Whatever aid and succour I can offer, you have."

"Oh, very nice." Simmering and derisive, the bearded man stepped past Seylon Heresar. "Do we thank you now, Couerveur? I presume we're to accept without murmur your so-convenient appearance? Believe you innocent of this assault?"

There was nothing of courtly feint about this man, hands curling and weight balanced on the balls of his feet.

He was spoiling for a fight, and though he lacked a sword he had the advantage of height and muscle in this place where magic would not be a factor in battle. Lord Aristide looked up at him with little of the veiled mockery he so readily turned on others. But nor did he betray any hint of perturbation, only saying: "I would not presume to dictate your beliefs, Prince Jurasel."

"Sun spare me these mealy-mouthed word mincers," the Crown Prince of Cya exclaimed to the air, before snapping his attention back to Lord Aristide. "Tell me plain. What is this place? What do you know of this plot?"

"At this stage, Highness, less than you. We merely followed your trail."

Prince Jurasel looked anything but appeased, but before he could respond the dark-haired woman, another Cyan, interrupted: "And do you have a way out?"

"You are the Lady Dhara Orlath?" Aristide bowed his head in apparently genuine respect. "I regret not as yet. Our investigations appear to have led us into the same trap which holds you."

"Then I hope you have food and water. We've had one flask between us, and the children are hungry."

"And that is naturally our priority." Flat sarcasm from Jurasel this time. He shot the woman a look of open dislike.

While tempers were hardly likely to be cool after a day trapped here, Prince Jurasel seemed to be positively eager to lose his. He was an impressive figure, vigorous and proud, and Gentian could easily picture him taking the lead on anything from a tavern brawl to a charge into battle. Right this moment, he seemed on the verge of swinging punches.

"I've a little food," she volunteered, aiming for distraction without provocation. Noticing movement further down the corridor, she added: "Are those your children?"

A miniature of Lady Dhara, about ten years old, was trotting along the corridor toward them, narrowly pursued by a girl of fourteen who more closely resembled Prince Jurasel. Both wore simple shifts. Lady Dhara clicked her tongue in exasperation, and turned to capture the girl by the shoulder.

"I'm sorry, Mama-la," said the older girl. "She would."

"Always. No fault of yours, Desseron. You need to learn to stay where you're put, Kassen."

"I wanted to see, Mama," Kassen replied, with a straightforward assurance that curiosity was total justification. She peered around her mother's legs at the newcomers. "Can we leave now?"

"I hope so," Lady Dhara said, with a grim look toward Prince Jurasel and Lord Aristide both. "We've camped ourselves at what we think may be an exit to this place, Lord Couerveur, but we're making little progress with it. Perhaps you'll have better luck. Shall we go?"

She was already turning away, her daughters' hands caught in her own. Prince Jurasel, although obviously nettled by her assumption of command, had lost enough momentum to merely glower at Aristide before striding in her wake. Aristide, in his turn, made an 'after you' gesture to his brother, and glittered at his brief hesitation. Capitulating with a sudden lowering of dark lashes, the man called Seylon followed Prince Jurasel, and Aristide Couerveur strolled after him.

Rua Ketu, having been left very much to one side during the encounter, bent close to her fellow hapt-guard's ear as they joined the troop, with Captain Djol behind them. Gentian, thoughts preoccupied with the fate of Vostal Hill, was about to join the procession when Lord Aristide's apprentice caught at her arm.

"Magister Calder," he began, glancing at Captain Djol's back.

"Call me Gentian. If I can call you Aspen?"

"Yes, of course," he said, shaking aside pleasantries. He was literally quivering, she noticed, with an equal mix of excitement and consternation. "Mag – Gentian, you understand that we were sent along to protect the Diamond?"

That was news. "If you say so," she said, blankly.

"And–" Another harried glance, though Djol was now out of earshot. "Look, that was Seylon Heresar. The Heresar family, probably Seylon himself, was directly involved in an attempt on King Aluster's life last autumn, one that would have finished the Diamond as well. Cya particularly considers Darest's recovery a threat and second to King Aluster suffering an accident, nothing would please Queen Rithana more than the Diamond's head on a platter. I don't know what would have happened just then, if we hadn't a few non-Cyan witnesses. We need to–" He broke off, perhaps unsure exactly what they could do. Neither of them were carrying weapons, and in this place without magic Gentian at least knew herself to be entirely negligible in methods of battle.

"Be on our guard?" she suggested, and he nodded gratefully. "Who is Lady Dhara?"

"Princess Kestia's wife. Very high-level mage, and heir to one of their largest dukedoms. Queen Rithana doesn't get on with the current duke, but together Kestia and Dhara have quite a power base, so the marriage is less than popular with the rest of the family. Heresar's the Diamond's elder by a year or so, and assumed their father's dukedom years ago. He's in the Queen's pocket, works with whichever of her children is heir of the moment, and plays no favourites." Aspen gazed at the group ahead, shifting abruptly from tension to speculation. "For a moment there I thought Prince Jurasel was going to grab the Diamond by the throat. *Quite* a handful."

With a tangled smile, he hurried after the others. Gentian trailed him thoughtfully, trying to sort out all these names and consequences. Travelling half her life, she'd had little involvement in politics. Always an outsider, not really concerned with anything beyond her gardens. She found she didn't like the idea of someone trying to scuttle Darest's fortunes by killing her King, and supposed she would be naïve to believe Aristide's brother wouldn't be ready to make himself an only child. What she could do about it was less clear. Aristide Couerveur she considered well able to look after himself when he had the resources of magic, but she wasn't sure he even knew how to use the sword he was carrying. And there was every possibility that the *saecstra* would soon take him out of the picture.

Leaving as soon as possible was the obvious course.

And escape was important for more personal reasons. Gentian knew this was still Darest – the overarching identity of the land hadn't changed – but the corridor itself was blank, as if it wasn't really there. The rubbed-over empty wrongness kept pulling at her. She suspected they were still in the Skorese, but couldn't be sure, and she didn't like the sensation at all.

Catching up to Captain Djol, she was in time to hear the kidnapping from the barge's point of view.

"Most of us were below deck, of course," the Lady Dhara was saying. "I was woken by Hapt-lo Dest giving the alarm, felt a wash of power, but no casting except his. Then I fell over, couldn't even make it out of our cabin. And was in this place."

"I, too, felt nothing I would call casting," said the Atlaran man, evidently Hapt-lo Dest. "At first it seemed to me that the wind had freshened." He shook his head, the beading in his hair clicking. "That is understatement. I thought it a gale, a storm-front. The mist began to stream past the prow of the barge. I found myself unsteady on my feet, and still did not understand. Then – then we were above the mist."

This scarcely made sense to Gentian. Magic of such high order should have shouted its intent, warning every true-mage in the area of casting. But then, between floating above the Cauldron and finding herself in this corridor, she had felt only a strange kind of surge, with no murmur of will behind it. Like the tide.

"The speed of it far outstripped any ordinary flight," the Hapt-lo added. "Miles in moments. I could see mountains ahead, shouted an order to erect shields. We began to slow, as quickly as we had accelerated, and were about to strike rock, hard, when we were brought here. We retained only a little of our speed, enough to bruise us against the wall, the most minor of injuries. To those of us who came through."

His pause was a question.

"All dead," Aristide replied, without elaboration.

"With such power, why not translocate from our original location?" asked Captain Djol, while those who were on the barge each tamped down on their reaction. "Rather than remove the entire barge, performing a feat a dozen mages would struggle to achieve?"

That was unanswerable. Lady Dhara considered him restively, then continued her story: "So we were here. We chose a direction and eventually came across a knot of Fae script, the only marking so far on these walls. There was a body before it." She glanced down at her younger daughter, but continued, "Some months dead, as best we could judge. The script is an enchantment, of that we are sure, and our hope is that it is a gate. Some of us travelled on, walked for hours, with only more corridor to show for our effort. It seems to be a very large circle. We had just regrouped when Aurak Bes told us he felt enchantment approaching. There is our camp."

The curve of the corridor had revealed the rest of the lost, sitting among a scatter of blankets and small objects. A strange sight, this collection of young and powerful in their bedclothes, their stances declaring tension and distrust.

Like an island of calm in their centre was Aurak Bes, fortunately in one piece. He smiled in surprised recognition at the sight of her, but before Gentian could respond Seylon Heresar, who had been murmuring quietly to Prince Jurasel, stepped once again to the fore.

"I'm sure it is hardly necessary," he said, with a suggestion of purr, "but allow me to introduce my brother, Aristide Couerveur of Darest, who is anxious to come to our rescue as soon as he discovers how." He looked with undisguised pleasure at Aristide's *saecstra*-marked hand and added: "I understand your title to be Councillor of Mages now, brother?"

"Currently," Aristide replied, displaying no particular concern at the intended barb. He bowed with a pleasing elegance, then spared a glance for the wall to their right, where an intricate medallion of twisting lines, pale purple in colour, stretched from the floor to well above their heads. Fae script as promised, with an elaborate border.

The first to step forward was a highly polished piece of courtly gallantry. His bed robe displayed skin of velvet cream and, while not muscular, he was certainly well-formed. Dark eyes were framed by extravagantly long lashes, and his curling black hair was lightly tousled.

"This is unexpected, Lord Couerveur."

His voice, with a slight Saxan lilt, matched the beauty of his face and Gentian guessed this to be Crown Prince Chenar. The most she knew of him was that he suffered from a land-hungry father. Beneath his muted dismay, the man seemed nervous, his eyes flicking between Aristide and Prince Jurasel before settling on the uniformed figure who stood between them.

"Djol, what has been happening?"

Captain Djol, with a precise salute, said: "Highness. After over a day's search the wreckage of your barge was located in the Skorese Mountains of Darest, along with the bodies of those...not here. No hint of those responsible could be located, but on investigating a trace of what must have been the translocation spell, we were brought here. Since we were not immediately followed by others among the searchers, I consider it likely that route has been closed."

"I see." Prince Chenar did not quite manage to hide the blow, but glanced aside as a younger, less highly finished version of himself touched his arm. "Rydan, you'll not have met Lord Couerveur before. If you have been caught in this trap on our behalf, Lord Couerveur, I can only offer my regrets."

"I imagine no fault of yours, Prince Chenar."

Gentian sensed something unspoken, but couldn't read the exchange. She heard Prince Jurasel shift position, still at a slow seethe, and wondered if it was even remotely possible this group would survive another day without coming to blows.

"You will be familiar with Princess Kestia, of course," Prince Chenar continued, bowing with toward a tall, red-haired woman standing between a boy of four and the girl called Desseron. The woman inclined her head a bare fraction, austere to the point of rigidity.

"Well met, Your Highness," Aristide said. He left a little pause, a kind of auditory underscoring, then with deliberate care unslung the water-skin he was carrying. "I understand you have been short of food and water?"

"Sweet of you." The speaker, her tone drawling, was the only one still seated, watching the encounter with lazy detachment. The last of the missing heirs of the West, surely: the Cerian Crown Princess.

White gold. Her hair, her skin, her brief silken shift. Even her eyes were a molten honey-brown. But beyond her colouring, with her long legs curled under her, and her head drooping almost as if it was too heavy for her neck, she was quite the most innately graceful creature Gentian had ever seen. Improbably out of place seated on a blanket in this stark corridor, but Aristide's equal for self-composure.

"Princess Aloren." Passing the skin to Lady Dhara, Aristide bowed again, this time with a flourish, ironic tribute to the display the woman made. For she was certainly beautiful, enough to make Gentian blink and look away from the figure hidden, flaunted, by the golden shift.

"Aristide." Heavy lashes dropped as she surveyed him, lazily critical. "I see you haven't grown any taller. But I like the black. I do hope you're going to live up to your reputation, for this is certainly the dullest place in all Sumica."

Lord Aristide seemed to find Princess Aloren highly amusing, and was probably well aware that Prince Chenar and Prince Jurasel were both watching the exchange with disfavour. "I see I must produce an exit without delay," he said, aplomb undiminished.

"For that, I suspect you may well have brought us a key."

Aurak Bes, never long to remain in the background, walked forward. Grand in an ochre bed-robe, he was six and a half feet tall and over sixty years old, though the advantages of being true-mage kept any hint of grey from his neatly beaded hair. He was very dark, and had the imposing build of Atlarus' south, with a deep chest that made his voice boom. Without a doubt he had caught and weighed every nuance of tension, but no hint of concern marred the warmth in his eyes.

"Lord Magister Couerveur," he said, a hand going to his chest as he inclined his head. "It is indeed a pleasure to meet you."

He nodded acceptance of Aristide's return courtesy, then turned to Gentian and held out both his hands, capturing hers and bowing over them. "*'Gentian, Gentian, meek and mild'*," he quoted, with great good humour.

"You are the very person I have been wishing for. It has been over a year, has it not?"

"Near to two, Sir." She smiled up at him, then freed her hands. "I could hope to have found you in better circumstances."

"I am whole. I breathe. I understand that is more than I can say for the other passengers." He looked back at Aristide. "I have undertaken to bring the Arachol's good wishes to your King, Lord Magister, and I mean to fulfil my commission. To this end, I suggest that together we turn our minds to unravelling this puzzle of the Fair." His eyes turned briefly toward the writing on the wall. "But first there is another matter I feel should be drawn to your attention. If you would follow me?"

They obeyed, Gentian pausing to unload her bags and hand Lady Dhara a box of rose jellies meant to be a gift to her parents. Gentian's experience of Kubara Bes had been full of these moments where he would sweep in and take control, and everyone would just do what he said because it was the best and most logical course. She could remember one of his daughters complaining about the total autocracy of a benevolent man. No doubt his presence was the reason the storm of tension had yet to break.

With half the castaways in tow, Aurak Bes led them a short way along the corridor, to where a blanket covered an unmistakeable shape. "We moved her here," he said, sketching the Moon's crescent. "Rather than leave her in the middle of our camp."

A curious quietude came over Aristide Couerveur's face as he lifted the blanket to reveal the pinched and shrunken features of a woman months dead.

It's not a pose, Gentian thought. He really has been enjoying himself. Despite the risk to Darest and his own life, this mess had simply put him on his mettle. But this, this he definitely isn't pleased about.

"Desia Metral," Aristide said, drawing the blanket back across the corpse's face with particular care. He straightened. "A diviner I sent to survey the Bonisen Mines, some eight months ago. I will be able to call off the search."

"Dehydration seems the probable cause," Aurak Bes said.

"Very likely. Shall we?" Aristide asked, turning back toward the intricate patch of writing. This time the undertone was 'enough games'.

Gentian could haltingly read Fae script, but she did not need to even look at these words to know them. They had been telling her their meaning long before she came within sight of them, murmuring, scratching, *sucking* at the edges of her mind. It had inspired a queer uncertainty, a reluctance to think about, to even look at the wall. Another new experience: she'd never been prone to fits of nerves. But she kept remembering the sea-fetch, staring up at her out of her own drowned eyes.

"*'Bow your head in shame before Telsandar'*," Aristide Couerveur read. And smiled.

"I am not such a scholar of the Fair as you, Lord Magister," Aurak Bes said, watching the smaller man with full attention. "I have never heard of a Telsandar."

"It is this land. It is the name the Fair had for Darest before it was given as gift to Domina Rathen."

This produced a spate of questions and demands from those behind them, which Aristide completely ignored. Gentian wondered what he felt from the medallion. The Couerveur bloodline was strong, but she'd not known the family to be sensitive enough to touch the soul of the land, had been surprised he'd known they hadn't left Darest. Still, he was true-mage, great-mage, and had quite a reputation.

The Couerveurs also had a reputation for turning into autocratic madmen as they aged. Gentian's mother had made it a policy to have as little to do with their regency as possible, and Gentian suspected that sooner or later she was going to come in for a lecture for finding this autocrat entirely too entertaining.

"The casting is too subtle, or perhaps too old, for me to read the intent," Aurak Bes said. "That is why I am glad to see you have brought Magister Calder with you. It is a gate, is it not?"

"Yes."

They said it together, more deliberately this time, and Aristide's eyes narrowed meaningfully. Gentian saw, with an inner curl of hilarity, that Aristide Couerveur had decided to be suspicious of her, of the convenience of her. He could well have said "We must talk of this later," as he had when he so unexpectedly fired up about her plans for Vostal Hill.

"It feels like it's one way," she added, turning away to gather up her bags. "Wherever this takes us, we'll only be using it the once."

"How can you be sure of that?" This from Prince Jurasel, obviously having had enough of standing about in the background. "None of us could read intent from that thing, just those words." For all he made no move toward her, his dissatisfaction, the vivid desire to strike out at something, anything, made her shoulder blades itch.

No need to tell this tinderbox of royalty she thought they were walking from one trap to another, and that she had no idea what the consequences would be. What gain admitting to a feeling of being dragged under whenever she came near the thing? Dying of thirst in this corridor was surely the worse option.

"Why don't we find out?" she asked instead, and put her hand through the wall.

Chapter Seven

Aspen had a new god. Anyone who could call the Diamond short to his face was worthy of the most slavish devotion, and he made no effort to hide his approbation. Like Prince Jurasel and Prince Chenar, he was going to make every effort to win her good graces.

He appreciated that she saw and accepted his admiration as her due, sparing a moment to look him up and down. At this stage that was enough, for it would surely be a difficult pursuit with two Crown Princes trying to annex her as territory. Not that both of them weren't worth second, third *and* fourth looks as well. Aspen was suffering from an embarrassment of riches.

Continuing her role as proclaiming oracle, Gentian had walked into the wall like it was wet mud, and was now only an arm, shoulder and bags projecting from the middle of the tangle of purplish script. She waggled splayed fingers, and the Atlaran ambassador took the hint, enveloping them before offering his free hand to Aristide. Seeing exactly where this was going, Aspen was caught between getting to hold the Diamond's hand, and jockeying for position by the golden Aloren.

But the Hapt-lo blocked Aristide and Chenar and Jurasel quickly bracketed Aloren. Aspen ended up between Lady Dhara and her blood-daughter. The girl, Kassen, was blinking back tears, which Aspen did not think was at all the appropriate response to escape, especially by means of filing absurdly hand-in-hand through a wall. She caught him looking askance and ducked her head, then glowered at him in an it's-all-your-fault way.

"How did they die?"

"Ah–" Aspen looked at Lady Dhara for guidance, but Kassen tugged imperiously on his hand.

"How? They said they were all dead. All of them. Michel and Nana and even Po. I want to know."

"Tell her." Lady Dhara's mouth was set, but her tone sure.

Aspen's tongue clove to the roof of his mouth at the prospect of translating 'Michel and Nana and Po' into the fragments of barge and flesh tumbling in the Cauldron. At least the other two children had already gone through.

The Guard Dog, last link on the chain, saved him from response. "The barge struck a rock and broke apart," the man said, blunt, unflinching. "They drowned."

"Quick?"

"Quick."

The girl's hand squirmed in Aspen's, then she bent her head. Grateful, Aspen nodded his thanks to the Guard Dog, and was snubbed for his pains: surveyed briefly and dismissed. Aspen rolled his eyes.

Lady Dhara started through the wall. What was on the other side? Darest might once have been part of The Deeping, the empire of the Fair, but he'd never heard of anything like this. The longer this little excursion went on, the less sense it made. At least the prospect of escape had distracted the lot of them from sniping at each other, and in the company of the Atlaran ambassador and Princess Aloren even Jurasel would surely hesitate to try to snap the Diamond's neck.

When it was Aspen's turn to be drawn gently into pearl white he found it to be cold treacle, not quite solid enough to resist him. Hand, forearm, shoulder. Just when he was starting to think that this was perhaps not such a good idea, he felt his fingers breaking through the other side. Warm air, nothing frightening. Lady Dhara let go his hand, and he started pushing through on his own, taking a deep breath before his head went in, and concentrating on moving forward, not thinking about the tightness in his chest, and making damn sure he kept hold of the warm, wriggling fingers behind him.

Sooner than he expected, his face broke into warmth and air. Free magic tingled promisingly at his senses and he blinked twice then gaped, disbelieving, at a valley bathed in afternoon light.

Bizarrely, he thought of the place Rua Ketu had described, a dark grey place which judged, a place with eyes. But this was nothing like. This – huge, miles across – was a city. Flowing, ornate, lovely, and frozen white: a city of the Fair iced like a sunken festival cake.

He turned, still pulling Kassen's hand, and looked out over a line of mountains he had recently seen from the far side. The Skorese. They'd been transported to the very north of the range.

Sumica's heirs were scattering along a neat pathway that ran around the rim of the almost circular valley. Balustrades to either side of the path separated the sugar fondant city from grassy mountain slopes where wildflowers had almost vanquished the last of the high mountain snowdrifts. A stone-paved road led down to the foothills.

"Sun and Moon! Thank you." With Kassen now almost completely through, Aspen let her go and took a few exuberant steps forward. They had done it. Out of the trap, back into the world. Free magic all around, ready for them to use to fly out, to let the world know where they were.

Wherever they were. How could this place be in the Skorese? Yes, the mountains had a reputation for getting people lost, but they'd been thoroughly explored. People had *flown* over them, for pity's sake. You'd think they'd mention a huge valley full of hundreds of buildings! And what was with the glazing? Houses, trees, gardens: the entire thing was covered over with a white sheen a little too reminiscent of the wall they'd just passed through. Nothing moved except his fellow escapees, clumping in little groups, exclaiming. The only sound was their confused voices.

The Diamond stood two steps down the nearest path into the valley. True to type, he was completely failing to act like a man suddenly delivered from a death sentence, instead talking calmly to the Atlaran ambassador. As Aspen started toward them, eager to hear what they were discussing, Kassen suddenly bolted to Lady Dhara's side.

"Mama!" she cried, equal parts excited and unhappy. "Mama, the sky isn't real!"

ooOoo

It was true. Even as the last of the barge's survivors filed out of an obelisk set into the balustrade, Aspen realised that at least half of what he was seeing was illusion. Everything not in the valley. If you looked hard enough, peered with more than just your eyes, the sky and mountains took on a tell-tale thinness. Behind was a familiar pearly wall, rising into a grand dome. Unbroken.

"Mount Garant," the Diamond said. "If the seeming is a true representation of our location, we are under Mount Garant."

"What does it matter *which* mountain it is?" Lady Dhara was ever-pragmatic. "How do we get out?"

"I am not able to sigil-call," the Atlaran guardsman said, breaking off an attempt. "There is a shield."

"A major casting," Aurak Bes confirmed. "Woven all around us. It is...unusual, and massive. Power here means we are not completely closed off–"

"But still another box." Seylon Heresar, with an air of prowling anticipation, moved down to join the Diamond and the Aurak. "I own, I prefer this one. It has a certain...sterile charm." He surveyed parklands and gardens, houses built in steps, and walkways curving down to what might well be a small lake, formed into a complex, four-sided cross. A pavilion on a small island formed a centre point. "What now?"

"We find an exit," the Diamond said. "Or overcome this casting." He gave them an extraordinarily bland look. "I suspect that will take some time."

Princess Aloren, sitting with an air of habitual weariness on a convenient bench, laughed. "How nicely you put it, Aristide. I do hope you mean to be an attentive host."

Aspen gazed at her with increasing approval. Even her laughter was rich with indolent power. Rua Ketu caught his eye and rocked her staff back and forth. Comment, agreement, a little mockery. Aspen grinned in return, then offered her the same appreciative glance. She had her own magnificence, and if they were going to be here for a while...well.

"We will have to conjure supplies," Lady Dhara was saying briskly. She reached across the inner balustrade and tried unsuccessfully to pluck a white-frosted leaf from the nearest tree. It could well have been solid stone. "Or break this preservation spell. Has anything else of this kind ever been found in Darest?"

Given the number of spies the western lands maintained in the Darien Court, Aspen half expected the Diamond's response to be sugared with arsenic, but he merely said: "No," and turned to study the winding path below him.

But before any of this temperamental audience could fire up, he continued: "Darest lay empty for centuries before it was given to Domina Rathen. Long enough that only vague tales remain of its occupants. I am told that during this span it was a particularly dangerous region to stray into, less...tame than much of The Deeping."

"Which is not tame." Lady Dhara's mouth twisted.

"It does not welcome intruders." This *did* have the finest dagger-edge. "When The Deeping withdrew its influence, and the land became Darest, little evidence could be found to show it had ever been occupied. Signs that the forest had once been orchard. Fragments of the foundations of settlements. Tor Darest is built on the site of one. But nothing whole. Very much as if a concerted effort had been made to erase any trace of the people who lived here. And the Fair will not talk of them."

"Their deep, dark secret." Seylon Heresar was looking over the valley with renewed interest. "An attempt at a coup, perhaps? This land's lord deciding that they would rather not be part of an empire?"

The Aurak moved at this. "I have long believed that it was a matter of Shaping."

Aristide nodded. "So have I."

This was not quite news to Aspen, who had enjoyed certain confidences from Soren about just how, during the previous autumn's confrontation, the Court of the Fair had reacted to the idea of one of their own being Shaped. Shaping was a finicky sort of casting which operated 'beyond the blood', as it were. Rather than making a plant or animal different by laying an enchantment over it, you tried to create one from the inside out. It was a chancy, tedious and altogether difficult process which Aspen had never wanted to attempt, but which had an immense advantage over enchantment: a Shaped creature did not require any maintenance, and could have children. A new species, tailored to your needs.

The Fair were past masters of the art. The Fair also lived centuries longer than any other people, were born true-mage without exception, and had a marked tendency to be tall and beautiful even before they had grown old enough to start improving their looks with castings. No great leap of the imagination to believe they'd been practicing on themselves.

While the assembled clutch of royalty immediately tried to pry reasons out of the Diamond, Aspen looked about for their own representative of the Shaper art. She'd wandered a little way along the rim-top pathway, and was gazing fixedly not at the city, but out over the foothills of the mountains. As he walked toward her, Aspen decided she wasn't paying the least attention to the discussion of Darest's past.

"'Gentian, Gentian, meek and mild'?"

For a moment he thought she hadn't even heard him, but then her face relaxed and she gave him a sideways look. "The Arachol's Court thought that terribly amusing. There's a whole series of rhymes to go with it, which I trust Aurak Bes will not repeat."

"Rhymes? Such as?"

"I think I'll spare myself." She reached with one finger to touch the balcony, and Aspen saw that there was a lizard sitting there. Its resemblance to a sugar-ice decoration prompted a vague impulse to pick it up and bite its head off. But through the layer of white, he could see it really was a lizard.

"It's alive," Gentian said, almost below her breath.

"What does your sense of place tell you about this valley, Magister?" a distinctly Eastern voice asked. Aspen had to hide a little start of shock, for he hadn't heard the Guard Dog coming up behind him.

Gentian gave the man one of those big-eyed, sombre examinations, then turned to look at the preserved city.

"It feels like Darest. Quite more like Darest than any other part I've visited. It also feels–" She broke off, frowning at the centre pavilion. "It's – it's in mourning. It grieves. It isn't – it's not what I would have expected. We should go down soon."

"Why? Is there danger approaching?" The Captain's hand went to his sword, as if Djol could think of no other solution to the unknown.

Gentian blinked at him. "I don't know. But I think the sun is going to pretend to set in a couple of hours. And I want to see this place in its own light."

This was a suitably nonsensical answer, but before Aspen could think of an appropriate response he noticed

Prince Rydan had followed them up. A pretty youth, seventeen or so, with an air of having not quite grown into his full height. He had possibilities, but Aspen's tastes didn't run to callow.

Captain Djol?" he said, and waited until the man had acknowledged him before continuing. "I wished to ask: those on the barge – is there no possibility of other survivors?"

"We found many bodies, Highness," the Guard Dog replied, blunt as ever. "We had yet to count them."

Rydan blanched. "I see. Thank you." He touched a hand to his chest, an oddly respectful gesture to give a bodyguard, and headed back to the main group. Djol followed him.

When Aspen looked back at Gentian, he found her still gazing unhappily down into the valley. She'd turned into a proper little cloud of gloom.

"So who do you think will win?" he asked lightly. "The Pirate or the Poet?"

He liked her for not saying: "Who?" but taking the time to puzzle it out before turning to look at Jurasel and Chenar, standing to either side of Aloren.

"The Playwright."

That was a new take on Aloren, and Aspen turned the term over semi-approvingly. The Cerian princess was certainly a far cry from the inconsequential cipher he'd initially pictured. Golden Aloren. Precious Metal.

Someone drew shield. Jerked out of agreeable fantasy, Aspen stared in consternation as shield after shield answered. An active personal defence was like a bared sword, proclaiming intent or expectation of an attack. Now that they were out of that corridor, this fractious group had access to an entire mage's arsenal to use on each other, but what in the name of the Sun and Moon had happened to set them off?

Hurriedly using true-magic to pull some semblance of shield in place for himself, Aspen dashed back to the tight knot of royalty. From the way they were all centred on Jurasel, he must have been the first to call power. But his expression was scornful rather than combative.

"What cause to be so white-livered?" he asked, obviously pleased by the reaction he'd provoked. "All this talk of searching about, hoping for an exit. What happened to the first option? We have our fists back. Are we going to leave this wall untested, merely because it is large?"

He began casting, carefully enunciated word-magic. Aspen didn't recognise the spell, but Lady Dhara obviously did.

"For Sun's sake," she said, sounding more than a little exasperated with her brother-by-marriage. "You'll just have that back in our faces."

Jurasel, mid-spell, showed no sign of stopping to answer. A little nimbus of light began to collect about him as his words took substance.

"It may give our investigations a starting point," the Diamond said. "Though good sense would urge a withdrawal to a safe distance."

He drew shield and stood studying the Saxan prince: a neat demonstration of his confidence in his own defences, and the fact that he'd not leapt to protect himself the moment power had been called. Aspen was not about to make the same boast, and joined the general exodus.

Gentian, he discovered, had remained by the ornamental lizard, and it was here that the Atlaran ambassador and his two guards stopped, along with Prince Chenar and Princess Aloren. Aspen chose the better part of valour, following Kestia and Dhara as they ushered their children well out of range. Prince Rydan and the Guard Dog, after a brief exchange with Chenar, ended up with them. Only Seylon Heresar stayed with Aristide to face the full impact of Prince Jurasel's attempt.

It was a spell and a half. Aspen, even from a distance, could see the effort it was costing the Saxan prince.

Jurasel, like most of those trapped, would be Maja not Magister: the journeyman or workman, rather than scholar rank of mage. But he seemed well equal to winding a great deal of power up into something he could hurl. And made a magnificent figure in the attempt: eyes alight, body braced for impact, smiling with anticipation. A true child of the Sun.

The nimbus of light surrounding Jurasel intensified, sending rainbows dancing through the valley's pearly shell. The illusion of sky and mountains around their point of entry thinned, revealing more of the smooth expanse of white. The flow of sheer force began to pick out the edges of the ordinarily transparent shields which surrounded the three men, and the highlights in Seylon and Jurasel's hair shone brilliant red. The Diamond burned white.

Jurasel released, and the bolt of force struck directly on the obelisk where they had come through. Aspen threw up a hand to protect his eyes as a lightning flash bloomed to cover the entire area, the edges of it streaming past the first group of watchers so that their shields also crackled into visibility, straining to protect. Aspen felt the remnants of the thing sweep past him, and even at this remove he had to grit his teeth and concentrate on pouring power into his shield.

Then it was over. The light vanished, leaving only spots before eyes as keepsakes. Aspen blinked around them, checking everyone was still standing. The trio at the epicentre had not shifted, though Jurasel now bent, propping hands on knees and gasping for breath. Nothing else had changed. The obelisk was unmarked, the illusion once again tight. So far as Aspen could tell, the prince hadn't succeeded in even knocking a marzipan leaf from one of the trees.

As shields were one by one released, Prince Chenar said, almost apologetically: "You weren't holding back?"

Jurasel was not stung, merely grinning broadly as he straightened, stretching out muscle kinks. "No fear of that. Worthwhile in establishing that there's no value in blunt force."

"And faint heart never won fair lady."

The words, barely loud enough to hear, had come from behind Aspen, could only be from the Guard Dog, though the man did not so much as blink when Aspen turned to him. Nor was he far off the mark, judging from Jurasel's expression when Princess Aloren glided up to talk to him. It had been a wholly impressive display.

Gentian and Aurak Bes were murmuring to each other in low tones, and Aspen hurried to catch up to them when they moved toward the Diamond.

"As an experiment, this has been even more valuable, Prince Jurasel," the Aurak was saying. "You felt it too, Magister?"

"What's this?" Jurasel sounded positively cheerful. "Gave you something you could use, did I?"

Aristide nodded. "An important fact. The shielding strengthened at this point before you released, Highness. It anticipated you."

ooOoo

With this little fillip to digest, they started down the nearest spiralling path into the valley. Aspen wasn't altogether sure why they didn't just fly, but supposed the Guard Dog, at least, wasn't really up to it. And the prospect of flying beneath that false sky conjured up visions of mages splatting painfully into concealed objects.

Besides, it gave him a wonderful opportunity to watch Princess Aloren in motion. It was almost as if, to spare her the effort of walking, the world shifted cunningly beneath her feet. Obliging of circumstance to dress her in that scanty scrap of silk. Jurasel and Chenar naturally strode to either side, which meant Aspen could feast his eyes on all three at once, and plot a most complex conquest.

Between admiring glances and listening to snatches of conversation, Aspen had little attention to spare for the city. But then, with it all iced over, there wasn't a great deal to look at. You couldn't actually go inside the buildings. None of the doors would move, and the windows were blocked and opaque. At a guess they were mostly private residences, built down the slope with balconies designed to take advantage of the view across the valley. Lots of space between them, with gardens and little plazas, the occasional curving park, even miniature fields with rows of marzipan corn. Around the park of grass and low gardens edging the frozen, pocket-sized lake they discovered larger buildings, temples and palaces and such. Magnificent, silent, frosted, dead.

"Do you hear music?"

From the faint murmur of agreement, Prince Rydan was the first to speak what many suspected. Aspen hadn't noticed anything, but when he strained his ears, he could just catch the faintest melody. The place wasn't as lifeless as he'd thought.

"This way." The Aurak started around the edge of the central parkland with its cross-shaped lake. The music became more distinct and Aspen guessed at a harp somewhere in the buildings ahead.

Rua Ketu's commander, Hapt-lo Dest, quickened his step, long legs effortlessly taking him to the front of the group. "Shields?" he asked, when the Aurak tilted his heavy head toward him.

The Aurak tipped his head in the opposite direction, meeting the Diamond's eyes. A little pause, then: "Not as yet."

Good manners. They'd already had one demonstration today of how drawing shield could be misunderstood. Which was all well and good, but there was something about this music – delicate, intricate – which got under

Aspen's skin to tickle and constrict. Like a net of cobwebs around his veins.

The Hapt-lo's steady pace faltered, and he looked again to his lord. In a moment, Aspen saw what had conjured clear surprise to his stoic features. There, in front of one of the buildings, was another misplaced festival confection. Seven foot at least, greyhound slender, her profile clean, beautiful and stern. A woman, frozen along with the trees and lizards.

She had been caught in a graceful, very upright pose, her head turned to look up a broad flight of stairs to the door of the nearest building: a large, square edifice with high columns supporting a decorated architrave. Music cascaded through the unblocked entrance.

With many wary glances at the doorway, they approached the white figure. Aurak Bes, after a close glance at the glazing, chuckled.

"Stone beneath. This is a statue in truth."

"It's not a statue up there, Lord," the Guard Dog said.

"No, indeed. And – I believe this composition shares a pattern with the valley's shielding."

"Linked, certainly," the Diamond said.

"Stop the music, stop the shield?" Lady Dhara mused. "It's never that simple, is it?" She exchanged a glance with Princess Kestia, their children gathered around her.

"Do we go as a group?" Aspen asked. "Or–?" He paused, and looked uncomfortably toward the three children.

"I'm sure we can find somewhere out of harm's way for you, sister." Jurasel's tone was still cheerful, the malice almost automatic.

Princess Kestia didn't respond, but Lady Dhara snorted and gestured toward the western rim of the valley where the sky was changing colours. "Whatever's able to maintain that shield – let alone an illusion lighting a place this large – is perfectly capable of swatting the lot of us, wherever we lurk. Let's get this over with." She mounted the stair, sweeping them into her wake.

Aspen awarded her at least ten points for taking a daunting prospect head-on, and by doing so somehow reducing it. For what she'd said was true. Here they were, some of the most powerful mages in Western Sumica, walking about a valley none of them could hope to produce. So far as he knew, even the entire Court of the Fair would struggle to manage this kind of effect. If they wanted to bring down whoever had built the thing, they'd have to pray for intervention from Sun and Moon both.

Time to find out why they'd been brought here.

ooOoo

A white marble box, leavened by slender lancet arches reaching from waist-height to within a hand's-span of the ceiling. Four great harps in the corners, polished and gleaming in shades of teak and mahogany. Smaller instruments scattered on divans and elegant cupped chairs. And, at the harp to the right of the door, the musician.

It was the original of the statue. Her hair matched the massive harp she was playing: a very dark mahogany dressed to a high chignon, caught up, looped and braided, with a cascading tail long enough to coil on the floor behind her, pooling on the train of her slate and sage gown. For a moment Aspen was entirely diverted from imminent bug-squashing by the reflection that as soon as he was back in Tor Darest he would absolutely have to put a picture of himself outside his room, to let people know of the delights within. But then the woman stopped playing. Long hands moved from the harp's quivering strings to her lap, and she looked at them.

Momentous thing. The Fair could be quite human at times, particularly those who weren't so full of a sense of their own history. They lived a long time, but they did the same things people did: ate and laughed and longed for whatever met their fancy. Falling into this woman's forest-black eyes, Aspen found no point of common reference.

For the first time since entering the valley he was acutely aware of their intrusion into the hidden past, as out of place as a mouse in the Feast-Hall of the King of the Cats. And about as brave of heart.

~To what purpose do you disturb Telsandar?~

There was precious little expression to the voice and no change at all in the smooth oval face. Her lips hadn't moved, and the words weren't Sumican. Translation didn't appear to be necessary: they reverberated, with the absolute clarity of struck crystal, inside Aspen's head.

He wasn't feeling anything he recognised as casting, but it occurred to him that the free magic in the room was behaving more than oddly. There was a kind of current to it, a general wash toward the near corner of the room where the woman sat. She was drawing on the ambient magic so massively that, even though he couldn't actually detect any intent to her casting, he could see the wake it left. That was...entirely outside his experience, and Aspen was certain he wasn't the only one in the room feeling an urgent need to back right out the door and find something to crawl under.

Aurak Bes took a step forward. With his head high, and his pale bed-robe settling in authoritative folds, he managed a complete and uncowed dignity. "No purpose of ours, My Lady," he said, polite in the grandest of ways. "We have been brought to this place unwilling, and would be glad of your assistance in leaving it."

~That I cannot give.~

Her impassive, unremitting gaze shifted past the Aurak and seemed to fix on Aspen. But she was looking past him, out the open doors, and a sudden surge in the tide of magic prompted him to turn sharply, to witness a spark of blue fire ignite on the crown of the pavilion that sat at the very centre of the valley. The light, burning water, flowed down the curving roof and the marzipan glazing went with it like melting wax, exposing green and brown marble, then a brighter green and blue beneath as the frosting was stripped off grass, and the water of the lake. Gardens were revealed, bordered by pathways of faintly pink stone edged in charcoal. The buildings remained white, but lacked the pearly gloss, and gained details picked out in charcoal, dusky pink, and a lighter grey. Brighter colour sparked: flowers, fruit, the rows of corn, and a flash of crimson as a red and black falsehawk launched from a tree, spiralled in a rising circle, and battered itself against the sky.

~Use what you will,~ said the voice in their minds.

Incredulity thick in the air, they turned as a group to look back at the Fae. She had lifted her hands preparatory to resuming play, and before this sorely-tried group the sight was a goad. Prince Jurasel made a choking sound and Lady Dhara seemed to be grinding her teeth. The Aurak had become grave with affront and the golden Aloren was decidedly less languid. Even the Diamond was frowning. Prince Chenar painted himself into a whole new light by being the first to manage to speak.

"Use what you will?" he repeated, diffidence falling away as he took two entire steps forward. "Who are you, to abduct and then dismiss us? You–"

~I am Suldar. Regent of this land.~

They were outside. Standing next to the now grey stone statue as the first deep notes of the harp sounded. There had been no sense of transition, no warning, no chance or hope to resist their dislocation. True to their insect status, she had brushed them aside and then closed – *removed* – the door behind them. The stair now led to an unbroken marbled wall, and they were left with one final statement, struck ringing into their minds:

~Your presence is no act of mine.~

Chapter Eight

"God?" Aristide Couerveur asked, lips curling. "Or monster?"

For the first time since she'd entered the valley the sick knot in Gentian's stomach relaxed, disarmed. "Face to face, it might be hard to tell the difference."

He nodded agreement, but turned away as Prince Chenar climbed down from anger, took a shuddering breath, then said: "I assume you are not content to remain in this place, Couerveur?"

"Not at all. However, I found nothing in that encounter to suggest we will escape tonight. Using what we need seems a most sensible suggestion."

"Water, food, a place to eat while we discuss this." Lady Dhara ticked each item off on her fingers. "Then rest. For you know he's perfectly right, Chenar. Unless you're capable of breaking back in there and forcing this Suldar to let us go, we're going to be chipping at these walls for weeks."

"We will aim for a quicker escape than that, My Lady," Seylon Heresar said. He emphasised the 'we' just enough to suggest that not everyone was working to the same goal, and coolly assessed the result. No doubt Cya would be delighted to set Sax at Darest's throat.

But Prince Chenar had recovered his quiet manner, and nothing seemed liable to strike more than glitter from Aristide Couerveur, who simply said: "Shall we choose a base of operations?"

They moved away from Suldar's building toward one of the mansion-sized houses, and Gentian again reached with all her senses for the place around her. Darest.

Intensely, inescapably Darest. But the hate wasn't there. She didn't understand.

And then there was the pavilion, the hub for the valley surrounded by grass and a cross with a complex border. The pavilion itself was stone: clean columns for trunks, stylised branches, and a lattice of pale grey leaves curving to a peak. It was beautiful, a work of art. Now that she'd recovered some semblance of equilibrium, she was able to study its frame without flinching, and begin to nudge her mind toward facing the implications.

"There's sure to be a kitchen around here somewhere," Lady Dhara was saying, pushing open the doors of the first house around the circle to reveal a simply lovely hall, all honey-toned marquetry. She strode onward with unstinting determination, opened another door, another, then was gone.

"It's been too long since I last played follow the leader," Aspen murmured in Gentian's ear. "Shall we move on to hide and seek?"

"King-in-his-castle's more likely."

He chortled, a delighted burble. "At least the Fair can be relied on to have littered this place with every comfort. There's something about abandoned luxury that makes me *itch* to take advantage of it."

"Abandoned is about right," Gentian replied, stopped by the crowd in the doorway of what had proven to be a kitchen.

Spacious, opening on a working garden, the room told an eloquent tale. Chopped and withered vegetables sat beside bowls of blackened meat. Pastry had been rolled into a sheet amidst a scatter of flour, and the shattered remains of a bottle twinkled in a dark stain on the slate flags. As if the residents had dropped everything and run. The scent of vinegar was still sharp in the air.

"This sat a week or more," Captain Djol said, prowling forward as others conjured mage-glows against the waning light.

"Before the preservation was activated." Lady Dhara followed him in and, with a nice display of perfectly controlled true-magic, lifted shattered glass, bowls, vegetables, and even the dusting of flour from the table. She walked it all out into the garden, then returned, shutting that door behind her. "Sit down," she ordered, with a sudden impatience. "Talk. Kassen, Desseron, help me find something to eat."

The two girls, along with Rua Ketu and Captain Djol, began to explore the kitchen's cupboards and pantries. Everyone else, after a hesitation full of sideways looks, collected chairs to cluster around the heavy table in the centre of the room. They were marvellously out of place, and not just because of the bed clothes. It occurred to Gentian to wonder how many of these people had actually *been* in a kitchen before, let alone used one. All this royalty, and barely a servant in sight.

She'd thought that Chenar and Jurasel would again be jockeying for access to Princess Aloren, but instead the seating arrangements took on a distinctly factional flavour, everyone clumping according to kingdom. Gentian felt very Darien, sitting at one end of the table at Aristide Couerveur's right hand, with his apprentice on her other side. Aspen had manoeuvred himself next to Princess Aloren and was making droll remarks, which the princess listened to with lazy attention. The two Saxans, Rydan and Chenar, were on her far side, murmuring together.

The Aurak had taken the other end of the table and, after setting down bowls full of apples, nuts and dried apricots, Rua Ketu joined Hapt-lo Dest in standing behind the ambassador. The three Atlarans seemed somehow removed from proceedings: as trapped as the rest but falling into the role of arbiters, with no stake in the tensions between Sumica's western realms.

On the final side of the table ranged the Cyans: Prince Jurasel, Seylon Heresar, Princess Kestia with her son on her lap, and empty chairs for Lady Dhara and the two girls. Cya certainly had the numbers. Not a good thing, if Aspen's talk of assassinations was true.

When the last of the chairs had been fetched, it was the Cyans who took the floor while Prince Chenar sat with head bowed, and Aloren, as ever, simply watched.

Seylon Heresar, gazing at his brother as a cat would a potential meal, started out with: "I own, I don't know what it is prompts me to turn to you for answers, Aristide. You've already told us this place is as much a surprise to you as it is to us. Perhaps, since you served your 'prenticeship among the Fair, you will forgive us for treating you as an expert and showering you with a few more questions?"

"If you wish." Perfect indifference, almost a statement that he and Darest had nothing to hide or apologise for. It was effective, but immediately undercut by Prince Jurasel.

"It's not Couerveur I want an answer from," he said flatly, his glower now directed at Gentian. "We spent an age trying to unlock the door to this place, with about as much success as a kitten trying to roar. Who are you to walk through it as if you had a key?"

"Laeth Varpatten's daughter."

The Varpatten reputation stretched well beyond Darest, and as a child Gentian had delighted in the string of mages bringing her father magical puzzles they hadn't the sensitivity to unravel. She had hoped her bloodline would provide enough of an explanation, and keep them from pressing her further, and thought it had done that.

"I do think I had a key," she added, feeling unsettled. "That door – I don't think you could ever have opened it. You don't belong here."

"True enough," Lady Dhara said, setting a jug and two bottles on the table. "But if you're suggesting that being Darien gave you right of entry, what about that wretched creature we found dead before it?"

"Saxan," Aristide put in. "Immigrated ten years ago." He glanced at Captain Djol, who seemed to have taken the role of cook to himself. "Transplanted, but not native."

Djol somehow managed to slice onions and gaze dispassionately back at the same time, not missing a stroke. Gentian wondered what the Easterner thought of the far more powerful mages he served. Not a native of the West, there was no guessing how he'd react to plots and intrigues against Darest.

"It seems this land has an excess of Regents," Lady Dhara said, sitting down as her daughters arrived with a fine collection of mugs and glasses. Her brusque manner was a relief, bare of the overtones of insinuation and attack which were making conversation such heavy weather. "Regent of Telsandar-as-was, I presume. Telsandar which became Darest, what, six or seven hundred years ago? And stood empty for centuries before that. With this Suldar hidden away here all that time? The Fair don't live that long."

"Nor do they own the kind of power displayed here. Nothing has that kind of power." It was the first time Princess Kestia had spoken. There was a dry, definite quality to her voice, and she surveyed them over the dark head of her meal-preoccupied son.

"Fae, but more than Fae," Seylon Heresar mused, sounding doubtful. "The question is, does she stay here by choice, or is this her prison?"

"If I am any judge," Aurak Bes said, "the Lady Suldar is the one maintaining this place. The illusion and the shield. There was certainly an echo of their shape in that music. What prisoner shores up the walls of their cell?"

"Warden then?" Lady Dhara suggested. "Or – is this better termed a museum, and Suldar the curator? Either way, if she told the truth about not bringing us here, we still have no idea who did."

"And what reason for the message on the door?" Seylon Heresar turned back to Aristide. "Another of the questions I am keen to ask, brother. *'Bow your head in shame'?* That is hardly typical–"

Princess Kestia lifted a hand. "We are going nowhere with this. Tell us what you *do* know, Lord Couerveur, so we might progress."

Aristide lowered his chin minutely. The group around the table watched him impatiently: no friendlier, but with the sharp edges of temperament restrained. They were anxious for answers.

"Three things," Aristide said, assuming the detached air of a scholar. 'Suldar', which means dusk, is a word I have only encountered in older works of Fae poetry. That is significant purely because the term is no longer in use. Essan is the most stable of the languages, with few archaisms. It is too closely related to Elachar for the Fair to abandon any word without reason. Secondly, the Fair maintain the strongest of Bans upon Shaping their own kind, far harsher than our own laws." He paused, and then his mouth, which had relaxed from its habitual curve, twitched at the corners. "The last thing I can say with certainty is that Darest is cursed."

Half the heirs of the West started in unfeigned shock while Gentian passed through a moment of complete disbelief. Everyone talked about Darest being cursed. It had been failing for centuries: a gradual, inexorable decline, and Dariens habitually blamed every setback or obstacle on a villainous Fae curse. But for the Fair to curse Darest would be to go against their own strict laws, and no trace of such a monumental spell had ever been discovered. No trace.

And yet Aristide had spoken with complete assurance, and now leaned back in his chair, brilliant eyes pensive. "This I have from the Fair," he continued. "Telsandar was a sacred place to them. A disaster they refuse to discuss killed its inhabitants and afterwards 'the region was held to be tainted'. Exactly what this taint is I don't know, but the Fair believe they cannot safely live within our borders.

They are forbidden from lingering here for more than brief periods, and even suspect that the taint affects the neighbouring kingdoms, causing friction, enmity. But not among humans, which was why Darest was given in gift to the Rathens."

Apparently entertained by his audience's fixed regard, he stopped, pouring himself a glass of wine.

While Gentian mulled over this unexpected explanation, Lady Dhara made a gesture, half appreciation, half disparagement. "So we have a Ban on Shaping Fae, and an ancient Fae who must surely be Shaped, whose name is abandoned, sealed in a city from centuries past. In a kingdom suffering from some malign horror that actually makes the Fair afraid to live in it. This Suldar could be the problem or its jailer, and in either case we had best lock our doors tonight. And our conclusions are all just so much air 'til we investigate further. Well, I would appreciate *some* speculation from you, Lord Couerveur. Did this Suldar speak the truth, when she claimed not to be our kidnapper?"

"The Fair rarely lie directly." With the faintest of shrugs, Aristide sipped his wine, then glanced distractedly at Captain Djol. The smell of frying onions was no doubt doing acute things to more than Gentian's stomach. "At this point, the best we can do is eat, sleep. Shall we reconvene this discussion tomorrow morning, after some preliminary investigation?"

No-one objected. Tired enough to accept simple sense? Or perhaps it was Captain Djol's cooking, which proved to be a kind of fried flat-bread, pleasantly salty, studded with onion rings and quite possibly the most delicious thing Gentian had ever eaten. The day had made her hungry.

Looking around the table, she decided that the lull in hostilities was a sign their situation was sinking in. Not so easy to digest, the prospect of being trapped here for days or months. Years? While their respective peoples searched, and their enemies moved to fill the vacuum they'd left behind.

And Darest was torn apart?

"Aurak Bes."

It was Prince Chenar who had spoken, and Gentian was not alone in looking up sharply. The words had a steely note, as if Chenar had worked his way to a difficult resolution.

Kubara Bes had certainly caught the warning. The smile he bestowed on the Saxan prince was positively grandfatherly: a sure sign in Gentian's experience that the Aurak detected dangerous waters. "How may I help you, Prince Chenar?"

"You believe that creature's performance is linked to the shield which traps us here?"

The Aurak nodded. "There is an echo in the patterns, certainly. The shielding is set enchantment, but–" He paused, then went on with an air of candour: "Such an enchantment needs to be fuelled, and the more I regard it, the more certain it appears that it is Suldar who maintains this place. There are at least no other visible candidates."

"So, whether we believe her protestations of innocence or not, it is this Fae who is our gaoler?"

The Aurak regarded him for a long moment, then inclined his head judicially. "That is the most straightforward construction, Prince. The shield keeps us here. The shield is maintained by Suldar. She has refused to lift it. I do not advise taking this path to its conclusion."

"I'm not dismissing the risks and the – the wrong of it." Chenar looked frankly miserable. "But, while of course we must search, investigate, while we can hope for some other solution, when invention fails we will have to face her. Deal with her."

"Yes."

It was Aristide who had answered so promptly, cold as his namesake diamond. Gentian blinked at his steady profile, and felt suddenly lost. What was going on, that they talked of death before looking for a way out, that they even imagined they could succeed? What was Aristide, to agree without qualm or hesitation?

"Deal with her *how?*" Lady Dhara asked. "Sun–!"

Princess Kestia put a hand on her wife's arm, and the woman bit back further response as the Cyan princess' frozen mask turned from Chenar to Aristide, the drowsing child resting against her chest testament to what she had to risk in any attack. The couple's two daughters were white-faced statues.

"What consequence, Couerveur?" she asked, her dry, definite voice low and uncompromising. "What alternative? This Suldar has given us...guest-rights? Does that not mean we enjoy a certain immunity, which would be lost in any attack?"

"It is rare for the Fair to kill when no offence has been committed," Aristide agreed, unruffled. "But their laws are harsh, and easy to break unintentionally. Under the strictest Fae codes, Suldar could have executed us for the trespass alone, and that she has not is an acknowledgement that we did not come here by choice. I would not interpret her words so broadly as guest-rights, but whatever the case we would certainly invite retribution should she notice us trying to murder her."

The word 'murder' was not well received, but since they had no hope at all of killing Suldar in open battle, 'dealing with her' could hardly mean anything else. For the crime of saying no. There was a brief pause, but though Chenar's glance wavered, he lifted his chin and gritted his teeth. And they all had to admit it was true: whether Suldar had brought them there or not, she was the one who prevented them from leaving.

Princess Kestia compressed her lips, but bowed her head a fraction. "If–"

Jurasel cut his sister short. "You needn't think Cya unready to face the matter."

"We are not yet at the point where this question needs to be discussed," Kestia continued, quite as if her brother hadn't spoken.

A red glint appeared in Jurasel's eyes and he straightened, emphasising height and muscle and reminding them all he was Cya's heir. *His* choice to commit, deny or delay. Kestia turned her head to stare at him coldly, and for a moment Gentian thought the simmering antagonism would finally explode. But Jurasel relaxed back just as suddenly, and waved a negligent hand. "We've no need to run head-first to the worst option. But it is one to keep in mind." He looked across the table at Princess Aloren, inviting her agreement, and the Cerian princess responded with a slow smile.

Then, as if they had set a case before a judge, they all turned to Aurak Bes. Gentian had tried to anticipate his response, working her way through the complexities of the Atlaran precepts. They were rules to govern the way mages dealt with each other, and with those who couldn't draw magic. But Suldar turned the precepts on their head: compared to this hidden Fae the mightiest of the true-mages around this table were ants. Were *senserel*. And that, of course, gave her the answer.

"I cannot like that course," the Aurak said gravely. "And fear the wrongs we might commit if we act before we have fully investigated. But I agree that the path of honourable challenge is not open to us. If this Suldar is proved *descoar* then–" He paused, his expression well-suited to a man at a funeral. "Then our freedom must be won by any means."

ooOoo

Gentian was so overwhelmed by the idea of Kubara Bes agreeing to contemplate murder that she barely took in the little scene that followed, with Heresar suggesting to

Jurasel that they should make their base in another building, and Jurasel promptly offering Aloren Cya's protection. Which inspired Chenar to a counter-offer, while Aloren smiled, and weighed their answers, and watched them look daggers at each other before announcing herself well situated already, enjoying the hospitality of Darest.

They were all tedious and bizarre. Gentian was glad when the Cyans and Saxans took themselves off, and even more pleased when Aloren joined the Atlarans in investigating the floors above for suitable sleeping chambers. Enough of temper and drama and dark plots.

Not that a bit of Sun-blessed silence brought her any answers. To be *descoar* was to be a monster in attitude or spirit. A creature of immense power which treated those less than itself as nothing: as toys, dirt. In robbing the less powerful of their dignities, *descoar* forfeited a right to existence, became a thing to be exterminated. Something you could kill in all justice to set yourself free. When she'd passed through the shield-wall, Gentian had thought she'd *wanted* to find a monster in Telsandar, a thing she could kill. But even if she could imagine a way to do it, she found herself less than taken with the idea of killing Suldar.

Aristide Couerveur cast a true-spell, something understated and too quickly done to catch intent. And then he sat sipping a dark red wine and considering her over the rim of the glass, his expression very like a craftsman faced with an uncertain tool. His apprentice, the only other person left in the kitchen, shifted uneasily, drawing that vivid gaze on himself.

"And how much time do we have to look for alternatives?" Gentian asked softly. "How long before we're supposed to start playing assassin?"

"The answer is likely to be 'however much the Aurak requires'. Between the advantages of Atlaran goodwill, and the minor point of not attacking until we think we can win, I suspect we'll have time enough to thoroughly explore other options."

"Oh." The flood of relief was dizzying, quite like she'd stood up too quickly and had to catch herself before she fell over. Gentian blinked, then let out a breath she hadn't realised she was holding. "I see. They'd have worked themselves up more if you'd objected. Aurak Bes is neutral enough for his opposition to be accepted. But he committed to it too. If he judges her truly *descoar*, he will be first in any attack."

Aristide's gaze was cool and steady. "You needn't doubt that I would consider killing this Regent of Telsandar, Magister, if the cost of remaining here rose too high. And I thought it actually possible. Justice rarely holds against self-interest."

"But is self-interest proof against temper?" Aspen glanced quickly at the door, looking almost as excited as he was worried. "They weren't just pretending to be angry."

"Anger is perhaps more of a threat to self-interest, but they are none of them suicidal, nor eager to spend the remainder of their lives trapped in Darest's past. Which in turn should afford us some protection."

Gentian remembered Aspen's warnings. "Are they really all so eager to kill you?"

"They'd not weep to see me dead. But, unless there is a straightforward exit to stumble over, leaving this valley will take a high order of magery, and our entrance will have taught them a lesson. They'll at least weigh the risk of depriving themselves of Darien mages."

He glanced at his apprentice.

"Exercise some basic caution, Choraide. Try to minimise the opportunities and reasons for anyone to find you an annoyance." He produced a particularly dry expression, and let it slide to include Gentian. "Don't forget who these people are, what setting them at odds might mean to Darest. If you must sleep with them, say 'thank you' nicely after."

Aspen, unabashed by this instruction, simply murmured, "I'll try not to disappoint," but it was all too much for Gentian, who choked into laughter.

"How very pragmatic you are, Lord Magister," she managed. "You almost reconcile me to being trapped in Darest." She paused, finding an unexpected core of truth in the words, and spoke unwarily when she added: "I didn't think anyone could do that."

Delicate brows rose. "You overwhelm me, Magister. Such praise."

He didn't understand the immensity of what she'd said. For Gentian, staying in Darest was madness, a kind of suicide. She couldn't, wouldn't do that to herself. Yet the thought of walking away from Aristide Couerveur brought a growing sense of loss. Not a good development.

"But I interrupted you, Lord Magister," she said lightly, while her blood fizzed in her ears. "Were you going to tell us anything other than to be careful who we sleep with?"

Aspen made a strangled noise, but her return to composure brought a hint of appreciation to Aristide's eyes. "Ask rather than tell, Magister," he said, with a mildness that simply shouted consequences. "I would like to hear your explanation for this."

He cast, sweeping illusion across the table-top. A hill rose from dark wood, was matched by a valley. Both were roughly circular. Each had at its centre a pavilion: one of living trees, the other stone. Both pavilions were surrounded by a square cross in a knotwork frame.

The sight had struck her a blow a few hours earlier, but had lost the power to dismay, dwarfed by this over-nice politician.

"You have an excellent eye for detail, Lord Magister," she said, idiot light-headedness receding but not entirely lost. And then she felt suddenly, overwhelmingly tired. One day was too short to lose herself and find someone else. Any more self-revelation would be an ocean too much.

She leaned forward, studying hill and valley while she tried to think what she could possibly say. The illusions were constructed with a craftsman's flair, only the occasional blurred patches on Vostal Hill – little more than swatches of leafy colour – to betray that he'd conjured them direct from memory. The valley, though considerably larger, was even more precisely rendered. He'd had the length of their walk down to look it over, and apparently was a type who did not forget.

But then, his reputation had told her that already, and painted him equally disinclined to forgive. He had his full attention on her now, an unnerving sensation, but despite his earlier darts she did not think him hostile. Merely focused on the problem.

Meeting that very thoughtful gaze frankly she said: "I wish I *had* an explanation. I've never seen this place before, neither heard nor guessed at its existence. I can't even claim convenient visionary dreams. I thought Vostal Hill my own creation and...I don't think it is."

It hit her again, that overwhelming sense of betrayal. She had seen Vostal Hill, and wrought from her heart a suitable frame for its crown. But that shape was not her own.

Aristide had listened without showing any sign of whether he believed her, and now turned his head away, gazing into nothing. The illusions sank back into the table.

It gave her a marvellous sense of powerlessness, to find herself suddenly so very interested in his reaction. A very sharp, not entirely unpleasant sensation that made her wish she *wanted* to want him.

"Do you suppose the pavilion serves the same purpose?" she asked restively, when he still did not speak. "A focus to bring together the Court of the Fair?"

"That is certainly worth investigating." And he stood up, adding only: "We will talk of this tomorrow, Magister."

Gentian glimpsed her own confusion on Aspen's face as Aristide carried his glass and plate across to one of the benches. Since the conversation had been heading in a direction she hated to go, she was relieved to put it off, but why had he?

Then she caught it. The faintest swirl of intent, of power shaped by will. A scry, shielded so that even she could barely sense its presence. They were being spied upon.

The spell Aristide had cast earlier must have been a detect. He'd anticipated this, guessed that one of their unfriendly fellows would try to listen. And heard, what? Certainly her comment about the pavilion. Possibly more. If it was a visual scry, they'd have definitely seen the design for Vostal Hill.

Gentian was almost grateful. The spy had bought her time, a chance to think about the necessity of talking about her childhood, about Suldar, gardens, and wanting someone who was devoted to a land that would destroy her.

And an absence of hate.

Chapter Nine

The Fair hadn't taken their clothes with them. Aspen, waking in slow degrees to birdsong and ever-brighter surveys of the bedroom he'd chosen, found himself waiting for the owner to step back in. It was the book, facedown on the wide windowsill. The way the chair was drawn back from the desk. Worst, a pair of gloves set down on a table by the door, still retaining the shape of slender, tapering fingers.

He was sleeping in that person's bed, crumpling their crisp sheets. By now Aspen had given up any vague hope that the people of Telsandar had packed up and left, though far too much time had passed for their deaths to linger tangibly. The Diamond's revelations, and the sheer absence of any packing, conjured instead a screaming rout from which no-one had escaped. None but Suldar, Dusk, thousand-year Fae. This was no place to linger.

On the other hand, there was Aloren, Rua Ketu, Jurasel, Chenar. And Aristide. Denied his Vaselte, his Robar, the rest of his small army of hand-picked servitors, Aristide had already started to draw Aspen in. Progress.

Knowing the Diamond to be the last person to have a lazy lie-in, Aspen rolled himself out of bed and puzzled his way through morning routines in an abandoned Fae mansion. He'd discovered the absence of chamber pots the previous night, and after tracking down a purpose-built lavatory had noted with a faint sense of foreboding that the functional enchantments had lapsed, despite the preservation spells. If they were stuck here for any appreciable time the whole system would need to be investigated and re-established. A tiresome, tedious and difficult task all too likely to be pushed Aspen's way.

Someone had been cleaning up in the kitchen, one of that strange race of creatures who thought nothing of greeting the cold light of dawn. Aspen poked about, noting that here, too, the functional enchantment was missing. The flat kindling stones were dead, without a trace of even Lady Dhara's temporary enchantment. The water barrel was nearly full, but the spout above unresponsive. More work.

After an apple and a glass of watered wine, Aspen headed out the front door, and immediately spotted the Diamond in the pavilion on the central island. Just like on Vostal Hill there was a throne for the Queen of the Fair, though unlike the pavilion in Tor Darest there was no matching seat for a human ruler. The Diamond was standing motionless before this version, but Aspen was too far away to tell if he was casting or just imagining how he'd look on it.

The rest of the valley flickered with movement: birds, and – was that a goat? It was also oddly damp, as if there'd been a heavy dew or a light rain. But the sky remained stone-backed deception, the air still and windless. Alive, but artificial, quite like a miniature garden Aspen had once seen growing in a large glass bowl.

That was not a pretty thought, and Aspen flicked it away, moving forward as he looked about for more activity. There was the Guard Dog, surveying him from the balcony of a house a level up, and Gentian wandering out from behind a nearby hall. She was carrying a flat basket stocked with greenery, and headed for the gardens around the lake. A short way in she put the basket down so she could thrust her arms into something low and hedge-like. Shaking his head, Aspen headed across.

"My dear unfortunate," he said, as she disappeared head-first into another bush. "If you truly have any desire to win the Diamond Couerveur – and I'm not saying I want you to succeed or anything – but do you really think scuffling about in the shrubbery is going to impress?"

"Depends on whether he likes eggs or not, I suppose," Gentian said, emerging with an undersized specimen. "Someone seems to have let loose a few hen-houses worth of bantams, and they've nested all over the place."

"And what's wrong with a little judicious true-magic?" Aspen asked. He concentrated carefully and the egg she'd just put down rose, turned over twice, and set down again.

Gentian was already poking about another bush. "In the grand scheme, I doubt hunting eggs will much change Lord Aristide's opinion of me."

"It would take a lot to get past 'you're almost good enough to stay here for'. As declarations go, I think that was the clumsiest I've ever witnessed."

She shrugged. "I wasn't actually meaning to make one. I gather you think I'd have little chance of success if I pursued him?"

"Far be it from me to predict the Diamond's tastes," Aspen protested, holding up his hands because he did, in fact, think she had no chance at all. The fastidious Diamond Couerveur and this gardener? Mage or not, she wasn't anything Aspen had ever pictured the Diamond wanting.

An odd expression flickered into her eyes, making him suspect she knew it to be a hopeless case, but she only said: "I'll have to sit down with you some time and work out how many of the rumours are true. If you're willing to talk out of turn?"

"Nothing I can tell you is likely to bother the Diamond," Aspen assured her, adding gleefully: "I've stories to curl your toes."

"Do you?" Her tone was off-hand, but the quick look she gave him suggested Gentian Calder wasn't nearly so sanguine as she'd have him believe. Not even close.

"Were you serious?" he asked, with a sudden spurt of sympathy. There were countless hordes who wanted Aristide Couerveur, but few fool enough to try and love him.

She straightened and looked over at the Diamond, still contemplating the throne. "I think so. I've not encountered an impulse to follow someone to the end of the world before."

On cue, the Diamond turned his head, and the pair gazed at each other across the small lake. A very po-faced and sombre survey, like two duellists before a bout.

"The end of the world and beyond."

"But he's not good enough to make you want to stay in Darest? That doesn't make sense," Aspen pointed out, then added by way of distraction: "I'm the first to extol the Diamond's many attractions, but folk who fix on just one person always get tied up in knots over nothing."

"*'All my peace is stolen and my plans have come to naught',*" she murmured almost cheerfully as the Diamond began walking across the lake toward them. "Do you know, Aspen, I think Aristide Couerveur is the price I'm going to pay for returning to Darest? I hope he's worth the cost."

"Just don't say I didn't warn you."

"For that courtesy, I thank you." She gave him that understated little smile, then turned her usual solemn expression on the Diamond. "This is a very confused valley, Lord Magister," she said. "Poppies under fruiting trees. Marrows and snowdrops. And rather a lot of plants I've never seen anywhere else."

"Hardly surprising for a settlement of the Fair." The Diamond was looking particularly crisp this morning, and wore the faint air of enjoyment which was his usual approach to business. "Tell me, Magister, when you were in the pavilion on Vostal Hill, could you sense any lingering enchantment?"

"On the pavilion itself? No. They're not very natural trees, but I couldn't feel anything actively bound to them. What about this one?"

"It reads as unenhanced stone. But you may catch something I cannot."

"Perhaps." She sounded doubtful, and bent to pick up her basket. "I'll look after breakfast."

This was all very polite and casual, enough to reassure Aspen that the Diamond wasn't about to succumb. He was wondering whether Gentian quite understood the concept of flirtation when, without warning, Rua Ketu and Hapt-lo Dest hauled themselves, dripping and mostly naked, out of the lake. It was a sight to make a man weep, and Aspen could only thank Fortune's munificence as the Atlarans came walking toward them.

"I knew there was a reason I got out of bed this morning," he said reverentially, once they were in earshot. "That was the loveliest surprise I've had for years. Thank you."

Rua's broad grin creased her face, but Hapt-lo Dest gave no sign of hearing. A pity: he had a frame any man would like to climb, and positively *gleamed* in the false morning light.

"Lord Magister," the Atlaran man said to Aristide, offering up an abbreviated, fist-to-chest bow. "There are outlets below the surface, as you surmised, but they are sealed by both shield and wall. Initial probes did not weaken them."

"Then we will leave them until the general survey of the valley is complete, Hapt-lo. Give my thanks to Aurak Bes."

With another brief courtesy the Atlarans turned away, off to dull their splendour with a layer of wholly unnecessary cloth. Aspen watched until they'd disappeared inside. And already the Guard Dog was moving forward to take their place, no doubt carrying a message from his masters. He'd at least cleaned himself up a little – enough to reveal a nice line to his jaw – but looked as stolidly humourless as ever as he started into the edge of the garden.

And stopped, eyes going wide and hand heading predictably to sword, staring past them. Aspen turned.

Gentian and the Diamond were already facing her. Suldar. Just standing there.

"May we assist you, Lady Suldar?" the Diamond asked, quite as if he'd expected the creature to reverse her attitude of the previous evening and come seeking them out.

But it was not Aristide Couerveur the Fae was interested in. From her great height she looked down at a woman carrying a basket of eggs and vegetables.

~You are not of the Blood.~

"...no," came the very blank reply. If there was ever anyone who looked less like a Fae, it was Gentian Calder.

Suldar's expression, or lack of expression, didn't change, but Aspen thought her intent study became even more focused. Then incomprehensible words again translated into their minds.

~That which brought you from sleep – has it touched you before?~

Gentian actually swayed, her shock as visible as a blow. "You *felt* It?"

~It has touched you before this?~ The words echoed with extra emphasis in Aspen's head, as if a storm had moved closer, the thunder directly overhead. The thousand-year Fae, the creature of impossible power...sounded worried.

And Gentian, eyes wide, replied in a whisper: "Every day I'm in Darest."

A silence, quivering. Aspen had no other way to describe it.

~I did not know.~

"Know what? Do you know what it is?" A plea, equal parts hope and disbelief.

But Suldar left. Turned her back on them and walked out of the central park, back into the building with her harps. The wall closed behind her.

Livid patches of red bloomed on Gentian's cheeks, and her fingers were white on the basket's handle. "No secret better kept than by the Fair," she said savagely. "No race so ready to ask but not answer."

"But what woke you this morning?" Aspen asked, thinking Gentian was hardly the person to complain about keeping secrets. Whether or not she'd been lying, there was obviously a good deal she should have volunteered. "What was she talking about?"

The Diamond reached out and steadied the basket before all the eggs ended up on the ground. "Captain Djol," he said, face dangerously blank. "Would you be so kind as to tell Prince Chenar we plan to gather in two hours to discuss our findings and further steps? There is a plaza near the building you have made your base, which will do well as a meeting place."

The Guard Dog produced a very flat stare indeed, then shifted his grip on his sword hilt and nodded at the ground. "Look."

Thin blurred ovals traced the path of Suldar's departure. Footprints. Burnt into the grass. After a moment's hesitation, Gentian crouched to touch the nearest print, then dusted her fingers. "Desiccated. Like it's been in a desert for years."

"She did that just by walking on it?" Aspen found the idea particularly horrible. "*Not* a lady to sweep off her feet. But how?"

"I think she must have drawn the fragment of living magic out of it. All the free magic in the valley flows to her, at least." Gentian was regaining her self-composure: that had been almost as solemn and unperturbed as usual.

The Guard Dog, standing his ground despite the Diamond's obvious dismissal, finally let go his sword. "You said before that the place grieved, Magister. Is it an angry mourning? Should we consider the valley itself hostile?"

Aspen had no idea where *that* question had come from, but Gentian seemed to think it logical. "No." She looked down at her basket, her fingers still white-knuckled despite surface calm. They waited while she carefully loosed her grip. "No. It's glad we're here. It wants people. It was responding to us all the while we were walking down, and when Suldar took the preservation off – it was like it was able to take its first breath in centuries. But it still feels bound."

"It wants people?" Djol sounded like he couldn't decide whether to be sceptical or enlightened. "Could it be the valley itself, then, which brought us here?"

"Not many places work magic. And most are very distinct in their borders. Mountains might look at what's approaching them, but usually a valley wouldn't notice you till you entered it, and not have any particular inclination to do anything to you. I don't think this place was...expecting us."

"I see. Thank you, Magister." With a curt nod to Aristide, Djol walked off. Gentian stood watching him stride toward the Saxan base, then turned to the Diamond.

There was enough ice in the famed star sapphire eyes to sink a fleet of ships, and Aspen was surprised when, after only the tiniest hesitation, she said, undaunted: "I suppose you're less than keen to put off explanations?"

"They are by now overdue."

Each word was so very, very restrained. In Gentian's shoes, Aspen would have wilted. Instead her mouth flattened to a straight line. "It's not as if it wasn't all laid before the Regent years ago, Lord Magister," she said, matching him for frost. "And I presume you'd not have it aired out here?"

Without waiting for any response she turned and walked away, and the Diamond followed, wearing one of the coldest smiles Aspen had ever seen from him. Aspen could only shake his head in exasperation and join the train. He didn't doubt for a moment that Gentian, no matter where she'd been living, knew the Diamond and Lady Arista had been at each other's throats for years. "Wonderful tactics," he muttered. "Throw his mother in his face. That'll get him on side."

Gentian had gone back to the kitchen, but no sooner had Aspen and Aristide caught up with her, then the room was made smaller by two over-dressed Atlarans.

"Lord Magister," said Hapt-lo Dest, "the Aurak would be grateful to consult with you."

"Of course." Without a backward glance, the Diamond followed the Hapt-lo out. Gentian was already chopping things, all set-faced and determinedly silent. She obviously wanted to wallow in a foul mood, so Aspen left her to it, turning to the far more pleasing prospect of Rua Ketu.

"Can we abandon all formality?" he asked. "I'm a little overdone with My Lords and Your Highnesses and whatnot."

"An excellent thought," Rua said agreeably. "Though did abandonment not come long ago for you?"

He grinned. "It's a continuing thing. So why the swimming expedition? Not that making it a regular morning feature isn't a very good idea, but you could have just scried to see what's below the surface."

"Eyes and fingers can be harder to deceive. To find our way out, we will need such care."

"I see you're going to be our voice of reason, Rua."

Her eyes crinkled. "And you our saviour from boredom's threat?"

"I do my humble best." He bowed, liking her again for the genial good humour she inhabited. "Are you going to head out for more scouting around?"

"Not yet. The Aurak is preparing for a *sel-deseva* divination, and we will attend on him."

"Do you think it will work?" Aspen asked, impressed. It was a kind of magic he associated only with the Apexes of the Sun and Moon, those who devoted themselves to a God's service. *Sel-deseva* was an attempt to achieve divine revelation rather than divination.

"The Aurak has been answered in the past. But here, who can say? Neither Sun nor Moon touch this place."

"Only Suldar."

"So it would seem." She shrugged, then looked across at Gentian. "Is there anything you would like done, Magister Calder?"

The smaller woman had fallen into a brown study in the midst of slicing tomatoes. She blinked, processed the question, then said: "How are you at milking goats?"

Rua laughed. "Well, we shall see. How much would you like?"

"A cup? I'm not sure how much her kid will have left to us."

"Ever a new discovery to make." Rua picked up a bowl and headed for the back door.

"Could you set those plates out on the bench, Aspen?" Gentian added, saving him from trying to decide whether he should brave goat-herding for Rua's sake. "And then go ask Princess Aloren whether she would like breakfast?"

"This is a morning *full* of gifts," Aspen said, brightening. He quickly lined empty plates up. "I'll think of a kindness I can do in return."

She wasn't able to hold back a flicker of a wry smile. "I gather I wouldn't be tall enough for her."

"You caught that too? Priceless, wasn't it? I must say," he added, judging it now safe, "just when I thought I had you pegged, you get the claws out. What happened to the meek and mild thing?"

She grimaced, but Aspen diagnosed embarrassment not annoyance. "And my thoughts have been less than gracious about everyone else's little displays, too," she said. "I imagine it would be a bad idea to excuse myself by telling Aristide that he was reminding me too much of his mother?"

"That would be one way to kiss any chance of romance goodbye," Aspen agreed. "You know Lady Arista?"

"We've met. It's strange to suddenly, ah, discover her son, since I certainly don't cherish fond memories of the Regent."

"Well, look at it this way: at least it's one thing you and the Diamond have in common."

He left her to mull that over, heading upstairs. The building had three floors and Darest's finest had taken a row of rooms on the middle level, while the Atlarans and the oh-so ravishing Aloren were well situated on top.

The stairs ended with two doors that led into matching suites. One was open, with Hapt-lo Dest standing inside. Aspen treated him to the sunniest of smiles and knocked on the other. No answer. But it was unlocked, and Aspen could never be accused of being shy.

"Your Highness?" he called, closing the door behind him and looking hopefully around a small entry hall.

That drawling, honey-soaked voice floated out of the room to his right. "Come tie me up."

"An order no-one would refuse," Aspen murmured, heading in. He found a bedroom dominated by huge windows overlooking the lake. The lid of every chest was raised and all the cupboard doors stood open, a selection of Fae clothing spilling out. Aloren was in the centre of the room, a vision of bronze and gold.

Aspen paused reverentially. Ancient Fae clothing apparently tended even more to impracticality than the current stuff: this was all flowing sleeves and an endless train. Even Aloren was not tall enough for the gown she'd chosen, but the colour made it hers.

Criss-cross lacing from nape of neck to base of spine explained her command. This was the kind of clothing that required a dresser, or a fine command of true-magic. Or Aspen, nothing loathe to step into the breach.

"I've been sent to offer you breakfast," he said, moving to stand behind her. The faint remnant of a heady scent clung to her hair, and he felt his heart start to race just because he was close. Astonishing creature.

Aloren didn't respond, only stood waiting for him. She was humming to herself. Delicately he hooked fingers into the lowest cross of the lace. The heat of her skin came through the cloth, and he had to close his eyes a moment. He'd spent a long time the previous night debating how best to approach the Cerian princess. She hadn't dismissed his admiration out of hand, but if ever there was a woman who was pursued on every side, and could take her pick...

Slowly he pulled the lace tight, and moved a notch up her spine, working his way along the lace with infinite care. It would be crass to grope, and no compliment was adequate. He simply took his time, not allowing himself so much as an unnecessary brush of the fingers, enjoying this privilege. Aloren still hummed: a slow, melancholic tune.

Finally, after hooking the ends of the lace into a complicated little clasp, he stood back. "Let me know when you want to take it off."

She turned. Golden eyes, burnished mirrors, surveyed him from head to toe. "And do you feel yourself equal to two princes?" she asked. Idle curiosity.

"Depends on the competition," Aspen said blithely. "I dance like a dream."

"And could prove yourself the better?"

Aspen hesitated. Aloren was a princess, a goddess. Outside this valley she had a kingdom to add a certain weight to her rancour. But he saw no sign that her ego demanded complete worship, so, greatly daring, he said: "Frankly, Your Most Very Royal Highness, what I'd like to do with Prince Jurasel and Prince Chenar doesn't need any proving. Where's the fun in playing them off against each other?"

She considered this with no sign of annoyance. "With Sax and Cya, is there any other option?"

"Well..." Aspen rolled his shoulders, turning over the possibilities. "I'm not saying it wouldn't be a challenge. Lifelong enemies, sky-high tempers, the no doubt vigorous disapproval of thousands..."

"The need for a very large bed." She was dry, but the slow smile curved.

"Well, we're not short of those," Aspen said delightedly, glancing at the central feature of the room. Lofty Fae needed furniture on a generous scale.

"Grand ambitions," was all she said, in a most ambiguous tone. She turned away, but he thought her not displeased. Enough for now.

"Was that a 'yes' on the breakfast?"

"It was."

He headed for the door, caring less about traps and mysteries than Jurasel, Chenar, Aloren. One bed, and Aspen. And the Diamond, of course. And Rua Ketu.

Grand ambition indeed.

Chapter Ten

It had long been Gentian's policy not to beat her head against brick walls. Accepting that some things were impossible and moving on had kept her sane. When presented with a sheer and glittering cliff, it was only good sense not to ram herself into it.

A few minutes of comfortable chatter with Rua had returned her equilibrium. It hadn't taken her mind off the morning's developments, but had made her feel more herself. The Atlaran, though physically very different, reminded her strongly of one of her first lovers: Thierry, a rare child of human and Fae, whose calm curiosity about all the world could make mountains into molehills. Thierry's reaction to the morning's scenes would be to open a bottle of ginger wine to celebrate. So what if Suldar wouldn't explain? She'd felt It. As for getting straight back to dagger's drawn with Aristide Couerveur, surely that was all for the good. She had, after all, resolved to give him up.

But when Aristide strolled into the kitchen, his apprentice at his heels, Gentian immediately found herself torn in two directions. It was hard to force yourself to not want a man when he was so unrelentingly...himself, and a mountain was stopping you from running from temptation.

Still, she couldn't relish this opportunity to try to explain just what it would mean for her to stay in Darest. Words had never made anyone understand, and she was finding her tongue strangely untrustworthy whenever she faced that eclipse. It did not help that she had never felt smaller in her life than she did beneath this mountain.

"Could we eat in the garden?" she asked, dishing out steaming portions onto the waiting plates. If she had to expose all her rawest parts, she'd prefer comforting surroundings.

"If you wish, Magister."

So they were back to being all neutral and polite. Gentian doubted he'd forgiven her little tantrum, but even if she'd killed any immediate chance of empathy, there was no hope for further delay. Handing them both a plate, she led the way outside, leaving Rua to take the rest upstairs.

Her morning explorations had shown the vegetable garden was linked to a very pretty formal area, all geometric symmetry. Steps took them up to a room of ivy-covered walls where stone benches were arranged in a three-sided square. The setting was more contemplation than confession, but it had a nice air, and she liked it.

"We should kidnap Captain Djol," she said, sitting down on the right and prodding scrambled eggs and fried tomatoes doubtfully. "My repertoire is strictly limited, and Rua says she can burn water."

"Smells fine to me," Aspen said, dropping on to the centre bench. He diplomatically took a big mouthful, then looked relieved. Edible.

Aristide avoided the issue by putting his plate down on the bench beside him, and casting. Word-magic this time, a sign of complexity since the man was a great-mage, so adept at the language of magic that he could cast many higher-level spells as a direct expression of will, as if they were straightforward true-magic. Gentian hadn't quite achieved that level of internalisation, but she did recognise the spell. A façade to not only keep their conversation wholly private, but also disguise itself so that they appeared silent rather than shielded.

During the wait Gentian started work on her tomatoes, but lost momentum by the time she reached the eggs, distracted by the opportunity to openly study Aristide while he cast. His skin had a wonderful quality: it made her want to touch his face to prove he wasn't carved of marble. Despite everything, she found herself enjoying her sudden passion. Even deciding against pursuing him wasn't enough to make her regret the emotion itself, just the circumstances.

"Am I too much for you, Magister?"

Gentian realised he'd stopped casting some time back and was watching her with that faint, ironic smile. But the edge of coldness was missing, and he seemed so completely entertained that she felt more heartened than embarrassed. He would not, of course, be able to fix anything, but she abruptly wanted him to see her properly.

"You do have a habit of framing yourself spectacularly," she said, making a vague gesture toward his arrangement of porcelain and charcoal against dark ivy and stone. "But, no – I was trying to think what to say. It's a long story."

"Then start at the beginning." Very focused now. There was a problem he needed to solve, and he meant to get on with it. Ah well. Sooner started, soonest done.

"When I'm in Darest...I'm woken just before each dawn by someone hating me, so much and so strongly that it's like being picked up by the throat and shaken. Ever since I was born – before, actually, judging from the last few days of my mother's pregnancy. It made me a less than easy child to raise, because I would wake without fail to scream myself blue, and have absolute hysterics if they made any move to comfort me.

"My parents tried to find out what was going on, of course. Put shields around my crib and sat up watching me, worked a thousand divinations, called in every healer they'd ever heard of. Fed me poppy-milk, even. And I would wake, and scream, and even when I was old enough that they could ask me what was wrong, there was little I could tell them. There was no sign of enchantment, of any outside influence or intent. It was just something I did.

"By the time I was, oh, four, I'd reached the point where I'd wake up and cry rather than scream, and would stop much sooner. My parents thought it was going away. And I...thought it was normal, I suppose. Hard to say. You can grow used to anything.

"At twelve I'd long since stopped crying about it. But for my complete disinterest in Shaping, and the little obsession about proving I was being attacked and hunting down whatever was doing it, I imagine I was everything my parents had hoped for. Perhaps more egotistical than they might wish."

Remembering that towering self-belief, she experienced a flash of wry amusement, then glanced curiously at Aristide, who offered her only polite attention in return.

"I wasn't nearly so capable with Elachar as I thought, but I considered myself ready to do some serious experimentation, and knew exactly what I wanted to try. What simpler solution to a rude awakening than to not be asleep at dawn? I always was, you see. I simply could not be brought to stay awake. Hardly natural, but again there was no sign of it being an outside attack. No hint of enchantment, no trace of lingering power. I was determined to prove this at least was being done to me and, being rather more ruthless than my parents, found a spell which would simply have to keep me awake, set up every divination I was capable of casting, and...was less than pleased with the result."

"What happened?" Aspen was leaning forward, as caught up in the tale as his master was not.

"I stayed awake all right, but my divinations still showed no trace of outside influence. And until the next dawn, until that unnatural sleep came again and It woke me, I could barely move from my bed. *Not* sleeping and waking was apparently bad for my health. My parents wanted me to swear never to try it again, and I refused. So they dragged me off to Tor Darest to see the Regent."

She carefully didn't look at Aristide, as much to hide her own memory of anger as to avoid sparking his. "Goldenrod's valuable enough to Darest that Lady Arista agreed to investigate my peculiarities. And my parents had me promise to abide by her conclusions, whatever they were. Which, after a week of watching me sleep, was that I was too sensitive, too powerful for my own good. That absolutely no outside influence was involved, and each morning I was putting *myself* to sleep. My mind, my strength, was turning in on itself. The enemy I had fought all my life, the thing that attacked me, brutalised me...was me."

Repeating Lady Arista's pronouncement Gentian didn't even try to keep flat bitterness from her voice, and wondered again how she had ever managed to fall for the woman's son. But then, she'd been more than impressed with Lady Arista, before the Regent had chosen the wrong answer. For it had been. Suldar, no matter how unhelpfully, had provided the final vindication. Gentian felt dizzy all over again, remembering that bolt-from-the-blue question.

Buoyed up enough to offer a ghost of a smile to the second Couerveur to completely overturn her, she said: "I didn't take her diagnosis well, particularly when she asked my parents if I was, perhaps, a not-very-legal Shaping experiment. I expect Lady Arista remembers me as a particularly vituperative little hellion. My problem was that I believed her. She'd used shields and divinations of such a high order, and she was so very certain. So I swore my oath and went home, and taught myself to accept that this was how it would be."

"When you are in Darest." Aristide said each word distinctly.

"Oh yes." She took a breath, then paused and frowned at him. "How *did* you know we were still in Darest, Lord

Magister? I've never heard that the Couerveurs could sense the soul of the place."

The corners of his mouth curled up. Disdain. As if she had disappointed him, been offensive, or manipulative. But he answered.

"Darest is my charge, Magister," he said, very coolly. "Naturally I would know if I had left it."

Gentian tried to make sense of this, could think of only one explanation, and said *"Crown* bond?" in blank astonishment. Her mother had told her Aristide Couerveur had assumed almost full control of Darest during the long years of Lady Arista's decline, when she had lost interest in everything except battling her son. But he had never sat Darest's throne, never openly ruled, and now served a duly crowned King. How could he have formed the rare monarch's link with his land?

A glittering and entirely discouraging smile was the only response to her question. She stared at him a moment longer, then carefully went back to her own story.

"I didn't cross Darest's borders until I was fourteen, after my parents had allowed me flight spells." She passed a hand over her eyes, wondering how to explain this to people who didn't feel place. "Have you ever encountered a sound, not loud, which you've been hearing for so long you don't hear it any more? And then it stops, and only then do you realise that it existed at all? When I went to Ceria, something went away. A background, a thing always there – gone. Out of earshot.

"I flew back and forth across the border a dozen times, and each time I felt it clearer. A thing I recognised, that I knew all too well. It was diffuse, unfocused, but there every time I crossed into Darest. Hate."

Aristide shifted minutely, and Gentian glanced up at him again, then stared. He looked pleased. Pleased in the way a man might be if he had hunted his family's murderer all his life, and now had him tied helpless to a chair. Like he was about to choose the first of many knives.

Bewildered, she glanced at Aspen, only to find he shared her surprise. Less than comforting. This was neither the reaction she had hoped for, nor the one that she'd expected. Something quite different.

She went on uncertainly. "All the time I was looking for an enemy, looking for what hated me, I had focused on my morning trial and not recognised that I felt It every day, all the time, waking and sleeping. Every moment I was in Darest. Only in Darest. I spent the night in Ceria. And woke before dawn. But out of habit only, for the first time in my life without shrinking from that blow."

And she had been furious, feeling none of the joy that should have been hers. This land was more than the home of her family. It was where she belonged, part of Goldenrod's greater whole, wound completely through her. And it hated her. "I swore on my name never to set foot in Darest again," she finished, voice shaking.

"You broke name-oath to come back?" Aspen exclaimed, almost shouting. "Why?!"

"Because I heard about the destruction of the Rose, and knew it was linked to the borders. Because a corrupt guardian spell could possibly explain what I had experienced." She grimaced. "And I had no other way of testing. I accepted the consequences."

"Do you think that's why we're trapped in here?"

"Because I broke oath? No." It hadn't even occurred to her to link them. "This valley is about more than me." And with that she looked sharply back at Aristide. "Are you going to tell me what it is I've said that you were expecting?"

Those exquisite lips curled. "Darest is tainted," he said, still looking at her as if he was deciding where to make the first cut. "And Darest is cursed. They are two different things. The first we did not even suspect, until Queen Daseretel explained the Fair's reasons for presenting Darest to the Rathens. But the taint, whatever it is, only affects the Fair. The second is the malison."

"Malison?" The word did not have quite the same meaning as a curse, was closer to a kind of disease. A slow tingle ran up her spine. Two things which were not quite curses.

"It is, as I understand the matter, the pure ill-will of every Fae who did not want Telsandar given to humans, who wanted us gone. Purpose arguably without actual intent, sunk into the very bones of Darest. Seldareth, the Lord of the Fae kingdom to our north, first divined it centuries ago, and last autumn they admitted its existence. Until it is lifted, Darest will continue to fail."

"The Fair *admitted* this? That they knew?"

He ignored the question. "Their Tzel Aviar is pledged to assist my investigation, to help us lift it. We have worked on the task, separately and together, since autumn. And have yet to successfully replicate Seldareth's divination, to even sense it." Brilliant sapphire eyes met hers, the eclipse all-consuming. "I trust you had no plans to leave Darest in the near future, Magister."

The hook through her chest twisted savagely. He hadn't understood. Not properly. Just like her mother, who had continually campaigned for Gentian to return to live in Darest despite that morning blow. The expectation, the demand in those eyes was clear: she might be of use, might be vital for Darest's future, and should have no thought of leaving to avoid a few minutes' pain each morning.

And should she? Did she not love Darest, long to return to Goldenrod, to be in this land that was hers? If that was true, surely there was no choice about any sacrifice she could make. And perhaps Aristide and the Tzel Aviar between them might be equal to It, might finally free her from her own curse.

No. Some things are too powerful to be defeated, and against It she had always been *senserel*, a gnat. Aristide, for all his brilliance, was merely a larger gnat, and one who had failed to see her clearly.

It was as bleak a moment as when her twelve year-old self had been told she was her own monster. Not just because she was sure to alienate him further, but because despite her best intentions she had started to buy into the myth, to think in terms of the Diamond Couerveur, inhumanly infallible. He would have made a marvellous Atlaran god-king, well worth worshipping, but she could not let herself believe in him.

"I did, actually," she said, giving her answer with flat determination. "But it's a moot point at the moment."

Pale lashes dropped, hiding his eyes. Then, inevitably, that exquisite mouth curved.

"You are correct, of course Magister." The tone was pure, satirical appreciation. "For the moment, we are none of us leaving. Shall we begin testing with the next dawn?"

She shrugged, seeing no choice about that, nor justification for delay.

"So which is it that wakes you in the morning?" Aspen asked, looking worriedly from Gentian to his master. "The taint or the malison?"

"I don't know," she said slowly. "Both? Neither? The thing I feel constantly matches very well to the description of this malison. It is a formless hate. Whether what I experience on waking is the malison, focused, or this taint–" She broke off. "No, whatever else, what wakes me isn't the malison. Because the malison isn't here."

Aristide went for a moment entirely still. "Not here?"

"No. This valley is more intensely Darest than any other part of it I've been, yet when I came into it I left behind that constant murmur of hate. I thought, hoped I'd have an undisturbed night, but nothing about my morning had changed."

"And whether that is the Fair's taint has yet to be established." He wasn't even looking at her any more, but into abstract possibilities. "It seems we have more reason than escape to investigate this shield. Do you feel any echo of either, Magister, when you are in Suldar's presence?"

But Gentian had been distracted by Aspen, by magic suddenly drawn in great volume, its purpose well hidden.

"What are you casting?" she asked, faintly astonished.

No less than Aspen. "I'm not!" he exclaimed, staring down at himself. "I mean – I *am*, but I'm *not*!" He lifted hands in perplexed appeal, channelling power all the while. It streamed toward the house, the bubble of the façade shield turning pinkish at its passage.

As Aristide dismissed the façade, Aspen rose uncertainly to his feet. He seemed to genuinely not know what he was doing, to what purpose he was drawing all this magic, and Gentian couldn't feel even a shadow of intent. She glanced at Aristide, who was looking up at his apprentice through narrowed eyes.

"If he'd set an enchantment which has only now triggered?" she suggested doubtfully. Usually she could at least catch an echo of the original purpose of a casting, especially one involving this amount of power.

"But I *didn't*!" Aspen wailed, somewhere between indignation and panic. He turned between her and Aristide as if he didn't know which one to appeal to. "I haven't cast anything beyond a clean-face cantrip since I got here! I'm not doing this! It's just happening! And I can't stop it!" Beads of sweat had started out on his face.

Aristide did not seem to disbelieve his apprentice, instead saying practically, "The power is going somewhere. If it's an enchantment, we may be able to divine intent closer to its centre."

"But how do we *stop* it?" Aspen exclaimed, then started down the stair, weaving on his feet. Magical strength was all about how much power you could channel at once, and for how long. If Gentian was any judge, Aspen was operating at his greatest volume, sprinting madly up an arcane mountain. Sustaining this kind of outflow for more than a couple of minutes was painful, and would leave him exhausted. And if he didn't stop – she'd heard of mages bursting their hearts.

Not to mention...

"There are other sources," Gentian said, and took Aristide's absent nod to mean he'd already detected the near and distant pyres of major casting. She followed the two men to the house, guessing at just who else was helplessly pouring out their utmost for no purpose of their own. And found an immediate answer in Rua Ketu and Hapt-lo Dest.

Aurak Bes, following his two guards down the main stair, was the only one of the three Atlarans not drawing power. He looked from Aspen to Aristide, but wasted no words, simply leading the way to the front hall and out into the central gardens of the valley.

A point of fire grew on top of the pavilion of stone trees. Unlike the spark of blue that had yesterday uncovered the valley, this stayed fixed, roaring its strength. Around it, like sailors siren-called, came those it fed upon. Chenar and Rydan, Captain Djol, Jurasel, Kestia and her eldest daughter Desseron. They joined Aspen, Rua and Hapt-lo Dest on the grass at the lake's edge, pale from strain, sweating with effort. The rest of the valley's stolen mages gathered impotently at their sides.

"Stop this. Now."

Lady Dhara hadn't directed the order to anyone in particular, and no-one responded. What could they say? The casting was on a grand level, but although Gentian could sense the stolen power taking on purposeful form, its intent remained completely, infuriatingly hidden. Since it seemed the mages being used as fuel were equally perplexed, those untouched had little chance of interfering. Attacking a spell you didn't understand was an invitation to catastrophe, especially when you wanted to prevent the inevitable backlash from striking those building the thing.

For the first time since they'd entered the valley, Gentian thought the whole company had forgotten animosity. A palpable horror gripped them instead. For they were ants in a flood: small, helpless, entirely lost to the current. They could only watch, hoping the spell completed before anyone died, and that they could devise some protection when it released. That no-one even suggested a prudent retreat was a measure of both the spell's power and the demoralising effect of its casting.

"It can't be the Fae," Prince Jurasel said, suddenly. His strength showed in his upright stance, head held high, though the veins stood out in his neck. "She hasn't even stopped playing."

It was true. Drifting at the edge of hearing was the complex cascade of notes Gentian had been catching notes of all morning. The general wash of magic toward Suldar's location hadn't changed at all.

"Who else?" Chenar's question lacked any hint of hostility, what attention he could spare from his own plight reserved almost entirely for his brother. A mage's ability to sense and channel power strengthened with age, and Desseron and Rydan were both growing increasingly distressed, not used to sustaining such an outflow. Gentian could only be grateful that the two youngest children had been spared. Captain Djol, by far the weakest mage present, was on his knees, gasping for breath.

"It just wouldn't make sense for the Fae to be doing it," Jurasel replied, taking an unsteady step closer to the lake's edge. "This is big, but we've already seen what she can do. Why use others to power a spell she could manage in moments? She doesn't need us."

"Then who does?" Princess Kestia's voice was flat, drained, but her eyes were bright with fury as she held Desseron upright.

"It's peaking," Aristide said tersely. He hadn't taken his eyes from the pavilion.

Aurak Bes drew a basic shield over them all: a bubble of force sparking rainbows at the flow of still-streaming power. Then, as abruptly as it had started, the draw of power ceased and the shield smoothed to invisibility. The point of fire on the pavilion's roof grew brighter still, and Gentian looked away, blinking, straining to understand its intent before it moved from preparation to action. A weird peace settled into the stretching pause, where all that could be heard was gasping breath, and, distantly, Suldar's harp.

Aspen sat down abruptly. "I swear if this place doesn't start making sense soon I'm going to scream," he said, voice high. "Does anyone have the least idea what the wretched thing is doing?"

"It's eating the sky."

"An illusion-breaker. The damn thing's an illusion-breaker."

Kassen's quavering pronouncement and Jurasel's half-reverential exclamation came on top of each other. The sky, blue, cloud-studded, was being *pulled* toward the valley's centre, stripped away to reveal a dome of unbroken pearl-white. The truth of the valley dragged into chill reality.

That clear view of their prison's dome faded almost immediately. For the illusion which had hidden it also provided the valley's light: the spell was sucking them rapidly into darkness.

And as the last shred of light was consumed, memory rose up to crush Gentian. Fourteen years of morning fragments. Always, that blow of hate, the accompanying revulsion and – held within it – the sense of being trapped. A furious, desperate need for escape from some place, some pitch black torment beneath a hundred-weight of stone.

Grass prickled beneath the palms of her hands. She was shaking, gasping terror into sooty nothing. Dimly she could hear voices, the others yawping useless reaction to the darkness, unable to see its effect on her. And she refused to let them see, driven back to her feet as much by pride as a suddenly active sense of self-preservation. Because she was certain now, retained no shred of doubt that the thing that made Darest unliveable was here, that this was It's prison, and that It was trying to get out.

Gentian barely managed to force herself upright before half of them were conjuring mageglows, blinking around at each other. She must have lost only a few moments to that too-tangible memory, and now worked on shifting her expression to something less than completely undone. Whatever the truth of the situation, revealing to this hornet's nest of royalty her lifelong link to their unknown attacker was anything but wise. She wasn't sure what to tell even Aristide, who had every reason to investigate rather than kill her.

Then she remembered Captain Djol, and realised it was too late.

"No music."

Lady Dhara had barely spoken before the current of magic toward Suldar shifted. A sudden surge in the tide.

"She's putting it back."

If ever there was an apt demonstration that it wouldn't make sense for Suldar to be tapping their power, it was the ease with which she brought back the sky. It flowed from every horizon: brilliant blue, streaks of white, a flare which became the sun. All trace of stony truth wiped away in moments.

As Suldar's harp once again began to speak, Gentian followed Aristide's lead and sat down, joining the rough circle of mages swiping sweat from their eyes and trying to regain their composure. But for their complete and evident exhaustion, it was as if the illusion-breaking had never happened.

"I own, I cannot fathom this Fae," Seylon Heresar said, sounding ever so slightly breathless. "It's as if she wishes to pretend we aren't here, and acknowledges all this with only the deepest reluctance. That was patently an attempt to break her hold on the valley, and what does she do? Waits until it's over, then wipes it away. We are – for I cannot see this little display any other way – we are obviously tools brought here to help...*something* defeat her, and how does she react to our appearance? She shuts the door in our face and ignores us. Like the child who hides by covering its eyes."

"Perhaps she doesn't consider us a serious risk," Lady Dhara said in a preoccupied voice, her attention taken up with soothing her and Princess Kestia's son while her wife checked over their wan and shaking eldest daughter.

And, as had been inevitable, Prince Chenar said: "Not ignored us entirely." He was thin-lipped, strained and weary. "Perhaps, Lord Couerveur, you would care to explain what brought Suldar to speak to you this morning?"

Gentian couldn't quite stop herself from looking at Captain Djol. The Easterner's head was bowed, posture utterly drained, attention unfocused. As if he was in no way a factor in this discussion. For all that he'd heard every single word Suldar had said, and seen fit only to pass on the fact of the conversation, not its content. More than curious.

Without any hint he was aware of Captain Djol's existence, Aristide said: "That, I believe, was progress. Magister Calder is able to detect an...entity, something other than Suldar. Suldar saw her reaction to it this morning – which says something in itself to how much attention she is paying us – and was disturbed enough to seek out Magister Calder and confirm what she had felt."

Nothing but the truth. Spectacular. Gentian forced herself to match his assurance when they turned to her. "I'm not sure if it's in the valley or not," she said. "I certainly don't feel it now. But there is something very powerful, and...very angry. What I felt was only a flash, full of hatred. I think it fair to say Suldar was shocked that I could feel it, and very worried."

"So, our first guess might be right. Gaoler and gaoled." Lady Dhara looked toward Suldar's building, then shrugged. "And any plan we might make a very public thing it seems. Was it trying to communicate with you?"

"I—" Appalling concept. "I really don't think so. Unless It's – unless it's unable to hold back its anger, no. No."

Aurak Bes had been watching her as closely as the others, but with a better knowledge of her usual manner. "Not by any means a potential ally?" he asked, softly.

"Could we even dare to risk that?" Lady Dhara shook her head at her own question. "Lie down with something the *Fair* are afraid of?"

"When the alternative's permanent exile under some benighted Darien mountain?" Jurasel had regained a little heat. "If we're in the same prison, working to the same goal – do we have any choice?"

"When did it offer one?" Chenar, hand on his brother's shoulder, managed a mournful anger. "Ally? Did it, perhaps, humbly beg your pardon? No. If we're to escape this place, it will be despite this, this *entity*, as you call it."

"That is certain." Aurak Bes was absolute. "To release such a thing upon the world would be intolerable. Our freedom will not be bought at such a price."

"Sir," said Jurasel, with evident restraint, "if you have any suggestions on how we are to make any difference either way, I would be glad to hear it."

"We might start by finding our enemy." It was Aristide who answered. He nodded toward the building marked by a statue of its occupant. "Suldar we have seen, and I agree that it makes no sense to lay blame for this assault at her door, but nor does it appear we will receive any help from that quarter. We are less than likely to prevent further attacks when their mechanism is hidden from us, so we must go to their source. Whether we are equal to facing what we discover is another question."

"Very optimistic, brother." But Seylon Heresar's silken tone was almost perfunctory, his attention to the problem. They were, Gentian was coming to realise, really rather alike. "So we search the valley. For?"

"Other Fae. Exits, concealed rooms, a prison within a prison. History. The key to escape may be found in the events leading up to Telsandar's disaster, and the Fair were ever record-keepers."

"Something for those of us who can read those knots." Heresar's smile thinned. "But if these attacks are frequent, we will hardly have time for leisurely research. What else?"

"Convincing Suldar to speak to us is an obvious route, but one I would not push. Discovering some protection against this usurpation of casting must be a priority, and I will work with Magister Calder on catching a greater glimpse of the entity she detected. But for the rest of this day I suggest that those of us still able work on an attempt at a keyhole breach of the shield. I doubt it will succeed, but it is our ultimate goal. There is no leaving while it stands."

Heresar glanced at his prince, then nodded. "Then let's hope it falls before we do."

Chapter Eleven

Aspen still couldn't find the right word for the way Aloren moved. She didn't glide, and he'd hardly call it a saunter. Certainly nothing so simple as walk, and stride was out of the question for one so luxuriously languid. There was something innately effortless, and yet commanding of attention. Progressed, perhaps. Even wandering off alone in an abandoned Fae city, she conjured cheering crowds, brought to mind a trail of courtiers and attendants.

"Do you believe in coincidence, Highness?" he asked, catching her up despite the need to hide from what had just happened, not to mention the screaming exhaustion demanding he crawl under the nearest bush and expire. But curiosity had long been his harshest mistress.

"When the occasion demands."

She was humming to herself again, pausing in providing her own processional music only long enough to answer. The melody matched Suldar's. And it was Suldar Aloren was moving toward. She glanced up at the statue's face, then moved to circle the Fae's blocky white building.

"Coincidences happen," Aspen told her, keeping pace. "But usually there's a deeper explanation."

"And what coincidence exercises you so?" she asked, indulgent but absent. Her attention was more for one of the high, lanced windows leading into Suldar's building. They began well above head height, were as blocked as the entrance, but with some kind of cloudy glass. The faintest shadowy shapes were visible inside.

"Two groups," Aspen said, watching her face closely. "I discount the youngest two, Kassen and the boy–"

"Prince Chiall."

"Chiall. The rest of us fall neatly into two groups. Those heading back to bed, limp as rags and just as useful. And that little collection out there trying to do something particularly difficult with magic. All our acknowledged Magisters, scholars with a passion for their craft, and I guess just a little harder to, ah, usurp than the rest of us. And then, Highness, there's you."

He'd won that slow, amused smile, and a moment's full attention. "Yours is a passion for people," she said, a simple statement of fact. "Tell me what you think of Suldar."

"I've been trying not to," Aspen said, then looked uneasily toward the nearest window. "I don't know – I have a hard time putting myself into her shoes. A thousand years down here, doing what? Playing those harps?"

"If she wasn't mad to start with, she would be by now?" Aloren was apparently not concerned at the prospect of Suldar eavesdropping on everything they said. "That lessens any need for this to make sense. Perhaps, being bored, she brought us here just to watch us try to leave."

Aspen could see this was an explanation that Aloren could relate to. "I guess, if we don't find anyone else in the valley, we'll have to ask ourselves that again. Are you going to answer my question?"

"You didn't ask one," she pointed out. "Perhaps you could answer one for me."

"Yes?" Aspen came alert, any thought of Suldar blown totally out of his mind by the hint of shared secrets, of camaraderie, in Aloren's honey-treacle voice.

"Why did Magister Calder fall over when the lights went out?"

ooOoo

She hadn't waited for an answer, and Aspen had been left to stumble off to bed, head full of unpleasant questions about the Fae taint and Gentian, and the memory of Aloren humming Suldar's melody. Tired as he was, all the worst possibilities woke him again and again, leaving him a frazzled tangle in a sour, stale bed. There were too many things that could be happening while he played hydra with his thoughts.

It was no wonder Gentian was such a repressed, squashed down little thing. Bad enough to wake without fail out of nightmare every morning, to have every sleepy lie-in stolen from you. For it to not be your own fears, but a cold and nasty, completely hidden thing that no-one else believed was real? Clawing at the inside of your head. Trying to get out?

And that was the question. Aspen was fairly sure Aloren wasn't going to go asking it of anyone else in the near future, but if things like this morning kept happening, the Diamond was going to need more than a few brazen half-truths to keep the little gardening mage in one piece. Pity he seemed to have decided she was Darest's best hope for getting rid of the malison.

And that was an interesting thought. Gentian wasn't going to make herself popular refusing to help Darest, but perhaps the situation could win Aspen some favour. Naturally the Diamond could arrange matters so that the woman wouldn't be going anywhere 'til he was done with her, but there were a thousand other things that would be requiring his attention as well, once they finally escaped. If Aspen could do a little judicious nudging and convincing, well, that would be a service surely worth a little reward? By late afternoon, making the attempt seemed far more attractive than lying in bed, so he started out with manipulation in mind.

He spotted Gentian immediately, out in the central garden teaching Desseron, Kassen and Chiall how to grub themselves up with dirt. Since Lady Dhara was in close attendance, looking faintly wry at the accumulation of mud, he decided to postpone the attempt. Especially when Rua and the Guard Dog were over by the lake, poring over a big sheet of paper.

"I'm guessing the Aurak didn't finish his divination," Aspen said, as soon as he was in earshot.

"It was a poorly timed interruption," Rua agreed. "Your Lord has agreed to assist him in another attempt this evening."

The Diamond would enjoy that. "Does that mean you'll be busy tonight?" Aspen asked, letting himself hope.

Those warm eyes crinkled. "Hapt-lo Dest is to assist," she said, placidly. "Captain Djol and I are detailed to the search."

"Sounds like fun." Aspen couldn't hide a certain glee when the Guard Dog looked up from the sheet of paper with a grimace. "Where do we start?"

With a resigned shrug Djol tilted the paper toward him, displaying a roughly drawn but very detailed map. "We'll move through the lowest circle and work up to the valley's rim," he said. "On the first pass, we'll be viewing every room, searching for the obvious and the unusual. Anything resembling a diary or history is to be collected. If it comes to a second pass, we'll be divining for hidden entrances, turning over every object. Can you read Essan?"

"Not enough for more than the vaguest guess." The language of the Fair and the language of magic were thoroughly related, and any well studied word-mage could usually puzzle out a hint of meaning. But both were hugely complex and completely tedious. Aspen was never going to claim to be well studied.

"Then we will guess," the Guard Dog said. "And aim for at least a half dozen buildings before dark."

Shuffling his map into a tight roll, he headed off toward the first building to the right of Darien headquarters, yet another oversized box, the entrance all columns and carving. "Yessir, Captain Sir," Aspen said to his back, then grinned sunnily at Rua. "Alone at last."

"Even so," Rua said, with that composed good humour. She began to follow the Guard Dog, but not too quickly.

Aspen admired the ripple of muscle, the velvet-steel skin, and was glad of her just for existing. And she gave him a chance to ease another point of curiosity.

"Is the Atlaran court rife with poetry, Rua? When we found him, the Aurak recited a phrase..." He trailed off hopefully.

"*'Gentian, Gentian, meek and mild'*," Rua said, very wry. "Well, that is a translation, but I have encountered the originals."

"*And?*"

She laughed, a clear, buoyant sound. "I cannot remember most word for word, which is as well, for they are not kindly intended. It is how I first heard of Magister Calder, how her name became known in Atlarus." She paused for a moment, then said: "*'Gentian, Gentian, meek and mild; Asks politely, then changes your mind.'*"

"That's it?" He'd hoped for something far more salacious. "What's that supposed to mean?"

"She is an artist, that one. Gardens do not ordinarily bring great fame, but the Aurak's valley has a reputation outside unusual, and it was even whispered that the Arachol himself had commissioned a work in the inner fastnesses of the Great Palace, a place few are ever privileged to see." Rua gave him an amused look for his impatience at this non-explanation. "There is one among the most powerful of our lords who declared that Magister Calder would create for him as well. He is renowned for his successes, and he turned upon her every persuasion."

"And she would not."

"It is her size, of course, which made it so amusing. Like a child, but so steadfast, a rock against all his power. *Gentian, Gentian, meek and mild; Walking the shore, she turned back the tide.*"

"Feh." That was nothing like so interesting as Aspen had hoped, so he contemplated a much more interesting prospect. "What are you going to be when you grow up, Rua?"

That made her laugh again, but she understood just what he meant. "Under the Aurak's guidance I have reached Maja rank. I am committed to his service until the year's turning, and he has offered me a student's year after, for me to further my studies. I am privileged to learn from him."

"But–?"

"But I will not continue beyond year-end," she said easily. "I do not have the love for magic. It is a craft to me, not an art, and it is not fair to those who are truly drawn, that I should take the Aurak's time."

"No love for it." Aspen turned that one over approvingly. "It's always best to follow your heart."

"The Aurak has been greatly impressed by your Lord," she added, quickening her pace to catch the Guard Dog as he tested a heavily decorated set of double-doors. "For him, it is a calling."

"No arguments there." Aspen shook his head at understatement, and set his back against the door to help Djol push. "Sun! If it wasn't for the threat to Darest, I'd say this is the most the Diamond's enjoyed himself for months. Rummaging through the Fair's dirty laundry *and* with his own study-group of magisters to play with? This is practically a holiday."

That earned him a disapproving look from the Guard Dog, who no doubt had very worthy opinions on things you shouldn't say about your betters. Then the door deigned to shift, and they stood looking in at a long, lofty-ceilinged hall. Afternoon light streamed through high windows, picking out motes of dust dancing in the air, and gold lettering on the spines of row, upon row, upon positive rank and file *battalion* of books.

"No Fae here," Aspen declared after a revolted pause, and made to shut the door. The Guard Dog blocked him irritably and strode into the room, disappearing among the rows of shelving.

"Ever record-keepers," Rua said thoughtfully. "This is a lifetime's study."

"A Fae's life." Aspen had been caught by a faint tickling, one of the first traces of lingering enchantment he'd felt in the valley. Following it to the back wall of the library, he found the Guard Dog before him, opening a book from a long set of shelves. Peering over the man's shoulder, he saw a page covered in runes, all neatly boxed off like tigers in cages.

"Their arcanum," Rua said, coming up at his elbow. "The Aurak will wish to hear of this immediately."

Aspen watched her stride away regretfully, then eyed the books with a mix of disdain and excitement. Spells. A collection of word-magic on a truly excessive scale, written down in a safely neutered manner so that it could be taught to others. Fors Cabtly, his former teacher, had owned two books: thin, worn, painstakingly preserved volumes he had guarded like the gold they were. Unless you truly understood Elachar, unless you were a devising mage like the Diamond, spells were something you learned to repeat. They were recipes which, properly followed, gave the desired result. And, while there were spells which almost every mage knew, most of the really interesting stuff was hoarded, guarded. Getting access to it required joining certain schools, 'prenticing to a master, and making the most stringent oaths imaginable. An arcanum like this was, was–

"The Diamond's going to *wet* himself," Aspen said, just soft enough Djol could pretend not to hear.

Still, it earned him a disapproving flicker. Closing the book, the Guard Dog put it back in its place. "We'll check the rest of the building."

"So which part of the East are you from, Captain Djol?" Aspen asked, as the man struck out for a door in the library's back-left corner.

"Sorania." Tight, curt, and entirely discouraging.

"Been here long? In the West, I mean. I'll presume you've not been plumbing Telsandar's murky past any longer than the rest of us."

This time Djol ignored him, though there was a sense of gritted teeth as he opened the door and looked inside. Aspen mentally rubbed his hands together. There were few things he enjoyed more than being cheerfully friendly toward someone who didn't like him.

"I've often considered going for a look at the East," he announced, entirely untruthfully. "If only to see if it's as fraught and dramatic as all the stories make out. Is it true that even accidentally bumping someone in the street's liable to see you with swords drawn at dawn?"

Djol failed to acknowledge the bait at all this time, but Aspen didn't let up, positively burbling in the man's wake as he moved systematically through the library's few side-rooms. They reached the entrance in time to meet Rua.

"They will be here shortly," she said. "Shall we–?"

"We'll continue as planned." The Guard Dog went down the steps as if a few of the more picturesque Deeping monsters were at his heels.

"Captain Djol has been telling me *all* about life back home," Aspen said gaily. "Have you ever been to Eastern Sumica, Rua?"

"This is my first visit to the north."

"Tell me something of your home," he demanded as they reached the door of another of the manor houses. "Are your parents scholarly types?"

She gave him that quizzical look, assessing, then shook her head and began to entertain him with tales of her home life, of brothers, sisters and cousins spilling out of every cupboard, and a family business which involved garments of most extraordinary cloth. Aspen in turn told her about his own family, about their surprise when he'd thrown back to some magely ancestor, and their indulgent exasperation at his ideas of 'prenticeship, and how he'd promised to smuggle his much-younger brother in to see King Aluster in a temper, just as soon as an opportunity presented.

And his voice grew a little high, the words coming too fast and then, somewhere in between the third and the fourth echoing hollow house, it all dried up in his throat until finally he found himself in a bedroom, one that belonged to one of the non-human races the Fair liked to keep about them. The scale of the furniture gave it away.

There was a little wooden horse on the floor, worn but polished. The kind of thing some grandparent had made, generations ago: passed down to each new child, lost and rediscovered, growing a little more battered each year, the bridle painted on again and again. It was just there on the floor, next to a plate with an apple core gone brown.

And Rua was holding him, because he was shaking and could not stop. "They died too," he told her, wanting her to make it not real, not caring that the Guard Dog watched from the door. "They weren't even Fae. All that's left are goats and chickens. And nothing we can do, nothing we can say or think or try or want can ever change that."

"No." Rua, solemn and restful and the best of creatures, failed to spare him. "Nothing will ever change that."

ooOoo

The wrong side of dawn and Rua was gone. But she'd kept the nightmares at bay, just as she'd brought sympathy and welcome distraction. He blinked in the dark, trying to cling to happy thoughts full of sensual appreciation, of a long, strong body that had wrapped itself about him and made the bad things go away. But he couldn't. Not when he remembered why he'd left a wake-cantrip to get him up at this ungodly hour.

Gentian, of course. The Diamond had told him he was to attend the experiments, which Aspen could only interpret in one way. Cut off from all his stalwart myrmidons, the Diamond had settled his eye on Aspen and seen in him the answer to a particular need.

Chaperone.

It was a delicious prospect, and Aspen knew he should be beside himself at the opportunity to play faithful assistant, with a front-row seat for more of Gentian's wholly inept handling of the Diamond. But he couldn't work up the enthusiasm.

He liked the little gardening mage. Over-quiet, yes, and with a faint tendency to forget a proper sense of decorum, as well as apparently being inconveniently stubborn. But good people. If only she wasn't possibly-very likely-all too surely being used by some massively inhuman evil intent on ravaging Darest. The thing that had killed everything in this valley, which he was supposed to go help prod out into the open. He'd yet to think of an acceptable excuse for not turning up.

One good thing about the *saecstra* was that if he concentrated, Aspen could hear its nearby whisper. Unless the Diamond put some effort into guising the thing, it would handily reveal things like the fact that the Lord Aristide Couerveur was still in his room. Aspen, provided he could force himself out of bed, would manage a creditably early arrival.

Clinging to thoughts of Rua, and the hope that she didn't plan last night to be a one-off occurrence, he fumbled himself out of his tangle of sheets, cleaned up and dressed before braving the cool corridor. His room was in the middle of the three, and a glance showed no light beneath the Diamond's door. Gentian's stood open, revealing her sitting up in bed, waiting to be investigated.

"Don't you have anything transparent?"

Complete incomprehension, then a faint, twisted smile as she looked down at soft grey trousers and a shapeless, long-sleeved shirt of blue stripes. "I'd be horribly uncomfortable in something transparent," she said, drawing up bare feet so she was sitting between her heels. "I spent too much of my childhood on mornings like this to, ah, have quite the right associations."

"A wasted opportunity," Aspen declared, looking with determined interest about a room very much like his own. "*I'd* certainly be buck-naked and oiled, with only a sheet artfully arranged." He grimaced at a huge vase of cushiony buds on long, hairy stems, like a collection of smirking sea-serpents. "Aren't you supposed to wait for the flowers to open before you pick them?"

She laughed. "Poppies look good like that. Besides, they'll open eventually, uncrumple their petals and become an entirely different arrangement."

"Very butterfly-minded of you." He moved restlessly about, turning over ways to make the woman agree to stay in Darest. "What's in these trays of dirt?"

"Cress. I want to see if it grows at the same rate under an illusory sun."

That earned her a disbelieving look, but she seemed to be serious. "Do you think we'll be here long enough to find out?"

"Yes." She shrugged. "Unless we die first, or It gets out."

This was *not* what Aspen wanted to hear. He pulled a face at her, then noticed she'd placed a couple of comfortable chairs on the far side of the bed, and plumped himself into one. "No talk of dying," he chided, trying to refuse her pragmatic fatalism. "For one thing, I gather the Diamond thinks it among my duties to keep an eye on you, make sure you don't fall off a cliff or anything."

"Indeed?" She didn't look surprised. "Bodyguard or watchdog, Aspen?"

"Maybe a little of both, who knows?" He pulled a face, as he had wanted to when the Diamond had issued this particular gem. "What he imagines I'll be able to do if one of our collection of delectables tries to wring your neck, I don't know. I've as much chance of stopping Jurasel as I would Suldar."

"None at all?" Her gaze drifted past him to the darkened window.

"Why hasn't your head exploded?" he asked, feeling the need to switch the subject. "Sun knows, the one thing that Fors did manage to din into my brain was the extreme peril of breaking name-oath. Don't you think you should shrivel up into a blackened lump, or at the very least turn into a frog?"

The understated smile for this, but then she glanced toward the door. The faint itching tickle of the *saecstra* was moving toward them. "The consequences of foreswearing name-oath are always apt," she said in a subdued voice. "Not necessarily fatal. What better penalty for breaking a vow never to return to Darest than to be doubly tied to it?"

"You said you didn't think being trapped here had anything to do with your oath."

"I didn't mean the valley."

Even though she'd said something like this before, it took at least two beats for comprehension to hit, and then only because of the wholly appreciative expression in the Diamond's eyes as he stood looking at her from the doorway. And all the good sense in the world couldn't hold back the sound which choked its way out of Aspen's throat in response. He tipped out of the chair and hit the floor with a satisfactorily solid thump. And laughed. Laughed until he sobbed, until his face ached and his ribs hurt and the Diamond had come over to look down at him.

"She thinks you're her punishment," Aspen informed him, too far gone to even care about legendary Couerveur vengeances.

"So I gathered. High flattery indeed." The thing Aspen loved most about the Diamond was that, for all his reputation for venom, something truly ridiculous would only make him sardonic, not send him up into high ropes of dignity. And there was not a hint of spite in the considering look he turned on the little gardening mage. "The question of your departure from Darest is, as you said, a moot point in these circumstances, Magister Calder. Shall we set it aside in the interests of finding the source of these morning disturbances?"

She shrugged. "I won't argue against you trying, Lord Magister. I doubt Aspen could take much more entertainment."

"Punish me some more," Aspen murmured, but knew enough to make it barely audible, for he was well on the verge of going too far. "Thank you," he said more loudly. "I needed that." He levered himself off the floor and settled back in the chair as the Diamond took the one closer to the corner.

"You are not optimistic of our chances of success, then?" the Diamond asked.

"No. It's no easy problem to solve."

Aspen gave Gentian points for composure, telling the Diamond Couerveur she expected him to fail. In fact, she seemed curiously undismayed, not concerned about whether she should alienate the more-than-edible object of her desires.

While the Diamond...just nodded and began casting. Aspen blinked and blinked again. Something had changed. No curling smile, no courtier's barb. This was almost the same manner the Diamond used with the King. Businesslike.

Fascinating. Aspen considered the cool profile of Darest's most stand-offish of mages. Surely not. But then, why the chaperonage, after all? It was obvious that Gentian wasn't the sort to take advantage of the setting. She'd keep her hands to herself until asked – fortunate given how fond the Diamond was of being pushed or manipulated. So why had the man dragged Aspen in to play raspberry?

Highly entertained by the possibilities, Aspen considered Gentian all over again. Brains and magery, which would certainly score high in the Diamond's books. Vastly different in style, but she did hold her own against him, parrying any darts with undiminished calm. She was shorter than him, which was to some men's tastes. Nor would it do to forget the Varpatten bloodline, which a mage thinking about heirs would find reason enough alone. Plus that story she'd produced yesterday had surely balanced her absenteeism.

Nor, he decided, had the clothes been a mistake. Gentian was far outside Aspen's wide-ranging tastes: he had a distinct preference for dramatic colouring, and had never been particularly drawn by small women. Tall and lush, tall and muscular, tall and lean. He liked someone he could wrestle. But Gentian, overwhelmed by the Fae-sized bed, was looking unexpectedly intriguing. Fine bones at wrist and ankle, a slender little neck, with the line of her back and shoulders pleasantly outlined and small breasts only hinted at beneath the shirt: the modest clothes only made you want to take them off. And there was a definite draw in this authoritative composure, the frank and uncowed interest with which she watched the Diamond make a circuit of the room casting a four-corners ward. Yes, she was, after all, a definite possibility. Up against a wall, for preference, and–

Aspen carefully redirected this thought, before he really got himself in trouble. It was an interesting idea, but so terribly unlikely. The Diamond's expression was certainly far from lover-like as he finished casting and turned to study the subject of the experiment. She could as well be a frog.

"So, what now?" Aspen asked.

"Cast this." Ward complete, the Diamond handed him a slip of paper with runes neatly boxed down one side: a divination, one which would monitor any power used within the ward. Compact script covered every spare inch, giving a precise translation, outline of intent and guide to pronunciation. It was a complex little spell, and Aspen wondered whether he should be insulted at the level of explanation, complimented at the relative difficulty, or pleased to contribute something other than a pretty face to the proceedings.

Or daunted. A test, a test, with every mistake a nail in the coffin of 'prenticeship with the Diamond. Did he even want that any more? What price the opportunity to make a fool of himself before a more exacting master than his first could ever have dreamed of being? What gain? It wasn't as if they had a hope of overcoming Suldar or her maybe-maybe not prisoner.

Gentian had drawn her knees up to her chest and wrapped her arms about them, no doubt wondering why he was just sitting there while the Diamond was well into the depths of something infinitely trickier. And Aspen reminded himself that this was Aristide Couerveur, who lived magic and politics, who would let nothing stand between himself and Darest's interests. If anyone was going to get them out of this trap, it was the Diamond.

Throwing doubts to the wind, Aspen reviewed the instructions three times over, and cast with every ounce of care, gloating as it eased into being like he'd been practising for months. Instantly his head was full of ghosts of intent. The Diamond's voice in five different places, words hissing over each other. *Block*, said each corner of the room. *Guard*, the door replied. *Watch, Pierce, Record*, said the nightmarish knot above Gentian's head. *Reveal*, said the glowing orb that had risen to adhere to the ceiling. *On my name*, muttered the *saecstra*, with a finality which was more than apt.

"Can you describe exactly what you experience?" the Diamond asked, settling back in his chair. Like a healer, asking where it hurt.

"No." No wry edge: just a straightforward answer accompanied by that solemn stare. Then she looked away, resting her chin on her knees, profound discomfort betrayed by her determined focus on the vase of butterfly-serpents.

"Put yourself in a place where you're utterly alone," she went on, in a voice colourless from control. "You know, with absolute certainty that you're the only person there, the only thing that can exist in that place. It is the place where you are. And then something, a huge, horrid, utterly wrong thing – a thing that has been standing behind you in the dark holding its breath – that thing leans, rushes, swoops forward and *screams* in your ear. That is not memory: I have the next moment, the waking moment, only remembering a hating, black, vast anger, an impression of great wrongness. Of a thing that hates me, hates everything, me most of all. A typhoon of it, surging forward, as if anger alone could push me away. As if I am crushing it, and must be crushed in my turn, as if I'm the wrong that blinds and cripples it."

She spared them a sideways look, only her eyes moving, gauging their lack of reaction. "Never more than a moment's touch, never changing, never any less. I react physically to it, as a mouse would being dropped at the last moment by the owl. Pure fear reaction, then the quivering aftermath of shock, and a profound revulsion, as if all the world is wrong. I feel trapped, long to get outside, but if I move about too soon I prolong the weakness."

"Weakness?"

"Take that dizzy moment just after someone's startled you out of your wits and multiply it a lot." The faintest shrug. "It's nearly dawn."

"You're able to feel its approach?"

"There's a slight heaviness."

She glanced at them again, then closed her eyes. It took Aspen a moment to realise that this was it, that she'd gone to sleep as easily and completely as an infant, still sitting upright with her cheek resting on her knees. Her chest moved, deep and even, as if she'd been dreaming for hours.

Creep up on a sleeper and scream in their ear. It perfectly described her waking: the jolt upright, eyes flown wide, breath gulped in surprise, horror. He could see the pulse in her throat, leaping madly as she stared at them, a shuddering moment completely without recognition. Her fingers closed white on her shins, and her face went chalky as she squeezed her eyes shut – for all the world as if she couldn't bear to look at them – and swallowed a tiny second breath that sounded like it hurt.

And Aspen felt nothing. Gentian had gone – been forced – into sleep, and then blasted out of it, and the clever little spell the Diamond had crafted and Aspen had cast so well had shown him nothing at all.

Chapter Twelve

Having Aristide there was worse than Gentian had anticipated. It hurt to hate him, to look at him and struggle with nausea. She blocked him out, shut away the world and hugged her knees until her heart stopped trying to burst her throat and her head no longer echoed. And even then, when she'd recovered enough not to gasp for breath, she had to turn her face away and blink at the door.

Gentian had lost count of the number of times she'd woken with an audience. Her parents had continually researched new divinations, and too many of the mages who'd come to consult her father had thought themselves equal to 'fixing' his daughter. She couldn't remember ever believing they'd succeed, or not resenting them for trying.

Aristide...Aristide taking up that so-familiar position by her bed was a very bad thing. True, he was a superlative mage. Yesterday's tests on the shield had amply demonstrated that. But high skill wouldn't be enough to unmask It, any more than skill had been able to punch their way out of this cage.

Turning her head, she found him as sleek and composed as ever, giving no hint of whether his divinations had been successful. Even in the near aftermath of It she wanted to reach out and touch him, if only to force him to stop looking at her as if she were a puzzle box he needed to open. On the whole, this strengthening, very physical desire was a welcome distraction, but Gentian doubted she'd long find it such a novelty to want so powerfully a lover she could not have. And, quite beside the sudden urgency brought on by the previous morning's attacks, Gentian didn't want to start the old circle of defeat with this man who made her ache. The myth of the infallible Diamond Couerveur could not hold true and she could not, would not, let herself believe in him.

"What happens when you keep yourself awake, Magister?" he asked.

It was as tidy an acknowledgement of failure as Gentian could imagine, and she was angry at herself for the spurt of disappointment it produced. Never, never could she quite stop hoping.

"It was a little like a fever," she replied steadily, ignoring the prospect of tomorrow being one of the worst in her life. "Aching bones, a temperature, interesting shooting pains. I grew very tired, physically weak, until I couldn't even get out of bed. My parents were seriously worried, but the next morning I fell asleep and woke as...normal, and then the fever was gone and I could sleep. They could find no sign that I was under any enchantment, that it was any kind of curse or casting."

"Just like all the rest of it." This from Aspen, who was looking a good deal less pleased with himself. "No sign of casting when you sleep and wake. No sign of casting when we were brought here, or when Suldar does her little spectaculars. And I certainly didn't notice anyone setting up that illusion-breaker yesterday. For all that it was the showiest thing *I* ever produced."

"We felt the power of the transportation, of Suldar's spells, and the release of the illusion," she pointed out. "Just no intent. For me...well, providing the mechanism is well-constructed, it would take only the tiniest amount of force to knock a person out. That could easily be lost in my body's living magic."

"And is something best discovered by attempting to keep you awake. We will try, first, to repeat your original experiment. If that reveals nothing, there is a casting I have in mind to craft, a variant of one of the healer's divinations, which may be useful for unmasking a hidden trigger."

Aristide was certainly not one to turn back at the first fence. His apprentice, however, had developed that portentous expression, which he seemed to wear when approaching uncertain ground.

"I was just chatting to Princess Aloren before," he said, in a very delicate tone. "She was asking why it was you, ah, fell over. After the sky went black." He grimaced, a jumbled mixture of apology and exasperation, and looked sideways at Aristide as if he was expecting the man to explode.

It had been too much to hope that no-one had seen, that every soft, sore place of her wouldn't eventually be dragged out into the open. At least Aristide's immediate response was limited to a steady survey of his apprentice. "What did you answer?"

"I didn't. I don't think she was expecting one."

"And what was the cause, Magister Calder?" he asked then.

The mild, genial tone gave Gentian a sense of deep foreboding, but she refused to go about apologising for her own upsets. "I don't really know," she admitted. "But it was me doing that – no outside force to blame it on. When the illusion was pierced, and everything went black, all I could think of was how much stone was above us. I'm not particularly afraid of the dark, or being locked up or whatever, but I've never liked the combination. Trapped in the dark. And I think that *is* because of what wakes me, because It is trapped, and I've had that imprinted in my head each morning, I suppose. A horror of being trapped beneath stone. And...at the time I thought, was quite certain, that It was in here with us. In the dark, under all that rock."

"At the time?" He was looking at her with that detached, analytical gaze again. The Sun at eclipse: cold white fire burning on dark blue.

"I did spend a lot of the rest of the day trying to find It," she explained. "Reaching out, seeking anything resembling that hate. That's what I don't understand, what eventually convinced me I was wrong. If It's here, why does It still only touch me for one moment of a morning?"

"A valid point." He frowned, considering her. "Aloren is the second to be given reason to link you to our attacker, so we must anticipate these episodes becoming open knowledge. I will prepare the ground, paint you as a possible solution, but there is much relief to be found in a scapegoat."

"Must you sugar-coat it?" she asked, wrinkling her nose at him, and was pleased to glimpse the faintest wry expression. "You'd think, if I were being used by something she was keeping prisoner, Suldar would have already removed me. The Fair's laws have a certain pragmatism at their core."

"Until we know more of this place, Suldar's motives will only be speculation. We are better able to foresee how our companions will react."

"The other one's Djol, isn't it?" Aspen put in, looking more than a little annoyed with himself. "The second with a reason. He was standing only a few feet away, and hasn't told Poet *or* Pup just what was said. Now that's positively interesting of the man."

Gentian had been mulling over Captain Djol on her own account, but hadn't produced any sure answers. "I guess that falls into the speculation category too," she said, with a glance at Aristide.

"It does. But also provides a reason to be wary. He may hope to gain an advantage, or simply be nursing a grudge. Prince Chenar might not be harsh, but his father has a reputation." He stood up, dismissing the last of his divinations. "We will reconvene this tomorrow, Magister. Since that experiment is likely to keep you from our other investigations for some time, there are several places in the valley I would appreciate your impressions of this morning."

"Of course," she said, and had to smile at her immediate glow of pleasure. When the focus wasn't on her own problems, she was more than happy to work with – and ogle – him. But there was something that had been preying on her, which she needed answered first.

"Lord Aristide–" She waited for the polite pause, then hurried on. "Vostal Hill. Putting aside my neglect in laying out some of the possibilities of my gardens, do you actually object to the intent?"

"I was under the impression you had grown disenchanted with that particular design, Magister."

"Oh no. The lower part of the hill, that's all mine. That the crest is more Fae than I first knew just emphasises what I was trying to do." Even though she was going to leave Darest, she thought it important to give that splendid crown a human touch.

The re-emergence of the amused glitter in his eyes told her Aristide had read her well enough to know her gardens were far more than a hobby, that this was a thing she wanted almost as much as she claimed to want him.

"Then, Magister, next time we are on Vostal Hill we must discuss the matter," was all he said, and with a faint, very sweet smile inclined his head and left her to stew.

ooOoo

Planting and weeding. It was Gentian's oldest memory, and her most soothing pastime. After a morning of intensive divinations, and an involved session restoring most of the function of one of the bathrooms, she was using an after-lunch break to work on one of the herbal borders in Telsandar's centre. A futile task given the valley's size, but it relaxed her, keeping the shadows away while she turned over earth and the prospect of Aristide,

It, and tomorrow's ordeal. The only one she wanted was the one she was least certain of getting.

She wondered if he would use Vostal Hill to hold her to Darest. And whether she would be foolish enough to let him. Good idea or not, Gentian was by now quite certain Aristide was no passing fancy. There was something in him which resonated with her. A bizarre choice considering he was an infamously ruthless politician who had looked at her garden and seen only its cost.

Closer acquaintance hadn't given lie to his reputation, but had revealed an intensely private man who – he did not hide *behind* the role of consummate courtier. She thought that was a sport to him, a game he was well-versed in playing, and thoroughly enjoyed. But his twin passions were Darest and magic, and not so completely divorced from her own. And she thought – hoped, trusted – that there was a sense of justice working along with that well-practiced pragmatism. How she was going to cope with walking away from him she did not know.

Her immediate problem was these experiments. She'd long loathed every attempt to unravel her mornings. Always that starting confidence, growing more determined in the face of initial failures. And then, nothing. Bright ideas grew fewer, lines of investigation dried up. Until they gave in, and went away, and left her waking each morning to It.

Those attempts were the only real shadow on her relationship with her parents. She'd always been angriest at them when they produced another mage wanting to fix her. She had good parents. They were caring and careful and they had taught her so much about the real magic in the world. And not only had they not stopped It from hurting her, they had continued to offer bubbles of hope. Her earliest lesson: there were some things that could not be fixed. And Aristide was going to teach her that all over again, and this time would hurt more than all those before.

"Magister Calder?"

Startled, she blinked up past the patterned hem of a too-long Fae robe to the handsome, hesitant face of Prince Rydan. What had Aspen called him? The Pup? It was oddly apposite to see he was holding a ginger kitten.

"I wondered whether you'd like a pet?" he asked, rushing the words out with an embarrassed but determined air. "My – we found her alone, no sign of a mother or the rest of the litter and Che–, my brother always goes into fits of sneezes around cats."

Nonplussed, Gentian stood to accept a kitten only six or seven weeks old. Immensely light, little more than a puff of fur with smoky blue-grey eyes, catching the skin of her hands with needle-prick claws. "Thank you," she said belatedly. "It's been a long time since I had a pet."

"Then I am glad to have served," Rydan replied, with some of his brother's smoothness, and a faint hint of relief. She was immediately suspicious. He'd been sent. Sent with this diversionary feline scrap to...what?

After they had recovered from yesterday's attack, the Cyan and Saxan princes had abandoned arguing in favour of searching the valley – a good deal more haphazardly than Captain Djol and Rua. Gentian had glimpsed them from time to time, and entertained herself with thoughts of rival gangs of children, trying to prove themselves the better. But these people played games for higher stakes, and the sea-fetch looked out of her memory, riding an unfamiliar current of excitement and unease. Her link to It would soon be known, and likely make her less than popular. Given how Chenar had broached the question of Suldar's death, it was well within the bounds of possibility that a very nasty confrontation was on the horizon. She'd hoped to have a few more days before the tide of suspicion hit.

"How have your explorations been progressing, Your Highness?" she asked, feeling her way cautiously.

"They haven't been," Rydan said, shrugging. "Oh, we've gone through a few dozen buildings, and found all manner of wondrous objects, not to mention rotting food and countless books. But prisoners, exits, or anything of actual *use*..." He sighed heavily. "It's the kind of thing that sounds a wonderful adventure when someone's singing about it, but only because the tedium and the disquiet are compacted down into a couple of lines between the heroics. But – I think we're all facing it now. We're not going to get out of here quickly. We mightn't get out of here at all."

"No." The kitten wriggled, and she began stroking the downy skull. "I wish I could say differently, Highness. But all our divinations have only shown us how thoroughly we're trapped. Even ordinary weather and time-of-day castings won't reference outside the valley, and we're left to rely on Suldar's sky." And Its inevitable dawn.

"I find myself wanting to go shout at the Fae's door until she gives us answers, admits she was behind that attack or tells us who was. Why do you think she ignores us?"

Gentian could find no overtone, no significant emphasis. For all she could tell, the question was simply that of a nervous boy trying to make conversation. Yet she was sure there was more to this encounter.

"I think she doesn't *want* to deal with us," she told him, truthfully. "Didn't expect us, doesn't like the implications of our sudden arrival. Doesn't know what to do."

Movement behind the young prince caught her eye. Seylon Heresar was strolling toward them, his attitude relaxed, but his pace deceptively fast.

"She can hardly plan to stay shut in that building indefinitely," Rydan said, then either noticed her looking past him, or heard a footstep, and turned. A pause, then, stiffly: "Duke Heresar."

"Prince Rydan." Heresar's hair glinted in the false sunlight as he bowed before turning to Gentian. "Magister Calder. I wondered if you had seen my brother lately?"

"In the Library still, Lord Magister." She was not at all surprised when he nodded his thanks but did not depart. She had a distinct impression he'd come over primarily to interrupt this conversation.

"You were discussing our elusive Regent?" he asked, considering Rydan's set expression with a kind of critical amusement.

"Speculating on her behaviour." Gentian looked back down at the kitten, feeling irrationally pressed. Given Aspen's dramatic warnings, she'd been surprised at what a low profile Heresar had kept. After the attempt at shield-breaking, he'd divided his time between assisting Jurasel in his searches and conducting divinations with Lady Dhara and Princess Kestia. Perhaps he had to spend most of his energy keeping them from each other's throats.

"I'm beginning to wonder if Princess Aloren does not have the right of it," he said now, adopting much the same air of swords-down approachability as Rydan. "Here we are, scrabbling for a way out, but the only way the lid will come off this box is if the Lady Suldar chooses to lift it."

"No-one's made any practical suggestions on how to convince her."

"But you notice that talk of killing the good lady has been abandoned?" The glance he gave Rydan held a neatly measured serve of provocation. "Certainly none of us have been hammering on her door, demanding she talk to us. Facing her down isn't quite on the order of putting out the Sun, but it feels very close to that when you sit down and think through the practicalities. Perhaps this little get-together of Aristide's tonight will produce a few ideas."

Gentian, who was not overwhelmed by the prospect of another round of royal tension and demand, simply repeated "Perhaps," in her most colourless voice and wondered if she could avoid going.

Heresar's smile broadened to something positively predatory. "Still, the valley itself is not unpleasant, don't you think?" he said. "I'm sure we can find ways to keep ourselves entertained, until Suldar's impasse is broken."

The scene became, of a sudden, remarkably familiar. The gift, the friendly conversation, even the deliberate interruption. This was nothing to do with It, and all about the Varpatten bloodline. They were sizing her up.

It was difficult not to laugh: at the absurdity, out of relief. Gentian had long ago grown accustomed to people fixing on her as a prime candidate for producing an heir. Power bred to power, and even Aurak Bes hadn't been above throwing every available grandchild in her path. She felt immediately sorry for Rydan, who couldn't be relishing this task, let alone Heresar's interference.

And Heresar! Aristide's brother. No doubt half the motive for both of them was the prospect of stealing a useful Darien mage – Laeth Varpatten's only child – out from under the Diamond Couerveur's nose. This was...going to be complicated.

Gentian decided a monumental failure to catch any hint was the easiest way to avoid offence. Even the broadest pass would be beyond her. "It's certainly a prime chance to study Fae history," she said, smiling at them both with a mild and marvellous lack of comprehension. "Though I imagine I've more than enough to occupy myself, with an entire valley of gardens."

"You notice that it rains each night?" he asked. "Our Regent pays enough attention to maintain us."

"Or simply the valley," Rydan said, his manner both combative and thoughtful. "She had locked it so completely away. Even the water was under that shell. Does she eat? Does she breathe? Do – Magister?"

Gentian had looked sharply aside, her senses giving her a few moments early warning before it became clear to all of them that there was a strong tug of magic, pulling toward the lake.

"Oh, not again." But the young prince's words held an air of surprised relief, for while there were several sources to the growing casting, Gentian, Heresar and Rydan had all been spared.

"Something a little smaller this time," Heresar murmured, sounding more interested than dismayed. "Not another illusion-breaker, I'd wager."

Gentian strained to discern intent, closing her eyes to better focus, but again she found nothing. Power, going somewhere, doing something. As fathomless as the sea. So she felt instead for the response of Telsandar itself, and found the Place muted, with an overlay of quiet attention. No, it certainly wasn't the valley doing this.

"I swear, given the chance, I'll tear the throat out of the one responsible for this."

Gentian opened her eyes on two angry princes, but it was Lady Dhara who had spoken. She, like Jurasel and Chenar, was one of the sources of the casting's power. The last, Hapt-lo Dest, looked no better pleased, striding toward them in Aurak Bes' company. Aristide was on the library steps, and Princess Kestia still some distance away, her children gathered around her, when, in an echo of yesterday morning, a man hauled himself out of the lake.

He was Fae, and naked, and blue. His skin looked like indigo suede, slick with moisture, and he moved toward them with a grace that was truly boneless. A creature of magic and water, holding a sword.

Hapt-lo Dest quickly stepped forward to meet him, hefting his heavy, iron-bound staff and setting his feet to signal that he would defend his lord but planned no attack. Despite the casting's steady draw, the Atlaran seemed well able to do battle. As Heresar had said: something a little smaller this time – and not nearly so debilitating.

The water-Fae had stopped as Dest came forward, and now surveyed the Atlaran from head to toe. Magic-summoned or not, this was a distinct presence, an actual personality. At least, the blue man seemed pleased as he lifted a sword as watery as his flesh, but with an ice-rime edge to the blade. Perhaps this was no conjuring, but Suldar's prisoner. For all Gentian knew, this could be It made manifest.

With a weird internal quiver, Gentian turned her mind to trying to think of ways to stop the thing. The shrouded intent made the task infinitely more difficult. Usually, even if she hadn't heard the spell, Gentian could discern the broad outline of a casting, with its subtleties becoming clearer after study. This must be what it was like for word-mages: stumbling through a maze blind-folded. With your arms bound.

Which left logic and guess-work; trial and error. As Dest leaned away from a first, flickering pass, Gentian began a major word-magic shield. It was difficult indeed to block the flow of raw power, but the most direct way of neutralising an unknown casting was to starve it. She would try to cut it off from its victims.

Adroitly avoiding Dest's return blow, the Fae turned and looked at her. Marking her, she felt, and also Duke Heresar, busy in his own casting. Then, smiling with an unkind pleasure, the attacker made a lazy-seeming cut toward Dest's head, which the Atlaran barely blocked. The sound of ice-steel on wood rang out.

No wavering attention now, as they engaged in earnest. Dest was no shabby fighter, but he was plainly outmatched, struggling to counter the Fae's blows. Gasping from doubled effort of battle and unwilling casting, he spoke in High Atlar, urging the Aurak away. But Kubara Bes shook his head, and sent out a spell, a banishment that briefly blurred the outlines of both combatants, then dissolved to no effect except to draw the water-Fae's attention to the Atlaran ambassador.

Without the Fae even looking in Dest's direction, the ice-rime sword flicked out, and carved the guard's leg open from hip to knee. The Atlaran fell, but swung even as he went down, and finally succeeded in connecting with watery flesh. The heavy tip of the staff impacted – passed through – the Fae's waist, emerging in a shower of droplets.

Unfazed, the Fae stepped past Dest, eyes on the Aurak. Hastily, Gentian finished establishing her shield, and had the satisfaction of seeing its walls flare and fade as the flow of power was, if not completely severed, thoroughly choked. An imperfect block, but perhaps it would weaken the thing. And Duke Heresar, with excellent timing, loosed a more straightforward shield, a wall of force to keep the Fae in place. He nodded at her in satisfaction. Between them, they had it boxed.

Almost immediately her shield flared again, and Gentian had to channel power at full strength to maintain it as the Fae began drawing mightily on all four of its sources. The kitten, forgotten in her hands, mewled as she gripped it too tightly and, head swimming from effort, she put it down.

The Fae lifted its sword and Dest – along with Dhara, Jurasel and Chenar – shuddered with effort. Both shields went down, and Gentian staggered, ears ringing, as the ties of her casting bounded back on her.

"Very pretty," Heresar said, setting his teeth. "True-magic, great-magery, and the power of four to support it. Certainly no illusion-breaker."

The Fae had stopped to once again fix Gentian and Heresar with a most meaningful look, and was unhurriedly turning back to Aurak Bes when Rua ran into the fray. She channelled her own momentum into a blow aimed not at any mortal vulnerabilities, but at the indigo and ice sword.

"Nicely done!" Heresar said, as the weapon shattered into droplets. "But I doubt it will serve any purpose." He began another casting as Rua took the opportunity for several further strikes, filling the air with spray.

The sound of blade on staff came as quick confirmation of Heresar's assessment, followed by a nasty, almost axe-like blow which forced Rua a step back. It had simply grown itself another weapon, and used it now in blurring passes, slicing at the binding at Rua's wrists. She retreated toward her lord, not badly injured, but less certain.

"*Enough* of this," Jurasel snarled, and drew a sword he'd evidently found in his explorations. Heresar immediately broke off his spell and hurried forward to block his prince's path, adroitly turning the move into a word of muttered consultation, a discussion of tactics rather than delay. Aurak Bes, meanwhile, loosed another spell, one of straightforward force, blasting their assailant several feet away from Rua, and nearly into vapour before the Fae sent his four sources to their knees establishing a granite-solid shield. He moved forward, the shield sweeping over Rua so he could finish the assault without interference.

"Ah!"

Prince Rydan, standing neglected a few steps away, gave the exclamation a satisfaction worthy of the arrival of a rescuing army. Gentian glanced around to see Aristide had almost reached them, but it was Captain Djol Rydan had been looking for. The Easterner was striding unhurriedly down into valley's centre, a puffing Aspen jogging in his wake. Discarding the sheathe of his sword, Djol made a peremptory gesture to Rua, an order to take the limp and bleeding Dest and get out of the way. Then he lifted his blade in a swordsman's salute, held the Fae's eyes for a long, still moment, and became a different person.

Gentian stared. Gone was the stolid, taciturn guardsman, all business and due comportment. This man, completely focused, fiercely joyful, blazed in battle.

He whirled through the Fae's defences, swayed away from the returning blow, and came back to a guarding stance unscathed. Then made the tiniest motion of encouragement with the tip of his sword.

The water Fae smiled as if he'd met an unlooked for treat, and launched a counter-strike.

A dozen kingdoms had given Gentian plenty of opportunity to watch people try to kill each other. Duelling was a way of life in the East and Atlarus both, but only in the grand competitions, where the best of the elite battled for acclaim, had she seen anything to match this. Djol was the better, face alight as he weaved around the Fae's longer reach, heedless of the tiny hits the other scored. A mist of water vapour filled the air from his own strikes, and he danced through rainbows, alive in the moment. His sword was singing.

Wholly caught up by this phenomenon, Gentian came close to leaping out of her skin when Aristide, silk-smooth and acidic, spoke from an inch behind her ear: "Perhaps we might contribute before the Captain is entirely dissected?"

Heresar looked back at his brother and grinned. "But you notice the Fae has grown shorter? I think, given time, this Easterner would come out the winner."

"He would," Rydan affirmed, heart-felt.

"But since Captain Djol can only bleed so much, shall we attempt re-establishing the shield Magister Calder used? One over each mage fuelling the casting. Sekestry's Block, was it not?"

"A useful idea," Aurak Bes said, moving slowly up with Dest supported on one shoulder and Rua limping behind. "I will cover this one," he added, lowering Dest to the ground.

"I'll take Lady Dhara," Gentian said, approving the straightforward logic of the strategy.

"My Prince?" Heresar asked, and Jurasel nodded irritably.

"Leaving Your Highness to me," Aristide said to Prince Chenar, who merely shrugged, watching the fight with a critical air. "As close together as possible," Aristide continued. "If you would release on my mark?"

Gentian began again, taking it slowly this time because her head was still ringing. Djol showed no sign of faltering, nor concern for anything beyond the next stroke, but he would inevitably tire and weaken. They would need to do this soon.

Aurak Bes and Heresar were a beat behind her, but Aristide wordlessly cast a different spell, one that he left waiting to be triggered. The speed of true-magic casting left Gentian only with an impression of something transformative. She didn't waste concentration on analysing it further, carefully wrapping the close of her shield in her own trigger, and waiting. The Fae was no doubt aware of their casting, but gave no sign of breaking off to respond. A bad sign, surely.

Aristide drew power again, lifting a hand to hold them. The shield pressed against her trigger, too large to be easily held back, and she narrowed her eyes, reducing Djol and the Fae to blurs beyond Aristide's finely formed fingers. The *saecstra* swirled on his palm, tugging at the hook so firmly embedded in her chest, but she set the sight aside as well. Casting required a clear purpose, precise focus.

"Now."

Four shields, flaring into immediate visibility as the Fae's draw of power surged against the block. Gentian opened up to her widest output, channelling power at full strength to maintain the shield. Lady Dhara, Dest and the two princes disappeared entirely in the light sparking around them. Amazingly, the Fae didn't falter, raining blow after blow on Djol while hauling mercilessly against the blocks.

But the shields held. Panting, Gentian tightened hers further, strangling the misbegotten casting at the source.

Surely it couldn't be getting enough power, now, to maintain this attack?

The Fae's physical shield went, a soap bubble pricked. He gave no notice, pressing the attack on Djol with such speed and ferocity that it seemed scarcely possible the Easterner could hold. But Djol kept the pace, still blazing with vivid joy, though he was now breathing in great gasps. And that sword–

Next, the light around Chenar vanished, although the block remained. Aristide had succeeded in completely severing the link between the prince and the Fae. He straightened, cast a judicial glance at the flaring shields covering the other three sources, and released the first spell he'd set.

Ice cracked. The sharp, echoing report of a glacier, or a frozen water-Fae shattering to fragments. Djol snapped to a defensive stance even as a wave of frost swept over them, and Gentian flinched from another blow against the block she maintained. The spell had lost form, but not drive, and now beat at the blocks, trying to wrench free enough power to regain cohesion.

And it could not. Gentian turned to catch Aristide's eye, smiling in pleased relief as she found the strain of the shield was lessening. The light sparking from the blocks faded, then shimmered out of existence, along with any hint of the conjured Fae. Done.

Chapter Thirteen

Blood.   Oozing from shallow cuts wherever Djol's
armour had not protected him, spattered across the green
and tan colours of Sax. Aspen, usually the last person to
look anywhere near an open wound, drank in every
crimson line.

And the man. Gods, Guard Dog had been totally the
wrong thing to call him. Aspen could hit himself for not
spotting the lie, but how could he have known that stolid
little yes-man was a front for all this? Passion, command,
arrogance.   Yes, definitely, in that cool survey of his
audience, and the economical production of a cloth to dry
his blade.   This was a man who did *not* see himself
surrounded by his betters, and deservedly so.   The
phoenix that had burst from the heat of battle trotted at
no man's heels.

Rearranging his mental list to place Djol on par with
Aristide and Aloren, Aspen looked around to check who
else was finding the Easterner by far the most interesting
thing in the valley. The Atlarans were oblivious, muttering
staunching spells over Dest, but most everyone else was
watching him. Jurasel's gaze was definitely speculative,
and Rydan's calf-love open. And Gentian. Gentian, who
was supposed to be safely obsessed with the Diamond,
was staring at Djol with a kind of bemused surprise that
surely boded no good. Aspen wasn't pleased. It was one
thing for the little gardening mage to batter herself
uselessly against Diamond cliffs. It would be outright
greedy of her to go hunting Phoenix as well.

"That certainly livened up the afternoon," Jurasel said,
breaking the silence with sudden droll glee. "Welcome to

the club, Dhara. You've gotten off more lightly than we did first time out."

"There's nothing light about this," Dhara replied sourly. She was watching her wife and children belatedly advancing. "I felt no hint of that casting being set upon me. Despite detects specifically designed to catch any attempt."

And she'd ruined his theory about Magisters being too hard to manipulate, Aspen groused silently. Unless...unless their hidden Foe was getting better at this game.

"Was that pure conjuring?" Rydan asked. "Or was that actually the one behind all this? Projecting himself outside his prison?"

"Who can tell? If nothing else, an apt demonstration that this is no ally in our attempts to escape." Chenar dusted the knees of his borrowed Fae clothing. "Unless anyone cares to suggest that mutual need led it to try to cut us to little pieces?"

"No." Djol, marching up with the cloth now tied about the deepest cut on his forearm, called the sheathe of his sword in one of the few displays of magic Aspen had seen from him. "My blows didn't injure him," he added, and Aspen was delighted to see those black eyes still full of fire and assurance. "He could have ignored them, had me at any time. Whatever else, that was no attempt to kill us."

"No doubt the whole thing was arranged to cut the tedium with a short athletic display," Seylon Heresar remarked.

For a moment, pure cynical disdain glinted in Djol's eyes, but then his face dropped into the business-first impassivity of the Guard Dog. "It's possible. But it appeared to be on the lines of a taunt. No point in the action itself, other than to demonstrate it can be done."

"For the Lady Suldar's benefit, rather than our own?" Heresar considered the idea. "But yesterday was surely ample demonstration that we can be used. If that was to show we can be killed, it suggests Suldar would have some reason to wish that not happen."

"More guesses." Chenar offered Djol a neatly folded kerchief, eyeing his Phoenix's injuries unhappily. "We aren't progressing, only reacting."

"We are at least eliminating false paths," Aurak Bes said, as he rose from tending his arms man. "We may not yet be able to prevent this commandeering of our strengths, but we have learned a way to combat the results."

"And if the victim next time is yourself, Ambassador?" Chenar asked, quite reasonably. "Or Magister Couerveur? All of us? We'd hardly be playing with blocks then."

"True. But the step, however faltering, still takes us forward."

Chenar nodded, then turned the motion into a more respectful inclination of his head. "I trust that we will make more, and soon." He cast a sideways glance at the Diamond. "And share them."

That only revived the Diamond's famous smile. "Full disclosure, Highness?" he murmured. "I look forward to it."

Chenar's long lashes swept down, and Aspen saw Jurasel glance at Seylon Heresar. He was suddenly more certain than ever that Darest had been the prime topic of conversation on that barge. And that the discussion involved something they were keen to keep entirely from the Diamond's shell-like ear.

"Captain, will you still be able to assist our hosts for this evening's gathering?" the Saxan prince said, side-stepping carefully. "Perhaps you should rest instead."

"No need," Djol replied.

"This one's injuries are no longer serious," Aurak Bes said, looking down at Dest. "But they will keep him to bed a day or so. I would prefer not to postpone the *sel-deseva* again, if you and Magister Calder are willing to assist in his place? Success would certainly give us something with which to open discussions."

"We'll leave you to it then," Chenar said, when the Diamond nodded his agreement. "Until tonight." Collecting his brother by an elbow he took himself tidily off, sparking a general dispersal. Rua produced a casting to give Dest a useful thistledown quality, and she and the Aurak supported him away. The Cyans withdrew into a brief cluster, then departed. Aloren hadn't even bothered to show up.

Djol, transferred at least briefly to Camp Couerveur, reattached sheathe to sword-belt and turned to the Diamond. "Your orders, Lord Magister?"

The words were quite without irony, the blank stolidity of the Guard Dog well back to the fore with no sign of the man who'd so recently dazzled. The Diamond's fine-cut lips smoothed till they held no suggestion of a smile. And he waited.

It was a demand, wordless and implacable. Djol, after a pause very close to too long, responded with the subtlest of shifts. The way he held his head, a certain change of posture, a more focused and direct gaze, eyes narrowing into an expression as much assessment as capitulation. "Your orders?" he repeated, and this time it was no obedient cipher asking the question, but a creature as fully cognizant of his strengths as the Diamond himself.

That Aristide Couerveur did not smile, did not offer more than the tiniest of nods, marked his measure of the man. "Choraide will assist you in tending your wounds," he said, at his mildest. "If, in return, you should succeed in investing him with some understanding of the function of a kitchen, I would be very much obliged."

Typical of Aristide Couerveur to effortlessly give this man his due. Aspen, unable to contain a look of shining gratitude, could have kissed the Diamond for his inclusion in this arrangement. Not that he wouldn't kiss the Diamond purely for existing.

Djol's response was far less effusive. His gaze – black, cynical – flicked to Aspen and away. "Very well." It was an acceptance of terms from a free agent, and he produced that curt, clipped bow again. But before the man could turn away Gentian decided to stop staring in bemusement and go back to being peculiar.

"Captain Djol. Would your sword take offence if you allowed me to look at it?"

Even the Diamond blinked at that one. Djol showed an instant's confusion, then a glimmer of wary curiosity.

"There's no enchantment on the weapon."

"I know." Gentian produced one of those deceptive, wide-eyed expressions. "But, well, it was enjoying itself so very much. I hardly ever encounter objects like it."

The Easterner went very still, staring at her as if he wanted to strip away flesh and discover her thoughts. Then, in one motion, he pulled sword from sheathe and offered it to her, hilt first.

"Thank you." The grave, punctilious courtesy of a well-trained child, falling away to open fascination as she grasped and lifted it from his hold. Truly more interested in the sword than the man, which finally proved to Aspen that she wasn't right in the head.

A quick glance showed the Diamond watching this scene attentively, content to let it play out. Djol was not so sanguine, waiting tight-lipped as she turned the weapon in the afternoon light. Aspen wished just once to know more about what was going on than everyone else.

Turning the sword again, Gentian paused. She looked past it at Djol, not quite hiding her surprise, and now it was her turn to hold the man's gaze in a wordless question. But those black eyes were shuttered.

"It's a family piece, isn't it?" she said eventually. "Very old."

A hint of care, then: "How can you tell?"

"Well–" She looked down at the hilt, a plain, leather-wrapped affair, then held it out to him. "It knows I don't belong to it. Doesn't want me touching it, because I'm not...right."

That earned her another wary look before Djol took the sword and sheathed it. Aspen couldn't keep quiet a moment longer.

"For pity's sake stop being mysterious just for the sake of it. Are you saying the sword's alive?"

"Oh yes. Things don't usually waken, especially when there's no enchantment involved. Most objects don't last long enough, have enough emotion invested in them, don't have enough...weight. I first met one, a stone, a piece of a shattered fountain, actually, in Surratlar. In uncertain light it looks like a head resting on an arm, and it's local custom, myth, that it was once one of the old god-mages. They say that if you whisper your heart's fondest hope to it at midnight, and wait in absolute silence, it will tell you what to do to gain your desire." She grimaced. "It's the most horrid gloating thing. So many people have come there, alone in the dark, and given it their longing and their fears and then waited with their hearts in their throats, clutching at every murmur of the wind, willing the answer to come. It glories in their need."

"Does it answer?" Djol was finding Gentian a little too interesting, staring at her face as if he thought to find some sore-needed remedy of his own.

"I don't know. People say it does. I was less than eager to tell it anything at all, let alone sit up with it at midnight." She gestured at the sword. "This – this is very different. Pride and craft and...joy. It was singing, a kind of wordless battle paeon. Exulting whenever you did something it thought particularly good."

"Singing?" Djol's face was a picture.

"Cheering you on, I guess. You don't hear that?"

"No. Feel something of the emotion." He flicked a glance at the Diamond and his face closed back up. "It is, as you say, a family piece. Thank you, Magister Calder. This has been...educational."

She shrugged, then added hesitantly: "Captain – I gather you've not repeated Suldar's conversation with me. Do you intend to?"

"Should the safety of my charges require it, Magister." This time the clipped bow had a very dry edge indeed. They watched him walk away.

"They have that man doing their laundry," Gentian said, with wondering delight.

"No doubt he manages it competently enough." The Diamond's tone was thoughtful, his eyes on Gentian.

"And what was the family name?" Aspen asked, delaying following Djol only because he was tolerably certain Djol wasn't what they should be calling him. "That chunk of metal told you, didn't it?"

"Delmar."

This meant little to Aspen, but the Diamond lifted fine brows in recognition. "Arleton Delmar?"

"It must be."

"I've heard that name somewhere." Aspen pummelled his memory. "Something about a war?"

"Sorania, about five years ago." Gentian stared after Djol – Delmar – who had revealed the faintest limp as he headed toward the Saxan's mansion. "I'd left the East by then, but the tale was everywhere. Their King's only daughter died a few decades ago – fell down some stairs when she was heavy with twins. They saved the children and, though I find it a little hard to believe, apparently lifted them from her at the same time. So they had a prince and princess, but no clear heir. The King held off on setting one above the other until he'd judged which was more fit to rule. Logical in some respects–"

"Ludicrous idiocy," the Diamond murmured.

She gave him a quick, amused smile. "Probably, but I understand the temptation. The main fault was leaving it too late, 'til they'd grown to adulthood and accrued their supporters. He died only a month after naming the princess heir."

"And left behind a civil war?" Aspen guessed, wanting to hurry her along so he could catch his Phoenix up. "Where does Arleton Delmar come into it?"

"A famous family, the Delmars. Sword-masters and generals mainly. This one seemed to be on his way to both, quite the blazing comet, and was either a long-time friend or a prized lover of the prince. But he swore his oath to his King's chosen heir, and he stuck to it when the prince raised an army rather than see his sister crowned. The prince won in the end: the better soldier, if not the fitter ruler. He's King there now."

Aspen shifted impatiently, and she gave him that sideways look. "Delmar had been sent out-country to try to raise support, which is probably a sensible thing to do with a man whose loyalties are suspect. He returned in time to join the remnant of the heir's defenders, hunted to some shattered ruin to be slaughtered. Exhausted, starving, hopelessly outnumbered, and no mercy on offer. There was nothing Delmar could do to turn that tide. So he challenged the entire attacking army to a duel."

"Ah." That had struck a chord. "There's a song about it, isn't there? Delmar's Stand?"

"I don't know how many of them he killed. Some of the figures seem scarcely possible, though having seen him fight I begin to almost accept. There was even precedent for the kind of challenge. One opponent at a time, with the shortest of pauses between each bout. Easterners take their duels very seriously. They're much more common than in Darest."

"And it was a delaying tactic, wasn't it? She got away?"

"Yes. He was still going when they discovered the escape. The prince ordered him struck down, and I believe there were several days of torture after that." Her voice dropped with disapproval. "An execution was scheduled, but there was either an escape or a daring rescue, and all that's been heard of him since is the increasingly huge price on his head. No doubt there's quite a tale to how he came to be playing bodyguard to the Saxan King's sons."

A bubble of anticipation was filling Aspen's chest. "A tale and a half," he said, unsteadily. "Do excuse me. I have to go learn to cook."

ooOoo

How was it possible to explore a city with someone without really looking at him? It wasn't even true that Dj-Delmar had been so perfectly hiding his light under the Guard Dog's bushel. On reflection, Aspen could name more than a few times where they'd glimpsed a flash of a fiery tail, which vanished before they realised they should be impressed. Well, the Phoenix had been flushed into the open now, and marked for the most intensive study.

Aspen, catching the man up before he'd quite reached the Saxan's mansion, decided first-off to think of him as Leton, which was a nice compromise between the two identities. Leton was just short of six foot tall, lean muscle rather than brawn, though the leather cuirass made him look bulkier. His skin was darkish tan with a coppery note, his black hair fingertip length, with the slightest suggestion of a curl. His hands looked strong. A nice jaw line and a narrow face, neither overly handsome nor unsightly. Creases were carved down from an aquiline nose, and a couple more speared up between his brows to give him a faintly wicked look. Mouth held thin and flat. With a full measure of contempt in black eyes as he noticed Aspen's survey.

This was going to be a challenge.

"And you've been nothing but disapproving from day one," Aspen remarked, more than ready to leap to the point. "I'd love to know what I've done to deserve such scorn."

"Would you?" Leton, pushing open a gate into a kitchen garden, didn't disguise his doubt. "Very well. Nothing. You've done nothing."

"You don't mean that in a good way, do you?"

The look said it all, but then that dispassionate shrug, passing the matter off into indifference. "You're what, twenty-five?" Leton asked, more weary than annoyed as he worked on the strapping of his armour. "Powerful, with a master like that, and not at first glance stupid. Yet you're still 'prentice, more interested in enjoying yourself than actually contributing anything. A waste of talent, a waste of your Master's time. A waste of air."

Aspen laughed, not the least bit miffed by this assessment. "Surely I have some decorative value? Though, to be strictly accurate, I'm not the Diamond's 'prentice. I was 'prenticed to the Regent's Court Mage, but lost that when King Aluster demoted him. The Diamond said he'll 'prentice me if I reach a certain standard, gave me a list of a few *thousand* things I should read, and is going to test me on it at midsummer."

"What chance of passing?"

"Minimal if all the learning texts are in Essan. Mind you, the Diamond's standards for 'prentice would probably get me passed up to Maja in all but the loftiest schools." Aspen shrugged. "Do you actually need any help, or do I just get to watch?"

Leton, who had been methodically stripping off his uniform, looked over absently and met Aspen's very appreciative gaze. He snorted. "Dare I ask how you are at staunch spells?"

"Well, I've got them in theory. The Diamond's list started me out with a very pragmatic set of basic spells to memorise, before moving on to theory. I suspect he shares your views on people being useful."

"Fine. There's a stillroom off the kitchen in there. Bring back bandages, scissors, a towel. And some honey and a mortar and pestle from the kitchen."

Aspen did as he was told, though who knew how the Poet or Pup would react if they found him wandering about. He came back quietly because his Phoenix, dressed only in thin draws, was tipping buckets of water over his head. That was indeed a thing worth seeing: muscles sliding sweet and clean beneath bare wet skin of paler bronze, the recent wounds bright stripes over a spattering of white lines on arms and legs. Aspen had once bedded a mercenary so seamed she made jokes about having been cobbled together from spare parts. That Leton had so few, and only one knot on his ribs, was no doubt a sign of his skill. There was no obvious record of torture, but then it was so much more efficient to hurt someone with magic. Magic could shred nerves, spirit, without damaging flesh, so you could do it again and again...

Veering his mind away from the image of his Phoenix bound, broken, Aspen surveyed the current injuries. Several shallow cuts on the upper arms, and deeper wounds on one thigh and the left forearm. None of them seemed really bad: Leton had certainly been meandering about in true guardly fashion, acting as if they meant nothing.

And in what cause had he gained them? Had he been right about the prisoner merely taunting them? Playing with them like toys.

A shiver ran the length of Aspen's spine. The conjuring could easily have killed them, cut Leton down in seconds if it had chosen. Even the Diamond's magery mightn't have been enough, if it had really been out for their blood, instead of making some obscure point. How were they supposed to fight back?

"And why would Suldar care one way or the next if we got ourselves slaughtered?" he wondered aloud.

"If the assumption's right, we've a quick way to find out." Leton's eyes flicked to his sword. "You want to volunteer?"

Delighted fascination rushed through Aspen's veins. How had he ever thought he was dealing with a mere

Guard Dog? He was going to get this man into bed if it killed him.

"Maybe I'll work my way up to it," he said, offering the towel. "I take it you don't want me to do more than seal the cuts?"

Leton looked irritably down at the slash on his thigh, which was trickling water-diluted strawberry toward his knee. "I can't cook and sleep. Just do the leg, and this." He touched the knotted cloth about his arm.

"Right." Aspen lined his collection of objects along a convenient windowsill. "Maybe you'd better sit down."

"Wait." A brief excursion into the garden, and back with a handful of leaves. "Do the leg first." He snagged the honey, sat down with the mortar and pestle, and began making green paste.

Not entirely sure whether this was for dinner or an excursion into herbal healing, Aspen took a deep breath and brought back a day last autumn, just after the Diamond had said possibly-maybe and his enthusiasm had still been high. A Staunch spell, a common but difficult casting because it meant dealing with a body's living magic, which wasn't quite the same thing as arcane magic, and resented any interference.

The words were there and waiting, so Aspen pushed them, fiery bubbles from his tongue. He stared directly at the biggest slash so that he wouldn't think about the man. Staunch was something that required the most focused intent, to push arcane power into flesh, to seal and knit and hurry along what was going to happen anyway. To not wreck what you meant to fix.

The edges of the fresh, freely bleeding wound melted together and scabbed over, the skin around it flushing angry red as the body reacted to the change. Aspen switched focus to Leton's arm, pushing it a few days along but no more, because the forced healing would sap Leton's energy. Too much and he'd be exhausted, maybe even pass out.   Aspen had heard of people being *killed* by Staunch.

More than a little smug at how well the casting had gone, Aspen watched his Phoenix flex his arm experimentally.   The edge of the scab tore, but it didn't split, and Leton nodded approval before smearing a glob of green honey over the damage.

Glowing inside, Aspen proffered bandages, scissors and water at appropriate intervals, and planned seduction. There was a chance his Phoenix could be brought to the hand by the simple lure of enthusiastic pleasure, but he was certainly one to slap down a straightforward assault. No, Aspen would have to draw his interest, and after that little homily about contributing, he did not have to look far for a plan of attack.

Convenient that it matched his campaign to win the Diamond.   If the golden Aloren happened to think being *useful* was a marvellous thing as well, then, Sun!   It was obviously meant to be.

Smiling to himself, Aspen let his Phoenix go get dressed, and dutifully cleaned up.

ooOoo

"Quick, Rua.   You distract him while I grab one of those pies."

Aspen blocked the oven door.   "They're not done yet."

"Then they should stop smelling so marvellous," Gentian said, poking her nose under the covers of the dishes keeping warm on the table.   "Roast chicken too. You've done us proud."

He swatted her away.   "It'll go cold.   Has the Diamond said to start?   Leton went to change."

"We have been tasked to help as needed," Rua said, smiling at him with easy good humour.   "This is a party."

"I think we all need one," Aspen said, leaving the pies to fend for themselves and crossing to squeeze Rua happily. "You're looking better. You look marvellous, in fact." She was out of uniform, had found a gorgeous Fae robe of plummy red. Even Gentian was wearing a fetching little shift that made her look delicately edible.

"I have slept while you have worked," Rua said, looking ruefully at the pink lines on her wrists. "My lord insisted on returning us to as whole a skin as could be managed."

"So where do we start?" Gentian asked, eyeing the array on the table.

"Take out the wine and spirits," Leton said, striding in and glancing around the room. It was, Aspen imagined, the exact same quick and comprehensive survey that the man would give a row of troops.

Briskly, the guised Phoenix began transferring the contents of the last bubbling pots to the array of serving bowls. He'd managed to find some Fae clothing that resembled his uniform, but rather crisper and less grimed with wear. Very nice.

Offering up a suitably brisk salute, Aspen gathered four of the bottles, Rua following his lead. They were eating in a far more formal setting this time, quite the little social gathering, and would then move to a cosy lounging room to brainstorm over the brandy.

The long, polished dining table gleamed with porcelain and crystal. Seventeen places as the Diamond had instructed, cutting the divide between royalty and lesser folk perhaps because it pleased him to acknowledge Leton's worth. It pleased Aspen too, and he began to hum, whisking about, wanting everything to look perfect.

Rua was watching him with that quizzical smile. "He is a remarkable man, is he not?"

"A god among mortals," Aspen replied, meaning it for both his prey. Hands free, he captured Rua's and danced her briefly around the room. "Shall we chase him together, Rua?" he asked. "Don't tell me he doesn't tempt you."

She laughed, full-throated, wholehearted. "You are the small boy at the candies stall," she said. "Eyes like saucers, barely knowing where to start."

"I'll eat my fill and go back for seconds," he assured her, then shook his head. "Sun, Rua, I never thought I'd enjoy cooking. I think I'm good at it."

"And your teacher so inspiring." Indulgent amusement.

"Infinitely. Honestly, actually. Leton just makes it seem so natural. Though I can't say I thought much of the chicken-plucking. We soaked grains to stuff them with, mixed with all manner of greenery, and basted them with the juices. I'm dying to see what it tastes like. Speaking of which–" He hurried them back, determined to have nothing go wrong with this meal.

They found Gentian leaning over an empty jug, casting with immense concentration. Conjuration, Aspen realised, and wondered if she was equal to the task. Creating things out of magic alone required a fixity of purpose, an exact visualisation, and was more than power-hungry. Few could make anything complex.

Keeping quiet, since it wouldn't do to distract her, he crept a little closer, and was just in time to see the jug fill with something thick and milky.

"Cream?" he guessed.

"For the pies," Gentian said, sitting back with a sigh. "Pies must have cream. It's one of the laws."

"It, ah, it's got little black specks in it."

"I know." She dipped a spoon into the jug, and licked it with decadent pleasure. "Also sugar. I've an *enormous* sweet tooth."

"It's still got little black specks in it," Aspen said, shaking his head and smiling. *She* was in a good mood. Surely the Diamond hadn't–?

Leton took a spoon and sampled the cream, then nodded. "Very good. We'd best get on."

"Ants?" Aspen suggested, wondering why no-one else thought cream shouldn't have little black specks. "Pepper?"

Gentian just laughed, and went to pick up one of the salvers, but Rua, with an affectionate squeeze of his shoulder, murmured: "Vanilla seed. Hurry now."

"Place the main dishes along the centre of the table," Leton ordered, and led them like a daily-drilled troop to get the whole of the main meal out on the table just in time for the Diamond to lead their guests into the room. A dazzling array of royalty, all dressed up and nowhere else to go.

Aspen put on his sunniest smile and played waiter with Rua until everyone was seated and had a full glass of wine. They'd even made juice for the children, though the look Kassen gave him suggested *she* thought herself more than old enough for a dark red. Fully aware he was providing his erstwhile master with a great deal of amusement, Aspen made an elaborate show of bowing to Leton before he lifted the covers. Leton looked tempted to roll his eyes, and for a second a very ambiguous expression flickered over Chenar's face, but the appreciative murmur of royalty bore the moment out.

It was a charmed meal. By some unspoken agreement, everyone pretended that the Fair did not exist, that there was no hidden ceiling of stone to force them into company, and they weren't batting about like moths getting nowhere. Aurak Bes and the Diamond, with a faintly suspicious degree of coordination, coaxed the conversation along, steering clear of dangerous shoals and pricking bubbles of animosity well before they threatened to burst.

And the heirs of the West let them, and enjoyed themselves: laughed and told anecdotes and left their daggers sheathed. The food was an immense success, and Aspen would swear by every lover he'd tumbled that it was the best he'd ever eaten. Even the cream with specks. When they moved into the lounge it was difficult to throw off the air of celebration. They settled in chairs, little Prince Chiall more asleep than awake, the two Crown Princes bracketing Aloren, Aspen carefully placing himself not too close, not too far from his Phoenix. There was more than a hint of reluctance as they looked to the Diamond to open discussions.

But it was Aurak Bes who, warm smile fading from his lips, said: "I cannot find the Gods here."

"The *sel-deseva* failed?" Lady Dhara looked disappointed, even though it was a rare thing for a *sel-deseva* – a call for an answer from the Gods – to be answered.

"Definitively. But more than that, after the temples here were located by our explorers I visited both and spent time in prayer. It is not unexpected, in a Sun's Circle shut from the sky, not to feel any echo of His regard, but never have I knelt before an arluna and felt nothing. This shield is quite outside my experience. To exclude the gods themselves..." He shook his head.

"Suldar is our Sun and Moon," Seylon Heresar said airily. He leaned toward Gentian, who he'd kept close to all evening. "This could give Suldar a motive for not wanting us killed. If Lady Moon cannot gather us back, this valley will end up filled with ghosts."

"Would that bother her so much? She's more than powerful enough to ward against ghosts." Gentian shrugged, apparently oblivious to Heresar's evident interest. Aspen was going to have to sit the woman down and give her a lecture on flirtation. Or, since it was Heresar, maybe not.

"We, too, have something to report," Lady Dhara said and touched her eldest daughter's arm. Desseron, who was a less-frozen miniature of Princess Kestia, straightened nervously, but nodded.

"We do not believe the people here ran," she said, each word clear and careful. "We have discovered no signs of flight, only of abandonment, of objects dropped and left.

But at the same time, no bodies, or burials. Every *person* in the valley – but not the animals – must have...disappeared at the same instant." Since this matched what everyone had already seen, there was a general murmur of agreement, and Desseron dropped her chin to acknowledge it before adding: "But people came here after."

"You have found evidence of this, Highness?" Aurak Bes asked gravely.

"One of the houses near where we entered. Since it was our gate, and the illusion shows a road leading up the hills to that point, we looked there first. In most of the kitchens they were preparing a big meal, like this happened just before dinner. In one they'd dropped flour and wine, and people had walked through it. Not any of us. The footprints looked the right size for Fae, and something smaller, with claws. But it looked like they hadn't walked there 'til the wine had dried sticky. Days after it happened."

"Hardly surprising that Fae came here after," Jurasel said, cutting short the exchange of proud parental glances between Desseron's mothers. "How does this advance us?"

"It suggests that our Lady Suldar didn't shut herself away without discussion with someone outside this shield," Seylon Heresar replied, quick as ever to distract his royals from fighting. "That the Fair know the details of the disaster, know that this city is still here, know where that door is – probably wrote that knot of script. The question, which I'll refer to you brother, is what they'll do about it."

The Diamond, who had been playing his usual trick of just sitting there listening, inclined his head to Desseron with pointed courtesy. "I would be obliged, Highness, if you would show me the particular house where you found these footprints," he said. "There may well be some significance in the location."

"Of course, Lord Magister," the girl said.

"As to the Fair, I understand them to be bound by the Ban of a former Queen against even speaking of Telsandar's past. Only Desteret can countermand the rulings of her predecessors, and that she will be...reluctant to do. I would not rely on the Fair to rescue us." The corner of his mouth curled the tiniest fraction and Aspen, who knew the Diamond's expressions well, shivered at this one.

"You're such an optimist, Aristide," Heresar said. He was making a little show of gazing at Gentian's profile through the amber contents of his glass. "It does make one wonder, though, just what is going on out there in the sun."

"Nothing any of us would like, I'd wager." Jurasel, who'd planted himself on a footstool close to the fire, looked from Heresar to his sister. "Who do you suppose our beloved mother favours now? Semille?"

Kestia's expression was unpromising, but then she touched Desseron's shoulder, and lifted her own. "Does it matter?"

Jurasel's eyes went wide, then he laughed. "No. Amazing, isn't it? Abduction has unexpected advantages." He toasted her. "But to return to the point. So far these little get-togethers have been very interesting, and we've learned dribs and drabs of Fae history, and achieved nothing much. Something happened long ago, and for some reason we were brought here, and someone is amusing themselves making pointless displays with our powers. Wonderful. But we haven't made any progress toward getting out. And that being the case, I think we should start looking at the practicalities of staying here."

Aloren, languorous in a high-backed chair between the two princes, lifted one hand.

"Are our researches so fruitless?" Her slow smile spoke of secrets and mysteries, caught them all up in its spell and left them envying the Diamond his brilliance as sapphire and crystal pulled honey-gold eyes. "I should like to know what other words have been erased from the Fae language."

She'd scored a hit. The Diamond blinked, then said: "Your instincts are as ever acute, Highness," obviously meaning the compliment. "Very few, as I said, but one other that is more than relevant to this discussion. Selvar. Dawn."

Aspen missed Gentian's reaction. He caught instead Heresar's response, the curiosity and heightened attention focused on a woman who was now looking abstractly into the fire, face composed and posture relaxed. What had the Duke seen? Shock, anger, pure hurt? Well, Aspen had warned her against loving the Diamond. One-sided devotion was like breathing knives.

"And why in the name of all that's sacred didn't you tell us that before?" Jurasel exclaimed, too astonished to be angry. "Sun, Couerveur! Anyone would think you wanted to stay here!"

"And wonder what else you haven't told us." Chenar was almost sad, as if he, like Gentian, had expected the Diamond to have shared his thoughts sooner.

The mellow ease of the evening had been stripped away. They were once again adversaries, stolen, in danger, and less than pleased.

"Names have power," the Diamond replied. The mildest of tones, and it held them all, banished the last shreds of comfort and left each one of them alone in a dark, lonely place. Names have power. They had met dusk, Suldar. Did they want to meet the dawn?

"As for research–" The Diamond lifted an equivocal hand. "My attempts to scry for records mentioning Suldar, or the events leading up to Telsandar's disaster, have brought...curious results, so I have been casting about more or less at random for texts. The official histories, those kept by the land's Aviemptor, have been removed–"

"By Suldar?" Lady Dhara, arm protectively around Desseron's shoulders, frowned as if the lack was the Diamond's own fault.

"More likely by a representative of The Deeping's Queen, before the valley was sealed. The Fair do not care to forget their mistakes."

"For pity's sake, Couerveur," Jurasel interrupted. "Does it matter what you haven't found, what you don't know? You must have at least made a few educated guesses on why we've been brought here. Spit it out, man."

An almost compassionate expression flickered over the Diamond's face. "Very well." He sat back in his chair, and the firelight caught pale lashes and turned them gold. "Suldar named herself Telsandar's Regent, not its Lord. Who does she hold the throne for?"

"The Lady Dawn one would presume," Heresar said.

"If the name is correct, and was abandoned for the same reason as Suldar's, then we must remember again the power of naming. It is at dawn that Magister Calder senses something trapped and trying to escape. Dawn when your barge was snatched from the Galassas. If you wish to try to shield yourself from the usurpation of your powers, then I suggest that you make your attempts just prior to first light.

"The names themselves are typical of the Fair. Dawn and Dusk. Times of transition. And in Dusk we are shown what change was being made. More than long-lived, more than powerful, more than Fair. I have seen no sign that Suldar eats or sleeps. I am not certain she even breathes. She is what the Fair, in their arrogance, thought to become."

"Gods." The Aurak breathed the word, as if it were too heavy to speak.

"Monsters." The Diamond said the word with more than even his usual precision. "We saw Suldar draw the living magic from the garden plants, simply by touching them. We can only speculate on how her mother brought her to term. And what Suldar thought of the creatures who made her."

"Her and her sister." Jurasel was gazing fixedly at his own sister. "You can breed your children for power, but you've precious little control over what they'll make of themselves."

The Diamond's faint, sweet smile was sufficient reminder of his famously toxic relationship with his own mother. "I have found absolutely no sign of another Fae in this valley, let alone one so easy to detect as a sister to Suldar. If there is a prisoner here, the shielding of their cell must be absolute."

"And what is this place if it's not a prison?"

"A haven." Gentian had whispered the word, was staring at Aristide disbelievingly. "It's trying to get *in*."

The Diamond held her eyes: a grave moment of consideration that brought Aspen cold shudders. Then he looked back at Cya's Crown Prince. "You asked for my guess on why we've been brought here, Prince Jurasel? I think we are siege engines. As soon as this Other has our range, our role will be to somehow bring down the walls of Telsandar's Heart. To attack Suldar."

And in the appalled silence which followed it was Aspen's Phoenix who roused himself from the Guard Dog's shadows to murmur: "No need to plan for a prolonged stay then."

Chapter Fourteen

The worst thing about an increasing sense of impending doom was not being able to do anything to escape it. No more than she could escape her mornings.

Gentian made her preparations an hour before dawn, trying to be practical in the face of dire warnings and certain discomfort. Foremost was to belatedly put together a makeshift litter tray. The Fair, in all their genius, hadn't bred pets which came already toilet trained, and the gift of a kitten brought practical considerations. Then she wrote out the spell she would use, ate a light breakfast, and stripped all but a sheet from the bed, adding a mound of pillows so that she could prop herself up. Two jugs, one of water and the other very sweet lemonade. Books full of pictures.

Finally, a gift brought from Atlarus for her father, a day-candle scented with orange oil and clove. In the long wait for tomorrow's dawn she wanted to look at it and think of orange groves, and her father's love of scent, and see how much longer she had to endure.

Out in the night she felt a whisper of power, distant casting. A little too far away for her to read intent, but she could guess the others were following Aristide's suggestion about shields. It was to be a morning full of experiments. Closer to, the murmur of the *saecstra* warned that her own was about to begin.

Last night had been bad timing. She'd been determined to enjoy herself, to buoy herself up in preparation for this, and had, right up until she'd come face to face with Aristide's capacity to hurt her. Not a deliberate thing, and well within character, but she'd stopped being quite so diverted by this unexpected passion. And he'd followed with a theory she couldn't quite refute, even after Princess Kestia had asked why Suldar didn't simply wipe them from existence. The party had broken on a distinct note of trepidation.

"What doesn't the valley's shield keep out?" she asked the man who came to stand in her doorway.

"Raw power. Your morning visitor." Those brilliant eyes narrowed thoughtfully. "Darest."

"Hardly coincidence that all this started a few days after I returned."

"Unlikely," he agreed, with what she considered unnecessary readiness, moving to settle in the chair by her bed. "Did the name strike any chord?"

"No. But it doesn't seem wrong, either. I would like to know where It – she – actually *is* if she's trying to get into this valley rather than out of it. I would certainly hope we'd have noticed her wandering about Darest. And there didn't seem to be any hint of her in that area of no magic which surrounds this place."

He answered this with a silence that was admonitory, the kind of pause a teacher would use to prompt a good student to think a little harder. Resentful, and feeling suddenly vulnerable, Gentian drew her knees up to her chest. Because she knew full well the most likely answer, one he hadn't spelt out the previous night. Selvar was nowhere.

"There are no Darien legends of ghostly Fae stalking about. And it goes quite against the idea of Suldar being Regent because she has an elder sister, if that sister is dead."

But it would begin to answer the question of why the heirs of the West had been brought here: the lost dead, those trapped between the Sun and Moon's embrace, could draw precious little power without a physical anchor. A ghost would have reason to usurp the strength of the living.

"You don't even need to be true-mage to see a ghost. If that's what she's become, why am I the only one to sense her?"

"Not only you." Aristide used the very mild tone she'd come to associate with things that annoyed him. "The Fair do not dwell in Darest for a reason."

Gentian stared at him. "My parents asked the aid of more than one of the Fair," she said, voice low and face hot. "They claimed to be unable to detect whatever it was waking me."

"Probably true in the most precise sense. But remember Suldar's words to you."

"'...you are not of the Blood'."

"Her surprise was that you were not Fae, not that you were woken. It must touch them in some way."

"And the *region* is held to be tainted." Gentian blinked, then thrust the possibilities away with a quick motion of her hand. "They do make it hard to like them." She gazed at Aristide, who had lived among the Fair and was equally trying. "I would have preferred not to have learned Its name that way," she added, wishing her voice would stop trying to stifle itself. She had thought them at least working to the same purpose, allies, whatever else he felt.

"I would have preferred you not learn that name at all," Aristide replied and, when her eyes widened, added: "Do you really wish this thing to gain even more power over you?"

"I should like some power over It," she said, with utmost sincerity. "And–" She frowned at him. "And, yes. Given the disparity in our strength, knowing Its name would not give me the advantage. Rather the reverse. Must you *always* be right?"

The corners of his eyes creased fractionally, giving them a warmer light, though his mouth did not alter. It brought a little frisson of awareness, underlining the fact that they were together and alone, and she sat in her night-clothes on a very large bed. Just a hint of surprise surfaced in his eyes, and they both went very still.

But then pure sardonic amusement swallowed all else, and he looked past her, drawing power. A moment later there was a strangled squawk, and a thud from the room next to hers. Aspen. A long pause followed this rude awakening, then muffled thumps suggested he was trying to dress quickly in the dark.

As a diversion this was excellent, and Gentian allowed it, appreciating the time to analyse that brief moment of exposure. He found her attractive? He found that funny?

"Does Aspen really do nothing at Court but gossip and look decorative?" she asked, to fill the silence.

"Choraide's own description, I assume?" Aristide accepted the change of subject without an eye-blink. "He is known as a devotee of scandal and conquest."

"And takes a good deal of pride in it," she said, having spent a portion of the previous night not quite enjoying listening to Aspen outline his plan to snare his three current favourites.

Aristide was still looking highly entertained – by himself, or just her? He tipped a hand to one side with a suggestion of a shrug. "Choraide serves the useful purpose of providing the Rathen Champion with a friend and confidant, and has proven an able intelligencer on her behalf, capable of keeping his mouth closed on occasion. If he poured the same amount of energy into developing his talent he would be formidable. As it is – perhaps Captain Djol will serve our immediate need by making a cook of him."

The subject of their conversation came at double-pace through the door, drew himself up and offered Aristide a deep and magnificent courtesy, rich with reproach. "How may I serve, my Lord, my Master? Your every whim, your most passing desire–"

"Sit down." The tone was flat, disinterested, and those sapphire and crystal eyes turned briefly toward the window to remind them of dawn's approach. Dawn. "What did you use to keep yourself awake, Magister Calder?"

She handed him the spell she'd written down, and drank off a glass of water while he read it. "No, not something my parents taught me. I found it in a collection in Goldenrod's attics. I've ancestors with exciting pasts, it seems."

This earned her a long, steady survey. Aristide was not pleased, but he made no comment, crediting her with the judgment to set this course – or at least seeing the lack of alternatives. Experiments limited to one moment each morning did not suit a race against time.

He handed the piece of paper to Aspen before beginning to cast, and Gentian, wary of being caught late, followed suit. Her spell was concise, designed to be held on trigger, and she had no trouble binding it off ready to be used. Looking back, she found Aspen staring at her in horror.

"This–"

"–is necessary. I can't shield against or nullify whatever makes me sleep. This overwhelms it."

"But...it'll *hurt* you."

Genuine abhorrence. Gentian found herself suddenly very grateful for Aspen. "All things being equal, I'd rather cast this than wake to It," she told him. "It's having to spend the day in bed afterwards that makes it a problem."

"The aftermath you described sounds very like a form of spell backlash," Aristide commented, as he looked down from the knot of divination he'd set on the ceiling.

"The fever and aches? I know. But not the increasing exhaustion." She shrugged. Lady Arista had fastened on those symptoms as well, and she had expected this. "You're the one always talking about doing things from fact, not supposition. See what your divinations tell you."

"As you suggest, Magister," he said, with an unexpectedly respectful inclination of his head. He may not have baulked at the nature of the experiment, but it seemed he honoured the cost.

Gentian lost herself to him all over again, astonished desire threatening to swallow her whole just as the Moon ate the Sun in his eyes. Only the approach of dawn was enough to drag her free of the eclipse and she looked away, feeling impossibly exposed, on uneven ground. What had happened to her, that the smallest taste of approval from this man could overwhelm her?

There was, at least, little time to feel embarrassed. Before sleep could take her Gentian tightened her grip on her knees and curled down to shut her audience away. Reluctant but resigned she whispered the trigger, and burned.

It was the thought of fire, a conviction of heat. Embers swimming beneath her skin, boiling her blood. She screamed, or tried not to, wasn't sure, only that it hurt, that she was dying, burning, that every part of her was char and ash and a dragon was eating her *bones*–!

And not.

How triumphant she'd been, that first time. A twelve year girl who'd cast a torture spell, whose screams had brought her parents running. And through the haze of her body's shocked aftermath she'd gloated that she hadn't slept, that she'd won. It would never touch her again. Her father had yelled at her, the first time ever, a furious scolding. And she'd shouted back, so angry that he wouldn't understand how necessary it was, that anything was better. Anything.

Then the tingling of outraged nerves had given way to an oppressive ache, and the spell's false fire transmuted to fever. Her day of triumph became an ordeal and she'd marked the cost of battle by the terror in her parents' eyes. Another lesson: she was no better able to fix this thing than anyone else.

Gentian took a slow breath, unlocking frozen muscles, then grimaced because a mountain had come to sit on her head. And magic had become a thing that itched and rubbed: the divination Aristide had set, the *saecstra*, and whatever he was casting now, all scratching unpleasantly behind her. It was only going to get worse, which was the other edge to the sword of knowing what would come next. She was already beginning to sweat.

Turning gingerly, Gentian found Aristide unpacking the divination he'd set above her head. His face was abstract, revealing no hint of triumph or frustration – or sympathy. Aspen was for some reason glaring at her, but right now Gentian frankly couldn't care enough to wonder why. She shut him from her attention and watched Aristide, beautiful and opaque. The man had had a lifetime's practice giving nothing away.

"If you would cast, Magister?" he said, having finished reviewing the inaudible results of his divination. She wanted very much to know what it had told him, but instead obediently drew true-magic to spark the candle to flame, and had to swallow against the accompanying rush of nausea. Her head pounded.

"Classic indicators of spell backlash." She'd never heard his voice so expressionless. "At the same time, absolutely no sign that you cast anything but a successfully triggered piece of unpleasantness. It is possible that your spell covered another, almost negligible expenditure of power, but the backlash for a minor casting would not justify the effect on you. Can you write out for me a general history of past attempts to diagnose this? With the obvious avenues of investigation unproductive, we will need to look for another approach, and I would like to avoid covering the same ground."

"What I can remember of it," Gentian said, wearily. "A great deal went on when I was very young."

Aristide nodded and rose, glancing at the ceiling as he reset his divination. "We will follow the development of this weakness, to see whether it reveals its source. Will you need anything during the day, Magister? I can place a numbing on you."

"No." She said that a little too forcefully, and winced. "No, my mother tried that. I feel anything cast on me too strongly for it to work."

"Then we will check with you around midday."

They departed, leaving her looking unenthusiastically up at the divination. At least the *saecstra* was now receding into the distance. It was going to be a long day, made longer by the reflection that it was wasted suffering, that for all Aristide's much-vaunted mastery, he was achieving exactly as much as his predecessors.

Nothing.

ooOoo

Gentian had discovered a great fondness for the kitten. While laboriously trying to write some kind of account of past failures, she had watched the little creature prowling about the confines of the room, far more confidant than the previous night's hiding-under-the-furniture performance. The return of Aristide and Aspen at lunchtime sent the creature back under a table, but after that she had apparently decided Gentian was an acceptable being, and allowed herself to be coaxed on to the bed by a piece of string.

This passed the time perfectly for Gentian, who couldn't settle to anything that required thought. The kitten savaged the string with satisfying enthusiasm, then settled down to be tickled, only occasionally deciding that Gentian's fingers were also worthy adversaries. Gentian was wishing Aspen would come back so she could send him out for milk when there was a light tap at the door, and she looked over to see Prince Rydan holding a large bouquet of flowers.

"Would you like a visitor?" he asked, obviously uncomfortable. "Maistrice Choraide said you were ill."

And your brother sent you straight here to try to gain a little ground, Gentian thought. Neither of the Saxans had tried to break Seylon's monopoly of her the previous night, but she had gained the distinct impression that she now primarily represented a piece of one-upmanship between Sax and Cya. Any idea of the game bothering Aristide had no doubt died after the single, sardonic look he'd bent on his brother's performance.

"I was hoping someone would come," she told Rydan truthfully, for all she found it unspeakably boring when people chased her for enhance-the-bloodline reasons. "And should thank you again for the kitten. I've been glad of her today."

This produced a more natural smile. "Then I'm glad as well," he said, promptly. "Have you thought of a name for her?"

"Koltai. A famous hunter in Atlaran legend. Could you do me a favour, Highness, and bring me up something for her to eat? I think there's some leftovers from last night's dinner."

"Of course. I'll find a vase for these as well," he said, waving the bouquet with just the faintest air of disparagement before heading out the door. Gentian shook her head, and stroked Koltai's stomach until he came back with the flowers in a vase, a kitten-sized bowl of milk, and a full jug – using true-magic as extra hands. "I noticed you had nothing to drink," he said, replacing the two empty pitchers by her bed. "I remember, oh, a few years ago now I had Semnes Fever, and was thirsty all the time."

Mildly impressed, Gentian thanked him and accepted the mug he poured out for her. He set the plate on the corner of the bed and they occupied themselves with watching Koltai.

At least, Gentian did. Rydan spent his time casting sidelong glances under long lashes. She supposed herself to be a less than appealing subject for courtship, all flushed and sweaty and lank. "It's a kind of spell backlash," she told him. "A not very successful experiment."

He nodded, seating himself tentatively on the far side of the bed. "So Maistrice Choraide said. You will forgive me for disturbing you, I hope." Then, unexpectedly, he snorted. "And for the wholly transparent pursuit as well. You must be wishing a pile of rock would fall on me and Lord Heresar both. Will you allow me to stay a little while, so I can make a pretence of having won your good graces?"

"Is it so important to do so?" she asked, pleasantly surprised.

"Easier, I guess. Dutifully obeying a long-standing–" Cheeks reddening, he met her eyes with obvious effort. "Games aside, Magister, is there any chance you would be interested in a contract as a third? And playing the part of leverage?"

Gentian, not quite up to dealing with propositions, tried to puzzle out the reason for it. "Captain Djol?" she hazarded.

"This is hardly a compliment to you, I know. But the Varpatten reputation is such that it might just be possible, should you show a partiality for Leton, that I could turn this encounter to *his* advantage." He stopped, gauging the expression on her face, and sighed. "Oh, ignore me. Pipedreams, I know, but I can see so few ways to help him."

"Is his situation so very bad? Your brother seems to hold him in esteem." she asked, struggling to keep up through the wool in her head.

"My brother isn't the problem. And he deserves better than this bodyguard role. Anyone can see that. But–" Rydan pulled a face, then leaned forward hesitantly. "I watched you speaking to him, after the battle. He gave you his sword."

"I asked to see it," Gentian replied neutrally. "It's an interesting piece."

"I've never before seen him allow anyone to touch it." Rydan searched her face, then continued slowly: "He has been with us six months, a little more. My father produced him one day, set him in charge of our safety, and...gloats over him. When he was tasked to be my swordmaster, I began to see why. But there is more to it, I know. Father would object to my courting Leton, I think, unless I can provide a high incentive."

"Like the Varpatten bloodline."

"But if you were going to have children to benefit someone else's ambitions, you'd have done so already." His voice was resigned, unsurprised, but long lashes swept down to hide disappointment.

"It's the first time anyone's suggested I rescue someone in the process. But, truly, Captain Djol doesn't strike me as a man in need of help. Perhaps he isn't exactly where he'd like to be, but–" She wondered how to put this. "He's not without resource."

"No." A faint smile, which made Gentian wonder what *she* looked like when talking about Aristide. Then Rydan lifted a hand to close the subject, and glanced toward the window where the light was shifting past late afternoon. "But sometimes being resourceful can't be enough. At least we've stopped these puppet games."

"You shielded yourself this morning?"

"Oh yes." There was grim satisfaction to his words. "Of course, we don't know for certain if that's what's made the difference, but, well, it's been a quiet day. Now if we could only make some progress toward getting *out* of this place."

Gentian blinked, then pretended not to notice his sudden check and change of expression. That wasn't about Captain Djol. Rydan – the Saxans – faced some urgency that had lent an edge of gnawing anxiety to the exclamation. And, for all the talk of thirds and children, he was not about to confide in her, so Gentian obligingly made a business of sinking into her pillows.

"I should let you rest," Rydan said promptly, standing up and offering her a pretty courtesy. "I hope you're feeling better tomorrow."

"Thank you. So do I."

She smiled wearily as he turned away and, forewarned by the whisper of the *saecstra*, was unsurprised when he came face to face with Aristide at the door. But the Saxan prince only bowed again, murmured "Lord Magister" in a colourless voice, and escaped. Aristide glanced after him, but he was not revealing any of his thoughts this afternoon.

Aspen, following Aristide into the room, pantomimed salacious delight: "Too, too popular, Gentian. We're going to have to give you a stick to fight them off with."

"Perhaps you can guard my door." She looked at Aristide. "Is there some reason the Saxans would need to get out of here more than urgently?"

"They have misplaced Atlarus' favourite lord. Beyond that? Quite possibly, but they have not told me it."

He was studying her intently, but she couldn't guess whether it was her deterioration or Rydan's visit that occupied him. Aspen made a show of admiring the flowers, shooting her mischievous glances all the while. Gentian checked the candle as it neared its halfway mark, and longed for tomorrow.

Resetting his divination, Aristide sat in one of the chairs by her bed, frowning faintly. "There is no sign you have been drawing power over the course of the day, nor any hint of an external casting. Yet the toll on you is evident, far greater than could be expected from a minor fever. I suspect that divining for arcane interference will continue to take us nowhere, and that we must focus on this ability of yours to sense...spirit. Since no-one has ever come close to detecting your attacker–"

He stopped. Perhaps her expression had changed, she didn't know, but fine brows drew together as he surveyed her closely, and then those exquisite lips lifted to a sweetly edged curve. "It would help immeasurably, Magister, if you gave up this habit of holding back relevant details."

Gentian couldn't help but laugh, making her head jangle in protest. "Do as I say, not as I do?" But she couldn't raise the energy to take him to task, and it was true there was one thing she hadn't cared to mention. "How relevant this is without my father here, I can't say..."

"Magister Varpatten has experienced the same attack?"

"A few years ago he told me that he thought, once, that he'd felt It." She shifted uncomfortably, remembering sigil-calling her father on his fiftieth birthday to find him caught in past regrets. "It had been weighing on him, I think. When I was, oh, two or three, I developed a habit of waking hours before dawn. I knew what was coming, knew I couldn't stay awake, so I'd sit there and cry. Father would come and sit with me, to rock me back to sleep." He'd tell her stories, or sing to her, and try to hide the ache in his eyes.

"Once, just once, he had what he thought was a nightmare. He woke feeling crushed, heart pounding, covered in sweat. I was having my usual fit, and he–" She stopped, unhappy to be describing this, though she couldn't remember it at all. "My parents didn't exactly have an easy time raising me. I think the helplessness must have been the worst, beyond the sheer exhaustion involved in these morning performances. They learned early on that trying to touch me when It woke me would invoke a new level of hysterics. I would scratch and kick, even gave my mother a black eye. That morning, my father looked at this screaming brat he was struggling to raise – and threw me across the room. He remembers being overwhelmed by a wave of revulsion, violent aversion. I don't think he's ever forgiven himself for it, for all that he only managed to wind me."

She sighed, wondering why she felt guilty, and whether she should feel angry. "This was well before I had the words to properly explain what I felt each morning. When

I finally was able to describe what was happening to me, he remembered that morning and spent years wondering whether that was a reason or an excuse. But he only felt it the once, and since he's not here it's hardly an experiment we can reproduce."

"You miss the relevant detail, Magister." To Gentian's astonishment there had been something in her tale that had sparked off Aristide's vivid appreciation of the ironic. His eyes were full of it, though he was polite enough to maintain an otherwise solemn expression.

"And what's that?" she asked, struggling with hurt hostility. She did not find her childhood the least bit funny.

"That he was asleep!" Aspen almost shouted it. "You said he woke up, flung you away. You must have both been asleep. And what you felt, he felt. I bet that's an experiment none of your parade of healers thought to try: getting in bed with the patient."

"Contagion," Aristide agreed, less boisterously. "And sympathetic magic. Basic principles which I should not have overlooked. Given our sheer lack of progress so far, we must certainly explore the possibility. Not this coming morning, since we cannot predict the effect of this weakness on the results, but the next will do."

Gentian discovered herself appalled. "You don't have the Varpatten sensitivity," she pointed out, very carefully. "You can't expect to repeat my father's experience."

"We will discover if the key was the person, or the situation." He was the essence of bland logic.

"I don't see what it would achieve, either. We're not trying to establish *what* I feel, but where it comes from. And how to stop it."

"Contagion is something I *do* have divinations to detect." His eyes glittered with unholy enjoyment. "No Magister, if we are to escape this place, we all must make our sacrifices. If you would join me an hour or two before dawn? That should allow me a chance to sleep again, should you wake me. I will leave the door ajar."

He stood and offered her a most eloquent courtesy, then strolled out. Gentian stared after him.

"I'm sorry. I have to do this."

Aspen leaned over the bed and, gripping her by the upper arms, pretended to shake her. "By all that's sacred, Gentian, I could *strangle* you! Two days ago you were gaping at the Diamond like you'd never seen a man before. The most delectable and unapproachable creature in all Darest, and you wanted him. Now, tell me if I've gotten this wrong. Tell me if there was some tiny fragment I failed to notice. Did he or did he not just say he thought it a good idea if you climbed into his bed? Were you or were you not just handed a written invitation to wrap your arms about him? I have been trying to get That Man to look twice at me for *years*, and you don't see what it would *achieve*?!"

"Please stop shouting."

He was instantly contrite, holding out his hands as if he could somehow stop her head from reverberating. Gentian ignored whatever he said next, closing her eyes and just breathing for a little while. When she opened them he was sitting in the chair beside her bed, hands folded in his lap like a child waiting for a scolding.

"That was inexcusable," he said, much subdued. "I'm sorry."

Gentian waved a hand to put it behind them, then sat considering this handsome creature who relished every moment of life and who Aristide would not look at twice. "Tell me about his lovers," she said, knowing she shouldn't go into this, especially when she was at such a low ebb, but the day stretched out before her and she was too fretful to leave well enough alone. "I know there's no-one he's shown any inclination to marry, but who does he trifle with? What are his tastes?"

This produced a strange expression. "Well..." Aspen screwed up his nose. "According to the Court, most recently he's been bedding one of the sons of the Baroness of Leverath. He was seen to talk to the young chub on three separate occasions, at least. Lord Merik's a very pretty creature, and almost certainly the source of the rumours. That's the problem, you see. Lady Arista now, she used to make a great show of choosing her current fancy, and would reward them lavishly afterward, usually with positions in the Court. The Diamond makes deliberate contrast, doesn't openly favour *anyone*, and thus, if you believe everything which is said, has slept with the whole of Darest at least three times over. His own people spread half the stories, you see, to hide whatever's true. Winnowing the wheat from the chaff's an epic challenge."

This didn't surprise her. She'd already seen how very private Aristide was. "And the wheat is?"

Aspen sighed. "Even I can only give you the most likely. One's the Captain of the Guard. She's a flinty-eyed, no-nonsense type, tall and strapping and a lot of people discount her for it. But he practices sword with her at least once a week, and I gather they play some kind of tactical game occasionally. For the Diamond, that's pretty much bosom-friendship, if not more. Then there's Vaselte, the most trusted of his servants. There's long been rumours that the Diamond keeps it in his household, and if that's true Vaselte would certainly be first candidate. Ah, the secrets Vaselte could tell, if only he would." Aspen smiled beatifically.

"Soren now–" He hesitated, then shrugged. "The Champion, you know, she doesn't think he sleeps with *anyone*. Before they destroyed the Rathen Rose, Soren could see everything that went on inside the palace. All the Champions were able to apparently. She says the Diamond didn't so much as breathe on another person in those first weeks after King Aluster's return. And thinks that he doesn't at all, ever, that he's just not interested."

This possibility hadn't occurred to Gentian, and she did not like the dismay it produced. "Do you think she's right?"

"No." Aspen snorted. "I doubt he makes bed-games a priority – the Diamond's married to Darest and always will be – but, I'm sorry, I just can't put Aristide Couerveur and virginal denial in the same room together. Now. Please. Are you going to tell me what flea got into your brain and made you try to turn the Diamond down? You get to go to bed with him!"

A wave of discomfort ran through Gentian at the mere thought. "It's not going to be a romantic interlude." She didn't know which would be worse: trying to sleep beside the person she wanted so much, or waking loathing him. And for what? Another possibility eliminated? Another failure.

"So?" Aspen had no qualms. "All right: he was fairly clearly not inviting passionate adventure. And one thing I can tell you about the Diamond is that you don't go leaping on him without encouragement. There's a few at the Court who learned that to their cost. But you get to hold him. Instead of languishing from afar, you can languish right up close. That Is Not A Bad Thing."

She wondered if Aspen ever saw anything but the best possibilities. "What would you do?"

A faint, dreaming smile. "Surprise him with propriety. Focused on the task, doing nothing but what is correct. But, you know, I sleep naked. And I'd be *there*. Wrapped around him, all warm and inviting. You never know what might happen."

When Gentian only shook her head, he growled, an exasperated little noise. "All right then, look at it this way. If he really wants to try to divine contagious magic – the transference of something happening to you to someone you're in contact with – wouldn't it make infinitely more sense for him to detail *me* to snuggle duty? Rather than set a divination to run while he's sleeping?"

A good point. She allowed herself for a moment to enjoy the possibility that Aristide desired her. He had, at least, stopped glittering at her, and treated her more like a colleague than an opponent. But– "I think he wants to feel It," she said. "After all, he's been fighting It as long as I have. The poison in Darest's heart. It must have come as almost as great a shock to him as it did to me, to give It a name."

"He's been fighting the malison, not the taint." But she'd given him pause, and he frowned at her. "Why in the world, if you're so keen on the Diamond, don't you make the least shift to fix his interest? Compliment him a little, act glad to have him around, compose a few love songs. Show some faint measure of enthusiasm when he invites you to his bed."

"Because I don't want that, Aspen."

He rolled his eyes. "Stop changing your story. You're the one squirming at the thought of snuggling up against him. Were you quizzing me about his love life out of pure intellectual curiosity then?"

She looked at the candle again, thinking about her father, about her parents and the joy they found in each other. The day felt longer than ever.

Aspen shifted impatiently. "Don't tell me it's just that you don't want to chase him? I'm not saying he's not an incredible challenge and more besides, but are you really not even going to try? What about this Gentian, Gentian meek and mild thing? Ask politely and change his mind."

Memories of Atlarus and Aurak Tel's imperious commands made her grimace. "Those rhymes are amusing, but don't reflect who I truly am. I know my limits. And I will not fight for Aristide. Not because I think that impossible, but because I can't succeed."

"Gah!" Aspen pulled at his hair in dramatic exaggeration. "You're not making sense again."

"I am. What could I do, if I pursued Aristide and won him? He's part of this land, part of Darest. Literally bound to it, if it is true he has some form of Crown bond. He would never leave it, and I couldn't ask him to. And I can't stay."

"Can't or won't? Why are you so keen to give up? I swear, you're the most bloodless of creatures. Why not aim to find this monster of yours? Fight it. Win."

"Is that what you plan to do, Aspen?"

She could see he'd not even considered himself in the context of the battle. "I–uh." He frowned at her, then recovered. "I'll do whatever's asked of me, but I'm only a 'prentice here. You need to have more confidence in the Diamond."

"Do I? We are all of us nothing to the kind of power we face, 'prentice or great-mage. We are *senserel* before their god-king. Don't you see? If we are right, if It is trying to get in here, get to Suldar – who could destroy us with a thought – then It must be greater than Suldar even. Or Suldar would not need to fear."

She glanced at the window, watching the march of the day. Soon night, then the inevitable waking. "Dawn. Aristide is many things, Aspen, but even he cannot hold that back."

Chapter Fifteen

It had not been a good day under the mountain. Aspen's elbow ached because a certain mage had dropped him without warning to the floor. The appalling spectacle that followed, of Gentian hurting herself and the Diamond letting her, had only been made worse by the later reflection that she preferred *that* to the way she usually woke up. The question she'd asked him after, about what he planned to do to combat Dawn, had stayed with him all morning. It wasn't as if he even wanted to sleep with the woman. There was no need to go trying to prove himself *useful* to her as well.

Then, to truly sour the morning, Prince Chenar had decided to chain a Phoenix.

Leton had met up with Aspen and Rua after breakfast, but only to tell them the prince had ordered him to see to the reestablishment of the functional enchantment of the Saxan's base. He'd been perfectly matter-of-fact, without any of the insult, the outrage, which should accompany a sword-dancer seeing to the plumbing.

It hadn't helped that Leton had dismissed Aspen's immediate offer of help, and sent him and Rua off to explore houses on their lonesome. Or that, beneath his usual dry efficiency, he'd looked uncommonly concerned about something other than bathwater.

Then Rua had finally made it clear that they would be the more boring sort of friends in future, and Aspen had been left to look at the shells of people's lives and try not to think about all the nasty possibilities. In fact, the only bright point of the day had been the Diamond inviting Gentian to bed.

Now that was something he'd never thought to find himself thinking, but how could he resist such a truly delicious development? Not that he believed for a moment that the Diamond would turn tomorrow's experiment into something really worth watching, but Gentian's squirming had been marvellous.

A pity she'd spoiled Aspen's enjoyment by refusing to take advantage of the situation. And by looking unnervingly like someone had just stepped on her. Which was why Aspen, instead of cleaning up after dinner, was in the library of all places, hunting about for picture books.

With an audience. Aspen had always been good at knowing he was being watched, so he was able to turn without surprise to discover Jurasel leaning against the library door.

"A little bedtime reading?" The prince's voice was lazy, but his eyes glinted with curiosity and suspicion.

"For Gentian. She's bored out of her mind, so I'm trying to find something with drawings of plants."

"Heard she'd done herself some damage." Jurasel looked thoughtfully around the shelves lit by Aspen's magelight, then reached down a few books from a top shelf and flipped through them. "Here," he said, offering one to Aspen.

Not only pen and ink drawings of leaves and flowers, but occasional pages beautifully painted in colour. Aspen was impressed: the Pirate was quicker with the Fae language than at least half the valley's captives.

"I take it Couerveur's experiments aren't going well?" Jurasel asked next, not keeping back a certain pleasure.

Pretence was pointless. "We've made a negative kind of progress, I suppose. No, that doesn't work. No, that doesn't work. No, that doesn't work. Our list of things that don't work is getting nice and long. A bit repetitive, but, well, we have to get a few points for persistence."

"Keeping score are you?" But the man shook his head, his smouldering intensity replaced by a reluctant appreciation of captivity's twists. "How are we supposed to keep up old rivalries when all we want is for your master to live up to his reputation?"

"You could throw an even more lavish party," Aspen suggested brightly, and won himself laughter.

"You're not what I would have expected from an apprentice of Couerveur. How long have you served him?"

Aspen gazed at opportunity walking right up to him, all shiny and waiting to be plucked. Should he take it? He could end up tangling his chances with Leton, not to mention putting Diamond and Gold even further out of reach.

"That's a whole story in itself," he said, greatly daring. "Why don't we go somewhere with less books and more wine, and I'll tell you all about me?"

Just the right amount of push, rewarded with startled appreciation rather than affront, and then a fuller survey of what was on offer. The smile moved into tawny hazel eyes. "Indeed, my calendar is clear this evening."

"I remember a particularly fine cellar two houses over. Let me show you."

"Very well."

Lit by a warm glow, but still taking care not to outrage any royal need for command, Aspen led the way out of the library, only to be stopped in his tracks by a sudden surge of magic behind him.

Jurasel instantly drew shield and Aspen followed his lead a half-beat later. They both turned on their heels to look up at a house one back from the valley's inner circle. There was a crash of broken glass, but the casting was too far away for Aspen to even guess at intent. He took a doubtful step forward, but stopped when Jurasel dropped his shield.

"Something's just gone up in their faces," the Cyan prince said, with a mix of derision and pleasure. And just an ounce of relief. "No magisters of their own, and can't bring themselves to rely on your master to set the pace."

Aspen was dismayed, not only for this interruption of good fortune, but because Leton was in there. If Chenar was experimenting without real understanding–

"Think I'd rather've had another display like yesterday than to jump at every trickle of power since the sun came up," Jurasel said. "We'll end up killing each other out of sheer nerves."

"Could you tell what they were doing?" That had been physical backlash. If Leton was in the room, his shields inadequate to the task...

Jurasel didn't answer, gazing over at Suldar's building. The man's restless energy was immense, and Aspen could feel the frustration pouring off him. "I don't know how much longer I can stand sitting on my hands myself," he added unexpectedly. "Dancing to the tune of that icewater Darien. We're going mad with nothing to do, because against our Lady Dusk and this possible Dawn there's nothing we *can* do. Just wait for the axe to swing." He looked suddenly at Aspen, perhaps remembering who he was talking to. "So where's this cellar?"

Trying to trust Leton to have kept himself in one piece, Aspen led the way to one of the nicer mansions, and through the kitchen to the array of bottles he'd already raided for yesterday's party. Struggling to recapture the mood, he lifted bottles at random.

"Wine? Spirits?"

"It's all guesswork with these vintages," Jurasel said, selecting a white and a brandy before gesturing mutely for Aspen to continue.

Distractedly, Aspen snatched up a couple of glasses on the way through, and headed for the stairs. All the buildings had begun to blur together, but he distinctly remembered – yes, a suite of rooms one floor up, with a warmly cosy lounge opening on to one of those expansive Fae bedrooms.

"Do you think much about the people who left this behind?" Jurasel asked, frowning at an elegant little carving as he chilled the wine.

Holding up the glasses to be filled, Aspen discovered he didn't want to drink. Worry, the day's creeping uncertainty, had left him open to all the wrong kind of thoughts, and he found himself babbling.

"What they looked like. What they were doing when it happened. What they'd think of us prancing about in their clothes and raiding their cellars. I can see their footprints everywhere, the things they've just put down, dropped; all the countless odds and ends of their lives left standing in a moment. But I can't taste them: they've faded out of presence, like the maintenance enchantments, and left only gaps behind."

"We're living in a graveyard," Jurasel muttered, and put the bottle down on the nearest table, face shuttered. "Jostling for elbow room with the memory of ghosts."

Aspen cursed himself for killing the last shreds of the moment with one of his stupid excesses of sensibility. But, though the mood was now less than light-hearted, the intention held. Eyes sombre, Jurasel lifted Aspen's chin, stole his breath in a kiss that was at once comfortless and comforting. His beard tickled, and his hands moved to touch Aspen's back, slide down his spine.

A little shiver followed them along their course. Jurasel was powerful in a physical, arcane and worldly sense. That blunt forthrightness was backed by an able mind, and the proud temper was certainly no act. And here was Aspen Choraide, between this man and a wall, losing clothes without even trying.

"Say thank you nicely after," the Diamond had said, and Gentian had laughed, but it was perfectly true. There was no better place to make an enemy than a bed, and if he offended Jurasel the consequences could be far more drastic then a few cold glances. This man was a prince, most definitely not loyal to Darest, and Aspen was playing with fire.

Delicious.

ooOoo

Happiness should always be shared, and unexpected bliss made all the sweeter when you could sit talking to a friend without telling, smiling just enough so that they knew. Aspen thought it entirely inconsiderate of Gentian to have gone and fallen asleep. Still, he supposed it meant the pangs of spell backlash had faded. She certainly looked a good deal less cross-tempered and headachy, slipped down from her mound of pillows and...really, not moving very much at all.

A well-timed breath spared Aspen the trouble of having a heart attack, but then there was a distinct pause before a repeat performance. Frowning, he peered at her in the dim light of the room's single candle. Gentian *had* said she had grown very weak toward morning: it would be a pity to get into a tizz about nothing and go waking her up. But it wasn't even midnight, and he'd taken the distinct impression that she'd not been able to sleep at all last time.

The Diamond's divination was still active, though it was the type he would have to come and unpack to find out what was going on. Aspen cast one of his own, just to prove her pulse. Steady enough, but irritatingly faint and when he touched her arm he found the skin clammy, quite the opposite of feverish.

"You do sick very badly," he told her unhappily. "You should have gone all pale and bravely stalwart and inspired the Diamond to sit at your bedside patting your hand." Aspen rubbed cold fingers. "Instead, I swear you looked relieved each time he headed for the door. What have you got against having a good time with the man while you're trapped here, and leave worrying about not living in Darest for when that's actually an option?" He took her by the shoulders, as he had before dinner, and shook her warily, then hastily stopped because her head *flopped* without any resistance at all.

Aspen followed the beacon of the *saecstra* the short way down the hall, knocked on the Diamond's door and never would have imagined the reluctance he felt when the command came to open it. The Diamond Couerveur's bedroom.

Beyond beautiful, he glowed beneath a magelight: cross-legged on a moss and pitch eiderdown, pale hair still damp from a bath and shapely feet bare. But for the five books sitting open around him, and the grim frown he wore as he read, it was a scene that fit the beginning of many of Aspen's choicest fantasies. Yet Aspen had never pictured himself unable to speak. Or wishing himself a thousand miles away.

The Diamond didn't ask questions. He took one look at Aspen, then drew power and gazed through two walls at an experiment gone wrong. His face lost all vestige of expression.

Badly needing reassurance, Aspen had to swallow down his stomach at least twice before Darest's unshakeable Diamond Couerveur remembered how to move.

"Fetch Princess Aloren."

"Aloren?" The last thing Aspen had expected him to say.

"Her Highness has long collected the esoterica of healing. Go."

After spending half his life at Court, Aspen had seen the Diamond Couerveur deadly displeased and coldly unconcerned, had watched him indifferently snatch impossible victories, and seen his face when he'd sworn his future away to an unexpected king. He'd never seen him look so young.

Aspen fled from it, out the room and up the stairs to the suites of Ceria and Atlarus. Both entry doors were shut, and it was a far different thing to burst in upon the Cerian Crown Princess in the middle of the night, but he would worry about royal temperament later.

A few loud knocks resulted in the wrong door opening, and he turned to see Rua, puzzled and concerned. "What is happening?" He couldn't bring himself to answer her.

Behind him, the other door shushed open and he looked back over his shoulder at a vision of gold and white, a grand ambition.

And said: "Gentian's dying."

The words fell clumsily from his lips, cringing before Aloren's golden majesty. What had death to do with a creature such as she? What business had Aspen to speak, and make it real?

"I must tell the Aurak," Rua said, and was gone. Aloren simply started down the stairs.

They found the Diamond standing at the window in Gentian's room, gazing out into the night. For a moment Aspen thought he hadn't heard them, but then he turned and said "Thank you for coming," and seemed almost his own self again.

Aloren ignored him, casting divination without word or gesture, leaving Aspen to stare. A great-mage. Aloren, dismissed as decoration by half the West, and she was so skilled, so intuitive with the language of magic, that complex casting had become a true expression of will. A thing few outside the Fair ever achieved and, it was very likely, few outside this room would ever link to Ceria's Crown Princess.

"I believe the Fair would term Magister Calder a 'land-seer'," the Diamond said, almost absently, as Aurak Bes arrived. "Sensitive to and affected by the boundaries and spirit of a place in a way that far outstrips a true-mage's ear for power. She has felt the Fair's taint since birth."

This won Aloren's direct attention, and Rua, behind her master, gasped. Aspen tried not to look sick: to save Gentian they were going to have to expose her.

With an air of preoccupation, the Diamond told the history of the dawn attacks, and elaborated on Suldar's reaction. He didn't once look at Gentian, lying so still and pale on the bed.

"Magister Calder was conscious, holding up well when I checked on her after dinner," he concluded. "My *sel-esta* shows her becoming increasingly listless, until she passed into this state perhaps an hour ago. I cannot identify the cause of this weakness, any more than I can detect whatever touches her each morning, but I see no sign that this is an attack – rather, as before, damage she has done to herself preventing this unknown's daily touch. And if that one is a sibling of Suldar – the mirror of dusk – then she may not be able to heal the damage until we next enter her time of power. The moment of dawn."

"You believe Magister Calder is the tool of our hidden foe?"

Never had the Aurak sounded so sombre, the planes of his face transformed to basalt and granite. The Diamond only said: "I cannot discount it."

"But you are not certain." Temporary reprieve brought the Atlaran's face back to life and he joined Aloren at the side of the bed. "I once offered her the best of my grandsons, and she told me she did not want to make another land her home. In my ignorance some part of me felt this an insult, because she had plainly not been in Darest for many years." He smoothed Gentian's short, rumpled hair. "I would that it not be too late to repair my error. Can we stop this?"

The Diamond didn't answer immediately, looking out the window again. "Feeding her with an *anaur* is the obvious move," he said finally, "but I wished to ask Your Highness' advice before making the attempt."

"There is little else to do." Aloren's honey-treacle drawl was casually factual. "But begin with a small amount only." She settled into one of the chairs, rearranging sheer white silk over burnished limbs, and watched with critical interest as the Diamond began to cast. Quite as if she would be scoring him on pronunciation.

An *anaur* was a transfer, a horribly fiddly piece of casting used as a last resort to sustain life. It wasn't anything so simple as pushing arcane power into your subject. That would be about as useful as pouring sand down the throat of a suffocating man. Instead, the *anaur* would tap the living magic of the Diamond's body, an energy quite separate from any arcane strength he might possess, and try to use it to bolster Gentian's. And, because healing was always unnecessarily complex, you had to ease it over subtly, else it be confused for some wrongness or attack.

Eyes narrowed with concentration, the Diamond pressed fingers lightly to Gentian's temple. It was not a loud spell, using a minimal amount of arcane force, and quite lacking any handy visual effects. All there was to see was the faintest flush of colour to thin cheeks, and then a deeper breath.

"Gentian."

The air vibrated. He'd called on her Name, put hooks of power into the word and tugged her to consciousness. Bruised lids shifted, and then she turned her cheek against his hand and opened her eyes.

It was a moment of naked vulnerability. Gentian, having fallen asleep, woke to the touch of this man she desired. Surprise and wonder competed with exhaustion, and her lips parted. But then burnished gold shifted beneath moon silk, and she looked past him to Aloren. All expression fled.

"What time is it?" The words were little more than breath, and she shifted to look at the steadily burning candle, moving, by no coincidence, away from the Diamond's hand.

"Near midnight, Magister." The words were formal, his face aloof. "Can you tell us how far this experience differs from your first experiment?"

Gentian turned her head with leaden care to mark the occupants of the room: Aloren, Aspen, Aurak Bes, and Rua by the door. For a moment it didn't seem she'd even heard the question, but then she blinked, and said: "I don't remember not being able to sit up. But – I think it's just sooner. Didn't...really flatten till nearly dawn, before. Perhaps because I'm older, more sensitive?"

Only then did she look back at the Diamond, staring straight into those sapphire and ice eyes as if she was trying to memorise every fleck. "I saw a sea-fetch," she told him. "Just after I crossed Darest's ocean border. Another relevant detail, I suppose, but I found it hard to believe." She smiled, regret leavened with a fleeting hilarity. "Does it count, if you strike your*self* down?"

"I do not know, Magister," the Diamond replied, without so much as a glimmer of humour, but she was already gone, slipping unresisting from consciousness. The Diamond stood a beat longer, then said: "The transfer should have sustained her better than that. Where is her strength going?"

Aloren's answer was to cast, a word-magic spell of painful complexity. Aspen tried to follow the intent, but his Elachar wasn't nearly equal to the task, and he was guessing at particularly esoteric divination when Gentian flickered into light.

A rainbow palette painted a fragile shimmer of green and blue, with a wash of gold flecked with red all around her. The spell stained the living magic of her body, but it was fading as they watched, the colours wavering up into nothingness.

"Her strength is not being taken," Aloren said. "It's evaporating. Mist in the sunlight."

"Do you know a way to stop this, Highness?" the Diamond asked, and Aspen wished he would stop sounding so remote, so disconnected from what was happening. So oddly...not there.

"I have read of a case of possession," Aloren replied calmly. "A revenant. The creature was successfully cast out, but some hours later the victim fell to exhaustion in just such a way as this. The envelope of living magic had been torn. The account states that their attempts to stop the outflow were 'like sewing shut a rain-cloud'."

"But it fixed itself last time." Aspen was swinging wildly between dismay and outrage. Selvar was possessing Gentian for an instant each morning? The implications were impossible to face, and he wanted to shout, only calming when Aloren's burnished gaze switched to him. "It woke her again and she was back to normal," he said. "Can't we keep her alive 'til dawn?"

"Very likely. What happens when she wakes is another question."

The Diamond turned away from the flicker of colour above Gentian. "The shock?"

"The reaction you have described must surely place a severe strain on her heart. In this state, I would not expect her to survive that. Nor would I recommend trying to build up her strength against it. That might further strain whatever is torn, possibly speeding her decline. Of course, since we are relying on this Other to repair her, perhaps it is capable of withholding the effect." Aloren's voice was quite impersonal, but she watched the Diamond's reaction with interest.

Which was not to react at all. Aspen was painfully aware of the waiting silence, and wondered if it was possible he hadn't heard. But then, "We will make our own attempts. Since we have the precedent of an earlier case, we will at least be able to eliminate what has failed already. If you will assist me?"

"Of course," Aurak Bes said, with just the faintest hint of affront. Aloren produced that slow smile, but inclined her head. They would do it.

The Diamond barely reacted, giving no sign of being relieved or grateful. "Choraide, we will need food," he said, after another of those uncharacteristic pauses, and began another divination.

Feeling a fraction dizzy, Aspen nodded and hurried out of the room. Arcane casting was energy-intensive enough. Repeatedly transferring living magic would leave them starving hollow.

One day's lesson did not make a cook. But a 'prenticeship devoted to avoiding Elachar definitely ruled out Aspen making any other contribution. He was *not* going to let that bother him. Instead, he gathered simple things, nuts and juice and cheeses, and kept half his attention on the flow of magic above. Aloren's spell cut out abruptly, and after a long pause an intense wash suggested a major shield, which vanished while Aspen was making his way upstairs.

They cast another shield as he arrived. Not trying to keep something out, but to hold a life in. Putting a bandage on a cloud. Biting his lip, Aspen poured drinks and passed them around, and held his breath as Aurak Bes brought a hint of pink back to Gentian's cheeks with another *anaur*.

"Well, brother." Seylon Heresar was at the door, a wolf sniffing out weakness, fixing unerringly on Gentian's still figure. "We've been sent to discover why you must keep such hours," he said, after a slight pause, "but perhaps I'll ask instead if you would like any help."

The Diamond dismissed the latest shield before turning to answer, his face still revealing little but distraction. "It seems we will need it. Thank you, Seylon."

At least the man didn't gloat, just nodded and stepped forward. A thrill of relief ran the course of Aspen's spine when Leton followed him in, offering up one of his clipped little bows as he made that brief, comprehensive survey of the room. "This goes beyond spell backlash," he observed neutrally.

"Yes." The Diamond recounted Gentian's history, adding the latest fillip about the sea-fetch. Again he didn't look at the bed while he spoke.

"A sea-fetch is a *uyruk-kedai*, yes?" Leton's mouth was flat with distaste. "Harbinger of an enemy attack, deadly peril. But it does not sound as if this fulfils a *uyruk-kedai's* conditions. More an unfortunate side-effect than a direct attempt on her life."

"Perhaps that will come." Seylon Heresar's gaze was thoughtful as it held his brother's. "Well, we will go and settle our lords. Shall I bring Dhara back with me?"

"Please."

Something about that distant tone prompted Heresar to lift his eyebrows, but he departed without further words. Leton, ever-correct, bowed his head before following him out. Watching the scene with languid interest, Aloren hummed a snatch of a battle refrain. If Gentian really was being possessed by Selvar, 'settling' their lords would be no small matter.

Aspen couldn't help but wince at the memory of Jurasel. Wine and kisses seemed centuries ago, and it was a sure thing that the prince, left brooding but replete, almost a friend, would have no trouble remembering old rivalries next time he met a Darien.

"I'll go get some more chairs," Aspen said philosophically. Two from his room, two from across the hall. He set the one for himself on the side of the window nearer the door so that he could return to the kitchen as needed. And nearly leapt out of his skin when tiny hooks batted his ankle.

The kitten, of course, lurking forgotten under the furniture. Aspen picked the creature up by the scruff of its neck and glowered into unrepentant periwinkle eyes. What Gentian thought she was doing adopting stray animals he didn't know. It was no doubt riddled with fleas. Then, because it gave him something to do with his hands, he tickled its ears and made it purr.

It was Aloren's turn to cast the *anaur*, which she produced with a minimum of effort. She had just drawn a blanket up to Gentian's waist when Heresar, Leton and Lady Dhara arrived.

"You'll be pleased to know that the question of whether to kill her has been postponed until after we see if she survives," the Cyan woman said, leaping briskly to the point as usual. "I gather that's a bare chance at best, but for what it's worth you have my strength."

"It may make the difference," the Diamond said, and again Aspen wondered at the withdrawn note in his voice. His every response was off-key, far from his usual precise and absolute self, and Aspen felt like he'd suddenly discovered a glorious castle balanced on a wineglass. The foundations of his world were teetering.

"My Prince asks that I stay and observe," Leton said then, without apology or challenge.

Aspen waited for Aristide's habitual faint smile to be resurrected, but "He is naturally interested," was all he said, and turned away.

It was true the man had never been one to waste energy killing the messenger, but this was still nothing like his normal self. Where was the Diamond's brilliance?

Leton took a chair, Rua leaned stolidly against the doorway, and Aspen made a third whose role it was to keep quiet through a fruitless cycle of *anaur*, shield, divination, discussion. Repeat, vary, start over from scratch. Even sitting doing nothing Aspen felt worn. The wait between each and every tenuous breath was enough to drive a man mad, and the scent from the candle Gentian had lit was giving him a headache. He longed to snuff it, but couldn't escape the symbology, only the room. Back downstairs to the sanctuary of the kitchen.

A scrape of boot on the stair warned him he had company. Aspen wiped his face and glowered at Leton, for that moment not caring about fiery tails at all.

"Death watch is never easy."

"It's not a death watch. It's a rescue."

"Both, perhaps." Leton, unfazed, gestured toward the stove. "Either way, they're out of food."

"I suppose so," Aspen said, then asked himself what he was doing. Here was this man he'd been wanting all day, this escapee from a bard's epics, obligingly following him about. Moping was completely the wrong response, and it wasn't going to make the least difference to Gentian how he killed the night. Not that Leton looked inclined to play that game. He was altogether a different kettle of fish from the fiery Jurasel, who would accept brief pleasure to keep away ghosts. In fact, Aspen had a nasty suspicion that Leton was a little too like Soren and Gentian.

Well, for the moment it would be easier to work than do anything else, anyway. "A drawn-out breakfast?" he suggested practically. "I suppose we should cater for the whole valley. They're sure to turn up – either way."

He headed off before Leton could respond, and lost himself briefly in the task of heating the cook-stone, then cocked an eyebrow for orders. True to his commission, Leton made it another lesson, setting chores with a dry dose of explanation, banishing any suggestion of funeral feasts. And Rua came down to do a little fetch-and-carry and spared them the necessity of returning until the night had almost given up its last gasp. And if he could *only* stop every *second* blasted thought from taking him where he didn't want to go–!

"Eat something yourself," Leton said, when Aspen paused in the middle of filling a tray. "Clear your head."

It was an unremarkable piece of advice. And Aspen would bet that every man, woman and child who'd ever served under this man had longed for just such a comment, worked to earn his attention, lived for the little flash of glory it brought. For he was a sword-dancer and a leader of men: deadly, detached, every part of him consummately professional, and he *noticed*.

"How did you start out cooking?" Aspen asked, desperately needing to think about living things.

A shrug accompanied the answer. "Military background. Armies march on their stomachs, so on, so forth."

"But–" Aspen hesitated, since exalted family names like 'Delmar' hadn't actually been bandied about between them, let alone the astronomical price attached to it. "Supply corps?" he extemporised.

Fooling no-one. Black eyes narrowed, the cynical glint replaced by something best kept to dark alleys. "Magister Calder is entirely too sensitive for comfort," Leton said. Flat, lethal.

"Now that's an understatement," Aspen retorted, though his heart was racing double-time. *This* was not where the conversation had been meant to go. "You can at least rest assured that she's got other things on her mind than collecting bounties."

Pent breath was let out in a little 'tuh'. And then an uncoiling and Leton nodded, and rubbed at his chin. "True enough. We stepped outside the past when we stepped into this one."

"A thousand years outside." Aspen shut his mouth on this precious chance to chat to a Phoenix, and returned to assembling the tray. He would not dwell on injustice or the question of what came next. He would not lure death to them with words.

ooOoo

Between midnight and dawn someone painted shadows beneath the Diamond's eyes. Aurak Bes' proud shoulders bowed, and Lady Dhara and Seylon Heresar seemed to be sharing a migraine. Even Golden Aloren's languid grace was a cut string from collapse. They had been pouring their vitality into a sieve. And none of them, no combination of their brilliance and determination, could produce enough moss to stop it up.

The Diamond cast the final *anaur*, timing it to anticipate the precise moment Gentian's sleep would take her, and transferring as much energy as he dared. If he tore wider whatever rent was draining her life, so be it. They would not be able to sustain her much longer anyway, and their aim now was merely to have her survive waking up.

The sudden influx brought a hectic flush to cheeks that had been grey and waxen, and *finally* increased the pace of that stop-start breathing. She even moved a little, shifted as she had not been doing for too long.

But the glow of borrowed strength only outlined hollow-thin cheeks, highlighting the toll the night had taken. Aspen remembered too well the convulsive start she'd given when her hidden stalker had wrenched her out of sleep, how she'd shuddered and gasped afterwards, like she'd been struck by lightning, or been running for her life. Something – any moment now – some dreadful, secret, grotesque wrongness was going to creep up on this husk of a girl, this guttering candle, and *scream* in her ear.

Aspen closed his eyes.

Then opened them, just as quickly. Power. Power was moving, a great wave of it, a cloud-front with no sign, no shred, no drop of intent to explain what it was doing. It swirled around the bed, heat-haze thick, then took on form, some kind of shield, a soap-bubble with a woman inside.

And Gentian woke. Woke with the smallest jerk of her head, more of a twitch, to lie there blinking at the pearly rainbow surrounding her for all of the moment before it popped out of existence.

"How...very odd."

The words were barely audible, and they all leaned forward to hear them, caught in a gust of relief and anti-climax.

"That was Suldar." It was Lady Dhara who managed to get the words out, looking about as confused as Aspen felt. "Was it not?"

"There...yes. Between me and It." The breathy whisper was puzzled, wondering. "It *laughed* at her. It thought it was funny."

She subsided, overwhelmed either by this latest twist or the effort of speech, and left them to look at each other in complete incomprehension. Aloren, with immense practicality, poured a glass of sweetened juice and, sliding a hand beneath Gentian's head, helped her to drink it.

"Bring her up to my rooms," she said, directing the order to Aspen. "I will monitor her until she wakes." That slow smile took the rest of them in, a sphinx who was pleased to find a new riddle.

"And we," Seylon Heresar responded, with a jagged glance directed at his brother, "will exhaust our imaginations trying to find a reason why our Lady Regent might want to rescue her enemy's best catapult."

The Diamond hadn't spoken, didn't respond, and the chill ghost that had been haunting Aspen half the night raked icy fingers down his spine. All through their time in the valley, all through his entire experience of the man, the Diamond had approached every twist with focused purpose and a level of enjoyment, leaving little doubt that he was equal to each new challenge. Aspen hadn't deep-down believed for a moment that they would end their days in this valley, purely because the Diamond was here, and infallible. He never faltered.

Aspen did not know what to make of a Diamond who hesitated, so he crossed to the bed and lifted Gentian into his arms. Bones and thistledown. The kitten weighed more. It was entirely against all nature to carry people around in your arms unless you were about to undress them, but the errand was easier than waiting to see if this flaw in the Diamond Couerveur was real, whether he was even going to answer Seylon's question. Aspen escaped, upstairs and away from the impossible.

"Put her on the bed."

Aloren had followed him up the stairs, but Aspen found little pleasure following her orders this time.

"He wasn't even relieved," he said, still at a complete loss. "We just spent half the night trying to keep her alive and he looked – he looked almost like he was sorry she survived."

"We are beginning to see the role Magister Calder is to play in this drama," Aloren said. She touched a finger to Gentian's cheek. "I wonder if she does?"

This sent Aspen straight back out the door, but he couldn't avoid the implications, couldn't run from his own thoughts. Just like the rest of them, trapped under this mountain, with no escape at all.

Chapter Sixteen

Someone was singing. Drowsy melody, wordless intoxication. It wound into thought, sank under the skin, sewed its way beneath flesh. Suldar's music. For the first time Gentian thought of it as more than a way of reinforcing the shield and illusion surrounding the valley. It was Suldar's purpose, her pulse. An intricate cycle, an endless web that locked her in place. A song of tranquillity and endurance: sanctuary with a price.

The saecstra. Aristide's hand against her cheek, while the saecstra whispered its vow into her bones. "On my name, then. I will not seek to harm you or your heirs. I will not attempt to gain the throne of Darest at your expense. I will protect and support you." Raised to rule, King in all but name, he had bound himself to serve another. Because it would save Darest.

Her cheek still burned from that brief touch. She had been somewhere very dark, and he had said her name, and she had gone to him. But when she looked up, she had seen only the Diamond Couerveur. And then Aloren.

It was Aloren who was singing. Gentian struggled out of leaden drowsiness to a room full of afternoon light, and a golden princess sitting in the window, combing her hair. So beautiful. It was impossible not to look at her without feeling privileged by the experience, without being tangled by want.

"I was dying."

"Yes." Aloren looked over at her, still humming in time with Suldar's melody. That languid, impersonal gaze, as if she studied some portrait, interesting but hardly real. "You will be hungry."

She was, echoing empty. Mages who cast a great deal often had trouble eating enough, but she'd never been this pared back. Strangely insubstantial, as if the previous night had scraped away all but the thinnest layer of flesh. She felt like there wasn't enough left of her to cast a shadow.

Aloren left the window, and Gentian tried sitting up, finding herself still tired, weary, but no longer weak beyond movement. And discovered a hollow in the bed beside her. She sat with her hand in it.

"The not-quite-apprentice and the more-than-Captain brought this for you."

A cake. Though her mouth was parched dry, Gentian automatically accepted the offered slice and broke off a corner to sample. Orange and almond, expertly done. It brought a lump of dizzy gratitude to her throat, this gesture to weigh against the circle of faces that had greeted her last waking, judgment heavy in their eyes.

"Eat several small meals over the rest of the day," Aloren said, settling on the edge of the bed and handing her a glass of juice. "Nothing too large, but a steady intake. I would expect you to recover strength rapidly with another day's bed rest, but to also suffer a long spell of low stamina." The words were practical, the gaze one of lazy interest. It was like having a honey-coloured panther for a nurse.

Deliberately, Gentian drank and finished the slice of cake, trying to work out just what had been happening, and pondering her consignment to Aloren's care. Not to mention to her bed, wearing a silky, over-long shirt and nothing else. An awkward setting for self-dissection.

"You're trying to reach Suldar through her music?" she said instead, and met the full force of Aloren's slow smile.

"Why search for answers when they are there for the asking?"

"Because Suldar doesn't answer," Gentian replied, not without frustration.

"If the situation is as we guess, Suldar has not spoken to anyone for more than a thousand years. And there is this matter of a Ban, and shame on the Fair. Knowing that race, there is every chance Suldar is forbidden from speaking to us about her own existence, let alone this other's. Does the music affect you?"

Interesting question. "I don't think I feel it differently from anyone else here," Gentian said. "It's not part of the *place*, but the net around it. The valley's aware of its isolation, but I don't feel anything from the net other than the fact of it. As music – I find it soothing, actually. I keep expecting it to be sad, isolated, but it's...in balance."

Aloren's molten gaze warmed as she considered this, then she dipped her head and stood. "I will help you down to your room," she said, picking up the cake.

Braced against an inquisition into her connection with It, Gentian blinked but accepted the reprieve. She clambered her way out of the over-sized bed, and found standing easier than she'd expected. Gentian Calder, strong enough to wobble her way down a flight of stairs with Ceria's Crown Princess merely in close attendance.

"You are unlikely to survive a third attempt of this kind," Aloren remarked, putting the cake on the table. "Twice torn and mended, the fabric of your life is worn thin."

"I'm not planning to try again."

"No." With another of those slow smiles, Aloren drifted out, leaving Gentian to wonder at the woman's apparent dearth of curiosity. And to chide herself for forgetting to thank the princess. Suldar may have stepped in at the last minute, but Telsandar's kidnapped Magisters had sustained her till dawn.

Why?

Aristide could not have escaped making some sort of explanation. They would know that It – Selvar – touched her each morning. They would have taken only moments to connect her return to Darest and their vanishment. To the deaths of their companions back at the Cauldron, and, very likely, the usurpation of their powers.

Gentian gazed around the room. It felt abandoned. Even the kitten was gone, though someone had been tidying, had made the bed and cleared her collection of glasses away. An excess of chairs kept pushing themselves into view: audience, saviours, jury. What had been said, between explanation and dawn? What had they decided to do with her? Aristide had obviously prevailed against any vote of execution, and Gentian rather thought Aloren had been extending a sheltering wing. Suldar's interference must surely have muddied the waters, but it had to be faced. This angry little group of the overpowerful now had good reason to call her enemy.

The sea-fetch's drowned eyes looked up at her, and then were replaced by Aristide's. Had he really looked down at her like that? So cold, so distant?

Gentian shook the memory away, then pushed herself into movement. All her life she'd been losing her war against It, so comprehensively that she'd been routed from Darest altogether. To stay in this room, unhappily alone, would be to give It another small victory. So, a second slice of cake and a comb through her hair before she pulled on one of the cotton shifts she'd bought in anticipation of summer. What was needed was a garden.

All these divinations and searches for prisons and prisoners had distracted her from the valley itself, from the beauty of the place. The Fair's Empire had not been part of her travels: she'd once crossed the border of one of their far eastern lands, felt herself unwelcome, and not lingered. But Darest, Telsandar, did not seem to care that she was not Fae.

Wandering from kitchen to the house gardens, and then out into the central grounds, she let herself think purely in terms of plant variety and placement, of the interjection of water and the comment of sculptured stone. There was no-one in sight and the hostile gaze of princes was a matter for later, yesterday, some other time. Just now she walked in magnificence, for the Fair understood gardens.

And then she had to think of the nearest bench, over by a shady clump of trees, because Aloren hadn't been wrong about her stamina.

The previous night began to press in on her. She'd almost died. It had almost won. Then Suldar had saved her, and It had acted like It had won anyway. Hopelessly perplexing. And she was left feeling as abandoned as her room.

"We're not supposed to talk to you."

This from Kassen, trailing up in her sister's wake, all curiosity and glee. But it was Princess Desseron, with an expression quite as stony as her mother's, who had come to see her.

"That is true," she said, chin held high, posture stiff. "We have been told we are not to talk to you, that we are to stay away from you. My heart-mother says that you are more victim than enemy. Even my blood-mother concedes that it is not fair and right. But they tell us it is necessary."

Gentian blinked. She'd made overtures to the Cyan princesses because her parents had instilled a belief that a child who has never planted and grown has missed a great wonder. She had not been strategising, and had not expected such a return. "Don't you agree?" she asked.

"I want to know if you do."

"That I'm not an enemy, that it's not right, or that it's necessary?" Questions she hadn't even asked herself, and she found the last especially hard to say aloud. "I hardly know, Highness. I certainly didn't want us to be brought here, and I don't think any of it's right. As for necessary–" She faltered. "I doubt it'll make any difference whether you avoid me or not, except in how you feel about whatever happens next."

Desseron considered this, then nodded: decisive agreement. "Because it would be easier to kill you if you aren't a person to us," she said, with a bald frankness she'd obviously learned from Lady Dhara. "Like Suldar."

"Suldar?"

"Suldar keeps us away because she doesn't want to start to like us."

So straightforward. "You could very well be right, Highness," Gentian said, as Kassen tugged her sister's sleeve and tipped her head to alert her to the approach of Seylon Heresar. Desseron grimaced faintly, but went on, deliberately raising her voice.

"Even if we knew for certain that this monster was using you, it doesn't do anything useful to suddenly stop talking to you," she said, her eyes flashing defiance as she met the Duke's gaze. "I know it wouldn't make *me* feel any better."

Seylon's faint, ironic smile made him look painfully like Aristide. He stopped before them, bowed, and said: "I believe you are wanted inside, Highness."

"If you say so, M'Lord," Desseron replied, pressing her lips together. She inclined her head formally to Gentian and left without further protest.

"You're making a habit of interrupting my conversations, Duke Heresar," Gentian said, wondering if she should be afraid of this man, and not feeling the slightest impulse to run away. At least not until she was sure she could stand up without falling down.

"Isn't it about time you started calling me Seylon?" He sat beside her with a sigh, and she saw that there were circles under his eyes. He had, after all, spent half the night keeping her alive, and probably had much less sleep after.

"It feels strange to owe so many people my life." Discomforting.

"I expect we'll all think of ways for you to make it up to us."

The words were not light-hearted, and she bit her lip. "You're not planning to avoid me for your own good?"

"I doubt that would make me feel any better, either," he said, still quite seriously. "You must forgive Dhara and Kestia. They've always had good reason to be protective of their children."

She shrugged. "Frankly, I'm surprised that's the sum of their reaction. This isn't a development I expected to be taken calmly."

"Who is calm? After Suldar so kindly stopped you from expiring, we all went down for the confrontation scene. Everyone was waiting, eager to haul my precious little brother over the coals for neglecting to share the more interesting aspects of your past. Chenar is proving most unexpectedly bloodthirsty – it doesn't match his reputation at all to ask why we should not go immediately to kill you. Do you know what Aristide's response was?"

"Not loud enough to wake me."

A pained smile touched Seylon's mouth, but he brushed any attempt at humour aside. "He said 'And then what?' And we couldn't answer him. Until we do, I think you'll find you're the safest person in this valley."

"Because, even if It is reaching you through me, without me–"

"We might as well put down roots. None of us have made the slightest progress toward getting out and we're all far more interested in escape than stopping this mystery Fae. If nothing else, killing you before finding out exactly what happened this morning would be less than practical."

It was a question, and Gentian saw no gain not answering it. "Nothing like how I usually wake," she said, as matter-of-factly as possible. "Suldar was there. I wasn't awake, just aware of Suldar, being there. I don't think she was there in the way that It usually comes. All I felt was her presence. Then It came. But Suldar was between me and It and It couldn't touch me. Or...did, but

Suldar drew off the effects. And It thought this was funny. I'm not sure which of them repaired whatever was draining my strength. Can I ask you something?"

Seylon was looking less than happy. His pursuit of her had been smoothly light-hearted, and he'd never made a pretence of being struck with any passion. But it seemed he was at least ready to feel sorry for her. "Anyone can ask," he said, after a long pause.

"What were you meeting about on that barge?"

The frown gave way to a wry grimace. "You choose your moments, Gentian. Right now, I'm almost tempted to forget our borders. Lost property, shall we say, and leave it at that? It's not my secret to tell."

"Whose is it?" she asked, but waved the question away. "It's funny – borders are very real to me, but I've never before been involved in the politics of them. We could be anywhere in all the world, but you would be in Cya, and I Darest." She wondered briefly where Captain Djol was, and what he felt about the land that had punished his loyalty.

"The politics of borders?" Seylon shook his head, and stared for a long while into the distance. Making up his mind about something. "There has always been a border between my brother and myself," he continued unexpectedly. "Among other things. We have met very rarely, but we've had plenty of reason to study each other. I have never seen him less pleased with himself than he is today."

"Pleased?"

He sighed, not looking pleased with himself either. "Positively subdued. You see, our elusive Dawn, whether she's trying to get in or out of this place, appears to be constrained by Darest's borders. Which means she, and you, mainly constitute a threat to Darest. And my brother is well-known for eliminating any threat to Darest."

Seylon rose, bowed to her, and turned away. Gentian wondered if he had genuinely thought to warn her, or was simply making mischief. She had of course already realised that if Selvar did free herself, Darest would bear the brunt of that escape, a fact which gave Aristide, above them all, a reason to kill her. With a hastier man, less devoted to certainty, she would probably be dead already.

"It is not wise to expose yourself so, Magister."

Gentian started, twisting to discover Aristide standing directly behind her. She stared at his hand, at the *saecstra* which should have warned her of his arrival, and he followed her gaze, opening his fingers to better view the knotted lines.

"I do not always need to shout my presence, no," he said and released a spell that must have been muffling the enchantment's distinctive whisper.

That was only the start of it. She had looked about often enough to have seen anyone approaching. He'd been completely guised, hidden from view and then shielded so that even she couldn't detect the power of his castings.

"Do you really think it makes any difference where I sit?" she asked, wondering if he was trying to deliberately unnerve her.

"Perhaps not. I believe Princess Aloren prescribed rest and frequent meals?"

When she didn't respond he held out his *saecstra*-marked hand, and after a fraction's pause Gentian clasped it, and felt his oath whisper through her bones.

He pulled her to her feet, and they walked back to her room. At the door she looked directly into those eyes: brilliant and distant, all reaction blocked away. Subdued, Seylon had said.

"You still wish to try the contagion experiment?"

"Yes."

"Then I'll see you tomorrow."

ooOoo

Some time after midnight and Gentian, not feeling at all inclined to sleep, wandered into the hall to look at Aristide's door, standing ajar as promised. She could feel the murmur of several divinations set to await her arrival, and wondered what he would do if he woke alone.

Drifting downstairs, she found something to supplement Aspen's cake, then left her candle and walked out into the grand inner garden of Telsandar to look up at the bright, false moon.

Harp music drew her from the illusion of sky, and she sought the pale light filtering through the opaque side-windows of Suldar's building. Stopping beside the statue, Gentian stared at the blackness where an entry should be, and let the harp's notes wind through her.

Suldar is our sun and moon, Seylon had said, and Gentian saw no reason not to take his words at face value. She had a prayer. Climbing until she reached the blank marble that was not a door, she leaned her forehead against it.

The music stopped.

"I screamed every day for four years," Gentian whispered. "And wept for six more. My parents learned not to touch me. All those broken mornings with no understanding, and not able to do the least thing about them. I haven't shed a tear since I was ten. I used them all up." She turned her head so that the chill stone pressed against one temple. "I long ago abandoned the idea of life being just, and learned to deal with what is. I know I probably won't see how this ends.

"The only thing I was ever able to do was leave, and I forfeited that escape by coming back. Breaking oath. That's all that matters, isn't it? Even knowing who, or why, it's not going to make any difference to me. And you – in this you're just like me. Caught with no choice at all, and no way out. As much *senserel* as I."

Gentian gave up talking and listened to the silence, and when the first notes of the harp sounded, she merely turned and wobbled back to her room. She was far too tired for the tantrum the situation deserved. Crying that it wasn't fair would be no more use than it had been when she was four, twelve, sixteen. Crying had never made any difference at all. Nothing had.

But she would go through the motions. Time for another token experiment.

For all her reluctance, and her doubts that it would work, Gentian agreed with the approach. Magic bound by word and thought was necessarily limited. Contagious and sympathetic magic might be popularly associated with the charms and curses of hedge-mages – tenuous and unreliable – but they were also the forces that moved the oceans, and returned souls to the Moon. They were vast powers that followed different rules.

Pushing Aristide's door further open, she found a corner room where moonlight streamed through gauzy curtains. Outside its reach the shadows were inky, and she could make out little except the faint sheen of pale hair in a dark, vast bed.

Wanting to get this over with, she walked into the room and felt every one of his divinations react to her presence. Aristide woke up. Facing away from her, he was little more than a shadow to her unenhanced eyes, but Gentian was quite sure he was no longer asleep. He didn't move, lay there waiting.

She climbed slowly into the bed, sliding beneath cool sheets to brush against him, every nerve tingling. Trying not to be too awkward, she settled along his back, laying an arm lightly across his ribs.

A faint sandalwood scent tantalised her, and the warmth of his body leached through the thin cotton robe he wore. Her arm moved with the steady pace of his breathing and his feet were bare against hers. No doubt Aspen would advise her to glory in the privilege, the moment, but not even Aspen's optimism could overcome thoughts of death.

Was that why he had withdrawn so far? To treat someone you contemplated killing as a colleague or friend – let alone a romantic prospect – would not be to Gentian's taste, and she doubted Aristide still found this experiment funny. She certainly did not.

Aspen had been wrong: languishing up close only hurt more.

Fingers brushed the back of her hand. A feather-light gesture, not repeated, but beyond what she had expected. Gentian accepted it, wrapped it up in a tiny glowing starburst in her mind, and let it take her back to sleep.

Chapter Seventeen

Aspen jerked upright. Someone had shouted. Straining to identify the source, he nearly levitated off the bed when a burst of power bloomed nearby. Wood splintered, was followed by shattering glass. In the Diamond's room.

Aspen threw himself from the sheets, snatched up a robe, then stumbled to a stop. It had all gone quiet. No casting, no sounds of a fight. Just the same divinations that had been there earlier in the night, and the familiar hum of the *saecstra*. What in the hells had happened?

Clutching at the robe, Aspen took a deep breath, then another, forcing a semblance of calm before drawing power. One of the most basic of the true-magic castings, a simple sharpening of senses. He listened.

Someone was...weeping? No. Gasping, breathing in great juddering gulps. Two someones, both in the Diamond's room. The morning experiment. Aspen hadn't been invited to watch, had had to content himself with imagining Gentian snuggled up to the Diamond. Hoping that this would somehow fix things, that the world would turn right way up, the sky become real. The Diamond Couerveur be himself again.

Alert to every sound, Aspen padded cautiously into the corridor to stare at a closed door. They weren't talking. What had been that spell? Even if the experiment had worked, if the Diamond had succeeded in sensing Gentian's morning visitor, there shouldn't have been any breaking of things involved. Could Dawn have attacked them physically? Actually manifested? Should he be running to the rescue?

But no. No more casting, no screaming or crashing, just breathing. One had slowed down. Appalling to realise that this must be Gentian, lying there as she had after each awakening, eyes squeezed shut. Which made the one still gasping, the one with breath sobbing in his throat–

The door opened. Aspen had been too caught up in disbelief to notice the movement from the bed. Gentian staggered through, clutching the wall as if she needed it to stand up. She flinched from him, threw up a hand as if she thought he'd hit her.

"What–"

"Quiet." The command was ragged but absolute, and she pulled the door shut before doing anything else, then leaned against the wall, panting. "Go away."

"Gentian–"

"Please, Aspen." Her face was turned into the wall. "Go downstairs. I'll explain later."

He'd seen that strained endurance before – the part of the morning attack that made her barely able to look at him. But she didn't seem frightened, or hurt, and Aspen most especially did not want to look past her into the room where his idol, his lifelong ambition, shuddered in the gloom.

Allowing his hearing to sink back to a normal range, he was glad there was something he could run to. Pots and pans were so much easier: they did what you wanted, and didn't go changing into things you never expected.

Discovering his robe still clutched in his hand, Aspen put it on and went to make breakfast. Peppering Leton with questions during yesterday's explorations had given him plenty of ideas at least, and he was regarding the results with partial satisfaction when she finally showed up.

"Sorry. I–"

"Don't try to explain yet." Aspen handed her a steaming plate. "Sit. Eat."

He frowned at her while she obeyed. This was his first good chance to look at Gentian since she'd stopped dying, and he was mainly inspired to pour more food down her throat. Frail. A strong wind would send her flying.

"Thank you for the cake," she offered, after picking without interest at her plate.

"No problem." Aspen made his voice close to normal as he added: "What went wrong?"

A blink. "Nothing. As experiments go, I guess that would count as our first real success. He felt It. He must have felt It every bit as strongly as I do, which I wasn't expecting. I'm sure my father only caught some echo."

She paused, considering this, and Aspen frowned at her. Like the Diamond, she seemed quelled, missing some vital spark. In her case it was probably just exhaustion, but Aspen wished she'd give him one of those sideways looks, or at least act concerned or worried, show anything but this...squashed lack of emotion.

"I needed you to go away, had to leave myself, because he'd made it worse by moving. And then by casting. Unless you stay as still as possible, the world feels more and more wrong and it's like your bones don't come with you and all people are monsters... With us there the need to get away would have been overwhelming, and I can't guess how casting must have complicated things. Once we left the pressure to escape us lifted. He's gone now, out into the valley. Walking it off."

She must have caught his expression because her own flickered. "You thought he'd handle it better than me?"

"Well, yes! I mean, I know you've had practice, but he's the Diamond! He doesn't do things like this."

"He's still human, Aspen."

"Maybe." He leaned forward urgently, needing her to understand. "But there's something very wrong. Didn't you notice? You should have seen him yesterday morning, barely listening to Chenar. It's like he's stopped caring whether we get out of here or not, like he's given up. And the Diamond doesn't just give up. He never has before." He realised he was glaring at her, heard the accusation, and protested: "But it can't be because of you. He saved you, and if the idea of you dying really and truly bothered him, then the last thing he'd be doing would be giving up. That's not how the Diamond is!"

"No." She said it softly, with a deep regret Aspen found peculiar. "Nor has he, or we wouldn't have suffered through this morning's experiment. But, you see, it was Suldar who saved me."

"What, so it's a fit of pique?"

She looked away from him, and he was immediately sorry for snapping.

"I think it does bother him." The words were tentative, as if she thought he'd up and shout a denial. "But he seems to have found that out just as we discover that It is quite happy to have me die. That It wins either way."

Aspen stared at her. "Do you believe that? That this thing wins whether you live or die?"

"I—" She bent to pick up the kitten, which had been lurking about the kitchen since yesterday morning, and watched impassively as the savage little creature tried to bite her fingers. "I'm short of other explanations."

"And the Diamond's out taking a walk?"

"It takes a while for It to wear off completely, and with the miscasting—"

"Miscasting?! The—"

"I think he was trying to draw shield. And, yes, I have some idea what miscasting means for him." She sighed and stood up, cradling the kitten. "If you don't think it's about me, then consider what this represents. After all, you've known all along his aim has been to protect Darest. Now it seems that the simple solution of just getting rid of me is far too risky. And that may have been an option he was relying on to save Darest."

Aspen frowned at her, not caring for the implications.

"How long do you think he'll be gone?" he asked eventually. "You do realise that the only reason why this morning's little snuggle-session wasn't a command performance was because he told them all that while you were recovering from dying we needed to focus on trying to detect and prevent any attempts to puppeteer them. They're all expecting to meet at midday to discuss what to do next, and no-one's in the mood to be put off."

"I expect he'll come back. But I wouldn't count on it." She didn't sound like it mattered one way or another.

Aspen's instinct was for denial. The Diamond was business first, always. With tempers back at tinder-point, he wouldn't indulge himself going off being upset somewhere. But then, if he'd really lost control of a casting... The Diamond was a mage above all else. A great-mage. Control was everything.

"I guess I'll go back to sleep," Gentian said, unenthusiastically. "I've stopped wanting to fall over every few seconds, and I think I'll try to consolidate that."

"These ladies of leisure, spending their whole lives in bed," Aspen said half-heartedly, making a face at the dishes he had to wash. "Off you go then."

With a faint, crumpled smile Gentian drifted out, and it was only after she was gone that Aspen realised what he had said. Feeling less than clever, he delivered breakfast to the rest of his guests, then returned to his room to dress. And then to stand outside the Diamond's door.

It stood an inch ajar, and there was no murmur of *saecstra*, but the divinations were still there, keeping watch over an empty room. A light push and he could survey the damage. Sheets draggling off the bed, scattered with fragments of glass and wood. Half a desk and a few sticks that had been a chair. All centred around a two-foot depression in the floor, the smooth-grained beams buckled as if a boulder had fallen out of the sky.

The Diamond, the ultimate in cool, calm and collected, had thrown himself out of bed, made it halfway to the window and tried to cast – it probably *had* been a shield. And true-magic drawn without due care had destroyed instead of protecting.   Pure luck the room wasn't decorated with fragments of Gentian and Aristide as well.

Aspen felt rather than heard movement behind him, and turned to find Leton.   Dark eyes made that brief, comprehensive survey – flick, flick, flick – and finished on Aspen's face.

"Come away from here."

Mutely, Aspen followed his Phoenix, wondering just what kind of explanation he wanted to make. And was faintly surprised to find himself being led upstairs to the Aurak's apartments, where he discovered the three Atlarans and the golden Aloren sitting over the remains of breakfast.

The Aurak gestured for him to sit down, and asked: "Is your master injured?"

Perhaps explanations weren't going to be necessary. "There wasn't any blood," Aspen said neutrally. "You felt the backlash of his casting?"

"Of course. Magister Couerveur had some concerns about the possible consequences, should he succeed in sensing our enemy's touch. He asked me to spend this morning attempting to discover any sign of castings linked to us. If we can find them, we may be able to discover a way to break the link before they trigger."

The Diamond had delegated.   The strategy of a drowning man, or simple good sense?   Whatever the answer, Aspen was heartened by signs of forethought and glad to put himself in the Aurak's hands, to spend a morning following orders and not thinking about what might happen next.   Scrying and casting minor shields and making himself feel like he was doing something useful.

He began to see why Rua was so proud of her lord. Aurak Bes might be just as far from a solution as the rest of them, but he went about his experiments with such genial interest that a desperate problem became a particularly tricky puzzle they would all enjoy solving. And Aloren and Leton stayed and were themselves, powerful and glorious and distracting, so it wasn't until it was nearly midday, when Aurak Bes tried and failed to sigil-call the Diamond, that Aspen found himself facing his worst thoughts again.

"Magister Couerveur must be shielded," the Aurak said, and though his tone was matter-of-fact, Aspen could see he was worried. "Come, let us go down. There is much to discuss."

No-one demurred. Perhaps even Aloren didn't want to question the Diamond's behaviour. Not only run off to be upset, but hiding now? A man who'd never flinched in his life? Who had barred *himself* from Darest's throne without an eye blink and managed to rule after by making sure the King never disagreed with him? The Diamond Couerveur putting magical hands over his ears so they couldn't talk to him?

What had he discovered? Surely Gentian's near-death and a handful of failures couldn't truly rob the man of the confidence that had brought Darest so far. Because, Aspen realised, that was what he hadn't seen in the Diamond this last day. It wasn't a question of whether he was upset, it was the lack of that ice-edged certainty, that rock-hard sense of purpose, direction, which made him so different.

With the day progressing so well Aspen was hardly surprised to see, when they reached the entry-hall, that Gentian had escaped the safety of her bedroom and seemed intent on throwing herself to the lions. Was Aspen supposed to protect her while the Diamond was off being upset?

But Dariens weren't Gentian's only friends. "Child, is this wise?" the Aurak asked, putting both hands on her shoulders, a greeting mixed with admonition. "You should be regaining your strength."

"I'm very tired of sleeping." Gentian's eyes had grown bright and strange since Aspen had fed her breakfast, and he was unhappily aware that she was not looking for a champion. That she thought herself past rescue.

"I think it's going to end today," she added then, with an otherworldly calm Aspen didn't like at all.

The Aurak considered her sorrowfully. "I have, I own, been feeling an air of expectation which I cannot explain."

"That is Suldar." Aloren, for once actually frowning a little, hummed as she came down the stair into the hall. "Her melody has changed."

It sounded like more harp music to Aspen, but after a pause the Aurak gave his definite nod. "I believe you are right, Your Highness."

"Is a change so significant?" Leton's hand was back on the hilt of his sword, knuckles white. "She can't have played exactly the same thing these past thousand years."

"Can she not?" Trailing a faint, sad refrain, Aloren went through the main door, and swept them all along in her wake, out to join the other heirs of the West standing before Suldar's statue.

And they were not what Aspen had been expecting either. The Cyans, even fiery Jurasel, were clustered together looking distinctly uneasy. Chenar and Rydan stood a short distance away, frowning up at the sun. The Saxan Crown Prince had evidently been continuing his dangerous line of experiments, and showed plain signs of spell backlash. Rydan looked exhausted and hopeless, like a half-grown boy facing a noose.

This at least explained why Leton had been so terse and preoccupied. There was something particularly upsetting his Saxan charges. Odd. Even if they thought a horde of Atlarans were right at that moment demanding the Aurak's return, there was no reason to go round acting like their kingdom was foundering while their backs were turned. That edge of imminent and catastrophic defeat had to be due to more than a change of musical tone.

Or was it? What was different about the song? These were some of the most powerful people in Sumica and they were *scared*. They were small, ineffectual things waiting for something bad to happen.

"Where is Couerveur?" Jurasel asked, with something very like concern. Prince Chenar merely glanced around wearily.

"Not here," Gentian answered, still with that unnatural calm. "I'm sure he won't mind if we start without him."

"And where do you suggest we start?" Jurasel asked, giving her a sharp glance. He was smart enough to see something strange in Gentian, though it didn't stop his questions. "Dhara and Seylon haven't produced any rabbits out of hats, and my own shields and scries were the usual waste of energy. All we ever get is more questions. We haven't made a jot of progress since the day we got here. No way out, and the only sign of this invisible enemy seems to be in your head. Can you at least tell us anything of use?"

"I can give you another question." She looked past him, gesturing at a stony woman at the foot of a flight of stairs. "Why put a statue of yourself at your front door?"

"Vanity?" Jurasel was impatient, but he looked at the statue nervously. "It's stone through and through, at least. Feel a strange affinity do you?"

"Nothing. We don't feel any of them, do we? None of Telsandar's deaths. But we can make a guess at a lot of this story. A thousand years ago the Fair Shaped themselves a pair of sisters. Immortal, immensely magical. By comparison the Fair were *senserel* – powerless. And one day all these *senserel* vanished, wiped out in a single moment. One of the two sisters must have been responsible. And the other..." She stared at Suldar's building, where the harp flowed on unheeding. "Came out here and looked down at her sister, the only creature in all the world anything like her–"

"And turned her to stone."

It was Desseron who had spoken, and perhaps it was the straightforward belief in the girl's voice that broke through to Gentian, because her eyes lost some of their unnatural brilliance and she looked down. "The death of a monster."

Walking blindly past Jurasel she stopped before the statue. "What is death, to someone that powerful? We know that around a week later the valley was put under a preservation spell, then sealed away altogether. And even that wasn't enough – the entire land was abandoned. Because Dawn was dead but not gone."

Gentian reached out, a negligible figure before the graceful height of the statue, the fingers of one thin hand splaying out. Aspen, whose whole world seemed bent on tilting toward disaster, felt it tip another inch and exclaimed "Don't!" even as she blasted stone to powder.

Not one of them managed not to flinch. Even Aloren cast a quick, concerned glance at Suldar's building. But sudden retribution failed to strike anyone down, and the music flowed on unceasingly.

Gentian was wide-eyed, but far from done. "The shield keeps her out of this valley," she said, staring down at the scatter of dust and grit. "And I let her in. I'm not sure why the rest of you are even here, but I'm sorry for it. As for what little we can do..." That too-steady gaze swept over Aurak Bes. "We are not quite *senserel* in this, Sir. Are the precepts not clear? We need to protect Darest–"

"We need to leave."

The Diamond, cold and precise and every bit as rock-hard absolute as his namesake, chose this moment to materialise from thin air, standing at Gentian's elbow. Not a hair out of place, not a crease in the unrelieved black of his clothing, and no measure of uncertainty in those star sapphire eyes as he added: "We need to leave today."

Chapter Eighteen

Gentian had gone through every option. She was Its primary tool and she had no way of changing that. But if her own fate was fixed, she planned to at least upset Its schedule. Anything was better than sitting in her room waiting for whatever happened next. To have Aristide, grim but no longer blackly frozen, suddenly materialise and talk of leaving, robbed her of numb acceptance and left her dizzy.

She was out of step with the rest of the prisoners. Aspen looked simply and profoundly grateful and, after a gaping moment while they assimilated the fact that he'd been prowling about invisibly, the heirs of the West shifted straight past shock and anger into taut readiness.

"You have something?" Lady Dhara stepped forward, dark eyes searching Aristide's face. "A new development?"

Jurasel was just as quick. "Bad news? Or are you actually proposing something constructive?"

"Yes and yes," Aristide said briefly. "Perhaps we could sit down?"

He took her by the elbow, which Gentian supposed meant she looked like she was about to fall over, and led them away from the dusty remains of It, to a circle of grass edged with stony benches. The whole scene felt unreal, with everyone falling back into the arrangement from that first night, when they'd sat around a kitchen table and talked of killing Suldar. Before the depth of their predicament had sunk in, and they'd still imagined there was anything they could do. Gentian was again sitting at Aristide's right hand, but with her head full of too-recent hurts and arm tingling where he'd gripped her.

"The bad news first, if you would, Magister Couerveur?" Aurak Bes said. He was, she could tell, less relieved than wary.

"We are out of time." It was perhaps the most direct Gentian had ever seen Aristide, gaze steady and mouth firm and unsmiling. But he was himself, far from the distant ghost of yesterday.

"Today I succeeded in experiencing the same touch as Magister Calder–" He broke off to glance at her and say, "It astonishes me that you ever contemplated returning to this land," before turning back to the rest of his audience. "My perception of Darest is different enough to see more of the mechanism 'Dawn' is using to touch Magister Calder, and through her usurp our strength. It seems this Fae is more trapped than I realised. The valley's shield is double, the inner making a haven and the outer a prison to keep her from running loose in Darest. But the outer shield is not as effective as the inner: she can reach past it in a very limited way, enough to keep the Fair from living in this kingdom. Like Magister Calder, they are something she can touch."

"So she's a bug under a rock." Jurasel was terse, holding himself in check. "Legs waving. Get on with it Couerveur. Does knowing more about the shield tell you how to get us out of here?"

His words conjured the faintest hint of a smile, but at the moment Aristide was far more magister than courtier. "It told me that while Dawn was able to bring us through the outer shield, she had nothing to do with our entry into the valley itself. And Suldar certainly did not want or help our arrival. We breached the inner shield purely because the Fair left themselves a door."

Disappointment was as intense as the hope it replaced.

"That's all?" Lady Dhara asked. "What's new there? We all know we came here through a door. The problem is, not only is it on the wrong side of the shield, it's not enchantment as I understand it. I spent too many hours staring at the thing and finding no rhyme nor reason whatsoever. Are you saying you've suddenly intuited a structure we couldn't even see?"

"In a way. It's not a technique I am any kind of expert with, but I have just come from reproducing it."

Aristide conjured illusion, a small image of himself standing before a blank white wall. Unlike the real Aristide, the miniature was dressed in white and wore a faint sardonic smile as he produced a stick of charcoal and drew a long rectangle on the wall, stretching from the floor to above his head. Then he drew a handle within the rectangle, reached out, and opened a door.

The image dissolved, sinking into a tangle of whorls that covered the circle of grass: the pattern through which she had brought them into the valley. A knot of Fae script wrote itself into the centre: 'Bow your head in shame before Telsandar'.

"We recognised it as a door, therefore it is a door." His tone was rueful. "No structure, no Elachar, nothing of the runic resonance we are taught to use. Still, it works."

Seylon began to laugh. "But this is the stuff of children's tales! You mean all we had to do was make a pretty picture of the thing we walked in through and we could have left? "

"Not quite. I attempted that days ago, trying to puzzle out its mechanism. Today, I abandoned the 'why' and simply used different centres." The illusion dissolved, and a new knot of script, bare of the border, wrote itself onto the grass. "The difficulty was finding a phrase that acted in the same way as 'before Telsandar', when we wanted to depart. I tried many possibilities, and this one seemed to wake to something more. And I put my hand through it. Through the shield."

"'Out of Telsandar...Darest'." Princess Kestia sounded only mildly incredulous as she translated the words. "You mean this? You have found our way of escape?"

Chenar leaned slowly forward, disappointment competing with something like despair. "Escape to what? Does this not simply bring us full circle, back out into that corridor?"

"No." Jurasel surged to his feet, eyes alight. "Not full circle. There was no free magic in that place, but our fed enchantments didn't lapse. And the outer shield is the weaker. Our fists will do us some good, so long as we pack them beforehand."

"Even so." Aristide's attention was on Chenar, who had gone shockingly white as he stared from Jurasel to Aristide. "Suldar cannot be maintaining the outer shield, which suggests it is a more traditional enchantment with either a large and well-hidden power store, or some kind of feeding mechanism. If we prepare sufficient shields, scries, dispells and demolitions, we may be able to force our way beyond the corridor."

"And where's the rub?" Captain Djol was ever-focused. "You were telling us we're out of time."

"Yes. The question of why you were brought here has always been a pivotal one. Even with all our strength combined, we are no match for Suldar. It is possible that the power born of the deaths of so many true-mages might be enough to overwhelm her, but if that was the case surely our stay here would have been a very short one."

"Cheerful." Seylon was dry. "I've had a few ideas on that count. Do you suppose the Fair don't live in your Darest because when they do they find themselves casting spells quite without meaning to?"

"Very likely. I suspect that when she lived Dawn possessed, if not Crown-bond, then something very similar. She has a link to the land itself, and it is that which allows her reach beyond her prison to touch any of her...parent race. But Telsandar has become Darest, overrun by a people who Dawn could not affect. Darest also currently possesses very few true-mages, which no doubt made a boat full of them a gift of fortune. Her power is limited without physical form, and she cannot be entirely certain that she will succeed against Suldar. So she has taken the opportunity to adapt to changing conditions." His mouth flattened. "Even if we succeed in leaving today, Darest may have become unliveable for true-mages."

The last couple of days of black emptiness became suddenly explicable. Disaster for Darest, and exile for this man who lived and breathed his kingdom. Because It had found a key to controlling human true-mages, and the door was already unlocked. They had moved too slow.

"But we can leave." Prince Chenar didn't care about Darest's future. He was transformed, lit from within. "Now." It was a demand. Rydan followed him to his feet, looking near to tears with relief.

"We cannot be certain this new gate will return us to the corridor." This was Aurak Bes, who would always see the weakness in any rash plan. "Let alone be sure of breaking through the second shield. Blast our way through a shield buried beneath a mountain? This seems to me a most risky idea, especially when we will only be able to rely on what we prepare. We will not be able to adjust to the conditions we face."

"We can't just wait here, Sir," Seylon pointed out. "And, after all, if the attempt fails the first gate should allow us to return to the valley. We can rest and try again tomorrow. Find something that will work."

Jurasel, watching Chenar with leonine indulgence, added: "But time's running out," and smiled to himself before looking back at Aristide. "What did you mean by that? Why do we need to leave today, now?"

"Before our experiments interrupted her, Dawn was becoming more and more adept at making use of us, better able to overcome the resistance of even the most naturally shielded. From what I could see this morning, she has nearly completed that adaptation, which makes our presence useful mainly as battle pawns. Today is our last chance to leave. Tomorrow she will usurp more than our powers."

"No-one's suggesting we stay another moment, Couerveur." Chenar's impatience was tangible, his sudden energy making him as vivid a creature as Jurasel. "When do we start?"

Aristide's eyes narrowed, but before he could speak Rydan flung up a hand, staring down at himself.

"*No!* Not now!"

But the trickle of power could not be denied, growing rapidly to a flood. Casting. All of them were casting. Even Princess Aloren. Even Kassen. Only Gentian and Aristide had escaped, and the princeling, Chiall, who was too young to be capable. The rest were pouring out power at an extraordinary rate, their faces tensing with shock and effort.

"You were *expecting* this!" Chenar spat the accusation between gasps. The power output of this casting was so far above previous efforts he had little breath left to spare.

Aristide looked at him, then crossed wordlessly to Kassen, drawing shield over the girl. Hurting and indignant, she flinched away, but then seemed to realise what he was doing and held still as power coruscated around her, the outflow choked by the shield.

"What's the intent?" Seylon asked brusquely, and grimaced as Prince Chiall, arms about Kestia's neck, began to wail from fright. "Aristide..."

"There is none." With immense concentration, Aristide succeeded in perfecting the shield around Kassen. Her outflow cut off immediately and she fell limp. "It's preparation for tomorrow. A power store."

"Gods."

Aristide turned away to construct a new shield about Desseron, and again began methodically choking off the casting. It was a performance Gentian couldn't match even at full health, so she went instead to Princess Kestia. Chiall's panic was growing, the infant flailing and clutching by turns, and the Cyan princess was barely able to keep upright.

"Highness. Do you want me to hold him?"

Kestia could not hide the flash of suspicion and affront, but she followed it with a glance at Desseron, standing white-faced but upright within a halo of flashes and sparks. Whatever Gentian's role in all this, Dariens were not quite enemies. "Take care," she said, stiffly.

With arms full of a now screaming and kicking child, Gentian staggered across to Kassen: "Sit down with me." She moved a few more steps away, then sank to her knees in the grass.

Kassen was slow to follow, but she did, brusquely detaching Chiall from Gentian and hugging and bouncing him while he howled louder still. In a few moments Desseron joined them and wrapped her arms about both of her siblings, which at least had the effect of muffling the noise.

"Can you stop this?" she asked over Kassen's shoulder.

"I wish I could." Inadequate words, feeble in the face of the accusation in the girl's voice. Gentian struggled with the mounting wave of responsibility. None of them would be here, if not for her. Their lives would not be at risk, and the disaster looming over Darest would not happen. "There's never been anything I could do."

"Then what were you going to suggest? Under the Aurak's precepts?"

"I don't think that will make any difference now."

Understanding rose in the girl's eyes, but Gentian looked away from it. She hadn't known what coming home would mean, but she'd been aware almost from the start that she was the cause of this mess. If putting herself out of reach had indeed been an option she'd left it too late, had done nothing since she got here except sit between disquiet and hope. Become *senserel* by behaving like one.

The casting stopped. Not all at once. Jurasel, Aurak Bes and Aloren lasted longest, slumping back drained and gasping almost at the same time. Even those shielded by Aristide were shaken, and the rest had collapsed one by one, most into brief unconsciousness. It had been a fast, furious vomiting of power and when it was done they were left to look up at a perfect globe of raw magic, sitting directly above the remains of the statue Gentian had just destroyed. It was scarcely visible, an ominous ripple in the sky.

Aloren laughed. She had subsided into a tangle of long limbs and elaborate gown, her hair streaming over a face shining with sweat. But she retained her magnificence all the same, and her eyes were glorious and alive.

"It would, after all, be a tremendous anti-climax if we left at anything but the last moment," she said, her voice rich with appreciation. "I trust you plan to bundle us out of this place a scarce moment before dawn?" Her heavy lids lowered. "I will at least give you the credit of assuming you would have spared us that if you could."

"It would certainly have been easier," Aristide said, without humour. "We will leave as soon as you are able." He glanced around the circle of royalty, most of whom were in no condition to argue, let alone get to the valley wall and try to blast their way through shields. "Midnight?"

"We were discussing risk." Lines of exhaustion and anger made Kestia more human, but no less absolute. "Before we rush to try this escape, I would like to hear just how dangerous it is." When he hesitated she added flatly, "Guess."

Aristide lifted one hand, then let it drop, suggesting a magnitude beyond measure. "Very," he said baldly. "Extremely. We cannot wait to fully recover your strength, and the spells we prepare might not be everything we need to break through. While the external shield is the weaker, it must still be immense. We will not be able to bolster our own shields against backlash in a confined space, and cannot guarantee our return here. I would not give us a more than even chance of survival."

"And if we simply stay here?"

"Rather less."

ooOoo

Gentian watched Aristide tidying up. Explaining patiently to Chenar that they were unlikely to have recovered sufficient strength before midnight, then checking over Captain Djol as he belatedly revived, and consigning him to the care of Aspen. Conferring with Seylon, who had rounded up his Cyan charges with an air of long practice.

Wondering once again if it were true that Seylon had been involved in an attempt on King Aluster's life, Gentian turned her attention to Suldar's building. The globe of raw magic distorted the lines of the architrave, but the music flowed on regardless. Gentian could not feel this was a good thing: if there was a way out of this valley, surely the Fae would be encouraging them toward it.

Or was it simply too late for Suldar as well? Having had her defences breached, she might not care about the fate of Its tools. Gentian had to admit she was herself less concerned with imminent death than the consequences of Darest being unliveable for true-mages. Her parents. Goldenrod. They would not be able to stand leaving it. And Aristide, of course. Aristide Couerveur, exiled from Darest? No wonder he'd been devastated.

"How are you feeling?"

Her turn to be tidied away. With no intention of being sent to her room, Gentian looked into the eclipse and wondered if she had imagined yesterday's defeat. She felt oddly inspired to hit him for recovering so quickly while she floundered in the same place.

"No longer perpetually exhausted," she said, as briskly as she could manage. "If we breach the outer shield, It will be free in Darest."

"But without Suldar's strength."

She was on the verge on asking him more when he cut her off, holding out his hand.

"There is something I wish to show you."

Gentian blinked, then took his hand. He immediately drew power: true-magic flight, lifting them both from the ground and straight up toward the false sky. She jerked in surprise, then adjusted to the sudden weightlessness, and gazed out at the counterfeit Darest appearing over the rim of the valley.

"Stop a moment."

He paused obediently, hovering near the apex of the dome, and she stared north over the shoulder of an illusory mountain to a dip of valley before some low, distant hills. "If that were real, we would be able to just make out Goldenrod," she said. She had very much wanted to see her home.

Aristide didn't respond, starting them moving again, heading directly for the obelisk that had been their door. He set them down on the walkway and let go her hand, glancing back down into the valley before gesturing to the right.

"This is the house Princess Desseron spoke of, which had visitors after the disaster," he said.

Beginning to feel curious, Gentian followed him, wondering what discovery he had made and why it was important now they were on the verge of leaving. It was one of the larger estates, the grounds separated from the walkway by a tall fence, with a sprawling building some distance in, overlooking a sharp drop. Aristide led her to a doorway through a high stone wall.

She was immediately distracted by the garden. The boundary was very distinct, and the place settled around her like a warm cloak, reminding her painfully of

Goldenrod. This had been someone's haven, a retreat, and they had loved and been loved by it. Everywhere she looked her eye was delighted by the natural and the exquisite. A pale stone bench gleaming in an ivy-dark nook. A single crimson highlight against a riot of interesting foliage. A bright corner, illusory sunlight warming a patch of grass surrounded by flowering annuals, with a stone railing and overhanging branches forming a window over the valley. Espaliered cherry trees made geometry against the high wall in an echo of the square frames of the glass-filled door leading into the house. It was graceful and full of joy and she let it draw her into its tiny rooms, each a different note in a glorious whole.

She drank it all in, feeling much revived, then remembered Aristide and said: "I'm sorry, what was it that you wanted to show me?"

"The garden. It seemed to me one you would like."

Gentian looked at him. He did not smile, or offer meaningful glances, or do anything but meet her eyes directly. And when he saw that she had understood, he turned away.

Aspen would tell her to shout with joy. Or throw herself on this Diamond Coueurveur, who had gone out of his way to show her a garden. A man of rigid priorities, telling her there was a conversation he had chosen to postpone. Gentian gripped the balustrade, then said:

"Why doesn't Suldar kill us?"

He considered the question, setting aside his reasons for taking her to this garden, as they had to be set aside while he balanced the tempers of the heirs of the West.

"While the shields appear to block our attempts to reach the Gods, a true-mage death is a source of enormous power. Most likely Suldar dare not risk killing any of us, particularly you or I with our links to the land itself, in case the shields are pierced. The attack with the swordsman certainly suggests that our deaths constitute a danger, although not the primary aim of our antagonist.

"The question I have been asking myself is why Suldar did not place us all under the Preservation she held on the valley. Unfortunately there was little opportunity to study the mechanism of that casting."

"Similar to Castrem's Restraint," Gentian said, remembering the lizard. "Time slowed immensely, but still progressing. That wouldn't have stopped It from touching me – I remember a string of related experiments around the time I was six. The Restraint would hold me still and unaware, but when they released me I suffered all the physical consequences at once, and the after-effects lasted longer."

He considered this, then nodded. "I suspect the moment we entered this valley, Dawn had her victory. We cannot be sufficiently shielded to prevent the manipulations made through you, and death is, as ever, only a matter of time. Suldar is unquestionably charged with keeping her sister in check, and I cannot be certain she will not attempt to prevent our departure. I gamble on the possibility that the destruction of the outer shield will be, to her, the lesser of two evils."

"I'm beginning to see why she shuts us out. We are instruments of ruin."

Too far away to hear Suldar's music, Gentian gazed down at the centre of the valley. Did the ancient Fae feel nothing but defeat, or did the prospect of the end of her long imprisonment make her heart beat a fraction faster?

Gentian dare not allow her own hopes rise too high. Thoughts of what would come after escape needed to wait until that escape had been achieved.

Chapter Nineteen

"Sleep and eat, sleep and eat. We have returned to our infancy."

Aspen, driven from his bed by hunger, made an effort to focus on a tall figure by the stair. Rua.

"Most infants don't feel quite so sat upon."

"It is to be hoped."

"Want me to fix something for you too?" He held up a peach.

She laughed. "You truly have found a calling, eager boy. Does it please you so to feed us?"

He shrugged. "Can't just sit around looking decorative. Feed the troops, my contribution to our adventures."

"A very necessary thing. And why I am here as well. Where shall we start?"

Aspen handed her a basket, and led the way outside, pondering a note of reservation in her voice. Rua must have opinions about being *useful* as well, or possibly living up to the strengths you'd been born with. But Aspen knew well enough his abilities, and tasty afternoon breakfasts were more than he'd originally expected to bring to this little jaunt.

His stomach complained, so he munched on the peach as he worked with Rua to put something more substantial together. He should have eaten before he slept, but it'd been enough to get Leton inside and then decorously stumble off to his own room. Fatigue and hunger would compete for their attention for hours yet, and he–

He stopped, then forced himself to think it through. They had been wrung dry. And in less than half a day they were supposed to crack open a shield big enough to hide a mountain.

Would they be recovered enough by midnight? Aspen had over-extended his casting a couple of times in the past, and knew this deep-seated exhaustion wouldn't be erased simply by a long rest. It would be days before he'd be at full strength.

"All in the timing," he muttered, and caught the faint nod Rua gave in response.

"To go into battle under strength is to gamble your life," she said. "But there are times when it is necessary."

"Saving yourself from the wolf by jumping off the cliff." Aspen sighed, and began to dish out.

With impeccable timing Hapt-lo Dest loomed in the doorway, and Rua sent him upstairs with trays for the Aurak and the Divine Aloren, following with a second. Aspen, aware that the *saecstra* was not anywhere nearby, covered plates with handy bowls, and then took a tray into a sunny room featuring a Phoenix sprawled on a day bed.

Setting the tray on a sideboard, he took his own plate and sat down to enjoy a survey of ambition, only to discover ambition regarding him narrowly between cracked eyelids.

"What was cast?" Leton asked, his voice rough from sleep.

"Nothing – a power store. We're going to make an attempt at midnight."

His Phoenix turned his head, enough to survey the windows to the garden, where shadows were stretching to late afternoon beneath their prison's false sun. He closed his eyes, took a sustaining breath, then sat up, fixing unerringly on the tray.

Only after inhaling half of the heavily buttered yam and onion concoction Aspen had reproduced did he cock a sardonic eye and say: "Not bad."

"Bah."

That earned him nothing, his Phoenix instead concentrating on eating quickly, apparently in order to make himself scarce. Not at all in the mood to be left behind, despite the dragging ache calling him to bed, Aspen followed him out of the building.

The globe of unspent force still hung over Suldar's building, near-invisible yet sucking all attention. Determinedly ignoring it was a cloying vision of youth: the three Cyan brats sitting with Gentian in the grass, making garlands out of flowers.

"Good to see our remaining forces working hard toward escape," Aspen said. "Now all I need is a bell to call them to dinner."

But Leton wasn't listening, making a bee-line for another late afternoon riser, just poking his nose into the central gardens, and looking as if it was all too much for him.

Aspen dogged his heels resolutely. Leton was barely up to walking, let alone all the cooking, cleaning and nurse-maiding the Saxans wasted him on. Truly a crime for a Phoenix to be stuck playing minder to such a tedious Pup.

"Leton!" Prince Rydan held out a hand as if expecting a Phoenix to light upon it, then let it drop. "I – I had something to ask you."

"Your Highness?"

Leton's tone was the Guard Dog's obedient neutrality, but the quick survey he gave his younger charge said volumes. The boy might well have greased his face for a melodrama, so largely writ were the lines of tragedy. More worryingly, he looked two gulps short of vomiting, so Aspen took himself a few steps away in a pretence of giving the pair some privacy. He wasn't at all certain Rydan even noticed his presence.

"At what point...at what point does duty...?" The Pup scraped his hands down his face. "I don't know what to do, Leton. Do I abandon myself for that which is my duty to protect? Chenar says we must place our trust in those outside this mountain, but the chance that, that..."

"Have you eaten at all?" Leton asked, cutting short any opportunity for interesting revelations. He wasn't one to forget flapping ears. "Decisions should never be made in haste or hunger," he added firmly. "Balance yourself physically, and you will be better positioned to settle questions of right and wrong."

"There's no *time*, Leton! We are past urgency." The Pup glanced at the false, sinking sun, noticed Aspen, and managed to catch himself up. "I–" He wavered, then sat down on the nearest bench. "You're right, of course. I'm not thinking straight."

Leton glanced about and stooped to select small, vivid strawberries from the nearest garden bed. "Eat these, and then come in. I'll have something ready."

They left him sitting on a low stone wall, staring at the berries as if he'd forgotten the trick of swallowing.

"A good opportunity for another lesson," Aspen said firmly, when Leton glanced at him. "I'll cook, you instruct."

Leton grunted, his attention shifting from Aspen back to the most irritating Pup, who had abandoned his strawberries to the wall, and wandered across to be offered a crown of flowers instead.

"Cooking is a useful extra skill," he said absently. "Not a reason to avoid harder work."

Aspen swore he didn't hear the noise of it, refused to have heard the noise of it, instead stopped at the jangle of harp notes, the shrill of children crying out in fright, and then Leton was shouting "No!", and Aspen turned again, to have that frozen moment burned into the back of his eyes: a small figure crumpled on the ground, and Prince Rydan standing above her, a heavy stone raised for a second blow.

Leton, barely walking let alone able to cast, still acted, thrusting with direct force over far too great a distance, enough to send that stone spinning away. He groaned and fell, clutching at his head and leaving to Aspen a field of horror made worse by floral ornament, and all Aspen wanted was to run away, but his feet took him forward, close enough to see the blood, the...the *dent*. But before he'd crossed half the distance the air twisted with an abrupt redirection of the valley's monumental flow of power, and Suldar was there.

Great gouts of magic made the scene ahead shimmer, but Aspen's feet did not slow, not 'til he stood panting at the edge of that focused intensity. He fumbled for a reason for the outpour. The...the *damage* had already vanished, with only a few smashed petals to mark the thing, the wrongness.

"He was right," Rydan whispered. "If she dies, the shield will be pierced."

It was the power, more than the princeling shrieking wildly in the arms of his sisters, that summoned true-mages from exhausted sleep, to run and halt and stare at the scene and react according to their natures. Lady Mara and Princess Kestia gathering their children. Seylon Heresar speaking a quiet word to distract Prince Jurasel's impetuous advance. Prince Chenar, grey and appalled, hurrying to his brother. The Aurak, paused in quiet prayer as Rua and Dest flanked him protectively. Golden Aloren, her expression judicial.

And Aristide.

The Diamond Couerveur was not smiling. Beyond that, Aspen could not guess at his emotions. Once past their early skirmishes, he'd treated Gentian with a directness he accorded very few, but if there was more it did not show in the glance he gave her crumpled figure before focusing on Suldar. Rydan he ignored altogether.

But Rydan would not be ignored. Chest heaving, he shrugged off his brother's restraining hand and took a step closer to the tight-wound maelstrom Suldar was channelling.

"Just let it end," he pleaded. "Why must you keep us here?"

The ancient Fae did stop, not in response to his words, but because she had completed her casting, leaving them in a strangely scrubbed moment, as if a storm had passed. Gentian lay as crumpled as before, with no sign of injury. Alive, within a certain meaning of the word.

Aspen had to grudgingly hand it to the Pup: he did not flinch as the Fae – dwarfing him in every aspect – turned to look down at him.

~My duty. My sworn vow. You will not find its failure benefits you.~

She turned, the only sound that of dead grass crunching beneath her slippers, but spared a parting word for those who had hoped to escape.

~I understand the outer shield to be designed to reflect internal attacks.~

ooOoo

"Choraide, take Magister Calder inside."

Aspen started, then reluctantly moved as the Diamond turned to Princess Aloren with a calm that was somehow worse than anger.

"It seems unlikely that we will succeed where the Lady Suldar has failed, but I would appreciate your assistance in the attempt."

"So, that's it then?" Jurasel had not quite lost his bullish energy, though he glanced uncomfortably away as Aspen stooped to collect a small and crumpled mage. "We're stuck here?"

"Until dawn," the Diamond replied. "Then I imagine Darest will detain you no longer."

He moved to go, but the Aurak forestalled them.

"I do not understand this," he said, and such was the man's authority that Aspen, who had contributed nothing to the situation, still quaked internally. "Why have you done this, Prince of Sax? Why, when we had finally determined a course of action, did you attempt to use death to pierce the shield?"

Rydan gulped like a lad about to be strapped, searched the ground for answers and found instead shattered petals. Flinching from that, he shook his head.

"It is a matter of the Skremmish succession, Aurak," said the Diamond, sounding only bored despite the muffled shock his words produced. "Skrem uses a Sun-blessed item to choose its ruler, a fist-sized knot of gold which relocates on the death of their monarch. The first true born of Skrem to hold it up to the Sun can claim their throne." The Diamond once again turned away, his glance warning Aspen to go inside or regret it.

"And this is relevant how?" the Aurak asked.

Arms full of a warm body that breathed but made no other movement, Aspen picked up his pace, but he heard Aloren answer, her voice rich with revelation and amusement.

"Skrem was once rather larger than its current size, and the Sun's Knot has been known to relocate outside today's borders. The only sensible thing to do when that happens is to shield it and have it hastily delivered...somewhere else, before vast hordes of ambitious Skremmish divine its location. But the Knot is a drearily powerful bit of metal. No shield would last for long."

You'd need a mage of Seylon Heresar's calibre to maintain such a shield, Aspen reflected as he followed the Diamond inside. Cya's Queen and Sax's King were far from friends, but Darest's revival was more than enough motive for a temporary truce. But why bring the thing to Sax, and tangle it up in a boating trip along the Galassas, instead of sending it directly into Darest?

"The Aurak was due to go from Sax to Tor Darest," he said aloud.

Aloren, a step behind him, hummed softly. She had been window dressing for the scheme, a role Aspen suspected she found ironic. Aspen doubted that Kubara Bes, Aurak and envoy of the Atlaran Empire, in whose company the Sun's Knot would most likely have travelled, found the matter half so funny.

"It's...it's too over-elaborate," Aspen continued, finding himself almost affronted. "Every man and his dog's been heading to Tor Darest this last month. Why not shove it in the hold of the next ship, then sit back and watch the fun?"

"The Skremmish are well aware of their own borders," the Diamond said. "There is no reason for the Knot to appear in Darest – or Sax, for that matter. Tracing its course back would be difficult, of course, but there would be a high chance of an attempt."

"And the Sun might well have an opinion." Aloren hummed a triumphal note, then touched the forehead of the still figure Aspen had laid on the bed. "How unlike Meneth. Bad enough to allow Cya to transfer the risk to him. To give the task to those two limp sons of his, instead of someone with his own pragmatism, was not at all wise. He's become increasingly erratic, these past few years."

The Cerian princess lifted her hand from Gentian's forehead, and briefly caressed one sun-browned cheek before stepping away.

"Just a shell," she said. "The Atlaran precepts have some definite opinions about revived corpses."

"Yes. The Aurak will not join us. He liked her enough to borrow time on her behalf. Besides..." The Diamond's eyes were veiled. "It may well be the best way to deal with Dawn."

"The shield wasn't pierced, though," Aspen said, because he could bear to follow through that thought. "Suldar stopped her dying. Fully dying."

"Stopped her returning to Lady Moon, certainly." Aloren hummed another note. "Death suppressed, not prevented. She has lost her link to her body, is as dead as any haunt or revenant. From what little I could translate of Suldar's intent, there was not sufficient response from whatever remains of the spirit."

"Death is a traumatic event." The Diamond, expression still completely absent, looked down at the body breathing on the bed, then bowed his head to Princess Aloren. "It is too soon to make any attempt. Will you join me after midnight? Choraide, lend Her Highness your arm."

Golden Aloren did not comment, merely accepting Aspen's hastily offered assistance for a walk upstairs. But when they reached her door, she hummed another note, then said:

"Diamonds are very lovely and very hard. But they can still shatter."

Chapter Twenty

Aspen spent the remainder of the afternoon sitting in a hidden corner of the centre garden, staring profitably at the toes of his boots. As desperately as he wanted to sleep, he lacked the heart to try.

Impossible for him to feel any lingering warmth where he had held Gentian's limp body, but still the sensation remained. There had been no resistance in her, no echo of the living person who had been so quietly assured, who had treated him with point-blank honesty, and had faced a daily beating because she wanted to return to a place she loved.

Aspen had no particular attachment to places. He would never hang about to be slapped awake each morning for one, let alone treat one as the be-all and end-all of existence, like a certain Couerveur.

How much pressure could the Diamond take, knowing the threats Darest currently faced? The combined wrath of the Western kingdoms, looking for their heirs. A Fae ghost liable to make the whole country unliveable for true-mages, and about to burst free of her prison. And the question of this Sun's Knot, sitting shielded somewhere, hidden even from the Saxan entourage. Had that shield, left unfuelled, failed and brought all Skrem down on Sax? Or had the Saxan King managed to have it located and moved on to Tor Darest? What would Soren and the divine Aluster be facing out there?

It had been the prospect of his own exile that had nearly made the Diamond falter. But even after that realisation he'd forged on, leading the effort to keep Gentian alive, and then to find a way out of their trap. The double blow delivered by a rock and Suldar's parting words hadn't even made him blink, immediately thinking ahead to the possibility of turning Gentian's breathing corpse into a trap for Selvar.

The revived dead – whole in all but spirit – were dangerous things to leave lying about. There were too many incorporeal things that might try to take up residence. Particularly Selvar, who had plenty of practice in at least momentarily possessing Gentian every dawn. That had been their vulnerability all along, the fact that had triggered the kidnapping of a barge of true-mages, then allowed an unkind spirit to reach into Suldar's sanctuary. It was entirely within the nature of the Diamond Couerveur to kill that possessed body in order to protect Darest.

Would striking down an ally he'd worked so hard to save be the blow to finally break him?

They were going to try recovery first. That, at least, had been clear. Gentian's spirit had been prevented from returning to Lady Moon and, in theory, could take up residence in her body once again. If she was allowed the time to recover a measure of coherence, understand what had happened to her, and summon the strength and determination to do so.

Gentian, Gentian, meek and mild.

The Atlarans had thought the woman hugely stubborn, and Aspen acknowledged that it took a certain level of willpower to stay more than an hour in a kingdom where you were savagely assaulted every morning. But haunts and revenants could take months, even years to recover from the shock of dying.

The thought of it all, of the sheer wasteful stupidity, made Aspen feel like he was suffocating. Particularly when he remembered Rydan's words, when Suldar had arrived to try to prevent a soul's escape.

He was right. If she dies, the shield will be pierced.

That idiot Pup. Led by the nose, and Aspen had no doubt which 'he' had fomented this piece of mischief. Just as Aristide was devoted to Darest, his brother was Cya's loyal dog. Those words were a titbit to choke on, and it was best to assume the Diamond knew or guessed whose hand had been at work, because Aspen most certainly wasn't going to–

It was not imagination. The air was thickening, power creeping around him. Unable to detect intent, Aspen heaved himself to his feet, wondering if he could bear to try to draw shield, and whether there was any point trying. His strength was nothing but a handy store for Selvar to tap, his skills too minimal to provide sufficient resistance.

But there was no outpouring, only a quietude, settling over an already hushed valley. And then, though harp music still cascaded from her sealed building, Suldar.

Astonished, Aspen took a step backward, belatedly recognising that the heaviness surrounding him was increasing layers of shielding. And this was dusk. Suldar's time of power, just as dawn was Selvar's.

~Hold out your hand.~

Running away would be pointless, but Aspen was still tempted. What was she going to do? What did she want with him, of all people?

His hand had crept out, against all better judgment, and he flinched as she raised her own, but somehow he managed to hold still even as a spur of white light appeared. But it was too much to expect him to just stand there when she thrust that spur down at him.

A deep, numbing jolt shot down his arm. Aspen fell back into a bed of daisies, unable to believe how quickly she'd moved, clutching at his wrist above a hand he'd surely pulled back before any blow could possibly land and it hurt, *hurt*–!

~The pain will fade.~

The daisies were dying. Aspen scrambled upright, staring from towering, too-close Fae to his hand, uninjured but for a faint silvery mark in the centre of his palm.

~When the time comes, you must strike.~

Already gone, leaving Aspen wondering if he'd imagined the last words. Hoping, *praying*, that it was imagination, because otherwise...what?

He curled his marked hand shut, and felt something there. Insubstantial, only present enough to be sure that it wasn't simply imagination, a cylinder. No, a hilt. And between the bones of his forearm, a blade.

A weapon. Suldar had given him a weapon. *Him*, a weapon.

Shaking, Aspen took a step, then another, and let his feet bring him inside. The Diamond would know what to do, would be able to put the Fae's weapon to better use than Aspen ever could.

The *saecstra* led him unerringly to Gentian's door, resting on its latch. It eased open at a touch, exposing the now-familiar scene of a Fae bedroom with several recently-planted pots by the window, an invested glow fading as the twilight deepened. The difference was in the shallowly breathing corpse on the bed, a ball of ginger fluff curled by her foot.

No Diamond. Aspen blinked, and for a wild moment wondered if Aristide Couerveur had spent the last few days disguising himself as an orange kitten. But a gleam of pale hair caught the eye, and he realised that the Diamond was sitting on the floor on the far side of the bed. Asleep, head resting on the mattress scant inches from one sun-browned and motionless hand.

Aspen caught the door and pulled it closed.

The only place to go was his room, to sit on a too-empty bed and contemplate options. Laughable to put himself in the role of the one who draws concealed weapons on Fae-possessed mages, and actually succeeds in striking them down. Ludicrous.

And yet beyond unacceptable, unthinkable, impossible to force Aristide Couerveur to do it.

ooOoo

Aspen sat himself in a corner of Gentian's room and worked quietly on the best shield he could manage. His private struggle had, of course, not altered the path the Diamond had already resolved upon: using the brief moment of possession, Gentian's daily torture, as an opportunity to strike at Selvar.

Was it only imagination that made the night feel so cold? Aspen had brought along his travelling coat, and huddled into it, wondering at his own presence. He had never aspired to be 'useful'. To enjoy life, definitely, and to lighten the trials of those around him, yes. Making the occasional witty observation, dancing divinely, and conjuring breathy gasps after suitable activity.

None of that involved killing anyone. Not even when they were dead already, and some kind of monster of spite. Especially not when it would probably destroy any chance of a little gardening mage recovering herself.

He glanced over at the bed, at the figure that had not moved or shifted since he'd put her there. She'd hated Selvar so much. Called her It. The last thing she'd want would be for her tormentor to break free, doing whatever it was that ancient Fae ghosts thought entertaining. Killing other Fae, perhaps? Gentian wouldn't want that.

Gentian wouldn't want a lot of things. She didn't get to have an opinion in the matter: choice taken away by a rock and an unguarded moment. Aspen didn't feel he had been given any real choice either. He had sat stubbornly in his room during the midnight session of trying to draw Gentian's spirit back to her body, but as dawn approached he'd again followed the whisper of the *saecstra*, supplemented by a half-dozen spells built to bring death.

As Aspen finished casting, other spells pricked at his senses. Outside, a reserve force waited against the possibility that the Diamond Couerveur, Golden Aloren, and Aurak Kubara Bes – the three great-mages of their company – should fail to crush one small gardener in the moment of Dawn's possession. What little he could make out of intent suggested defensive spells, and ordinarily Aspen would have most sensibly joined them. He could still do that, could get up and go downstairs, perhaps take comfort in a Phoenix's profile.

Leton. Why hadn't he thought of him before? A brilliant swordsman, decisive, practiced at leadership and death, and unlike Aspen demonstrably...

The Diamond glanced at him. He had not objected to Aspen's unhappy presence, but he was clearly aware of unusual behaviour. Aspen closed his silver-marked hand on the sensation of not-quite-there and held himself still.

What made Aspen *useful* was his failure to present any significant threat. That had to be why Suldar had come to him. Though whether Selvar knew enough details of her tools to make that distinction was another question altogether.

"I don't recognise that casting, Your Highness," Aurak Bes murmured, breaking a long period devoted only to inventive death.

"I've placed a bent sliver of bamboo into her heart. If the casting is removed, the sliver will spring open."

Aspen flinched, not at the terrible image the princesses' words conjured, but because his shield had responded to some outside touch. But it was only the kitten, nosing about his ankles. He relaxed his shield and scooped the ball of fluff up, depositing it to wriggle in a coat pocket, then hastily brought his shield to full strength as Aurak Bes murmured a note of warning. Only the Atlaran revealed his sorrow in the moment. Aloren was, as ever, the detached observer, and the Diamond...

Expression as calm and unperturbed as a Deeping pool – and likely just as deceptive – his gaze never wavered from Gentian's face. In all Aspen's long observation of the man, he'd never found him so opaque. The Diamond usually made a play of mockery, acrid little displays of derision and courtesy, and clearly enjoyed the verbal joust. Those who knew him well could spot the tiny signs of displeasure or true amusement, but Aspen now found only an absence. Would this new–

Light. Aspen flinched, threw up a hand to protect his eyes, and then concentrated frantically on his shield as the world seemed to float around him, and he was lifting, tumbling. An impact into pink, a riot of petals, and he bounced and slammed downward, then lay gasping until his mind churned through to an understanding that a cherry tree had not hurled itself out of nowhere to attack him. He'd been flung from the building.

Rolling over, Aspen gasped again and jerked to avoid crushing the kitten. And then staggered drunkenly to his feet, searching wildly through the myriad shades of dawn for movement.

The mountain opened.

Aspen sat down again beneath a shower of scented petals as the false sky unfolded as gracefully as any blossom, if flowers could shake the earth and set bones to rumble. A brisk breeze caught falling specks of pink and whisked them skyward, to compete with the stars fading into dawn's chill light.

The extravagance of the mountain's disrobing left Aspen's inner ear quivering and overloaded, but did leave the valley marginally brighter, enough for him to finally spot movement.

Light washing from the room of instruments picked out a tall figure walking with a curious lack of grace into the gardens. Beneath the curving stone leaves of the central pavilion her goal waited. It took Aspen several blinks to recognise the reluctance embedded into each step, and to begin to sort the flow of magic between the pair. A massive, one-way wash. Not an attack, but a channel. With each day Selvar had become more adept at taking and using the magic of the captive true-mages, but on this last morning she ignored all but the true prize, finally won. Suldar.

He had to get closer. To somehow reach that water-guarded pavilion unnoticed, and strike the blow that would stop this, and he almost broke down laughing at the idea of that, of him, and a creature who could open a mountain with the ease the rest of Darest sliced off the top of an egg.

A voice spoke out of the grey. "We are but *senserel* in this. And yet, knowing ourselves gnats, do you not wish to sting, to at least be a nuisance?"

Rua, grave but upright, reached down a hand, and Aspen took it.

"Our lost friend would tell me that I reveal in this pride the precept's prejudices, thinking myself a gnat merely because I cannot compare myself in power. But the precepts also tell us that in times of great peril it is the responsibility of all who can act to lend their strength, no matter how small that strength is. Shall we see what we can do?"

"Rua, you are ice in midsummer. I think I might love you."

"Just a little," Rua said equably, proving she had taken his measure well. "Come, we may at least be able to offer up a distraction."

"You think we have any hope of reaching her?"

Rua raised her iron-shod staff toward the sliver of moon visible over the rim of the valley, and then struck the path beneath their feet, the sound of metal striking stone ringing out like a judgment. From the upper tip of the staff bloomed a twin spiral of glowing smoke, taking the shape of two long-eared and lean hounds.

"Shield," she murmured, and Aspen hastily resurrected some measure of protection as twin trails of light and smoke loped through the air, paths crossing and crisscrossing in faster and wider loops until finally they came back together one last time, converging on the central island and its stone pavilion, only to flatten into nothing against an implacable wall.

"Shield indeed," Rua murmured, even as the pavilion was lit by a second attack, a crimson light washing across it, setting the water on fire but not troubling the occupant at all.

"No counterattacks," Aspen muttered, shoulders tight with anticipation of unfallen blows as he searched for whoever else was casting.

"I think perhaps the Lady Suldar is resisting? Come, let us close on them."

Aspen thought that if Suldar was resisting, she was not doing so very effectively. The ancient Fae had reached the bank of the valley's tiny central lake and, as Rua and Aspen dropped their shields in favour of stealth, Suldar ponderously lowered herself to her knees, gazing across the water at the gravely unsmiling face of the twice-dead.

~How many centuries? How long would you have sacrificed yourself to their cowardice? And for what?~

The mind-speech rang out clearly, though Aspen was not certain if he heard because he'd moved into range, or if the Fae pair had been silent until now.

~I have come to recognise that my reasons are beyond your understanding, sister.~

~I understand that you talk of duty as if it were a chain about your throat. That you buried yourself alive by Daseretal's command, and she left you to rot. Will you ever weary of the price placed on your loyalty?~

~Sister, it has never been Daseretal exacting this price from me.~

The mind-voices were almost identical, both dignified and sorrowful, and Aspen wished he could better tell them apart, so one could clearly be the monster. And now what? The pavilion was protected by a shield, not to mention its own little watery moat. Any approach would be obvious, and need to overcome a shield so completely indifferent to attack that the Fae wearing Gentian's body didn't even glance aside when another bloom of fire spent its force just short of the pavilion.

Drawing closer had allowed Aspen to spot the other players in this drama, scattered in clusters a short way beyond Suldar. Aurak Bes and Jurasel, with Hapt-lo Des hurrying to join them. The Diamond and his brother. Lady Dhara and Golden Aloren, who had blood spattered down the side of her face and over the shoulder of her dress.

And there a Phoenix, glorious shadow to Poet and Pup, and Aspen was struck by the fact that even the Saxans had stayed with some thought of fighting, despite how close the borders were, and how so much more sensible it would be to simply fly off and leave Darest to her angry ghost.

So they were at hand at least, even if most were holding back. If he somehow could coordinate these forces to attack all at once, would that be sufficient to break the shield? And then he could hurl himself at the pavilion – he'd need a flight spell, and he had nothing prepared and this was still madness, ridiculous, and yet his feet took him forward as Suldar bowed her head and shuddered from some invisible blow.

"Here."

Rua tugged his shoulder so they crouched by a spreading bush covered in flowers in shades of lavender, a handful of metres from Suldar, and with only a tiny lake to travel to reach their target.

"They prepare to place a shield over the Lady Suldar, as your lord did previously with the child, Kassen. When her sister is starved of the source of her power, we must strike with everything we have. Set your spells."

Aspen grit his teeth and made himself concentrate on casting a flight spell. This was everything he did not want to do, and, no, he would concentrate on the casting and nothing else. Just a flight spell, something he'd managed dozens of time. And when Selvar was unprotected, he would fly over the water, and draw the knife as he rushed forward and then, then...

Shuddering, he cleared the casting and started again, forcing himself to think only of the words. Exact pronunciation, crystal clear intent. A matter of flight, no...

"Sun."

Rua, preparations forgotten, straightened to her full height, staring upward. And Aspen joined her, startled out of all thought of death.

"I thought they were myth."

The sky-ships of the Fair. All the old stories of their Empire talked about sky-ships, but they had fallen far out of living memory, until it seemed that even the Fair themselves, long-lived but not immortal, had never seen one in flight.

Aspen had worried about the armies of Skrem, or the West, or even Atlarus invading Darest while the Diamond was sealed beneath a mountain. But instead it was the Fair, a half-dozen ships skimming into view, and more cresting the rim of the valley as he watched. Hulls of golden wood, sleek and simple, beneath great layered networks of sail, planes of cloth set at complex angles and picked out in all the colours of the dawn's light.

~now~

A tiny word, inserting itself into his mind, and Aspen looked away from the sky in confusion. The shield protecting the pavilion remained, solid and undisturbed, though the wash of power from Suldar to Selvar had suddenly increased, and the small figure worn by an angry ghost was staring upward with a clear and vivid pleasure as she wound all that strength up toward a blow to knock beauty from the sky.

And then Aspen understood, and he flinched, giving Rua a glance full of an appeal she did not even notice. He fished in his pocket and handed her a kitten and left without a word. It wasn't far, perhaps a half-dozen steps, and he moved quick and deliberate, because there was no space left to doubt this course.

Dead grass crunched beneath his feet, and she raised her head. Even kneeling she was nearly as tall as he, and from a still, cold place he saw that she had tears running down her cheeks, but that she smiled. Behind him a massive casting released, but he was in a tiny room where only two existed as he pulled the weapon she had given him, and ran it into her heart.

Death leaves claw-marks. Gentian had said that, an eternity ago when she was alive. The death of a being such as Suldar went so far beyond that one could only reach for superlatives. Rent. Gouge. Rift. Chasm.

All Aspen knew was that he was hurled into the lake, and that his arms hurt. His left felt like he had removed a bone along with the weapon. The right hand...

He held it up, between his face and the receding surface of the water, and then he took it away and thrust it into a pocket of his coat, and was glad he'd removed the kitten, which was unlikely to have appreciated these circumstances. He thought about other movement. There was surely some flailing or kicking appropriate to the occasion, and yet that was beyond him and he did not seem to care, could only think of a smile both beautiful and rare, and gone forever because of him.

Was this sinking sense of peace Suldar's? The deaths of stronger mages could leave more than a wound wrought with power: echoes of thought or feeling lingered, until even non-mages might shiver at an unseen past. What effect would such enormous power have on the hapless passer-by?

A twist of intent reached through the heaviness, and then the brightness that was the surface of the water and the sky all rushed toward him, and he was lifted effortlessly from the lake and deposited...not next to the body, thankfully, but some distance away from a scene which barely looked real. Princess Aloren, bloody and alone, kneeling like a handmaiden by the fallen, gently rearranging limbs and smoothing the overlong dress.

Aspen blinked, coughed, then turned his head and stared up into an infamous pair of ice and blue eyes.

"Now I know I'm dreaming."

The faintest of frowns lifted from the Diamond Couerveur's brow. "He'll live."

"Indeed." Rua, kneeling on his other side, had a background of flying ships in disarray, no longer under attack but most definitely damaged.

"It's over, then?" Prince Chenar asked, drawing tentatively closer. "We can leave?"

"But what did you use on her?" Jurasel asked. "What was that?"

Aspen shot a second brief glance at the body Aloren tended. The hilt of something, barely visible, projected just below the breast bone. The air looked bruised, over that place, darker and rubbed thin.

"She gave it to me. To use...when...when it was time. They're both gone, aren't they?" Remembering, Aspen hauled himself onto an elbow and stared across at the pavilion. A puppet with cut strings lay discarded.

The Diamond turned too, and that little pile lifted, and floated across to him.

"I believe the Lady Suldar used the strength of her own demise to end her sister's hold on this world," Aurak Bes said, watching gravely as the Diamond settled Gentian's body into his arms. "There was a substantial link between them."

"Bound beyond death," the Diamond said, looking down at the figure in his arms. Still breathing.

There was something exceptionally horrid about carting around the empty body of a lost friend. How long did you preserve it? At what point did you choose to stop its heart?

The Diamond turned to the largest clump of royalty – or perhaps simply to Prince Chenar, with his brother a wan shadow in his wake – and said:

"Goldenrod Steading, which is Magister Calder's home, lies at the northern foot of these mountains. No doubt you will wish to offer your regrets to her parents."

Aspen thought they all flinched a little at that, at the thought of the Diamond arriving with both corpse and murderer in tow. Or perhaps it was at the man's smile, faint and full of promise. For the mountain was open now, and while there were sure to be all manner of forces rushing to follow the Fair's ships to a newly-opened valley, the main threat had been disposed of, and the Diamond Couerveur could indulge in other business.

Chenar immediately muttered in his brother's ear, shaking his head. But Rydan, with the air of a martyr, drew a breath and nodded.

"Of course."

Chapter Twenty-One

"Show me your hand."

A Phoenix, narrow-eyed and determined, briefly leaving his charges to the argument that had followed the Diamond's departure.

"No. Can't do that yet." Aspen watched the Diamond waft over the rim of the valley, then took a hasty survey of those nearest: Leton and Rua, with Princess Aloren approaching. "Why is he taking her so far away? Won't distance make it harder for her spirit to find her body?"

"Aristide is far too much a realist to cling to a lost cause." Princess Aloren lifted a languorous hand to her bleeding upper ear, drew something out, and held it up for study. A sliver of bamboo. She flicked it away. "The possession alters the circumstances completely. Like a borrowed dress, reeking of another's scent and, worse, half the seams burst and the hem shortened. Unrecognisable to a spirit's limited senses. Particularly given that it was Selvar, a creature Magister Calder has been trained since birth to recoil from. So now we will have instead a salutary little lesson to Sax's cost, and I rather think your new king will have a difficult time of it in future."

Sax's King Meneth would definitely retaliate if his son was killed, no matter what he'd done to deserve it, but Aspen knew that wasn't what Aloren meant. The Couerveurs had been brilliant regents, but all of them had eventually been warped by the strain of rule – or the doubled curse lurking beneath the Darien Gift. Soren had once said that the biggest threat Darest faced was the moment Aristide Couerveur decided not to act in its best interests.

"You're not a realist, though," he said urgently, to a woman who would be a queen, and was great-mage, and rarely stirred herself because, perhaps, she was rarely stirred. Was it worse to be useful, and choose not to act? How could he move her? "You're a playwright," he added. "And tragedies are so dull."

"Playwright?"

"So Gentian said. Find a different ending to this. Please." He gauged her expression, then added: "The Diamond would never live it down if you do."

That won him an amused narrowing of golden eyes. "You will never be accused of subtlety."

"Pussyfooting around never got me anything but delay. If all the logical and proper methods have been exhausted, isn't this the moment for the mad chance? If Gentian's spirit's drifting about this valley, surely there must be some way we can *force* her back into her body."

Rua walked off abruptly, moving to join Princess Kestia, casting a flight spell on her younger daughter.

"A *farvelti* binding would do what you're talking about," Leton said. "But for the minor point of being against the precepts *and* Sumican law, and thus the form is not commonly known. A *farvelti* compels the lost into a specified object, obliged to obey your will – it's usually done for purposes of interrogation – but that is not the same thing at all as drawing a spirit to rediscover their body. It causes considerable distress, and the strictures of the spell itself would be a barrier preventing full union."

"But it would make her aware, yes? And place her at her body. And then we could release the spell."

"At which point her spirit, diminished by the toll placed on it, will dissipate, lost even to the Moon." Aloren hummed two slow notes. "Only an extraordinary feat of will would alter that outcome."

"Given that's the outcome we already have, doing nothing seems the worse option. Besides, we're talking about someone who cast a torture spell on *herself*. Twice.

Who returned to Darest against a vow on her name, and stayed even when she had to wake to something she thinks worse than torture, every morning. The Atlarans have all these little ditties about her legendary stubbornness. You think she'd just give up?"

"I think that it would be most interesting to watch you ask her parents' leave to cast a *farvelti*. But I have no objection to teaching you the form."

That hadn't been what he wanted, but all that was important at this stage was that she knew a useful spell and was willing to repeat it.

"Thank you, Highness," he said, and drew a shaking breath.

"Look to your own needs first," Leton said. "Dry clothes, and–"

"Dry clothes," Aspen agreed, cutting short anything more. "Dry clothes and then, for the Sun's sake, let's get out of this valley."

ooOoo

Aspen did not go near Suldar's body before he departed, but he bowed his head to her, and hoped that she had found the Moon's peace. The place where she had died would inevitably draw others after her, so strongly was it imprinted with her choice. And an act of his that would echo for decades.

He had found another coat with pockets deep enough to bury his right hand, and tried to put that from his mind as he rose and followed the trail of royalty heading north. The air had been full of sigil-communication, and the ships of the Fair had regained control above, but it seemed that no-one was inclined to stay in Telsandar to greet them. Instead, they all headed north, to the broad stretch of blue that marked Goldenrod Steading.

The colour was flax flowers. Playing about with fields of it seemed the dullest thing in the world to Aspen, but

Shapers were a peculiar breed, and the results of the Calder-Varpatten experiments were profitable to Darest. A sprawling set of buildings surrounded by all manner of other plants sat on the slope of a hill on the eastern edge of all the flax. It looked idyllic, a drowsy place of peace, and it came as a considerable shock to fly within its bounds and strike a morass of grief and fury.

Aspen had never felt anything like it, and followed the lead of the flyers immediately around him, dropping quickly to the nearest stretch of grass in the wake of Aurak Bes. It took several gasps before he managed to stand upright, and see that he was not the only one with tears suddenly streaming down his face.

A tethered goat watched him laconically, and Aspen wiped at his face, struggling to separate his own tangled emotions from that born externally.

The Aurak was clearly receiving sigil-communication, and looked back toward the southern mountains. Dozens of flyers were already drawing close: the search parties, considerably augmented from their initial numbers, sighting their goal at last. Aspen had not known there were so many mages in Western Sumica.

It all grew a little chaotic then, as flights of mages each in turn homed in on their lost, came to land, and experienced the same bewildering wave of grief. A portion of the newcomers seemed to be Atlaran, quickly forming an honour guard around their Aurak, but most were Sumican. Among the well-armed mass Aspen struggled to spot any familiar faces.

"Is that *mother?*"

The low, astonished question had come from Princess Kestia, and was followed by a muttered curse from Jurasel.

"With Eneka and Thon. Lovely. Look about for a nice puddle to have our faces rubbed into. Might as well get an early start."

"Not with Meneth looking on." Lady Mara nodded toward another arrival, exchanged a glance with her wife, and then with an air of loins girded, the group headed toward the Cyan Queen.

Royalty and mage blood might be commonly aligned, but it was incredibly unusual for Sax and Cya's monarchs to join the notoriously hands-on Cerian queen on the search, even when it was their own children lost. Aspen suspected that their presence was more than a little linked with a certain conspiracy regarding Skrem.

The royal he was most interested in was also dropping gently from the sky, his reaction to the atmosphere at Goldenrod only an already etched-deep frown. King Aluster had a lone guardswoman in his wake, a discomforting illustration of Darest's current strength compared to neighbouring kingdoms.

He must have spotted Aspen before he landed, since he headed directly for him and said: "Tell me."

Ordinarily Aspen would enjoy few things more than spilling his heart to the divine Aluster, but under the circumstances he focused instead on speed and detail, and felt a measure of relief to have his king nod as if he was making sense. Aluster Rathen might still be catching up to the time into which he'd been transported, but he fully understood the dangers of Aristide Couerveur.

"I presume he's not contemplating imprisonment and execution. Does he have grounds to seek personal redress?"

Finding it difficult to put an unguarded moment into words, Aspen raised his hands, and his king grimaced.

"He's barely known the woman a week. What chance of persuading him to accept blood price? No, stupid question."

The Diamond himself appeared then, descending the path from the house in the wake of a lean blond woman. Beside him...it could only be Gentian's father, far too like her for comfort. And with them a tall and beautiful man whose soft brown hair had inspired Aspen to several complicated dreams the previous autumn: the Tzel Aviar, Damaris, Warden of the Borders and representative of the Deeping. A useful reminder that Darest was not necessarily an easy target, but also typical of his kind in refusing to involve himself in human affairs unless there were no other options.

King Aluster started over immediately, but Aurak Bes reached the group first, and took the blond woman's hands, bowing over them and offering condolences.

Red-eyed but composed, the woman shook her head, then said in response to a murmured question: "No, it's Goldenrod itself. Laeth's family has worked with it so long that the tie has become tangible. Despite all these years of absence, Gentian was part of this place. We felt the blow yesterday afternoon."

The woman turned then, and surveyed the assembled throng.

"So which of you murdered my daughter?"

As questions go, this was one to conjure silence, even out of complete confusion. And then all the side players moved away, and a down-cheeked Pup pulled free of his father's hand to step forward. White-faced, shaking, but on some level stalwart.

"I understand that you felt some urgent need to avert a crisis. Did you succeed?"

The Pup flinched, and glanced over his shoulder at his father and brother, and the Phoenix in obedient attendance behind them. King Meneth, a more muscular and vigorous version of Chenar, didn't say anything, just narrowed his eyes. It was Leton who made a minute shift of position, commanding some form of answer.

"It – it had been..." Rydan jittered to a stop, then swallowed. "Others had taken – there was...it had already been prevented."

"A senseless death, then." Gentian's mother deliberately turned from Prince Rydan to the Diamond. "I have no objection to the course you propose, Magister Couerveur, if that is the one you must take."

Her husband took her arm, and the pair returned along the path to their house, no doubt to contemplate the breathing corpse the Diamond had presented them with.

By this time King Aluster had reached the Diamond, who appeared perfectly composed as he offered the king formal greeting. But Aspen was near enough to hear the barely-audible words that followed:

"Give me this, Strake. I find there are some things I cannot swallow."

An ignorant few called King Aluster the Diamond's puppet, obedient to his lead. And many others privately mocked and delighted in Aristide Couerveur's *saecstra*-enforced servitude, revelling in the circumstances that permanently barred him from the rule of a kingdom he considered his own. Aspen was well aware that the situation was far more complicated, a form of partnership based on mutual pragmatism and respect, and perhaps even friendship. Fragile still, but strengthening, and it was a good sign that the Diamond chose to ask for permission, for all he clearly didn't intend to accept any refusal.

"Very well," King Aluster replied, and while his voice was dry, he showed no sign of indulging his difficult temper.

The Diamond murmured a few more words, too low for Aspen to hear, then moved toward the waiting crowd. King Aluster shot Aspen a look of clear command before following him. Aspen, who had hoped the King would take over the difficult business of casting, searched unhappily for Aloren, only to find Rua leading the Cerian Crown Princess and her mother, Queen Myentra, toward him.

"Her Highness would appreciate a place to tend her injury," Rua said, as regal and reserved as a queen herself, despite the ginger kitten riding proudly on one shoulder.

"Of course," Aspen said, glad despite where this was leading him. Rua might have barred herself from the details, but she was sympathetic to his cause. "Right this way, Highness."

They turned toward the path, Rua neatly drawing the Queen's attention back to the Diamond just as he stopped some twenty feet from Prince Rydan and lifted his voice to carry over the crowd.

"The Tzel Aviar informs me that the Fair do not consider Telsandar to have been part of the Darien gift. Blood price can be negotiated with him at a more convenient juncture."

That sent a ripple of shock through the crowd, and though King Aluster did not look surprised, he could hardly be pleased. What would it mean for Darest's future, to have a Fae city planted in its northwest? Did the removal of Selvar mean the Fair would seek to undo the Darien gift, and take the kingdom for their own once again?

If the Diamond was concerned by that prospect, he did not show it, still wearing the faintest and coldest of smiles as he continued.

"Magister Varpatten's staff are arranging for food and places to rest for those who need it, though you will no doubt be anxious to return to your homes. But first there is a question of a life deliberately taken. Aurak Bes, would you adjudicate a *Tejustra* challenge to settle this matter?"

The Atlaran ambassador bowed his head. "Of course. Do you act in the stead of Magister Calder's parents?"

"No, I claim injury entirely on my own account. We had been fully an hour betrothed."

This caused a minor sensation, of course, and Aloren paused on the pathway to look back, brows raised. Aspen barely managed not to show his own astonishment. He'd known there was something there, yes, but he'd not begun to guess it had progressed so far.

Aurak Bes turned to Prince Rydan. "Are you willing to meet Magister Couerveur in *Tejustra* to answer for your act?"

"That's – you mean a duel, yes?"

"Combat to the death." Aurak Bes, although he could not know for sure that the Saxans had planned to use him as the Diamond had suggested, was clearly out of sympathy with them, speaking with considerable reserve. But he was also a kind and a fair man, adding: "There is no onus on the challenged to accept a *Tejustra*. It is a by-pass of the normal processes of law."

"The law in question would be Deeping law," offered Seylon Heresar from the edge of the crowd. His attention was on his brother, his usual air of light mockery replaced by a hooded watchfulness. "Of course, the Fair may not be interested in applying it." He inclined his head to Tzel Damaris, who failed to appear to notice.

The Saxan king, Meneth, turned from speaking to Captain Djol and came forward, face a welter of emotion, with caution currently in primacy. He had enough mages with him to make it impossible to stop him leaving without a fight, but while Darest did not have mages or even a strong standing army, Atlarus and the Deeping's involvement meant no-one was going to rush quickly to war. But he clearly had no intention of watching the Diamond neatly despatch his young son.

"It gains nothing to pile another tragedy on the events of the past week," King Meneth said. "I deeply regret your loss, Couerveur, but step back from this. It can bring no good."

A warning cloaked in sympathy and reason, and the worst of it was the audience of Cyan royalty, close behind Seylon Heresar. Aspen was quite certain it had been Aristide's own brother who had set Rydan on this course, and perhaps the Diamond even guessed at that. But it had still been the Saxan prince's choice to act.

"The challenge has been issued," Aurak Bes said, the man's authority rolling over the rising noise. "Rydan, Prince of Sax, it is for you to accept or refuse."

"I accept," Rydan said, voice breathy but determined. He shrugged off his father's hand. "I have to face the consequences."

"But I do not give you leave." King Meneth was absolute. "You are still a child, and should never have been brought to such a pass."

To Aspen's horror, a Phoenix joined the Saxan King. "Prince Rydan was in my charge," he said. "In such circumstances, I must stand in his stead."

Rydan went red, then white again, and all that blood rushing about set him swaying. "You – you would do that for me, Leton?"

"Is that acceptable to you, Couerveur?" Leton asked, with all the Guard Dog's flint.

Aurak Bes forestalled the Diamond's answer. "Prince Rydan, should Captain Djol fail, Magister Couerveur is free to pursue his grievance against you. Do you understand?"

"I understand."

No-one should look so happy after receiving a challenge from Aristide Couerveur, and there was something indecent about the Pup's shining eyes as he bowed with formal gratitude to a Phoenix.

"Couerveur?" Leton repeated.

"If you must," the Diamond said.

As Aurak Bes told them his Hapts would prepare a Circle for the battle, Aspen turned and barely prevented himself from dragging a golden goddess off for a tutoring session, merely striding ahead of her up the path. He didn't want to cast that spell, wouldn't trust himself on something so important even on the best of his days, but to have a Phoenix added to the pyre was...he would stop that. Absolutely.

The buildings above sprawled widely over the slope: a series of houses linked by covered walkways. Aspen guessed the largest would belong to Magister Varpatten, but hesitated in a boot-cluttered foyer, listening for voices to guide his direction.

"To the right," Princess Aloren said, drifting up behind him.

Aspen glanced toward what he could glimpse of a high-ceilinged room bright with morning light, but then turned, unable to stop words bursting out.

"That idiot thinks it's a gesture of love. He doesn't see at all that his father must have ordered it. What can he be thinking? That it's romantic to have the Diamond kill them both?"

"Gauche, earnest and heartfelt." Aloren's expression was as judicial as Aurak Bes'. "That is what sends this awry. This form of tit-for-tat justice shows its brutality when exercised on someone so young."

"Old enough to kill."

The quiet voice behind Aspen was, again, far too like Gentian's for comfort.

"That is a grievous injury," Laeth Varpatten added, not to blood-spattered Aloren, but to Aspen, who instinctively thrust his right hand deeper into its pocket.

"I suspect I might need your aid with that, Laeth," Princess Aloren said, and offered Aspen a slow smile in response to his confusion. "There are few Magisters in Western Sumica who have not found reason to consult Laeth on some problem or another. The Varpatten sensitivity surpasses all but the strongest of the Fair. I'm very sorry to meet you again in these circumstances, Laeth."

"Strange that you met Gentian ahead of our plans."

"Yes. Though, given events, perhaps all those suspicions were not so unfounded."

"Plans? Suspicions?" Aspen was feeling particularly out of the loop.

"The Varpattens have long been accused of practicing Shaping skills on themselves." This was Frid Calder, emerging impatient and weary from the sunlit room. "We knew that wasn't true, but it occurred to us that Shaping might provide a solution to Gentian's exile. However, our expertise lies with plant life." She and Princess Aloren embraced, clearly on the best of terms. "Would you like a clean dress, 'Lore? I should be able to find something that will fit you."

Princess Aloren glanced down, and then flicked her fingers. Blood turned to dust, scattered, and was gone.

"No, I would like to see if there is some last chance of salvaging your daughter. And this ridiculous boy probably needs to sit down before he drops."

ooOoo

Aspen had been completely taken in. But correct in his first opinion: Aloren of Ceria was entirely worthy of worship.

"You knew all along," he said softly, as they followed the two Shapers through a sun-swamped breakfast room looking over fields of blue. "Gentian's history."

A softly hummed note was all he had for answer, and then they were past the breakfast room and, around a twist of corridor, filing into a bedroom made heady by the scent of at least three flowering vines competing to suffocate the enormous window.

The room had clearly been refreshed in preparation for a daughter's long-awaited return, but otherwise preserved for the girl who had left it at fourteen. She probably wasn't much larger, a slip of a thing lying as if asleep.

With a dispassion that shouted refusal to display grief, Frid Calder touched her daughter's forehead, then stepped back. "Is a *farvelti* binding possible over the distance she's been moved?"

"Range is only limited by the strength of the caster," Aloren said, and drew the room's sole chair to the bedside. She nodded Aspen toward it before turning to carefully inscribe the spell's form on paper Laeth Varpatten pulled from a drawer. "Not all Magisters take oaths against forbidden casting when accepting the rank, but it is very common. You, however, have the strength, but are not bound by oath. Do you feel able to try?"

"I have to." There couldn't be any wavering now, not with Leton at stake.

Magic was ever a double-edged sword, bent readily to any purpose, and all too liable to spring back into your face at the first mistake in composition, pronunciation or purpose. All students of magic had to overcome the fear that followed their first warped casting, to learn not to dwell on the things that could go wrong. Focus was everything, and something Aspen had always lacked, giving him more than enough reason to shy away from difficult tasks. Worse still was casting a spell that would make you feel awful even when successful.

After studying the form, Aspen closed his eyes, sorting words and intent, and trying to shut out what his body was increasingly disinclined to let him ignore. The *farvelti* was a dreadful spell, not the sort of thing he'd ever want to cast, with too many non-common words, and it would feel awful, hateful...

A cool hand brushed his cheek. "Hold the binding only long enough to ensure that she is aware of this place and her body. Don't touch her while the spell is in effect."

Simple expectation should not buoy him so. And urgency should not be the goad to drive him on. But still the first word filled his mouth, and then came the second, and along with the form he had to build the intent, the certainty of the thing this spell would do, and that it was a thing he wanted to happen, to take the spirit of a solemn creature called Gentian, who looked so insignificant and fragile, but was stubborn as a rock, and fix her here where she could be *useful* to him – and perhaps to her own self as well.

"Tell me your name," he said. "*Speak.*" The binding word, the command, and he only just managed it because into the grief and anger that filled Goldenrod came confusion and shock and *pain.*

~...~

It was an inchoate fragment of sound. Aspen, who had cast with his eyes shut, opened them hastily, but the body had not moved, remained a living wrong, empty.

"Did I fail?"

"No. Command her to answer. Force the response. Stop hesitating."

"*Speak,*" Aspen repeated, voice high, and the Elachar rushed too quickly from his mouth. He could feel it distort, taking on his own hatred of being pushed. He was someone who laughed and invited, teased and sought the pleasant way. Not ever someone to take a friend by the throat and choke them until they cried out and did what you commanded.

The spell fell apart, leaving him with a stinging face, as if he'd been slapped. Which would probably have been Gentian's response if he'd tried such a thing when she was still alive. Or an elbow to the throat.

"I – I'm so sorry," he said, overwhelmed by all that could be lost to a single hasty word. Gentian's parents, hopes raised and immediately crushed. The flames of a Phoenix snuffed. The Diamond, with nothing to stop that first crack forming, and all Darest to pay the price.

"Wait." Laeth Varpatten's voice was husky. "Can't you feel her? Daughter. Welcome home."

The body still didn't move, thin chest rising and falling at the same unhurried pace. But Gentian's father wasn't looking at it, but at the window framed by leaves, and a reflection in the shape of a girl.

Chapter Twenty-Two

Goldenrod. The strongest Gentian had ever felt it. A place she'd once thought as much a part of her as her heart, and at long last she had returned to it. Its joy was an ocean, embracing her, lifting her up.

The balm of reunion could not hold back an awareness of pain, of having been scalded, and of pins driven through all her joints, and yet there was no weight to it at all. Instead a cascade of shadowy sensation, and she drifted away from it, only to find focus again when she realised her father was there. She could barely see him, could catch only an echo of his voice, but with effort she could make out his face, and there her mother. Beside her...Aloren? Aspen, seated, and...

She faded, surprise breaking her concentration, but Goldenrod rose to support her and she didn't entirely lose the image of her room.

Had she been injured? She focused again, trying to move toward the figure on the bed, a body with her face. Could she simply insert herself into – !

Loathing. Gentian shattered beneath it, that giant's blow, all too familiar, but this time there was no feeling of being crushed, no waking, no racing heartbeat.

No heartbeat at all.

Fragmenting and recoiling, she fled, and Goldenrod swelled around her. She felt more a part of it than she'd thought possible, as if the long stretches of flax clothed her flanks, the secret paths of water danced with her pulse, and the riot of plant life breathed with her, turned with her to face the glory of the sun.

A crowd of feet intruded, trammelling one grassy slope. A stitch in her side, it helped keep her separate, able to think.

Had she been ejected from her own body by her hated enemy? It. Dawn. Selvar. But...no, what she'd felt had been an echo, a residue; poisonous slime from a slug that had crawled through her veins.

Intolerable.

Anger was helpful. Anger, and an overwhelming sense of having been cheated out of her right to battle. How had It won so easily? Though the odds were impossibly against her, she would have fought to her last breath, fought every moment of possession, done everything she could to sabotage her enemy's plans.

Whatever the case, she could fight now. Slime was nothing. She had plucked countless slugs and snails from her gardens. The pain was beside the point. She had endured it every morning. The hate only conjured rigid determination, and an unexpected rush of pity. What had led those sisters to such a pass? The Fair had created them and thought them an experiment gone too far? Treated them with honour and feared them and put walls about them, and...

Gentian blinked.

"Oh, thank the Sun."

"No, don't touch her."

Her mother's voice and then Princess Aloren, sharply commanding.

Gentian turned her head. That wasn't a simple achievement. Her body kept slipping away from her, as if it had been greased, and at the same time it stung and pinched and simply did not feel like hers. More a puppet whose strings she did not have the knack to pulling, and she struggled to lift a hand, her fingers jittering spasmodically. But it was her hand, hers, no other's. She held it out to her mother and did not flinch from the sting of contact.

It became noisy then, as Gentian tried to hold on to herself, and greet her parents. Aspen interrupted to babble out a stream of explanation that was less than easy to follow, though his urgency at least was clear.

"That seems a little unfair on Captain Djol," she managed, because the rest of it, the idea of her death, and then Suldar's and Selvar's...

"A travesty," Aspen fumed, tugging his left hand through already disordered hair. The other...there was something very strange about him. "I – there's no time, I'm sorry. Do you think you can stop them?"

"I think that I'm not likely to be able to walk."

She was finding the knack of talking, but only if she focused on it absolutely. Still, she had ready hands to keep her upright, and she thought she could hold on to herself at least long enough to make some pointed comments about duels to Aristide, and about other unexpected things.

"What's wrong with Aspen's hand?" she asked, after he had hurried off ahead of them.

"A price paid."

Aloren had answered, and Gentian spent some of her attention turning her head so she could look at the princess. Magnificent as the sun, and twice as inscrutable. Had she paid a price? Or would she...

"What's this? Alive after all?"

They had descended far enough to see the crowd in the west meadow, only to meet Prince Jurasel on his way to the house.

"Not precisely," Gentian replied. "But I am trying very hard to be."

"And out to spoil the entertainment, hm? That explains the flight of the eager apprentice." He indicated Aspen, thrusting his way toward Aurak Bes.

Although the *Tejustra* circle looked to have been already marked out, stopping the duel hadn't truly been an urgent task. Even non-mages would sense Goldenrod's reaction to her return: joy overlaid by concern and lingering anger. Aristide most certainly had, and while he was standing opposite Captain Djol, he had turned to look not at the flurry caused by Aspen, but at her.

The straightforward pleasure this gave her provided a helpful surge of energy, but the strain of clinging to her body was becoming marked. Not knowing for certain if she could continue to do this did not put her in a forgiving frame of mind as her parents guided her through the hastily-parted crowd to consider the person who had killed her.

Rydan looked satisfactorily like he'd been flaying himself internally, and he had an entertaining back-and-forth struggle to meet her gaze. His mouth moved, formed a word, but produced no sound. The crowd shifted around them, but Gentian could not spare the energy for them, refusing to drop her own eyes.

"I trust this settles the matter, Couerveur," said a dark-haired man, moving to stand beside the young Saxan prince. "There's no need to pursue this injury now."

"It is no longer my question to answer."

Gentian smiled, not so much for the words, but for the faint shifts of a superb mouth that told her that Aristide Couerveur had decided to enjoy himself.

"I don't understand why the *Tejustra*," she said. "Knocking someone on the head with a rock hardly warrants an honour duel."

"Because it had marginally fewer consequences than arresting him or incinerating him on the spot."

Aristide could be very frank when he chose to be, and the Saxan king responded with cold affront, while Gentian looked back at Rydan, and then past him to a lean man with close-cropped dark hair, and lines of care etched into a face kept otherwise blank.

"I'm curious, Prince Rydan," she said. "I somewhat comprehend what drove you to cave in my skull. I do not understand at all what impulse leads to you sacrifice Captain Djol."

"Sacri–! Magister Calder, I am truly...I would pay anything to undo my stupidity. But be assured that – ah..." He glanced awkwardly at Aristide, drew a steadying breath and managed a quiet dignity to add: "I am sorry, but Leton is an unparalleled duellist. It was not his life at risk."

She almost laughed and, indeed, she thought that Captain Djol did as well, raising his eyes to the Sun as if he despaired of idiocy. The considerable audience was not so restrained, and Prince Rydan stared about him in confusion at the murmur of reaction.

"A *Tejustra* is often fought with the aid of weapons," she explained. "But it is a duel made by rule of the precepts. The laws that bind true-mages."

Comprehension dawned, and Prince Rydan whirled to face Captain Djol. "Leton. I didn't – I would never–!"

"I know that, cub." Captain Djol lifted a hand impatiently. "You were still my charge, and I did not anticipate the path you were taking. But now you must face the judgment of the one you injured. Raise your chin and accept it."

Rydan gulped, and Gentian wondered dispassionately if he would faint, but he spun on his heel again and gave her an unexpectedly defiant look.

"Enough of this." King Meneth snatched at the chance created by her interruption. "Accept blood price and be done. I am taking my sons home."

"No."

"Do you think you can stop us? If you wish to push this pathetic remnant of a kingdom to the brink, try to strike him down."

The crowd shifted, Saxan mages backing up their king's warning and making their presence felt. She hadn't the energy to try to measure numbers, but they didn't truly matter.

"I don't need to," she said. "King, you are in the place where I was born. The place that carried me through fourteen years of dawns. That longed for me over fourteen years of exile. That felt my death, and helped me back over the brink from it. And you are threatening me."

Rydan cried out as Goldenrod responded not to the conversation but to her emotions, to her marking of an injury against a down-cheeked boy who Gentian saw no reason to simply forgive.

"We are all *senserel* here."

ooOoo

"A young birch," her father observed, and glanced about. "Carly, are you by? Put up some fencing, or the goats will ringbark it."

"Turn him back!" King Meneth's face had taken on a choleric hue, and he loomed over her. "Blast you, do you think I'll accept this?"

Unmoved, Gentian did not step back, but was aware of a foreboding tightening of her mother's grip on her arm.

"I can't," she said. "I didn't change him."

"That was...this place." The scholar in Aurak Bes had come to the fore. "The land itself. Remarkable. I had no idea you could command it."

"I don't command Goldenrod. I am merely important to it." She looked from the corner of her eyes at the Saxan King. "And you are still threatening me."

If anything, this drove King Meneth's colour from red to purple, but Prince Chenar managed to somehow insert himself in front of his father.

"I am very grateful, Magister Calder," he said, rapidly. "For your forbearance in sparing Rydan's life."

And not having your steading turn the rest of us into trees, his expression added. Goldenrod's attention was focused fully on them now, and this disparate collection of mages could not fail to be aware how small they were.

Into a hush built by held breath, Chenar forged on desperately. "May I – may I plead for a further mercy? If you are able to...to communicate with this place, at some time in the future, when you feel that he has had... At some time in the future, would you consider asking this place to turn him back?"

King Meneth made a choking noise, but then waited, hands clenching and opening.

Gentian had had no plans to do anything of the sort. She had been attacked deliberately, as part of a larger scheme to damage Darest. Why should she be merciful? It wasn't even that simple a task, since Goldenrod did not possess language. But–

"I will," she said. "If you give me Captain Djol."

She'd startled them both, and the Saxan King looked in outright confusion past her to where Aristide stood, managing to annoy her and at the same time remind her that she had far more interesting conversations to have than this.

"It seemed to me his life was in the process of being thrown away," she said, watching Captain Djol produce a spectacular imitation of a rock. "I'm offended by the waste."

Nothing could be clearer than King Meneth's reluctance, but the weight of Goldenrod's regard was only increasing. Climbing down from anger, he raised a dismissive hand and said: "It is not for me to command Swordmaster Delmar's future. He is his own man."

Spite. To announce Captain Djol as Arleton Delmar, subject of a fabled bounty, was to set countless hunters at his heels. Gentian had no idea what hold King Meneth had had over the man, but the Saxan had revealed a vicious streak in relinquishing it.

Delmar smiled, an expression spectacular in its cynicism, but he seemed more energised than daunted. "Then I will take my leave, with thanks."

He nodded at Gentian and walked out of the crowd, and the Saxan royals curtly headed in the opposite direction, King Meneth gesturing for his people to prepare for departure. Gentian sighed with relief, then eyed the birch now spoiling the sweep of the west meadow.

"I wonder if he'd end up with scars if I let the goats have the occasional nibble," her mother mused, just barely audible, and her father laughed, then let go of Gentian's arm so he could hug them both. Gentian managed not to flinch from the pain of the contact, but he still felt her response and let go.

"Are you feeling any better at all?"

"Getting tired," Gentian murmured, watching Aristide ask Aloren a question. The Cerian princess shook her head then nodded toward Aspen, standing with Rua. "I don't think I should sleep."

It was something to watch Aristide's face while Aloren spoke. Puzzlement, and a flash approaching disbelief, and then an expression that was stunning for its straightforward warmth, something Gentian suspected almost no-one had witnessed before.

Then Aristide, the Diamond Couerveur, feared and coveted, bowed his head to his apprentice, deeply and respectfully.

Gentian joined him in the gesture, as did her parents, and then Aurak Bes, the rescued Cyan royals, and even Princess Aloren, highly amused. Honour where it was due. They were all alive thanks to Aspen.

And to one who had had even less choice about her life than Gentian. Suldar. To the very end she'd been bound about with oaths and her own sister's hatred. The most powerful being who had ever lived, and still unable to escape.

Silently Gentian hoped Dusk had found freedom in the Moon's embrace.

Chapter Twenty-Three

"Through those trees there? I can't see anyone."

Aspen raised himself on tiptoe atop a borrowed chair and strained his eyes for any sign of the objects of his intense interest. Gentian, still moving far from easily, had decided to conclude her morning with a walk up the hill to what she called Goldenrod's Heart, and she'd taken Aristide along to keep her upright. There would undoubtedly be a most affecting scene, and who was he to pass up a chance to glimpse the Diamond being romantic?

"Come down from there."

Leton. A piece of magnificence standing impatient and assured at his feet.

"Are you suggesting I should be looking at you instead?"

"I'm suggesting you should give the man some privacy. And save me the trouble of picking you off the floor."

Aspen hesitated, then obligingly stepped off the chair, so that he came down with a scarce inch to spare between them, and could look more directly into dark eyes. Still faintly contemptuous, but there was more to it now, Aspen was sure of that. Just a hint of reaction, of charge.

"Are you going to kiss?"

The bright, interested question emanated from a spot roughly level with Aspen's right elbow, and he flinched away, moving hastily to gain some distance from the younger of the Cyan princesses.

Laeth Varpatten, who had been helpfully showing Aspen the best way to spy on his daughter, dropped to his haunches before the girl.

"Are you lost? Who are you looking for?"

"The Darien king. He's supposed to invite Mama and Mama-la to his festival."

Aspen was reasonably certain the divine Aluster wanted nothing more than to send all Cyans hurtling over the border at record speed, but was saved from tactful attempts to point this out by the appearance of the girl's older sister.

"Kassen! Why must you–! I'm sorry. Somehow she always finds a way to slip off."

"But you want to go too, Dess." The mercurial younger girl's face crumpled. "You want to go too."

With an air of long practice, Princess Desseron folded her suddenly weeping sister to her chest. "Kassen's just glad that your daughter came back," she told Laeth Varpatten. "She...she is properly better now, right?"

"I believe so, yes. It is a difficult time for her at the moment, but the first step was the largest." Magister Varpatten produced a conspiratorial little grin. "And if you want an invitation from King Aluster, here is your opportunity."

King Aluster, following Princess Aloren into the breakfast room, was not quick enough to escape a tear-streaked Cyan princess. He managed not to grit his teeth as an invitation was duly extracted, but gave Magister Varpatten a less-than-pleased glance after the girls had left.

"Another assassination attempt or two will certainly enliven the festival."

"I understand they witnessed the attack on my daughter," Magister Varpatten replied serenely. "It will be a kindness to reassure them."

"And, for all Queen Rithana's game of heirs, Kestia is most likely to succeed her. There are opportunities in the ties built there." Aloren ignored King Aluster's muted scowl, crossing to survey Aspen. "Sit down please."

He didn't want to do it. There had to be another crisis or two to deal with. What were they all doing here, wasting time on something irrelevant, when the steading was heaving with mages and royalty tried beyond bearing?

A firm grip on his shoulder took away argument, guiding him into the chair he'd been using as a footstool.

"Hand," Leton ordered.

Squeezing his eyes shut, Aspen pulled his right hand from his pocket and held it out.

Silence.

It went on too long, enough to panic him, to pile rocks in his stomach, stuff cotton in his throat, and finally to crack one eyelid, just enough so that he too could look.

The sight made it impossible not to move to shove the thing back in his pocket, but Leton caught him below the wrist and held firm.

"Careful!" Aspen gasped, but Leton's grip didn't waver.

"There is no sign of anything similar to the life-draining effect suffered by that unfortunate Fae," Magister Varpatten said, correctly guessing Aspen's primary concern.

Aspen took another glance. Squinting did not make it any less horrible. Silvery skin, similar to the dot in the centre of his left palm, spread like an old burn scar over most of his right hand, giving it a crinkled appearance, like paper that had been wet and then dried. And everywhere his skin had come in contact with the weapon there was an absence, a haze like dark smoke, and a suggestion of depth, as if those parts of his hand had become a window on to some place else, somewhere cold, and desperately lonely.

"Can you feel this? This?"

"I...it's just cold. It's like holding ice with edges."

"Painful? Hm. Well, in the first instance we should do something about that. A little selective deadening of the flesh immediately surrounding this less tangible region. It appears stable, and is not actively drawing on your strength. It will take some experimentation to establish what exactly is occurring, but I see no transformative effect on yourself or objects you touch, so I'll have you rest first. I would very much like to examine the weapon that did this."

"Given that the Tzel Aviar tells me that their precious city is forbidden to humans, that might be difficult." King Aluster rubbed the back of his neck, clearly having had his fill of the Fair. "They don't want us anywhere near it. He's not even able to talk to me about it, beyond a few oblique observations, which...Sun, I could have strangled him a dozen times these past few days. Why must the Fair choke themselves with Bans? And in this case a Ban set by a former Queen, making it twice as difficult to overturn. The only thing he has cared to be direct about at all is you, Choraide."

"Me? What?" Aspen opened his eyes properly.

"That cloth-mouthed...Tzel Damaris saw fit to inform me that it would be several weeks before a ruling could be made on whether you needed to be handed over to them for the murder of one of the People."

"What? But–!" Black spots hazed Aspen's sight. Handed over to the Fair? Him?

"The fact that she arranged it herself, and it was done to avert disaster, is apparently beside the point." The King eyed him restively, then switched his attention to Leton. "Delmar, was it?"

"Arleton Delmar, formerly of Sorania." There was no concern in a Phoenix's voice.

"I'm looking for someone to escort my ambassador on a reciprocal visit to Atlarus, joining Aurak Bes when he returns after the festival. Would you be available?"

"Perhaps. How is this related?"

The King was, amazingly, again studying Aspen. "The role seems a more suitable use of his particular talents than playing Aristide's apprentice."

Aspen gaped. Never had he had a day of such extremes. The worst thing he had ever done, and then that scene out on the grass, where the *Diamond* had bowed his head to him. And now...could the divine Aluster be joking?

"You'll need to learn High Atlar, of course, but the Aurak has offered one of his Hapts to guide you about, and she'll tutor you." The King frowned down at him. "It may be a tour of a year or two, until we can clarify the intentions of the Fair. Think you can manage it?"

Serious diplomacy? But a mere reciprocal visit, with such a distant power, would be more a series of parties than negotiations. He would need new clothes. He would miss Soren – but also that awkward time revolving around a squalling infant. And...was it Rua who would be their guide? With a Phoenix, in attendance on *him*.

The smile he gave his king was brimful.

"I'll try my absolute best to be of use."

Chapter Twenty-Four

The walk had caused the pins-and-needle sensation to recede, but Gentian still did not feel like she belonged in her own body. The effort to keep hold of it had not decreased, while the need to sleep grew stronger. She was hoping that the visit to Goldenrod's Heart would centre her, and complete her transition back to life.

Aristide had chosen to fill the walk with a more detailed account of all that had happened while Gentian had been dead, and she listened without comment, enjoying his dry observations while working through the unpleasant implications of the current situation.

"I can still feel the malison," she said, as they started up the last rise toward the source of Goldenrod's water. "But – there is a difference."

"There is a very good chance that Selvar provided an anchor for it. It's unlikely to disperse entirely of its own accord, but I have several plans for countermeasure, now that I have a better understanding of...the shaping of places."

He was going to concede on her plans for Vostal Hill. If she had more energy she'd be delighted.

"No sign of a Skremmish invasion?"

"Not as yet. It's possible that Meneth was stupid enough to send the Sun's Knot on to Tor Darest, but forewarned we can move quickly to get it out of our borders."

"Do you intend any reprisals?"

He didn't answer immediately. Instead, as they reached the top of the slope he began fashioning one of the more complex shields. Gentian glanced at the round-leafed lorams, sheltering a spring burbling out of a fissure of stone. Water spread widely over a flat shelf of rock, and fell in a sheet over the lip. As Aristide constructed his shield, she slipped off her mother's soft shoes and used all her concentration to walk alone into the sun-dappled water. Every step brought a faint shift in temperature as she walked to the very edge of the rock and stopped in a swirl of warmth and cold, gazing out over her beloved home, and beyond that the Skorese, missing one peak.

Goldenrod wrapped itself around her. It was no longer at the high pitch of awareness that had greeted her revival, but remained powerfully focused on her. Gentian allowed its delight to give her strength, to buoy her up and fill her.

And then she hastily pulled away, clamping down on her body with everything she had. That had been a mistake. Instead of reinforcing her link to her physical form, Goldenrod had almost drawn her out of it.

She focused on breathing, determined not to give in. Yes, she had broken her sworn word returning, but how unfair to not be able to see through her design for Vostal Hill, or to discover why Princess Aloren seemed to know her parents so well. Especially to be denied more time at Goldenrod, with Aristide Couerveur.

If she could not achieve that through willpower alone, there were several castings she could attempt, and if they weren't successful then there was a convenient collection of mages to consult. Living magic was irritatingly resistant to arcane, but perhaps a binding enchantment would get her through the rest of the day...

Aristide wrapped his arms around her.

Startled, though far from displeased, Gentian leaned back into warmth, strength, the faint scent of long-preserved Fae soap, and the tickle of his breath.

"That...that's actually helping."

"Of course. Life calls to life. Now that the reaction pain you were feeling is gone, this should allow you to reclaim yourself.

A sadly prosaic reason to be embracing her, but his arms tightened, and he bent his head so that his cheek pressed against hers, making clear this was not pragmatism. Aristide was an extremely self-contained man with a very distinct presence, and though he had had as much chance as she to defeat It while It haunted Darest, his determination was more than enough to combine with hers and sweep away the last traces of an angry ghost.

Finally, her true homecoming. No longer struggling, no longer hurting, all sense of slime washed away. She stood in Goldenrod's Heart and, through their contact, made Goldenrod particularly aware of this person who had become a part of her. And, for a moment, she felt an echo of something vastly larger than her steading.

"You truly do have Crown bond."

"For years now. Darest is mine. It will always be mine."

"And yet you accepted a Rathen on the throne?"

"The advantage to Darest was too great to pass up. Pride is not worth crushing the things most precious to you." The tiniest exhalation followed, and she knew that that choice had not come without cost. And then he went on to answer her earlier question.

"Queen Rithana is the motive force behind most of the current attacks, and removing her will direct Cya's energies elsewhere. Arrangements are in place, waiting for the appointment of one of the more tolerable of her children as heir. It will appear a natural death."

Gentian recognised this as both a gesture of immense trust, and Aristide making clear exactly who he was. The person with his arms around her had enemies, and a reputation for dealing with them. The idea of murdering people for political gain was not one she was ever likely to be comfortable with, but she could hardly say it was an unreasonable response to repeated attacks.

"Do you assassinate people often?" she asked, needing to know how far a step over her own personal lines she was facing.

"Once before. I prefer methods along the line of what you did today. But it is clear that Queen Rithana will continue to interfere with Darest."

It was never a good idea to fail to kill an inventive mage. And not necessarily wise to become important to one. Gentian's relatively carefree life of the last fourteen years would most certainly become complicated if she added Aristide to it, and that wasn't even considering the Couerveur family's famed instability. That might be the result of ruling a twice-cursed kingdom, or might be an inevitable tragedy, and she rather suspected she didn't care.

"I hear we're engaged."

A scarcely noticeable tension dropped from the man who held her, and then his arms tightened. "Yes."

"As best I can make out you've taken me saying that 'you almost reconcile me to being trapped in Darest' as a proposal?"

"It was certainly a singular declaration."

"And showing me a garden was you saying yes?"

"You understood me."

She laughed, and felt well and whole and happier than she ever had in her life. "You are so very entertaining, Aristide. Of course, there could be no other interpretation. How dim of me to think that you were simply suggesting we get to know each other better."

He let her go, only to circle and stand on the very rim of the pool, so that those blue and ice eyes blocked out the world. "What need do I have for half-measures? If I care for you enough to speak at all, I care for you completely."

It was only after long kisses that he added: "You almost made the prospect of exile bearable."

Books by Andrea K Höst

Fantasy:

Arabaya
Hunting

Darest
Champion of the Rose
Bones of the Fair

Eferum
Stained Glass Monsters

Medair
Part 1: *The Silence of Medair*
Part 2: *Voice of the Lost*
(Collected together as *The Medair Duology*)

Science Fiction:

Sydney Apocalyptica
And All the Stars

The Touchstone Trilogy
Part 1: *Stray*
Part 2: *Lab Rat One*
Part 3: *Caszandra*
Part extra: *Gratuitous Epilogue*

www.ingramcontent.com/pod-product-compliance
Lightning Source LLC
Chambersburg PA
CBHW070647180626
46817CB00006B/2272